CW0086S759

Yangsila

Yangsila

Love Across the Himalayas

Hari Raj Bhattarai

Translated by

Mahesh Paudyal

Cover Artist: Devendra Thumkeli

Library of Congress Control Number:		2020901176
ISBN:	Hardcover	978-1-7960-8138-1
	Softcover	978-1-7960-8137-4
	eBook	978-1-7960-8139-8

Print information available on the last page.

Rev. date: 01/21/2020

To order additional copies of this book, contact:
Xlibris
1-888-795-4274
www.Xlibris.com
Orders@Xlibris.com
807688

YANGSILA: A MODERN POLITICAL ALLEGORY IN MEDIEVAL SETTING

Mahesh Paudyal

I T BECOMES QUITE a task for readers and critics to sort out the allegorical, especially the political shred in a romance when it is modeled after a traditional fantasy, and the story moves around love, sex and amorous infatuations. Most often, the readers are likely to be carried away by the plot threaded to a legendary love story. The brilliant novelists often camouflage their political agenda so artistically that unless one reads the story between the lines with a barometrically critical sense, there is no likelihood that it would be revealed, and the story will, in most cases, continue to be a pure romance—the 'once there was a king' type of story.

The same happened with *Yangsila* ever since it was published in its Nepali version in 2017. Most of the critical acclaims it received got a notice of its story, the brilliance of language the author has used, his knowledge of the Eastern social and religious traditions, especially that of the Kirats and the Tibetans, but very few unearthed it allegorical edge. There are two obvious reasons for that. First, the setting of the novel is medieval—around fourteenth century to be precise—inspiring awe and admiration in the minds of the readers as done by fantasy tales with a lot of magical and surrealistic happenings, and second, the tip of the iceberg is dominated by multiple love relations among visiting Nepali artists and maidens in the Chinese soil hosting them. The bucolic setting, the hillside trails and river banks, the majestic mountains and the lovely gardens are grand enough to sweep the readers' concentration on the romantic camouflage of the narrative.

The story is linear. Following an invitation by Chinese Emperor Timur Khan, a group of Nepali artisans, under the leadership of

Panchashar, move toward the mainland China, via Tibet. The story echoes the visit of Nepali artist Araniko, together with his friends, at the invitation of Chinese Emperor Kublai Khan in the fourteenth century for a similar task.

With Panchashar are other artists of whom Mauni, a speechless but highly intelligent artist, is his confidant. They enter China through a trail in eastern hills of Nepal, walking past Baraha Region, bank of the Tamor and mountain passes near Olangchungola in Taplejung of Nepal. Before they enter China, the team is received by the Kirats living in this region, and they are introduced to their glorious history and rich art and culture. The Kirats also offer two of their daughters—Sanjhang and Teejhang—as wives to Panchashar. Panchashar promises to return, and moves into China making his newly-wed wives wait for him.

The mission in China is to construct luxury palaces for Timur. Panchashar and his team do it efficiently, erecting one palace after another, and extending their stay far longer than the stipulated time. In the meantime, Panchashar gets close to Melamchi, the official deputed by Timur administration to oversee the construction work. His friend Mauni gets close to Omu, and their affairs continue with occasional jerks here and there. Finally, Panchashar and Mauni get back to Nepal together with Melamchi and Omu as their respective wives. After getting his family settled, Panchashar moves east to meet Teejhang and Sanjhang and bring them home.

Apparently a simple, linear and straight narrative, the novel has deeper shades of meaning, which are far deeper than the traditional love-marriage-settlement romances. There are at least three discernable political allegories embedded in the apparently innocent narrative.

The first political commentary the novel makes is on the gradual decline of the ancient glory of the Kirat civilization, an issue internal to Nepal. The Kirats are people occupying the northern mountainous region in the eastern part of Nepal. They belong to the Mongolian race, and are believed to have descended from regions around the interface of Nepal and Tibet in the ancient times. Over the years, they developed their own culture, and earned fame as a brave, fearless, united and homogenous community, having its own religion, pantheon, deities and rituals. The novel depicts them as a community in the verge of disintegration, requiring people from external communities to come and rescue them. This is a political comment against the weakening internal solidarity, and the interference by external forces. The reference is to incessant proselytization of the Kirats these days, and the cultural disintegration therefore. It also is seemingly making an observation: Real welfare of the Kirats, and of all communities in Nepal for that matter, lies in the invention of their own glories, instead of letting external actors enter and interfere with the internal decorum of the community. This also is a comment on recent decision to make Nepal a secular state, which in spite of having many merits, has opened doors for religious missions to come and perform as they wish.

The second allegorical meaning lies in the way the author observes cultural and familiar relations in the trans-Himalayan region in eastern Nepal. By showing families connected by lineage, marriage and trade, he is foregrounding the polemic that boundaries of the modern national states make no difference when communities on both sides of the international border come from the same stock. Governments, guided by documented rules, often stay far away from the awareness that communities occupying international borders often form an interface far thicker than the brick walls and barbed wires that demarcate international borders. This is an appeal to revise the concept of modern nation states that stands on the grounds of border division and overlook the undercurrent cultural connections that are not only indelible, but also eternal. The relation between people in Tibet and the eastern hills of Nepal makes a unique example of an antithesis to the concept of a nation state.

The third allegorical aspect of the novel is the author's proposition to review Sino-Nepal relation, which is most often eclipsed by non-issues. Instead of engaging in mere eulogies, the novelist has shown how the political community in China, at least in the medieval times, was a patron of lavish luxury and expensive life style. The unreasonable attack on the gardens of Tibet, and the forced migration of the people there, including the monks, has a strong political connotation. All these things force the readers to look at modern political relations in the new light.

There is one last thing to be critically viewed. One might wonder why the novelist Hari Raj Bhattarai, a seasoned professor and writer, gives his 2017 fiction such Arcadian hue and medieval touch, when there were so many contemporary and realistic issues at his disposal to pick and forge into stories. Having lived through a time when Nepal was passing through one major revolution to another, one constitution to another and one turmoil to another, the novelist seems kind of frustrated. Apparently a cavalier approach, this is also a strategy of escape. It has been evidenced in the world literary history that when reality becomes too mean to live with, writers tend to escape it by resorting to fantastic models, including extra-realistic fictions and romantic imaginations. Novelist Hari Raj did the same in *Yangsila*, but left enough rooms for the readers to see through the lines and discover the political subplots. In fact, novelist Bhattarai saw Nepal change from an oligarchy to democracy ushered by the fall of the Ranas, and the dawn of constitutional monarchy, which regressively evoked monolithic Panchayat, only to change into multiparty democracy headed by the king, and ultimately a republic without the king. At the major turns that underpin these changes, there were movements, and there were armed groups that launched war against the establishment. One of the longest of such conflicts was the one launched by the Maoist party, lasting through the 90s and early part of the first decade of the twenty-first century, making Nepal a secular, republican and federal state. But it is understandable that many of these changes came with a cost, and one of the most detrimental of them has been that, Nepal's cultural sovereignty has become porous, and external elements are trying to weaken the internal strength of

Nepal, socially and culturally. Bhattarai's novel fundamentally is a criticism of this development in Nepal.

Whatever be the motifs, the novel is a wonderful read for international readership. It engages the readers in a trans-Himalayan voyage, through its hills, rivers, valleys and gorges, and exposes them to the hidden treasures of Tibet and China, which are in most of the cases unmentioned chapters in world literature. After Laxmi Prasad Devkota's epic *Muna Madan* and Dor Bahadur Bista's novel *Sotala*, *Yangsila* is yet another major creative work that connects Nepal with Tibet and China, and inspires newer studies in this line.

I am thankful to the author for entrusting me the responsibility of translating the work into English. I have tried all my best to do justice to the text. I wish the book a global success.

Central Department of English
Tribhuvan University
mahesh.kathmandu@gmail.com

ACKNOWLEDGEMENTS

THOUGH NEPAL SHARES an extensive border with China, much of it falling along its autonomous region Tibet, very little of it has been incorporated in creative literature published from Nepal. Barring a few epics, novels and travel writing, this aspect of Nepal's regional link has been evaded. The few works that have dealt with the issue have limited themselves to trade and political relations. The larger cultural framework of the inseparable relations among people living in both parts of the international border as a homogenous community with a common lineage and genealogy has largely remained unexplored.

Having come from Taplejung, a hill district in eastern Nepal bordering with Tibet in the north, much of my upbringing took place in a cultural matrix where the Kirats in these hills on the Nepalese side interact with their brethren in the north, namely Tibet, and their relations are informed not merely by trade, but also by familial and marital connections. I grew up watching boys and girls on the Nepalese side freely visit their relatives in the Chinese side and vice-versa. Much later, I realized the social relations along the international borders cannot be defined by the modern provisions of international relationship true to national states. As I grew, I could see that beyond the narrative of artistic exchanges through Nepali artists like Araniko moving into China to construct temples and palaces, there were deeper relationships made possible by the cultural and familiar overlaps that exist between communities living on both sides of the border since ancient times.

In *Yangsila*, I wanted to unearth these interfaces. I thought, the ancientness I have maintained in the novel would give the subject its best treatment, because I did not think these subjects will have much meaning in the modern, politically ripped and culturally threatened setting. Having seen so many quick and aberrant movements in Nepal leading to nothing formidable, my mind flew to take refuge in the distant and imaginative past, where only such partially magical stories could do the trick. And I did the same. I feel deeply pained by the rifts and uncertainties that have been forced into the otherwise integrated and peaceful community life of Nepal, and think, renewing our civilizational glory and redefining cultural relations will be our surest resort in the days to come.

I am thankful to novelist Krishna Dharabasi, who suggested me to get this work translated into English and make it available for international readership. He brought me into contact with translator Mahesh Paudyal, who kindly agreed to render it into English, and the book got its shape in the present form. I thank the publisher........for launching the book, and expect critical observations from my esteemed readers.

Hari Raj Bhattarai
USA

CHAPTER ONE

T HE TRAVELERS' EYES fell on the unfathomable body of water. They moved ahead in a state of astonishment and curiosity.

Seeing the travelers approach him, the boatman was delighted.

The travelers' threw their burdens on the shore and looked out in astonishment with wide-open eyes without a single blink.

As many suns glittered as there were eyes. The image of the sun made the eyes dazzle.

It was not easy for them to tell if it was a vast lake or a dynamic river. The big body of water was, however, extremely tranquil.

The travelers were lured by the aquatic grandeur. They grew more and more impatient to walk near and touch it.

"Is this the Koshi?"

"Perhaps it is."

"There's so much of water. This must be Mahakoshi, the grand river."

"Are we supposed to walk across such a huge flow of water?"

"If we need to cross, there must be a way."

"That's true. After all, we are not the only travelers here."

They were obliged to travel. So, these travelers, who were expected to head north right from the beginning, had gone in the wrong direction, and had ended up on the bank of the Saptakoshi River, walking past the forest in the plains.

The saying, 'God does everything with a good purpose,' must be true. The Tarai or the southern plain of Nepal was a haven for indomitable wild animals. So the path running through the interior of the forest was not safe and secure for travelers. Yet, in the company of pilgrims heading toward the Pashupatinath Temple to participate in the Shivaratri festival fair, a group of artisans moving toward China had reached the Koshi bank.

The boatman was keenly observing these travelers. They were constantly moving toward the Koshi, stepping on anvil-like stones and heated shingles.

Though it was spring, the heat from the plains had not been able to slash the coldness in the water of the glaciers emanating from the high snow-capped mountains in the north. So travelers coming from distant lands could hardly surmise that water in Koshi could be so cold. In such a hot place, it was natural for travelers, tired of walking and carrying their loads, to find Koshi colder than expected. Having felt the surprising coldness in the river water, they gazed on one another's faces.

They cleansed themselves by sprinkling water from the Koshi, went knee-deep into it, and cleaned their bodies, did *achaman*[1], chanted some mantras and appeared extremely contented. They washed and cleaned, and made use of the river water in their own ways.

It was past midday now. After some rest, the travelers in this group walked near to a boat, together with their bundles.

The boatman ushered them into his boat with great respect. He maneuvered its balance carefully considering the flow of the Koshi, its nature, the destination and the proportion of the travelers, and started pushing the boat toward the central stream. The boat reached the other bank without any difficulty. The travelers appeared quite assured. A glow of joy spilled over their countenances.

"Brother, you helped us cross such a majestic river. We are indebted to you. I commend your courage, and thank you on behalf of all of us. Many thanks," said Panchashar, expressing his heartfelt gratitude for the boatman, and gave him the expected fare.

The boatman got more money than expected, and expressed his joy. He moved his hands left and right.

Other members of the trip sat beside their bundles and started taking their snacks and water. Panchashar, on his part, appeared

---

[1] a Hindu practice of self-cleansing by sipping holy water from palms in several bouts

HARI RAJ BHATTARAI

absorbed in some sort of contemplation as he stood on the bank facing the river.

His eyes fell on a boat. It was a huge boat made by carving a tree bole with a girth more than double a man's arm length. The boat, some forty-one feet long, had been carved with Kirat[2] art patterns. This made Panchashar delighted beyond measures. He joined both his hands and said, "Venerable Brikshadev[3]! I was able to cross such a mighty river with your help. I am thankful to you, and tender you my valedictory greetings. Please accept my devotion." He bowed down with a feeling of gratitude.

Panchashar's eyes then fell on the expansive body of water in the river. The Koshi, rendered grave and solemn by its vastness, appeared holy and magnanimous. He thought, 'I have crossed, and at places jumped over such a huge river. By that token, I must be guilty of defiling its holiness.' In a tone of utter humbleness, he added, "Jaladev[4], I shall never forget your help and goodwill. Accept my greetings." He lowered his head.

"Traveler, you shall be successful in reaching your destination. Your trip will bet accomplished without any trouble," said a woman, whose voice fell into his ears. He raised his hood and looked all around with curiosity. There, in front of him, stood a woman, glittering in a glorious halo. He paid his veneration to her, standing with both his palms locked, keeping utter silence.

"Traveler, this is Kirats' land. You are welcome to this land. All your wishes shall be granted, and your trip shall be peaceful and calm."

"Who are you, Devi? What orders have you got for me?"

"I am the Devi of the Kirat region. I am called Khambani Devi at some places and Limbani Devi somewhere else." After a brief pause she added, "The queens in the kingdom of Kirat are all my

---

2   The Kirats are people of Mongoloid race living primarily in the eastern hills of Nepal

3   Tree God! The word 'Briksha' in Sanskrit stands for a tree and 'Dev' for God.

4   Water God

parts, my manifestations. They shall ensure your safety in all parts of the Kirat region."

After a long time, Panchashar turned toward himself. He found himself standing in a posture of *namaskar*[5], folding both his palms together. The Goddess that stood in front of him a short while ago, and the conversation he had with Her appeared like a dream to him. Considering this fact, he grew more and more introvert. He barely cared how quickly time passed.

When he was shaken back to reality from the dreamlike vision, Panchashar could see the boatman very much there, where he had left the fellow travelers a while ago. A flash of thought occurred to his mind: 'Perhaps the boatman overheard my conversation with the Devi. He also perhaps saw Her.'

He therefore treasured his encounter and conversation with the Devi, and the context related with the meeting, in the deepest caverns of his heart, and locked them firmly, thinking that when needed he could retrieve them and analyze. He then raised his eyes and started looking far and wide.

To his east, on the bank of the Koshi, he could see Tapoban[6] glistening in the setting sun. The travelers moved in that direction, for their destination lay thither.

As soon as Panchashar and his men entered Tapoban premises, they heard two boys run to them and say simultaneously in reception, 'Atithi devo bhawa', meaning, the guests are gods.

"Guests, you are welcome to the ashram of the wards of Kulapati[7] Vishwamitra's realm. Welcome!" said the boys, walking close to the newcomers.

On behalf of all his men, Panchashar gestured the acceptance of the boys' offer for hospitality.

---

[5] An eastern way of greeting someone respectable by folding both the palms together

[6] A grove meant for penance and meditation

[7] Kulapati is equivalent to the chief of an educational institution, like the Chancellor of a modern-day university.

HARI RAJ BHATTARAI

"Guests! We, the disciples bound to the disciplinary order of the revered royal guru and devout pursuer Vishwamitra, are wards at this ashram of our revered guru. It's our highest duty to welcome you, who have turned up as our guests. Gurudev has moved toward Ramdhuni[8]. So, please pardon us for the lapses in our hospitality, if any. We are new boarders at his ashram, and we take the lead in welcoming you in the absence our guru."

This way, the boys showed their readiness, staying within the expectations of the gurukul[9] disciples.

The boys accorded their hospitality befitting the culture of Tapoban and the manners of the gurukul. The contingent of Panchashar rested for the night in that ashram that stood on the eastern bank of the Koshi.

A new day broke. Right from the brink of the day, the ashram ringed with auspicious activities. Soon they were done with blowing the conch, doing their prayers, and reading the scriptures.

The eastern horizon heralded the rise of the sun. Though the range of the mountains to the east of the ashram kept the morning light at bay and retained the darkness of the receding night for a long, there was soon enough daylight to help a traveler tell his way ahead. The morning songs of disparate chirping birds doubled the excitement of their trip.

Panchashar considered it worthwhile to take leave from there and depart. So he entered a room lighted by a lamp. This room used to stay open for everyone all the time. Inside it was an old tapasi[10] in the posture of rest after completing ajapa, a voiceless incantation. He opened his eyes when Panchashar entered the room. Allowing a gentle smile to ripple on his lips, he spoke in a soft but serious tone, "Pursuer of art! Your destination is defined. But you are caught in a dilemma as regards your way. What decision did you take? Would you move straight from here passing through Baraha Region and

---

8   Votive fire that buns ceaselessly
9   an ancient school in which the disciples stayed in the ashram of their guru until they graduated
10   a spiritual seeker

move along the bank of the Tamor, or first have a holy view of Budha Subba and move from there via Siddhapokhari?"

Astonished, Panchashar said to himself, 'The sage knows my work, my destination, my path and my dreams. On top of everything, he also knows my dilemma.'

He asked himself, 'In a dream, I had received a signal to move ahead after having a holy beholding of Budha Subba[11], and not take a diversion. The sage knows this fact as well. Isn't it a great miracle that he knows of our prior determination to move east along Tamor bank, walking past the Baraha Region?"

His soliloquy continued, 'I had heard a lot about the vision and power of the Aryan sages. But I witnessed it myself today. The saying that the sages are omniscient and cosmic visionaries came out to be true.'

Focusing himself on the sage's question, he said with utmost modesty, "O the greatest of the seekers! I consider it better to move after having a holy view of Budha Subba. What do you suggest?"

"Your decision is wise. On your way toward the summit, you shall meet Kirat sages."

Raising his hand in blessing, the sage said, "*Swasti shubhante panthanah.*"[12]

The brief conversation with the sage made Panchashar almost hypnotized. He was not much interested in making a quick exit from the sage's room. He felt great intimacy with the sage even with the exchange of so few words. Yet, he left the room with tears, leaving his heart behind.

Once out of the ashram, the team of the travelers dispersed in two groups. One moved across the Baraha region toward Maiwa-Dhulé confluence along Tamor bank, via Moolghat[13], aiming to reach Olangchunggola. This group was comparatively bigger. There were

---

[11]   A deity of the Kirats, whose grand temple stands at Dharan in eastern Nepal

[12]   May your journey become a happy one!

[13]   The word *'ghat'* is usually associated with that part of a river bank where dead bodies are cremated according to Hindu rituals.

nine members in it, and it had all the equipments and tools it might need. It moved north toward the source of the river Tamor. The other group moved east toward Budha Subba Temple, seemingly pulled by a magnetic power. This group had two members: Panchashar and Manthan. Manthan's popular named was Mauni.

***

As soon it entered Vijaypur Township, Panchashar's group came to become an issue of general curiosity and mystery. The townsmen gathered at many places to have a glance of the people coming from Nepal. The state administration turned more and more alert in maintaining security, and exercising control.

The townsmen saw the newcomers exactly like themselves in yellow complexion and thought they were, like themselves, wage-labors. Yet, they considered their wears quite strange. They were clad in home-spun *khandi*[14] vests, and had a ten-yard long girdle cloth around their waist, into which, a sharp-edged *khukuri* had been tucked. The Nepali shoes they had worn were, however, quite new and attractive. With a touch of the Tibetan art, the shoes were handiworks of artisans laden with wonderful skills. This context was not altogether meaningless. This internal bliss had been transmitted to everyone.

"Should such a thick crowd throng to see an eighteen-year lout coming here? And why such alertness in the administration? It is nonsense, foolish Kiratis!" said someone in a tone of hubris, criticizing the entire business.

"Let the maidens see him instead. The lad seems fine; he can keep a family going. Someone can go with him, or make him stay in the family," said yet another voice from somewhere.

"Why should we care for these vagabonds?" said a third voice in a listless tone.

Those who overheard these voices thought, 'There is some truth in these statements.'

---

[14] Home-grown cotton

Around Vijaypur and Budha Subba Temple, Panchashar and his friend were now recognized as simple and decent people. The civil community thought, these religious Nepalis were there on pilgrimage to have a holy visit of Budha Subba, bearing for Him great reverence in their hearts. The *phedangba, bijuwa, Budhi Boju, jhakri-pujari, tantrics* and the accomplished sages of the Kirat kingdom took no time in recognizing them as guests in possession of great skills, and presented themselves as grateful inquirers and hosts. In no time, Panchashar and Mauni were surrounded by sorts of people from the Kirat kingdom, including general citizenry, cultural spokespersons, social gurus, religious leaders, acquaintances and distinguished businessmen.

No member of the royal staffs appeared there. The ordinary citizens of that region didn't know which region Panchashar and his team were fond of or expert of. They however knew that they were artists. So a man representing the crowd came forward and said, "Dear guests! You bequeath a model of our skills here before you leave. We, the citizens of the Kirat Kingdom shall treasure it, considering it a gift from you. This is what the dwellers of this region request you."

Cashing an apt opportunity, another one said, "We, the Kirat people, have everything we need. We don't ask for anything with anyone else. So the only request we have with you is this: We want to establish a warm relation of friendship with you. This is an invaluable goodwill of ours. Since we are people who respect others' sentiments, we are humbly placing our request. We don't, however, pressure you. We therefore tell you: Either leave a gift to us from your side, or accept one from us before you depart."

The speaker was a representative of the people. Panchashar considered his proposal straight and uncorrupt. The words of the speaker impressed him. Inspired by the obligation to tender an answer, he said, "I express my due greetings to all the honorable citizens of the kingdom of Kirat. I also appreciate the goodwill and love for art you have exhibited." Adding one more paragraph to his speech, he said, "This is Kirat region. One must see the glory of Kirat art here. In order to create art, one must have absolute dedication and a lot of time. If there is dearth of any of these, creation of art becomes impossible. I am a traveler. I came here merely to have a holy view of Budha Subba, making some alteration in my usual route. I beg your pardon."

The Kirats appeared quite eager to listen to the words of their guests. Panchashar said, "Besides creating new artworks, I feel the need to conserve the older art forms. Otherwise, artistic creations will have no value here."

After a brief pause, he said in a serious tone, "In the future, preserving art and culture will become an uphill task. I advise the Kirat region to stay alert on this issue."

He further said, "There is such a huge turnout from the Kirat community here today. There also are learned gurus. We got this opportunity to meet you all here. We are blessed." With utmost humility he added, "I was invited here by Budha Subba. I, and we all, arrived here to have a holy beholding of His grand manifestations. We have ourselves become blessed. On your part, you are very much under the refuge of Baba Budha Subba. I consider you far luckier."

Glancing at his companion Mauni, Panchashar presented the summary of his speech. He said, "If chances favor, we will come to the shrine of Baba once again." Folding his hands together in respect, he said, "We now take leave of you."

One could hear side-talks continuing among the people present therein. There were minor movements here, and apparent haste there. In the meantime, a distinguished scholar of culture came forward and said, "Sewaro[15], respected guests!"

He was standing with his hands joined. He added, "Our guests happened to be in a hurry. We have realized that. So let's stage a cultural program from our side in their honor. Let's accomplish it with participation from all three Kirat regions: Wallo Kirat, Pallo Kirat and Majh Kirat[16]. This shall be a visual gift for our guest."

---

[15]   A word of greeting, usually used by the Kirats

[16]   The land of the Kirats, which fundamentally is the region of the Eastern Himalayas in Nepal, is divided into three sub-regions: Western, Eastern and Middle Kirat.

This announcement sent a ripple of joy among the commoners. The youths appeared more excited. Certain that they ought to stage the event, the youths divided the responsibilities on their own, according to which, maidens from Wallo Kirat played the *binayo*, and those from Majh Kirat played the *murchunga*[17]. Dancers from both these sub-regions performed a glimpse of Sakela[18].

Pallo Kirat was waiting for its turn. The adult men from Limbuwan[19] surprised the onlookers by presenting all the eight variations of Chyabrung Dance, while the maidens performed Dhan Naach presenting ample introduction of individual freedom endorsed by social and cultural considerations and of a lifestyle laden with utmost liveliness. The highly accomplished, saintly, wise and righteous men had become guardians for them. These events, performed under the guidance of their gurus, devotees and distinguished scholars were matchless examples of liberal thinking and intimate behavior of the Kirats.

Panchashar was delighted beyond measures with this honor and reception the Kirat community accorded to him. He expressed his heartfelt gratefulness to the community. Conscious of time, knowledge, age and rights, the Kirat community appeared completely disciplined. Respect for the learned ones and their sayings were a natural trait of the Kirats. Panchashar was obliged to wonder if the Kirats were the inventors of various significant codes related with personal inclinations, freedom and rights within the limits of their social decorum.

Joining his hands in reverence before Budha Subba, he prayed, 'Let no one ever forsake the freedom of the Kirats. Let their morale never slash, and let not this community ever accept anyone else's

---

[17] *binayo* is a stringed instrument played with the mouth. *Murchunga*, like a *binayo*, consists of flexible metal or bamboo tongue or reed attached to a frame.

[18] A culural dance of the Kirats performed in group during festivals

[19] The land of the Limboos. The Limboos are a tribal community of Mongoloid race living in the eastern hills of Nepal.

HARI RAJ BHATTARAI

servitude. Father Budha Subba, make the future of the Kirats secured, and let this community become the defense of this region in the future.'

Having made this wish, he left.

Escorting its guests as far as Sanguri Bhanjyang Pass in the north, the cultural troop of Limbuwan returned toward Vijaypur township toward sunset. Before the group returned, the chief of the cultural trip said, "You have hinted that it would be difficult for us to safeguard our culture and have also cite the need for us to stay aware of this fact. But we could not fully understand your words. Can't art stay alive in future as it has survived till today? There must be a reason or mystery why you gave us such a suggestion. If you have surmised the future of our art dark, do please tell us frankly. We cannot tolerate seeing ourselves robbed of our culture. We the Limboos inside the Kirat community do not like to see our art or culture destroyed or forgotten."

Making the issue clearer, Panchashar said, "In future, the ruling clans rising to power with revolution, and the unworthy representatives of the people will prove a curse for this land. A political culture that grabs power through intrigues shall strengthen its hold. Dynasties that conceal their real clan identity, engage in killing their kinsmen, and plunder the existence of the general public will arrive, one after another. Worse will be the fact that non-believers shall alter their culture, and will, with time, establish themselves as the gods of this region. The people will not put any effort to understand their tricks and intrigues."

Paying a quick look to the cultural troop seated on a wooden *chautari*[20] at the pass and eager to listen to his words, Panchashar said, "Idols shall disappear from shrines. Smugglers shall make away with archeological artifacts. Bricks, wood-carvings, idols, paintings and important archival scriptures at your historical sites shall become the most coveted objects for the smugglers. Worst

---

[20] a small, wayside mound usually under a big tree, constucted for on-foot travelers to sit and respose for a while

of all, members of the royal family shall be the leaders of such smuggling gangs."

"The smugglers eye our livestock. Do they also eye things like bricks, wood carvings, idols, pictures, books and manuscripts? If they do, what kind of smugglers are they?" said someone in the middle in a tone dotted with surprise and mysteriousness.

Panchashar's speech didn't pause. He added, "Your community and culture will see gross dishonor. With support from foreign powers, the royal family and the institution of monarchy shall be wiped out. A new political culture will brew up, which will monger after power, sacrificing the lives of the innocent public. Before its ultimate decline, the political fragment that survives the royal massacre shall appear quite powerful, albeit for the last time, and the nation will act as desired by foreign powers. The nation shall lose its original character. In due course, the country shall adopt the veil of a foreign constitution. The national flag and language shall change; the nation will disappear."

Rather irate, he added in a tone of hatred, "The uncultured administration that sends its youthful human resource overseas to work and diverts the tax, remittance and post-death compensation to the families of the deceased thereof to its personal account shall become stronger. Leaders of the latest generation and their henchmen shall become active in the loathsome culture of trafficking daughters from the country to lands abroad for prostitution, and keep themselves going from the income coming thereof."

After a brief pause, he tried to conclude his speech. He said, "I can foresee that in the near future, the Kirat community will have to come forward to safeguard the existence and historical glory of this land, and the Kirat dynasty shall come out victorious in this endeavor. The day this land awakens, the Kirat dynasty shall make an appeal for the same. The dynasty shall be able to retrieve its lost power, and launch a new term of its excellent administration. I have staunch belief in the guiltless, trustworthy and powerful Kirat community. I have my best wishes. The bright future of this land

HARI RAJ BHATTARAI

rests in your hands. If that happens, this land shall stand among the most developed regions of the world."

At the moment of valediction, the leader of the cultural troop expressed his desire to know something about Mauni. Picking up the context, Panchashar said, "I didn't introduce him to you, maybe because I was preoccupied. He is my right hand, a friend and my everything. By age, he is elder to me by six months. We call him Mauni with love, but his real name is Manmath."

Mauni smiled like a flower and said many things with his eyes. He made everyone present there get a glimpse of such gestures. An entire line of Kirat maidens smiled back to him. He was even more delighted because Panchashar had spoken highly in his appreciation.

In the human race, Mauni was such a creation that listened, comprehended, remembered and expressed, but had no voice. His speechlessness had become one of his significant traits. In regards to original art works and artifacts, his talent was beyond description. He could decipher the scripts of several languages and read them in silence. He had made himself known as a diligent young man, a faithful friend, a helpful companion and a knowledgeable person.

Manmath's introduction turned out to be the last issue therein. Toward dusk, the cultural troop reached the premises of the Budha Subba Temple and got dispersed. Panchashar and Mauni moved north, lumbering uphill with speed, targeting the majestic mountains up there. Though they were two in the tour, there were moments when Panchashar felt lonely. It was not unnatural for their trip to become mute.

Before stepping on the foot of the mountain, they heard a beautiful folk tune being sung somewhere. They sat down on the chautari[21] therein to rest. Mauni appeared unusually happy. He signaled Panchashar to listen to the tune. The duo listened to the words with care. The song resounded in the voice of two maidens:

---

[21]   a wayside mound built manually, usually underneath a big shady tree for travelers to rest for a while

Sanghuri pari tyo pallopati Leuti khoLama
Ekkais choti janghara tarné ko hola mardama?
Yo manko bhari kina ho eklai ma thamna sakdina
Tijasto kohi dauntari paye hudaina bhandina.

[Is there any hero among men who crossed the
river Leuti beyond Sanghuri twenty one times?
Why can't I drag the burden in my heart alone? If I
find a partner in such a man, I shall not decline the
proposal.]

Panchashar signaled Mauni to stand up and resume the walk,
for they had to reach a place where they could put up for the night.
But Mauni's heart was still reluctant to move. He begged to grant
him some more time, fished out his flute from his bag and started
playing it in the tune of the same song. Drawn by the tune of his
flute, the maiden duo crossed the ridge of their farms and came to
the spot where they had been sitting.

The parties stared at each other for a while. No word could
escape any lip. Panchashar was in a hurry; Mauni gestured his
willingness to stay on for some more time. The maidens stepped
onto the *chautari* and played the same tune on their *binayos*.
The musical charm of the *binayos* at once hooked Mauni's heart.
Harboring the pain of a fish just freed from a hook, the two men
plodded toward River Leuti. The Kirat maidens fell onto the hard
rock of reality, coming round from a momentary dreamlike spell.
They now started singing plaintive songs, making the hills and
slopes overflow with the sound. But the murmur of the river
dimmed the sound of their song. Crossing the serpentine Leuti at
several passes, Panchashar and Mauni finally arrived on the bank
of River Tamor.

"Come; you are dismally late. I have been waiting for you," said
the boatman. He was the same man who had met them at Koshi
bank before. He was waiting in the same way, and his boat was the
same too. Panchashar was wonderstruck. He grew more and more

introvert. Mauni also performed a new act, signaling that he was equally surprised.

Panchashar started musing in himself, 'This boatman, the Devi of the Kirat region, that Aryan sage, Buddha Subba's appeal in my dream, the words of the sage, my dreams and the realistic envisioning of my trip, and the exact study of the state of my mind! What a matter of wonder all these things are! How much are they real and how much imagined?'

After this self-contemplation, Panchashar returned to a state of normalcy and said, "This is Kirat land. Its strength and mysteries are unfathomable. Everything that took place and we experienced till today are in our favor. More, we are travelers. We don't need to fear or be suspicious of anything as long as we are inside its territory. My innermost convictions say our trip will get accomplished without any hindrance. The Kirat land, with its immensurable power and accomplishment will prove benefitting and complacent for us. There are moments when usual and mysterious incidents take place, but they come as back support for ourselves. We must receive them with a feeling of grandeur. This is how I feel, Mauni. This is what I have got to say."

Mauni nodded in support of Panchashar's statement.

Having crossed the Tamor, they took leave of the boatman and moved ahead. Panchashar stood on a mound beside the trail and had a monologue with the Tamor: "I am moving uphill from this very spot today. We may meet you again at your confluence with Mauwa Khola at Thum. From there, let's move toward Tibet without parting from each other. We shall be together for many days." He had the feeling that he was deeply connected with the Tamor.

They moved uphill, passing through flat plains, groves of star fruit, goose-berries, slopes lush with pineapple and groves of guavas. Their hearts were clung to thatch grass and sabaigrass they encountered at times on the way. Having short-term respite on the neat stone-built *chautaris* on almost every major bend along the uphill trail with wooden, wind-swept benches to sit on, they hurried up until they reached Hilé, past Debrebas and Nigalé.

To their north, they could see the east-west extension of the Himalayan ranges. Since the Mahalangur and Kanchenjunga ranges were at a formidable distance, they had to stretch their eyes to have a glance of them. These ranges appeared golden at times and silver some other moment. They often felt nature on the sky and on earth was presenting these majestic displays of snow in their honor.

Panchashar considered himself extremely lucky and accomplished on having a glance of these pristine Himalayan glimpses. He told to himself, 'I have the privilege of calling these Himalayan ranges *mine*. After all, I am the son of this very land.'

Envisioning the upcoming future he expressed his doubts: 'Generations to come will gradually lose the right to call these mountain ranges theirs. When the organized royal dynasties shall gradually disintegrate and the bandits shall not flinch from declaring themselves leaders and people's representatives. In that case, the people will lose their rights to call these mountain ranges theirs, and themselves the progenies of this land. Such a day too will come when with time we shall become a part of history.'

Mauni was enchanted whenever he saw the Himalayan ranges. At such moments, he forgot the rest of the world. Panchashar, on his part, shook Mauni back to reality.

They now took wide steps. At one point in time, a shrill enrapturing voice of a female singer fell into their ears:

> *Sindhuwako sireto teekho kamchha mutu pardachha tharthara*
> *Bayan bagne Arun khola dayantira garjanchha Tamor*
> *Eklai-duklai nahide yatri! palki baschha duikhutte taskar*
> *Udhauli ki Ubhauli bhandai lainu-tharu sanket bolero*
> *Akkarma khayera thakkar aafno boli aafailai daraune*
> *Charo muso boldaina kohi maryo-bachyo ko hunchha sunaune?*

[The cold wind at Shiduwa sends one shivering and chills the hearts. The Arul flows to its right, while the Tamor roars on its left. Traveler, do not keep this way alone! A bipedal smuggler is habituated to hunting here, sending forth false signals asking people if they are going for Udhauli or Unbhauli[22] festivals. Having faced such betrayals on the hard rock of life, one starts fearing her own voice. If that happens, no one else claims to speak out the truth. Who will come and inform if you are dead or alive?]

Analyzing the tales they had heard before and the message carried by this song, the duo lumbered ahead, taking heavy strides.

As for shelter, they put up sometimes under the trees, and some other times in caves just for name sake, the green, one-night makeshift huts of leaves, or fragile sheds of bamboo nets and silos left unattended after the animals had been moved elsewhere. Such were the verbal images of the shelters Panchashar and Mauni rested in on their way.

Water at some spots was so delicious that it would not suffice to call it tasty or ambrosial. The mountain water in this part of the world seemed quite nourishing. They felt that this drinking water oozing out of cracks on the mountains enhanced their physical power by a huge degree. In the water that came flowing across forage and grazing area, one could feel the reek of cow-dung and cattle urine, while at some places, they had to deal with the abominably acrid taste coming from petrified leaves that someone got mixed into the water stream. On the sides of their trail, they could see the fur of strange wild animals, the footprints they had never seen before, the reek of the animal bodies altogether new to them and the sight of animal droppings, which made them loathe it with heavy hearts. Adding curiosity to the existing fear, doubt and surprise, they gave continuity to their trip.

---

[22] Spring and summer festivals of the Kirats in which they move their livestock uphill (*Ubhauli*) and downhill (*Udhaili*).

At some place on the way, they could see stone piles decked with flowers, leaves, twigs and votive flags offered by the passersby, and at such spots, they also followed suit by adding more flowers, leaves and stones. They knowingly endorsed this tradition of bowing at such a stone pile with faith before moving ahead, done with the wish that this would ward off every potential hardship, sickness and impediment that might make their movement impossible. They felt that this system of treatment handed down through folk belief was a sparkling union of psychology and culture.

The travel of Panchashar and Mauni was a joint trip of two friends having two different sets of mindsets and difference viewpoints. When one got heavy with fear, the other looked indifferent and guiltless. Seeing the carefree life of Mauni, Panchashar unconsciously envied him, while on his part, he felt a sort of trepidation emanating from his balanced and active organs, and when that happened he suffered from a depressing agony.

In the same trip of these two people with the same mission, at the same time and in the same geography, one writhed with fear chilling his heart while the other stayed so indifferent to everything that he seemed unlikely to react even if a wild beast came and mauled them dead. In the same atmosphere, one was impatient with disturbed temper, while the other appeared cool and devoid of desires, resembling an accomplished recluse.

Finally, Panchashar developed a mental tonic for himself and drank the same. Inclined toward a conclusion, he said to himself, 'Our life is secured under the canopy of the blessings of Kirat Devi, the sage at the ashram, Budha Subba and the Kirat tantrics. In fact, this is Kirat land. So we are safe here. There is no need for a traveler to feel unsafe here." He made himself assured, but Mauni had received a blessing never to raise the issue of fear and doubt. So he was busy in himself, mindless of the world around.

They took three days to reach Siddhapokhari from Vijaypur Township.

***

The topography of Siddhapokhari composed of stagnated water of the Tamor and Arun rivers flowing into it from two sides looked beautifully decorated with geographical diversity. Yet it looked dry and listless for want of natural vegetation. This deserted look seen in the middle of a green mountain range competed with the life of the citizens rendered desolate by monarchy, selfish leadership and terrorists. Though the weather was sunny and quite pleasurable, the incessant slapping of winds flowing through the Tamor and Arun had stripped the greenness there, making the landscape look as though youthfulness and beauty had never been able to touch it, and was like a human body living without purpose. Yet, Siddhapokhari has a great significance in that part of the world.

Siddhapokhari thrives, letting an old and lonely rhododendron tree stand on its ridge. Some distance away, a green mountain with all its majesty stands with its peak jutted skyward. It seems it is the lively statue of a Siddha Kirat[23] personage sitting there as foreseer of all times, looking at the universe without blinking its eyes even for a second. The plains to the eastern side of the peak is the head and the fountain of the Mangmaya River, and was safe as a thick, wide and awe-inspiring wilderness rich with inexhaustible natural vegetable including invaluable medicinal herbs. Since accomplished pursuers attained enlightenment through their stringent penance and meditations performed in various caves and crevices in this very wilderness, the pond also came to be known as Siddhapokhari—the accomplished pond. In fact, Siddhapokhari is also called Guphapokhari, 'gupha', meaning a cave, and 'pokhari', meaning a pond.

Guphapokhari is another name of the same place. When people accorded equal honor to the cave and the pond, the composite name 'Guphapokhari' possibly became popular. In that part of the world, this pond was the only place that had become the surest stay for travelers. Since there were no forests, cattle farms, yak farms and traveler's rests and inns here, the travelers no option but these

---

[23]   An accomplished person with miraculous and divine powers

caves for their shelter. The caves and the pond were quite close to one another. So the travelers putting up inside those caves made use of the pond.

Dhaap is a beautiful, sunlit and extensive lawn. When watched from the mouth of the cave, the lawn appears extending eastward across a long distance. It is at an extremely low altitude. When observed from the entrance of the cave, the people and animals on the lawn appeared only as big as ants, but the snowfall has never affected the geographical harshness and natural diversity of this place. Whenever there is snowfall, it covers each yard equally here, and the entire region looks clean and pristine. The significance of the pond, the apex of the green mountains, the beauty of the lawn of Dhaap, the pond therein, the sunlit lawn and the unimaginable meditation grove have become meditation spots, excursion sites, refuges and everything for the accomplished pursuers of this region. Whoever arrives here is sure to harvest mysterious influence and becomes overwhelmed with an extraordinary impression.

Panchashar and Mauni decided to take shelter at a cave beside Siddhapokhari.

The arduous highland trail in this wilderness, the thick forest with night-like darkness at midday, the never-ending trail, and the way inflected by steps made of tree roots had made their feet bruised beyond telling. How much more were they supposed to walk? Was that trip an obligation or a choice? Such questions too were not appropriate to that time perhaps. But then, such questions popped and tormented their minds from time to time.

From inside the forest, they could see a faint light at a distance. They walked following it, and come out at a small clearing. They stepped into the clearing and felt as though they had come out into the free world after a long session of meditation inside a cave.

Thick woods on three sides, while the fourth side was fenced by a naked, rocky cliff. This was how the topography of the highland, locally called 'akkar', looked like.

Drinking the stunning beauty of the lawn with his eyes, Panchashar thought, 'Nature must have gifted beautiful lawn to *Kinnar-Kinnaris*[24] to play cricket.'

Seeing a huge, round-shaped rock lie on its own on one end of the lawn, Panchashar said, "Perhaps the gods come here during leisure and make a shot-put of this stone and enjoy."

Seeing the lawn divided roughly into two halves from the middle, he made an acrid remark: "How beautiful it would have been, if they had let the lawn stay undivided!"

The human, however, cannot bring changes in his thought easily. He could push his movement along keeping himself aloof from the utmost utilization of natural beauty, and such a journey could be enjoyable and complete too, but the reality is that beauty is not considered beauty in its own term if it is not brought to humanly use anyway. Underutilization of beauty is its sheer neglect. After all, if this trail had not passed by the side of this lawn, how could the description of this place's attractiveness and constant freshness be ever made? Isn't this thread-like trail that passed by the side of the lawn the most trustworthy companion and the lone umpire to the lawn, the fence-like forest, the tall, stone-like mountain standing there like an umpire and the tradition of its utilization and historical eulogies? Why should one overlook so many merits and make negative comments?

With their eyes filled with contentment and hearts filled with joy, they moved ahead toward their destination. The trail entered a forest once again. They had hardly taken a few steps when they saw a brown-furred cow sitting right on the trail, posing an impediment to them. They walked near to the cow.

"If there is anyone barring the way, the traveler should stop. He should not swerve, return or make a diversion. One can move only after the path is cleared, or permission is procured." This was what someone had told Panchashar once, giving a glimpse of the Limbuwan tradition. The same started ringing in his ears

---

[24]   men and women singers from heaven as mentioned in Hindu scriptures

repeatedly now. "*Gaumata*[25], accept my reverence, and give us a way," he said, praying with utmost modesty.

He was careful lest cultural decorum should be defaulted from his side. If he was proven guilty of ignoring *Gaumata* and ignoring cultural expectations, nothing would be worse than that in his life. Considering the same, he stood there stupefied.

Caught in this difficulty for a long time, he paid a quick look on Mauni, expecting a way out of the fix. Mauni wrote on a stone, "This is a roaming place for Siddha Kirats. Who knows if we are being tested at every step?"

Panchashar scanned Mauni's face as well. It was rippling with excitement and enthusiasm.

In the meantime, the cow stood up, stretched its body, and took a sigh, giving a twist to its snout. Letting them their way, it said, "I was waiting for you. Come; let's go. I also will go with you."

The cow accompanied, being their co-traveler.

After they had traveled for a while, they saw a huge deer sit on their way. On seeing them, the deer stood with a start and stretched its body thoroughly.

"Please give us our way," said Panchashar with modesty, praying to the deer with his palms joined.

"I will also walk with you," said the deer announcing its decision and followed them. Its well-developed antlers, rendered pointed, sharp and glistening by repeated use, were by nature dangerous enough to send chill down anyone's spine in solitude. How could understand that it had developed and toughened its antlers merely for the sake of self-defense?

After they had moved along a few more yards, they encountered a dog barring their way. Seeing a cow, a deer and two men approaching it, the dog stood up. Jutting out its long tongue and taking a sigh, the dog said, "I will also go with you. I was waiting for you." The dog followed them.

---

[25] "Mother Cow!" The cow is considered a mother by the Hindus and worshipped as a goddess

Mauni grew even more introvert with curiosity and surprise. Even as they were dragging their feet in the midst of bewilderment, Mauni and Panchashar sat down helplessly on the ground. The cow took the lead now, following by the deer and the dog, and the two men started following them.

After walking for a long time, they all arrived at the same beautiful lawn. This time, an enormous elephant had been waiting for them on the lawn. Declaring that it would also join the troupe, the elephant started walking in the lead.

Panchashar's contemplation no more helped him now. Mauni could sense that his friend was now trapped inside a labyrinth. He thought, 'Are we at the same spot again? Was our walk all through these hours pointless? How can we free ourselves from this mess now? These cannot be ordinary beasts. They must be transformed incarnations of some distinguished personages.'

Mauni ran his eyes all around and watched the lawn, the forest, the rocky cliff and the path that divided the lawn into two halves. With great self-confidence, he then said, "It's not illusion; this is the same place where we had been before. It is we who are in illusion."

The cow, deer dog and the elephant stood in front of them, making a line. Their eyes were soaked with tears, simmering all over.

To search out the cultural and aesthetic significance of the eyes of the cow and the deer, Panchashar started rummaging the literary and cultural arena. Who could understand the internal feelings of these gullible animals that could not defend themselves in need? Yet, feigning to understand their internal feelings through the reading of their tearful eyes, Panchashar spoke in a humble way, prioritizing his own convictions: "I am ready to walk with you, and I won't opt out of this journey. But the main problem lies in defending lives, which I cannot do because I am myself a traveler in an unknown land, and it is not easy for me to defend even myself. So you all ought to forgive me and bless me instead. Our journey and mission shall both be fruitful. Tell us the way out of this labyrinth. We are caught in sheer illusion. This is the only request I have got to make with you all."

The animals surrounded them from all three sides and said, "We will also go with you. Do not abandon us here."

They reiterated their decision. Seeing that the situation was not changing, Panchashar said, "I cannot save you from the arduous path, selfish human, merciless wild animals and inhospitable nature. So I beg your pardon for my obligation and incapacity."

Stealing a chance, he added, "If I return along the same route, I can take you along to any place I go." This way, Panchashar announced his final decision.

The cow, elephant, deer and the dog stared at one another and shook their heads and ears in a gesture of satisfaction. In a single voice they said, "Never think of an alternative way for return. You ought to keep this very path. There should be no trick in that. Come with us here for a while."

All of them mounted on a stone. Together in a single voice, the cow, elephant, deer and the dog said, "Until you return, we shall sit on this big stone and keep waiting. Never forget this place, this stone and your promise to return. If you forget us, we will leave our footprints atop this stone here and go. Those footprints shall be the testimony to the fact that we died waiting for your return. Let no one in due course be obliged to hear a story of our death while waiting for your return."

They drew a long breath and added, "Traveler, keep this fact in your mind: avert a future charge from the mass that the animals kept their promise but a man didn't. This is all that we have got to say."

The cow, elephant, deer and the dog finished their say.

Panchashar woke up and analyzed every shred of his dream. He recalled the promise he had made with the cow, elephant, deer and the dog. It was a story-like dream. He made it sure that it was some time past midnight now. He told himself, 'How come I had such a long dream and the night hasn't waned yet.' He was partly distressed.

The chill there was quite unruly. It was coldness that had shaken him up from his sleep. This is what he surmised.

There was no fire inside the dark crevice of the cave anymore. The fire too was asleep, perhaps. Panchashar focused his ears to every corner of the cave; they were filled with sounds of other people snoring, scratching their bodies and hair, shivering in the chill, occasional low murmur and long, monotonous self-conversation.

Composing the pace of his organs in himself, he tried to collect some sleep. He fell asleep again. Soon he was in the world of the dream, only to make an abrupt comeback.

This time, he didn't revert to sleeping. He passed the rest of the night waiting for sunrise, but Mauni continued to sleep without any care.

He made good attempt to study the soul of his dream. He felt as though someone was giving him an advice in the fashion of an *akashvani*[26]. Announcing his agreement, he said, "That's fine. I shall go only after beholding Mangmaya's descend."

In order not to forget these words he uttered in his dream, he repeated "Mangmaya, Mangmaya…"

***

---

[26] a mysterious sound coming from an unknown source in the sky

CHAPTER TWO

THE LIVING WORLD started ringing with commotion. The birds started their morning lays. Panchashar realized that it was morning now.

The eastern horizon displayed the crimson hue. The snow-capped mountains glittered with flame-like radiance. When this redness was over, it was replaced by a yellowish hue. With the passage of time, the peaks in its vicinity turned golden, when blondness emanating from the juvenile sun spilled over their summits, and the entire panorama looked stunningly pristine. The greenness on the ground, however, had to wait for a longer time before getting the warm touch of the sun's rays.

The cave at Siddhapokhari used by travelers as shelter faced east. The land in front of it was unusually sloppy, descending steeply down to the large lawn therein. So the sunrays fell directly on the mouth of the cave without any impediment. The first touch of the rays painted Panchashar's countenance red. He experienced the addition of altogether new types of life-rays entering him immediately. He soon finished his yogic postures to hail the sun and ran his eyes on the rest of the world in front of him.

On the north-eastern direction from the cave, one could see Chuli, a green mountain, jutting quite high in its mighty physical existence. Panchashar's eyes fell on the same. Its east-facing part looked pristine with the fall of the morning sunrays, while the part on the west looked grim with a paint of darkness, for the time was still at the junction between day and night. Focusing his eyes in this in-between moment, Panchashar concentrated further. In it, he could see fuzzy, dim, dynamic, linear and moving pace of life one sees when the eyes shift suddenly from light to darkness or from sunshine to shade.

Smoke rising from the cowsheds and meditation centers in the mountains stopped meandering in the clean sky now.

Soon there was change in the color of the sunrays. The mountain ranges spread along a distance as far as one's eyes could see, now turned silver. Before long, peaks like Kanchanjungha, Kumbhakarna, Jaljalé and all peaks in Singhaleela mountain ranges turned white, like a yogi clad completely in white, pure and clean robes.

In a while, the dynamic life seen on the western side of the green mountain in the dim light of dawn came near to the cave, playing all sorts of tunes to Kirati instruments and turned into a huge gathering. But now, such a huge human congregation standing in the strip of land between the cave and the pond was now utterly silent.

Seeing such a huge human gathering at such a desolate place, Panchashar was tickled by several questions and curiosities rising in his mind.

In that community, an old man seemed taking the lead. It seemed that he was the guru, director, cultural spokesperson, leader or a yogi in that group. His looks, pace, dress and jewelry suggested that he was a distinguished and highly revered person.

At a signal from that leading personality, a troupe from the community started playing musical instruments from which an auspicious melody of welcome and reception emanated. After his instrumental piece, the leader came a few feet ahead, joined his palms and said with humbleness, "Dear guests, we are people of the Kirat Limboo community living around Mauwa Khola Thum that falls under Limbuwan. We welcome you into our land. Welcome."

Once again, the band played an auspicious tune.

Panchashar sent the gestures of welcoming their reception by folding his hands and bowing down to the group.

Mauni stayed alert, observing all these contexts. He was astounded, though he went on receiving all those scenes with love.

The leader turned his eyes toward his people. Taking immense degree of spiritual inspiration, he turned to Panchashar and said,

"Guest, you happened to be an expert of architecture. We in our part are short of a beautiful palace for the kingdom of Kirat. Please build a royal palace for us which can assume a historical significance. This is what we expect from you."

After a brief pause, he again said, "The palace should be ready by the end of this day. We shall supply all the construction materials in ample quantity. You have such a huge human resource standing in front of you. There shall be no dearth of working hands." He added, "At the moment, we are short of stones. I shall manage them shortly."

Panchashar was astounded on hearing the words of the leader.

Mauni moved his eyebrows many times.

The spark of a mysterious thought rose and started smoldering Panchashar. He said to himself, 'A devilish royal dynasty shall extend its hand into this region some time later. That moment, the Rais and the Limboos from the Kirat dynasty shall forget their power and ethnic consciousness, and in a cowardly manner, volunteer to surrender their power. Why then do they need a royal palace then? If ever they can reclaim their power a royal palace befitting that age can be constructed for the kingdom of the Kirats. Why this haste? Materials are built and stories for the sake of consumption. If there is no possibility of consumption, what worth is constructing and collecting things?'

But the leader was firm in his mission. Pointing toward Jhyaupokhari, Nundhiki and Milké, he said, "Build it somewhere here, at a spot you think proper, or where it stands best or you consider fine."

A huge stretch of land on Arun bank lying as a flood-swept basin looked extremely attractive. It appeared that the people had procured in gift this sunlight and extensive plain land near to Guphapokhari. One could easily speculate that the mountain ranges that appeared standing far away could work as inaccessible forts for the palace to be built here. Panchashar's eyes were yet to be satiated with the natural beauty of this place. So he stood focused with deep concentration.

Even as he was observing, a patch of dark cloud appeared suddenly in the pure, clean sky. Soon the patch changed, and it turned even darker and appeared enraged and terrific. The sky overhead was soon overcast, and soon it canopied such a huge, extensive flatland until it was almost invisible. The cloud descended to the ground, and surprised everyone by throwing opaque veils on the eyes of the onlookers. Soon the people present there started feeling that they were in a different world.

The environment there suddenly turned dark and fearful. Thunder started shaking the entire sky. Lightning started terrifying everyone with its whips. There were terrifying voices like that of landslide, flooded river sweeping down boulders, and the wind slapping with fatal blows, pushing each moment toward inevitable end. There was a deafening thunderbolt when this natural calamity was at its climax and its manifestation was macabre, and the same froze every heart with terror.

But this state of natural ghastliness and terror didn't last long, for it was a calamity devised by will, like an artificially devised event, which had been done by Siddha Kirats for a specified purpose. So the day smiled once again as before, and everyone appeared happy. They shared happiness among themselves. They all experienced utter darkness and dazzling light within a short interval.

Giving his directives in a joyous mood, the Kirat leader said, "Guests, please look there. The stones have also been managed." Pointing as his people now, he said, "These people of mine shall do as you instruct them. You can finish constructing the royal palace before sunset today."

Panchashar was left gawking by the extraordinary power of the Kirat leader. He felt as though the whole of Kirat land was a land of magic. A person who could deploy natural forms and powers to procure an object of his desire as promised could not, at any rate, be an ordinary one. In the Kirat leader, a special being had become manifest in the human form. There was no doubt that he was an accomplished man. Panchashar thought so and told himself, 'I should not exhibit any short of erudition here. Else, my mission will be defeated.'

Mauni was keenly studying the gestures of the Kirat leader. The people of the Kirat community gathered there sat in discipline, observing those incidents and dialogues.

Panchashar walked two steps forward, folded his hands before the Kirat leader and said, "Revered one, who happened to be an accomplished personage. After having an audience with you, I consider my life successful. I honor your power and commitments in high terms. I believe that under your guardianship, the life of the people in Kirat land is well provided for and is highly developed."

He drew in a long breath and added one more paragraph to his speech: "Venerable one! I am a child in front of you. I can never know what powers lie inside you and what your viewpoints are. I had heard that there are great and accomplished men and women in the Kirat community. Today, I saw it myself, met you and came to know about it. I consider this an outcome of your special compassion upon me. And this is for me, and for all of us, a matter of pride."

Ending his statement, Panchashar paid a quick glance to Mauni. Mauni was quite happy and in a joyous mood as always.

Running his eyes on the people who gathered there, Panchashar started speaking once again, "Siddha Baba[27]! I appreciate the love, honor and compassion you showed on us with my open heart. I am a traveler who set out with a fixed goal. I have to reach there in the stipulated time. Else my journey and my reaching there later in time shall all be worthless. Please consider me a child and pardon me. I have no time to construct a royal palace for you."

Siddha Kirat leader was left stunned. His bright yellow robes suddenly turned red. The Kirat people started observing these changes in him with stupefied eyes. The leader considered that young Panchashar was not disobeying or defaulting on his promise, but was showing his reluctance. But he controlled his words and

---

[27] The accomplished one!

turned introvert. His ears started ringing with the recurrent echo of the words 'child', 'pardon', 'traveler' and 'goal'. His eyes turned crimson, and before long, turned moist. His body started trembling from within. For a short duration of time, he turned completely mute.

The air turned gravely silent. None could predict what would follow next and how such an uncomfortable moment would be over. But they could at least hope that Siddha Kirat leader would take some immediate and balanced decision and control the situation from getting worse.

Pondering over the situation, Panchashar counseled himself, 'At any rate, I should not annoy the Kirat leader. That will invite a disaster. Instead, I should receive his blessings."

Conjuring some courage, he spoke in clear terms, "Siddha Baba, I wish for great fame and progress of the Kirat royal family and all the Limboos living in this part of the world. Let this community come out successful in reclaiming power in its own hands, and let it rule in the fairest way, brining prosperity to all its subjects."

Pausing for a while and running his eyes on the people there, he said, "Today, this community has become like a domestic elephant tamed by a *mahout*[28]. By that token, it doesn't know what its real power is. It's like a tiger whose teeth and claws have been taken out; it has no estimation of its real power and might. Let this community that established the Kirat dynasty and ruled for a long time awake once again. Let it rise and get committed to reclaiming its waning existence. This is my good wish for you all."

In the fashion of a speech, he added, "At any rate, a tiger doesn't eat grass. It should never descend to the rank of ordinary animals; that doesn't suit a tiger. This community should not tolerate the seizure of its regime and the obligation to become someone else's serf." Lending stress to his words, he said, "It's a coward's trait to accept defeat or relinquish power without fighting. I ask you: How did the Kirat committee face defeat in a land that has accomplished

---

[28]   The person who is in charge of an elephant

personages like you? How was it disposed from its rule? How come this community is trying to forget this acrid fact? How is it tolerating such a grave agony? Why does the community accept the position of a servant to sustain others' regimes, throwing or losing its own? I want to throw hundreds of such question before every learned Kirat scholar so that they become awakened."

After a while, he added, "Venerable one! One should bear whatever happens on his land and region. So, my proposal is that the adage '*birbhogya basundhara*'[29] should come out true here. May you be reminded: a fox cannot be the master in the tigers' land!"

There was silence once again. Siddha Kirat leader stood mute as though he had been forsaken of his speech. Panchashar turned silent too, apparently tired of speaking. Mauni appeared busy studying the time and context therein, looking at the Kirat lasses carrying flowers in their baskets or at placid mass therein, or the sudden silence and compassionate gestures of the accomplished leader or sometimes at his friend Panchashar.

Panchashar came two steps ahead, and lowering his head in front of Siddha Kirat leader said, "Respectable Baba! We need to take our way now. Please give us your permissions." While making this request, Panchashar stood with his hands folded together.

The accomplished leader raised his palm in the fashion of blessing and from his tear-soaked throat spoke, "Let your journey succeed without any trouble." After this, he could not utter any word.

Within seconds, the Kirat lasses made a shower of flower petals and changed the entire atmosphere. The situation now turned quite comfortable and normal. In fact, the silence of their leader had become a matter of concern for the Kirat community. When he resumed his speech while giving permission to the travelers to launch their journey ahead, they all felt a relief like the one they feel on being freed from a smothering nightmare. Ceasing a moment, the Kirat lasses showered rhododendron petals in the air once

---

[29]   The brave ones rule the earth

again, sending forth a current of joy to everyone. The air turned joyous, believing that the choking session of the formal program was now thankfully over. Harmony returned to the atmosphere now. They were at ease finally and experienced a sort of lightness.

At this moment, a gentleman came forward from the Kirat gathering. His external looks suggested that he was a people's representative. When he came forward, the accomplished leader moved a few steps back. Seeing the situation changed and the atmosphere transformed, one could surmise that the episode of the accomplished leader was over and a new chapter was beginning.

Siddha Kirat, Panchashar and this new gentleman stood facing one another roughly at the three vertices of a triangle. Mauni was five to seven steps back.

"Guests, we are highly impressed with your decent and cultured manners. We are happy. So today, at this moment, we shall gift you the dearest and the best thing in our possession, and by that token, we will make you ours. You must accept it," the gentleman said in a modest language. Like a ripple rising on a placid pond, a peal of curiosity rippled through the silent gathering of the Kirat people. It was moved by curiosity and impatience.

Siddha Kirat was not familiar with this situation. So he also stayed alert, eager to see and hear the new thing. He ran his eyes through the mass once and stayed mute.

The gentleman, who looked like a people's representative, looked at the maidens with eyes simmering with kindness, compassion and honor. Seemingly deciphering the signals of his looks, two beautiful Kirat maidens came out of the group of girls and stood between the gentleman and the accomplished leader.

Clasping the two maidens gently on his left and right, the gentleman turned toward Panchashar and spoke in a tone resembling that of a request and a prayer, "Taking you for a dear and honorable guest, we offer you these two maidens. You must accept them." He then turned to the maidens, one at a time in turn, and placing his palm atop their heads said, "Go. You both go with him."

The maidens were in dresses, cosmetics and jewelries that reflected Kirat culture. They went close to Panchashar and stood on the left and right sides of him.

The people standing there watched this spectacle with joy, and treasured its memory in the core of their minds. Such an incident had never taken place in the past and was least likely to recur in future. Nor had anyone heard of anything like this. The Kirat spectators stood flabbergasted, considering and thinking about such mysterious happenings.

Introducing the maidens, the gentleman said, "The one standing on the left side is Sanjhang. She is the elder one. One on the right side is Teejhang, and is the younger. You must accept them."

Folding his hands, Panchashar said with humility, "I accept them."

Perhaps considering his mission fulfilled, the gentleman moved two steps backward. Everything took place as though it was a pre-meditated program. The task of receiving the guests was undertaken like in a traditional ritual.

Taking two steps forward from his standing place, Siddha Kirat said, "Respected guest, these maidens are timeless. Their youthfulness never wanes. They have received the blessings of eternal youthfulness from our accomplished gurus." He stopped for a while and said, "A man that comes in contact with them shall also be eternal young."

He uttered the remaining sentences to himself. He said, 'These girls shall never become mothers. They shall ever stay in the glory of their virginity, and shall always stay revered in the society. They shall become monumental.'

The people gathered there were wonderstruck on hearing the accomplish Kirat's words. No one there knew before about the blessing of eternal youthfulness their sisters had received from their accomplished gurus. A peal of curiosity ran through everyone. There was whispering in the traditional fashion for a while. After that, the atmosphere turned silent again.

Panchashar joined his hands and said in a tone of request, "Accomplished Guru! How should I walk along such a long way through Tibet, right up to China, having with me such tender young girls who have just entered adolescence? You please be the patrons of these daughters yourself. Let them stay under the warmth of your love and care. Let them face no dishonor and feel no insult. I shall return to take them later."

"That's fine. After parting with you, they shall live in a cave in the Chuli Mountain there. They shall be waiting for you, and shall always remain impatient to meet you as their dearest one. There shall be no change in the love and care we had been lending them. I make this promise from the side of our people's representative. There shall be no wanting of anything."

The gentleman who had presented the Kirat maidens moved two steps forward and said, "Dear guest, we respect your feelings." Turning his eyes toward the mass, he said, "You addressed our prayers. So we express our thankfulness to you. I now make a special request from the side of all of us gathered here. We need to accomplish a small ritual. We will take you toward our village now. You must accept this request as well."

Panchashar turned toward Mauni. Mauni showed his writing on a slate: "*Shubhashya shigram*[30]!"

At the beginning of their journey, a Kirat ceremonial melody was played by the band. After this, they commenced their journey. The adult Kirat men and women moved toward the village of Sanghu together with guests, like in a nuptial procession, dancing, hopping, moving back and forth, whistling, playing their pipes and hollering at places. As desired by the gentleman, Panchashar had, that moment, become the central figure.

Owing to different costumes, cosmetics and decorations of various colors, this procession of the Kirats looked like a moving garden of flowers. It suggested a light of innumerable and colorful butterflies flying over a green, velvety lawn. On seeing a pile of

---

[30] (Sanskrit) The sooner, the better

stones meant for constructing a royal palace for the Kirat kings, pulled down on earth by Siddha Kirat just a while ago, the procession stopped for a while. The sight amazed every member of the procession. These stones, scattered over a huge stretch of land looked like books of the same size that had fallen from a basket and were laying there, one staked upon the other, each asserting its own identity. The travelers stepped upon the same and moved ahead, keeping their tract along the pre-existing trail.

On knowing about such power and capacity of Siddha Kirat, this group of travelers grew even more faithful to him. It was not an ordinary thing on their part to see such a man from the Kirat clan in their own lifetime, to see his miracles and experience the same first-hand. Everyone present there felt proud of the personality of Siddha Kirat, and thanked themselves for the luck. All along their way, they discussed his accomplishment and power. In a matter of short time, he became the talk of the day inside Mauwa Khola Thum.

People keeping this route to observe Udhauli and Ubhauli took rest on the bank of the pond on reaching Jhyaupokhari. This community of the Kirat travelers did the same that day. The eyes of everyone once fell on the lofty land above the back wall of the pond. This wall of this east-facing pond, lush will a burst of blooming rhododendrons, was stable seemingly eager to welcome the travelers. Like others, Panchashar and Mauni also enjoyed the fragrance of the natural beauty here. As a matter of fact, nature's panorama one could see here was matchless.

Neruwa, the main tributary of river called Mauwa Khola emanated from Jhyaupokhari. This region and the green fields in its vicinity looked covetous, alluring one to roll over their grassy surface. Jaljalé, the mountain range in the shape of an arc standing on its north-eastern side was standing like a fort seemingly giving it its security. That had made the natural beauty of this place uniquely extraordinary.

The eyes of everyone were caught by the nourishing, wide and flat plains in Neruwa. On seeing the flock of mountain sheep and the huge Tibetan dogs—that reminded the onlooker of bears—reaching here to escape winter chill, everyone was delighted. Though they didn't read the Tibetan scripts on prayer wheels, they took them for instances of faith and reverence. At short intervals, they could hear the faint bleating of the sheep. But the Tibetan dogs, meant to defend the flocks of sheep, barked at times, breaking the silence of the entire region, sending tremors across the earth and heaven.

At this time of the year, the spring hue of nature seemed to have aroused natural excitement in the entire animal kingdom.

The lower banks of Neruwa had become fertile grazing grounds for the *chaunris*[31], yaks, horses and mules. From their dresses, their stewards and merchants looked like people coming down from the highlands. As soon as they met the villagers here, they asked if they would be willing to buy wool, salt, gold, *jimmu*[32], *hing*[33], butter from sheep's milk brought down from Lhasa. They also asked if they would barter these stuffs for maize or millet. Their accent used to be unique and musical to some extent, but was rather incomprehensible for the local people. So they needed repetition many a time to grasp the words.

The Sherpas, Tamangs and Gurungs living in the remote high Himalayan locations like Mauwa Khola, Muwa Khola, Tamor Khola, Tokpé Gola and Olangchunggola, also moved to various locations with their homemade products like woolen blankets (called *radi* or *mandré*), *pakhi*, *chharra*, *chukut* and carpets. But the quality and value of stuffs these people brought as they came down once in a year used to be quite high and commendable. Normally, things were bartered instead of selling for cash, and they did it by measuring in traditional ways. So in their transactions, measuring units like *mana, pathi, muthi, doko, dalo* or *thunse* were used more than *dharni, bisauli* or *aathpol*.

---

[31] *chaunri* is the female and yak the male of the same species of mountain cattle reared in the upper Himalayas of Nepal

[32] a herbal spice used in lentils and vegetables

[33] a spice

These migrant trades that looked simple, dirty, dull and filthy from without were quite smart and visionary from within. They traded in a myriad of things from simple to highly valuable ones. Besides *chaunris*, horses and Tibetan dogs, they also traded in *kasturi bina*, *shilajeet* and many other medicinal herbs of the rarest kinds. At places, they also established *miteri* relations. If pleased, they gifted carpets, blankets, coral necklaces and *churpi* necklaces before leaving.

At the time of Ubhauli and Udhauli, the plains of Phalaté, Neruwa, Milké, Jhyaupokhari around Mauwa Khola Thum region used to be filled with flocks of yaks or horses or animals coming from Uttarakhand or with bands of traders once or twice a year.

Since this region was a green, fertile and sunlit rich in fodder, its lower part had a huge settlement of people living in thick villages. Since people didn't have to worry about leafy boughs, firewood, water and security, the traders came here with ease and ran their business activities safely.

The way leading to Kantipur from Olangchunggola, Sinwa, Mauwa Dobhan, Mewa Dobhan (Dhulé), Tembé, Sanghu, Milké, Chainpur, Bhojpur and Khotang, the upper part of Sanghu Village, especially Milké-Maidané and the lower plains to its vicinity became centers for people trading in vehicles and livestock. Panchashar and Mauni moved, collecting information about all these activities.

The group moved downhill with a gush, reached Pati Danda hill, and stopped for a short repose. The people sat on wooden benches, branches of the banyan tree, stone slabs on the *chautari*, the shade of *hattibar* tree, and the clean stones scattered therein.

Panchashar sat on the wooden bench moving his feet. Sanjhang and Teejhang went and sat on his two sides. Sanjhang and Teejhang looked extremely delicate, tender and seductive, maybe because of walking or the burst of their natural beauty. 'These maidens are timeless. Their youthfulness never wanes.' These words spoken by Siddha Kirat some time ago started echoing in his ears. He turned more and more introvert. He tried to keep his amorous musings under restraint, and instead, tried to grasp a dramatic, dream-like vision. Finally, he reached a conclusion: 'These are not from this mortal world. They must be young incarnates, who have descended from a different world to accomplish a certain mission. My relations with them should be interesting and energetic and not fatal at any cost. It should be a blessed one, instead.'

He drew this conclusion.

That procession of the Kirat community managed a shelter for the guest and their sisters at a place called Sattal inside the village of Sanghu. After they were knotted in a relation, the Limboo people accomplished their social rituals as well and shared their joy. Under a care of some helpers and patrons, they arranged private places for guest and the brides to rest peacefully, while the rest of the villages moved homeward.

The Kirat brides prepared dinner with help and instructions from their friends. Sanjhang started serving meals while Teejhang walked near to her beloved husband Panchashar with a pail of water for him to clean his hands and feet.

"Ouch, how cold is this water!" Panchashar exclaimed, touching the water.

"This water is from Mangmaya."

"It's quite thick too."

"Everyone says the same," said Teejhang, tendered a complete reply in a few words.

"Mangmaya! Mangmaya!" Panchashar remembered the word. The previous night, he had learnt the same word and heard it. Resolving on his own, he said, "This is the name I had heard in my dream. I should reach Mangmaya once at any cost." Turning toward Teejhang now, he said, "Sani, what is Mangmaya? It is a river or a tap?"

"It's a river, but it flows like a fall," said Teejhang.

"Can we reach there? How far is it?" he asked, expressing his curiosity.

"It's up there. We can reach in a while," she said and smiled. Panchashar was glued to Teejhang's countenance and her style of answering. He was left gawking by her guiltless dialogues, cool countenance and leveled teeth. She held him by his hand and led him into the kitchen for dinner.

Inside, Sanjhang had been waiting for them. Others sat in line waiting for the guest before helping themselves. A separate place had been stipulated for Panchashar to sit on. As soon as she saw him there, Sanjhang appeared like a flower.

"Thuli, I beg your pardon. I made you wait too long." Turning toward the people waiting for him, Panchashar said, "I also beg your pardon. I was asking Sani about Mangmaya." He gave a short but bright clarification.

No one tendered any reaction to the words of their guest. Instead, they were pleased to see his modesty. Before sitting for dinner, he said, "I am yet to learn your practices. Today is my first day here. Do you have any rule one has to observe at mealtime?"

"We have a small request," said one from among the people who had sat in line to eat. He said, "If all three of you sit in front of all of us and eat from the same plate, a new flavor would be added to our feast." Having said this, the speaker laughed out, and others added their laughter to support his proposal. The petty atmosphere therein grew quite lively. The man stood up from the line and said, "This shall be a souvenir for all of us. It shall make us even more intimate and we will come to love one another even more."

Drawing in a long breath, he said, "I am not sure if my proposal will make you feel uncomfortable. In that case, I apologize, and take my proposal back. I don't want an indecent thing to happen in our society and tradition."

For a while, people gazed at one another's faces. A man that looked more aged than others stood up and said, "We, the Limboos in the Kirat community mould our mores and practices according to the changing time, and adopt and start new mores and practices. Therefore, we experience life and with awakening, and share the same with others."

He further added, "We accept the practices our elders and respected ones handed down to us, and we follow their advices. We support them, considering them the words of our king, gods and the society. At this home today, in fact in the whole of Sattal, I am the eldest man. So, on behalf of my sons (turning toward men) and daughters (turning toward women) I announce, "Our guest and brides should accept our proposal."

"This is a matter of happiness for me. Your daughters can put this proposal into action," said Panchashar, expressing his mind clearly.

Sanjhang and Teejhang blushed with embarrassment. Then they faced each other.

The old man gave some signals to a Kirat maiden. The maiden placed three cushions, made of maize husks, so that they made three vertices of a triangle. Panchashar, Sanjhang and Teejhang sat one each. The rest surrounded them as onlookers.

The helping girl served the trio, arraying every item artistically on the same plate.

A member from the brides' family present there said, "For us, you are our guest and respected ones. You start helping yourselves and feeding one another. Whenever our gods, guests and daughters eat, we consider that our goddesses have eaten. We don't need a different ritual anymore." The speaker made the procedure quite plain.

Panchashar, who was silent for a while, returned to his form and fed Sanjhang and Teejhang a measure of rice each. The brides also fed him in the same way. Then Sanjhang and Teejhang fed each other, thereby launching a new practice.

Soon the feasting was over. Arranging comfortable stays for the guest and his brides, everyone went out into a plain and fallow terrace in Sattal. The Kirat boys and girls performed Dhaan Naach all through the night and sang until it was dawn. The seniors and the middle-aged ones entertained themselves performing Chyabrung dance.

But Mangmaya stood awake all the night.

Panchashar didn't care where Mauni slept and how. But Mauni fully embraced one segment of the Limboo culture until he was fully satisfied. When there were short intervals between songs and dances, he played local tunes on his flute, and reached everyone's heart.

One painful aspect of the whole affair was that Panchashar had not introduced Mauni to others in that community till now. Everything was progressing smoothly on its own accord and there was no need for anyone to be especially focused on any individual.

At the break of the day, the romantic Limboo folks wound up their nightlong singing and dancing, and took their ways homeward.

To make the next day even more special, Sanjhang and Teejhang organized a picnic. Inside a farm at the north-eastern side of Sattal, there was a goose-berry tree. The picnic was organized at its base. With help from their friends, Sanjhang and Teejhang prepared their meals, and served it for everyone with their own hands. The day passed as a joyful day, and a day of rest. After this, the two brides started losing themselves in their own imaginations, impatiently waiting for the sun to set soon.

Many things were quite easy that day, devoid of any conflict.

***

The cock crowed. The birds started chirping. There was a spell of awakening in the human society.

That was the day when they were set to visit Mangmaya. Clear was the sky, and the morning light had started spilling everywhere in its rosiness. The stars had started disappearing fast from the face of the sky. The main road had woken up long back.

Sanjhang, Teejhang and Panchashar moved uphill from Sattal, expecting to reach Mangmaya. On the way, they were pursued by a huge black Tibetan dog. They took him for their security guard. Walking along terraces, ridges, fringes of the farm and steep slopes, they reached the path leading to the main canal. Walking past Karim-Karim, they moved ahead along the foot of the hill and the top of the village, until they arrived at Mangmaya, the spot from where people observed the water fall. From no other spot did Mangmaya Fall as beautiful as it did from here.

The white, foamy water falling off a black, blue, green and verdant mountainous world looked so beautiful before the touch of the sunrays that it resembled a flow of milk. It appeared like the natural topography here had put on a vertical *tika* of sandalwood as the Vaishnavs[34] do. It looked like a loin of an ideal personage, having deep faith in culture had strewn there to dry in the sun after a holy bath. The local eyes could see that it was not merely Mangmaya Fall but was a loom set up by a Limboo maiden to weave indigenous cotton clothes. In fact, it was an amazing spectacle of an entire river falling in the form of a cascade in the middle of a green, sylvan province. All three of them got deeply absorbed in this mesmerizing panorama.

Panchashar assured himself, 'True! Mangmaya is a huge mountainous river descending in the form of a waterfall as Teejhang said.' From the fall of Mangmaya, the wind used to carry water sprays and take them far and wide. The plants to its left and right always stood completely soaked. The spectators that came here to see the Mangmaya Fall also got drenched in no time.

Even as they were watching, the rays of the sun started bathing in the Mangmaya Fall. The fall of juvenile sunrays in the spray of water led to the development of a rainbow entrance in no time. It seemed, Mother Nature had prepared for herself a bathroom. The water birds, in terms of pairs, flew on their own accords and played in the water here. The mesmerizing scene opened yet another door leading to an imaginary world. In fact, the place wherefrom the gush of Mangmaya sprang had a pool that seduced every spectator to take a dive and play in the water. The aquatic and terrestrial beings came and played here freely according to their time and interest.

Standing on the right side of Panchashar, Sanjhang took an imaginary flight and dived into the pool together with Panchashar

---

[34] The followers of Lord Vishnu, a Hindu deity

for water-play, holding him tightly in her arms. Chilled by the freezing cold therein, Teejhang who stood shivering on the right side of Panchashar, got hold of his arms and said, "Our sweats have dried out, and it's very cold now. We should return, shouldn't we?"

Panchashar's concentration was disrupted. He looked at his two brides turn by turn. On their tresses, eyebrows, eyelashes, lips and chins, there were a drop of water each, clung with the exposure of their existence in entirety. Panchashar first touched the drop on Teejhang's tresses with his palm; his palm was soaked. He then turned right and run his fingers over Sanjhang's eyebrows, eyelashes and lips, wiping the water drops. Following this, he clasped Teejhang with his arms and said in fondly, "Sani, as you said, we must return now." By letting her eyes meet those of Panchashar, Teejhang sent forth a new sort of emotion. On her part, she treasured an unprecedented experience deep inside her heart.

All these acts were intimate and easy. Some of them were permissible by right, while others were harmonious. Sanjhang and Teejhang made such estimation of those acts: pure and thrilling. At the touch of Panchashar, they both experienced a sort of movement and thrill touching them in an unknown way. They felt that ripples of ecstasy were tickling the core of their hearts like waves of electric current in repeated bouts. They also felt that the currents were gradually developing into sources of bliss and curiosity.

Whatever Sanjhang and Teejhang experienced with their bodies and minds gradually developed into mutual curiosities. They could not, however, share with the other the types of feelings they had in their cores. Instead, they opted to keep those feelings concealed inside their minds safely.

A flock of emoiselle cranes was seen flying northward over the sky above this sylvan, hilly place. On seeing them Panchashar considered that these birds he had seen, and the name 'Mangmaya' he had heard in his dream, had finally come true. He repeated to himself the fruition of his dream. He then turned toward his brides standing on his left and right, looked at them with love-filled eyes and sent forth a new but curious spell of smiles.

All three of them turned introvert now. They started getting absorbed in themselves, and started taking several rounds inside their own mental worlds. Each of them started emphasizing the fact that they should decipher others' mental status. They grew more and more passionate, probably because they were being tickled by amorous feelings. As its result, a change could be noticed in their style of looking, talking and even walking. In fact, their minds started surmounting upon their bodies for the pursuit of a meaningful thing and the experience of a mysterious reality. Could their tripartite thought and the focus of their gaze be the same? Why were their minds turning so powerful? Such questions gradually started twining them.

As soon as they had turned back and taken a single descending step, the same dog followed them as their companion. Sanjhang said, "Our friend has turned up again. It had left us here and entered the village."

"It seems it is here to learn everything about us." Having said so, he burst into a loud laughter once and blushed, before sitting with ease. Panchashar lent his hand to help her get up. She caught hold his hand and stood, and started walking.

When they talked about a companion, Panchashar remembered Mauni. He was distressed, considering the fact that he had not seen or met him for the past two days. He wondered where Mauni was and what he was doing. Caught in such thought for a while, he returned to his normal mental condition before long.

They didn't take much time to walk the distance between their shelter at Sattal and the Mangmaya Fall. But the mysterious and unimpeded tour of the various bends of their minds, curiosity and impatience rendered the limits of many things seamless. So, even inside the limited purview of geography and time, they had been walking, devising their own limitless and unconstrained worlds within themselves.

From the mountain up above, Sanjhang, Teejhang and Panchashar saw a huge human gathering at Sattal below. They wondered what it was, and that was natural because no one had seen such a huge human gathering in that part of the world before.

On hearing from a distance the fuzzy, collage-like commotion emanating from people talking on their own accords, they caught a strange reverberation of voices. It seemed it was the voice of bumblebees humming together.

"Oh, God! What a big gathering of people," said Teejhang, astonished.

"You're right. From where could so many of them have gathered?" Sanjhang added.

"They must have come together with a purpose," said Panchashar with ordinary formality, drawing a conclusion.

In fact, it was an arranged program, slated for that moment at Sattal. The Limboos of Mauwa Khola Thum area had chosen this full moon day with commitments to grant the day a historical significance and start a new tradition by observing the joy of Panchashar's arrival and the honor of their two daughters Sanjhang and Teejhang. The gathering had, with a consensus, resolved to mark every full moon and new moon day by letting a bazaar come up at this place. Since that day, such a bazaar takes place on every full and new moon day at Sattal. Members from every family living in the villages of Sanghu, Tamrang, Phedap, Nundhiki Badha, Namlok, Phakumba, Hambhabung, Sangluppa, Ghoretar, Kharté, Oyakchung, Santhakra, Change, Sosinala, Tellabung, and Tembé that fell under Mauwa Khola Thum region. In fact, this is the first historic bazaar in the Limbuwan region. So it has its own glory and tradition.

It is said, the Kirat people consider it a matter of glory to visit this bazaar at Sattal in Sanghu. This bazaar inside the Limbuwan region also has a great cultural importance. Therefore, such markets have great significance among the Limboos for the way they back-up the chain of social life and the nourishment it offers to it. With time, similar practices were launched at other places, stipulating a particular date and staging a bazaar in the same way.

The human gathering at Sattal that day felicitated Siddha Kirat, the gentleman who had offered the maidens to Panchashar. They also honored Panchashar and his two brides Sanjhang and Teejhang. Following this, they sat uniformly on the same line and feasted together. After the feast, they sang and danced and the event came to a closure.

***

Both Sanjhang and Teejhang knew it very well that Panchashar was a traveler and he could move away any moment. So they focused on preparing themselves so that they would be able to stand the upcoming departure easily. With this thought, they rippled in yet another world of emotions, reached a state of bliss and satisfaction, forgetting the fated possibility of the imminent separation and came forward to congratulate themselves for the rare fate they had been blessed with. Gathering the tripartite feelings into one strong determinations of unity, they conjured the guts to face the separation, and thus they made themselves strong, and stayed pacified.

Mauni was lost in his own world. Keeping himself liberated and free, he studied the customs, traditions and practices of the Limboo community. For him, other things and criticism were irrelevant. He always stayed happy and wished the same for others. The people there made him take part in Dhaan Naach, inspired him to hop in Chyabrung Naach and poured on him a huge measure of love.

Mauni has a weapon with him: the instrument of seduction. He didn't have voice, as the goddess of voice was unhappy with him. The flowers, the light, the sky and the youth had gifted him a single weapon: the smile. Whenever he sent forth a wordless smile with the lines of his teeth exposed, people were hypnotized. As far as he could, he kept his hypnotic powers hidden. If he had pending issues at which he was obliged to laugh, he did so in seclusion, filling his heart with delight alone. Even Panchashar didn't have the exact estimation of this power of attraction Mauni possessed.

Mauni showed Panchashar a slate, where he had scribbled with a chalk, "Shouldn't we be moving now?"

There was a triangular exchange of looks. The eyes of Panchashar, Sanjhang and Teejhang were silent anymore. The ears were not prepared to hear anything acrid; the voice started turning futile.

They all experienced the same thing at one: it was time for them to part. The eyes and Sanjhang and Teejhang turned moist. Panchashar appeared extremely grave. Mauni felt a deep prick of pain considering the fate of the love birds.

At the moment of separation, the Kirat maidens present there seemed to value Mauni more than Panchashar and his two brides Sanjhang and Teejhang. Their guiltless eyes were glued to Mauni.

The context of the imminent trip had duel effect of joy and compassion in the Kirat community. The old and the adult ones appeared satisfied. The youths were more tearful. The ordinary folks enjoyed the moment.

Most of them saw Panchashar and Mauni off from Sattal itself. Sanjhang and Teejhang followed them, deciding to escort that as far at the hill of Panchami. Together with them were nine pairs of Kirat, especially Limboo young men and women of their age. They were with them, probably because they wanted to give Sanjhang and Teejhang their company on their way back. All these young men and women were very close and intimate friends of Sanjhang and Teejhang. So they were bound in their own pairs.

Once they crossed Mangmaya and started moving along the flat stretch of land, Teejhang started singing:

> *Pathibhara tyo ago danda*
> *Thumkimathi Deviko mandira*
> *Panchamika pugera hami*
> *Darshan garaun sangsangai hajura.*

[There is a temple of a Devi on top of Pathibhara hill.
Come; let's walk up to Panchami for a holy beholding
of the Devi.]

Sanjhang also followed the lines of the song. Other maidens
also added their voices to it. The northern border of the village of
Tyambé resounded with the sound:

Euta chithi khasalnuhola
Pugepachhi Olangchunggola
Arko pheri pathaunuhola
Lhasa puri belaima.

[Drop a letter when you reach Olangchunggola. Drop
another one when you reach Lhasa. They will reach
here in time.]

Sanjhang and Teejhang sang a duet:

Kasam hajur liyera janu
Pharki aaune yai hamro choLama
Birahama naparnuhola
Bainsa khulyo hajurkai naunma
Raji khushi janu hai hajura
Bato gari Tamorko gadhtir
Hajurko aarami herun
Simé Bhumé deu-deuta hajara.

[Go, making the promise that you shall certainly
return in our present lifetime. Do not leave us
bereaved; our youth was destined to tie with you.
Go happily, our lord, walking along the bank of the
Tamor River. Let Simé, Bhumé and thousand other
deities take care of your comfort.]

Even as they were singing, their throats got smothered. They sniveled, as drops of tears rolled down their faces. Drawing deep breaths after a while, Sanjhang and Teejhang composed themselves. Panchashar had tears in his eyes. Mauni appeared rather grave, only to become emotionally moved and he stood in rather an oblique gait.

On reaching the Panchami hill, all of them have a holy view of Goddess Pathibhara simultaneously, albeit from a long distance. They also viewed the shrines of other deities that represented the revered goddess Pathibhara. Sanjhang and Teejhang had expressed their goodwill and wishes in songs. But the changed hue of their faces, the inconsistency of their looks, the tremor on their lips and their frowns manifested the deep worry inside their hearts.

The friends allowed Sanjhang and Teejhang to have a dialogue with Panchashar in privacy. Panchashar held the hands of both and said something in a tone of request and assurance, consoled them, made promise and took leave of both. Panchashar and Mauni departed from this very spot, aiming to reach their destination. Sanjhang and Teejhang returned to their village Sanghu together with their dearest friends.

They walked past the plains at Tellabung, the hill at Changé, the *chautari* underneath the cottonwood tree, the low, trickling tap called Tirtiré and the downhill trail at Sosinal, the travelers crossed Mauwa confluence and arrived at the bank of the river Tamor. They crossed the river from a pass beyond Dhulé and came out into the wide road across it. With Tamor to their left hand side, they walked straight on the flat land, moving their feet as fast as they could. The foot of Pathibhara Hill and the bank of the Tamor were one and the same place.

Panchashar said to himself, 'Only now did we meet the Tamor we had left at Moolghat. We'll not perhaps lose the company of the Tamor now.'

Mauni was delighted to see the gush of water in the Tamor.

The village of Sawa that occupied the land between the foot of a high hill and the bank of the river Tamor was happy and beautiful, though a small one. Once again, the high, naked and sloppy mountain peaks posed a challenge to the new travelers. The onlookers often thought that the tip of the peak could fall on their heads anytime soon. Though the peak never tumbled, the caps and the turbans of the onlookers did.

They reached the village of Sawa, seeing and experiencing the hair-raising cliffs and slopes, the terrifying woods and the monotonous murmur of the Tamor.

When they inquired about another faction of their group that had moved along Baraha Region along the bank of the Tamor, they came to know that that group had moved north from Sawa some five days earlier. They were pleased and reassured with the news that they would be waiting for their friends at Olangchunggola.

At the place they had taken shelter, the locals asked them, "Are you here looking for your lost friends?"

Mauni looked at the enquirer with shocked eyes.

"No. We have been walking almost together. They are ahead of us by a few days."

"Oh. I happened to make a wrong guess," he said. Changing the context, he asked again, "Are you Udhauli or Ubhauli?"

They didn't understand his symbolic intention. So they kept starting on one another's face.

"Where are you going" he asked straight.

"Toward Olangchunggola and Lhasa," Panchashar said.

"There was news that *sokpa*[35] picked someone moving toward Olangchunggola recently. Could it be that you are looking for the same man?"

Both were startled. None of them could decide what answer they should give him. After a while, Panchashar tendered an extremely careful reply: "What sort of man did he pick? And where? Please tell us whatever you know and heard of. We are also keeping the same path. I am chilled what you just said."

"You don't need to fear. When you walk together with *chaunri*, horses, mules and their stewards, there is no much fear. More, such

---

[35]   a mythical, wild, man-eating spirit

incidents take place only occasionally, barely once in many years. No one but knows what the truth is."

"What is a *sokpa*? What does it look like?" Mauni asked to Panchashar, writing on his slate and showing the latter.

Panchashar passed Mauni's question to the local man and added his curiosity in it.

"No one has really seen a *sokpa* till now, but they say it looks like a human. Some say, it is like a woodman or a snowman."

Recalling yet another anecdote, the local man said, "People from Modibung have their cattle farms in Sangsabung. Once as they were moving uphill together with their herds, a *sokpa* caught a cowherd boy. They say they were father and son herding their cattle. How bad could the father feel when his son was lost midway?"

He added, "You don't need to worry. Such a thing doesn't always happen. It's a hilly trail; sometimes people slip off and fall into the gorges and disappear. Some bump against something and fall into the river. This happens with cattle as well. Sometimes, friends push down their friends in revenge."

He drew a long breath and said, "No one can tell what happens next. It also is a matter of predestined death, or a matter of fate."

Mauni thought, 'Let no such thing happen to our friends. This is Kirat land; we should be safe here. This is my firm faith."

"Sinwan occurs on the main way leading to Tibet. So when one stops there, he or she hears and sees many a thing," said another local man, lighting a pine twig. He added, "It has been two to four years now…a pair of travelers heading for Tibet had slept inside a cave. In the morning, the bed was very much there, but one of the men was missing."

Mauni raised his eyebrows. Panchashar appeared frozen. The hearts of both the men seemingly said together, 'Such tales are wroth avoiding."

"There was a huge commotion thereafter. People doubted that a *sokpa* or a leopard could have picked him. Since then, people stopped coming out of their homes after sunset. Wasn't that a case of disaster in the village?" the second local said.

HARI RAJ BHATTARAI

Mauni and Panchashar feigned to be listening, though they didn't want.

Drawing his hookah for two more times, he patted the first local and said, "They combed every village, slope, hill, cave and cliff. When the villagers insisted that they should find at least a portion of the mortal remain, and offered to help them in the search, they discovered that the victim was a woman. They both were spotted after twenty days."

"Could that be possible?" wrote Mauni drawing his slate inward and erased it before anyone had seen it.

"What happened next," Panchashar asked with curiosity.

"The boy tried to trick the girl by moving away, saying that he would return to take her later. The girl, knowing of his intentions, followed her, not letting him go."

"And then?"

"When they were out on the village road, she happened to scream in Limboo dialect, asking others to help. In no time, the villagers happened to surround the man with rods and *khukuris* in their hands.

"I hadn't heard such a thing," said the first local, interfering.

The excited speaker added, "The villagers discovered every detail about the boy. He was a boy of Suttar caste. They forced him to confess. The boy paid his fines. The villagers organized a feast with happiness. The issue was settled."

The listeners were all quiet. They didn't ask any question, nor showed any reaction. The speaker added, "Even more surprising is the fact that he came back walking along the daylong trail and made off, taking the girl along, right from the middle of a fair."

"It's possible that he had set the plans with the girl in advance."

"It's a matter of age. All feelings of the heart come hooked in the gestures of the eyes. But no one can do anything to a Limboo girl, unless he has her consent. This is a special power of theirs. If they don't like a thing, they never endorse it, even if the entire earth turns upside down."

The speaker received the hookah from another man. He smoked it two to three times and said, "This time, you happened to make it is very hard; seems I will nauseate."

A maiden came from inside carrying some water in a tumbler. The speaker took two quick gulps and stood and left for his home sauntering, holding a lighted pine twig to show him the way.

To the woman who stood there having placed the tumbler of water on the ground, a local man asked, "Aren't you asleep yet?"

"We are grinding maize; that's why," said the maiden, giving a clear reply.

"I briefly heard about the girl who picked a boy from Ramduwali fair and eloped," she said, making herself clear.

"What difference does it make if the boy picked the girl or vice versa? It's just a matter of conversation now," said the speaker, getting up from his place. He added, "Here I go to sleep. Guests, you also go to bed now." Seemingly recalling a forgotten issue, he said, "Leave only after taking your meal in the morning. Siwan is neither short of food, nor does it have too many guests. Nature has loved us in this matter."

The speaker prepared to leave.

"You were talking about eating something," wrote Mauni and showed it to Panchashar. The latter conveyed Mauni's curiosity to a villager. The villager said, "You can carry maize, soybeans, corn-grit or sugar molasses as you go. Up there, one suffers from altitude sickness. These stuffs can come in handy. They will make it ready; you pick them up as you move. You don't need to give us anything for that."

"Isn't this place Siwan? How far from here is the place where a *sokpa* once picked a passerby? How many days does one take to reach Olangchunggola from that spot?" Panchashar asked.

The local gentleman said, "You are both young. If you don't have the hassle of cooking on the way, you can reach there in three days." After a brief pause he said, "I don't know how fast you can walk and how tired you grow. I think, the *sokpa*-haunt is roughly midway from here."

They left Siwan. On the way, Panchashar shivered from time to time, for having heard tales about the *sokpas*, their kidnapping of people from midways, sedating them and sending back whole after killing them. At times, the hairs on his body rose with thrill. But Mauni had no care for any of such things.

All along the way, Panchashar and Mauni remained depressed, fearing if any member of their group had gone missing on the way. Several thoughts rose and crisscrossed their minds. Direct conversation was not easy between the two. Owing to that, they were unable to purge the pent-up worries and repressions of their minds easily.

Yet, they did not find it very difficult to walk together with traders and their *chauris*, horses, mules and dogs commuting between Lhasa and Olangchunggola, Siwan, Phungling, Mauwa Dobhan, Sanghu and Simlek.

To keep themselves safe from the chilly weather in the Himalayas, the travelers coming from Kantipur dressed themselves in the Tibetan cultural fashion making themselves look like the local dwellers, once they crossed Olangchunggola.

Even after a wait of three days, when Mauni and Panchashar didn't reach Olangchunggola, the first group moved toward Lhasa, only to receive them at the entrance to Lhasa, when the second group arrived there. On seeing Panchashar, they felt that they had rediscovered their lost leader. At moment, Panchashar felt that his personality had risen to its pinnacle.

Mauni appeared like a flower.

***

CHAPTER THREE

T HERE WERE SEVERAL interfaces of bilateral relations between Lhasa and Kantipur. In the background of their geographical proximity, the cultural, business and socio-familial relations had been prioritized on both the ends. So the travelers reaching Lhasa from Kantipur (Nepal) were accorded lots of honor.

Lhasa, located on a high altitude was in itself a centre from cultural and economic perspectives. It would be unwise to say that the description of Lhasa, introduced by the rule of Lama, a religious leader and a ruler, was exaggerated. The city of Lhasa, those days, expressed its liberal thoughts in a guiltless way at locations under the rule of monasteries by lighting four wick-lamps representing love, peace, cooperation and good conduct on four corners.

Lhasa left no stone unturned to welcome the guests from Kantipur, who had reached there at the invitation of the rulers from China. In honor of Panchashar and his troupe, the royal dancers performed a dance comparable to the one performed by celestial dancers in heaven, at the orders of its king Indra to welcome the great warrior Arjun. This made the environment both thrilling and curious.

Arrangements for accommodation of the royal guests had been made in a special room in the guest house lavishly decorated with Tibetan art and cultural works. The atmosphere of the bedroom had been rendered tantalizing by the use of fragrant plants and flowers bestowed upon the humankind by nature. An inspiring and blissful environment had been especially devised inside the royal guest house of the royal city of Lhasa, adopting everything to the tune of the local methods and culture.

At a time convenient to them, the guests staying here availed the majestic exhibition of the local culture and kept themselves physically and mentally satisfied. By adapting themselves to the tunes of many dramatic ways and implementation methods of curiosity and playfulness and thus considered themselves launching a journey along the highway of an illuminated life, and left Lhasa with lasting impacts. In that case, the question if chords and formulae kept the guests from Kantipur bound was a non-issue.

The topography of Lhasa, its folk culture and the environment inside the guest house were quite different from what Panchashar had thought about. He didn't even need an interpreter. There were two maidens there, who conversed with him in a language he could understand. So, instead of taking any decision on his own, he considered it wise to follow whatever they suggested.

Sleeping accommodations for Panchashar had been made on a spherical room on the top of the guest house. For the convenience and comfort of the guests, four small cabinets had been made on the side of the spherical room. In those four cabinets, four maidens in beautiful make-up stayed ready and alert all the time to serve the guests as and when demanded. To address the guests' call for any sort of service at any time, the beauties had been kept ready. But they came forth and presented themselves in accordance with the guests' mental readiness, bodily culture and the signals they sent forth. This was an unannounced culture practiced inside the royal guest house.

That room where sleeping arrangements had been made for Panchashar shone with moonstone fixed on its ceiling. At places, alternative lighting arrangements had been made with *ujeli kath*, bright wood that sent forth dim white light. If anyone entered that spherical room, the light dispersed, making it easy for anyone to go in and come out.

Wishing the guest a sound sleep, the stunningly beautiful maidens entered the four cabinets—one in each of them—and got absorbed in the works of their own departments. Yet, they kept a vigilant watch over the royal guest with their minds and brains. They even took note of the turns a guest took on his bed. This was both a rule and a gesture of courtesy. Yet they wished for uninterrupted and sound sleep of their guest. The attendants of the guest house were experts of physiology, psychology, medicine and defense.

While lodging in the guest house, Panchashar also inspected the architecture there. This was, however, its physical aspect. He also studied the elements and the things used in it. He also observed the condition of ventilation, lighting, acoustics and spatial orientation. He then observed their hospitality, the grandeur of the Kinnar's world, their service and their presentations. This experience, however was neither expressible to all, nor wholly comprehensible.

***

In the afternoon that day, they had to leave Lhasa and set out for Beijing. Every member of the travelers' group was quite happy. Telling his friend that he would be back 'in a while', Panchashar entered a monastery. Mauni, however, didn't look quite contented with this decision.

On reaching the monastery, Panchashar made a round of it formally. He also set the prayer wheels rotating, chanting "Om mane peme hum...Om mane peme hum." He then went in, had a holy beholding of the Buddha there, and asked the Lama for his blessings.

The Lama said only this: "May all your wishes be granted! Always stay healthy."

After a keen observation, the Lama said to himself, 'This traveler happened to receive the blessing of staying young forever.'

Showing that he was accepting the Lama's blessings, Panchashar started making efforts to exit from the entrance of the monastery.

"Guest," the Lama uttered.

Panchashar stood still and turned toward the Lama.

"Guest," said the Lama again and stopped. Panchashar peeked into the Lama's face. He appeared in an extremely serious mood. Panchashar scanned the Lama's eyes; he was standing motionless and still, throwing his eyes far way.

Panchashar continued to stand there until the Lama's words had ended. The Lama was a tall man with a robust body. From underneath his thick, wide eyebrows, he glued his eyes at a distance far away from the entrance to the monastery, he said, "Guest, you return to your shelter. Make it quick."

'It seems, the Lama has premonitions about a certain thing. So he is advising me to stay alert.' This is how Panchashar explained the Lama's words. Analyzing the gestures of the Lama, he moved out of the main entrance of the monastery.

The *chauris*, horses, mules and dogs present in the premises of the monastery and around the Royal City of Lhasa were startled for no reason, and appeared frightened. Their demeanors looked strange and their looks were so strange that it seemed they were amazed and frightened on seeing a thing they had never done before. For that reason, Panchashar grew even graver in deciphering the meaning of the suggestion the Lama had given him.

Nature had premonitions of an upcoming upheaval. Having a sense of the same, Panchashar rushed toward his destination without any delay.

The inner conviction of the animal kingdom got articulated in a single voice: "Man that survives at our mercy and help doesn't even turn and look when we are in peril. He stays shut, concerned only with his safety as though animals were the elements that invited havoc to him." The people-friendly animals living inside the premise of the city of Lhasa aired their frustration in a single tone: "Fie on man, the selfish creature!"

The painful scream coming from the *chauris*, horses, mules, goats and rams that wished for support and refuge from the human being made the atmosphere sound terrifying and distressful. A few moments before the emanation of the appalling commotion and the nature-induced terror, Panchashar entered the building he had lodged in. The type of rebellious contemplation that had started among other guests in the guesthouse, when one of their mates was out of it, ended as soon as Panchashar entered the guesthouse.

Everyone was reassured now and pleased too. Smile started spilling over everyone's countenance.

Panchashar was aware that everyone was grim as long as he was out, and was happy to see him return. The situation was so appalling that any time a devastating natural calamity could befall them. Everyone was impatient to see the havoc come and recede as soon as possible and that was quite natural. But no one could imagine what the calamity would look like, with how much power it would come, and what it would do or bequeath before it returned.

In the meantime, the wind started blowing. Wishing for safety and peace, they sat where they were, praying.

The concentration of the people coming from Kantipur was not here. They remembered the greenery that decked their locations. They also recalled the evidence and outcomes of season cycles. They remembered summer and fall, autumn and spring. They brought back to their memories the festivals and occasions they observed and the joy and excitement they brought home. To such reminiscence, they tagged their hearts in their bid to stay unaffected by the approaching calamity and its impact, and thus tried to stay composed in the resorts of their own hearts. In fact, this was an attempt to keep themselves free from worries, what if quite briefly, at this moment of dilemma caught between life and death, albeit by choosing the elixir of distant memories. It was both role-play and practice of the same, though it was abstract.

After a gusty wind that lasted for about half an hour, the doors and windows of the guesthouse opened. Life experienced its freedom from oppression. Inside, life got elated, feeling that fear and terror had left simultaneously but outside, no one instantly cared for the devastating outcome that had been left behind.

The scriptures mention *saptamahavayu*—the seven winds. It's needless to analyze how many of these winds work together to bring about the devastation of the city of Lhasa.

The wise men say it suffices for one of such winds to descend a little.

HARI RAJ BHATTARAI

Many a number of houses were demolished at those places where the wind had more impact. There also were reports that people got buried inside the ruins of many crumbling houses. The fall of the houses also crushed and killed goats and sheep much more than the number of *chauris,* horses and mules that were killed. Human life was even more panicked with reports of the loss of children who had been out of home to play.

People could see the sight of children—out of home to play— roll over and over again in the gusty wind, get trapped in crevices between houses, and get killed. The townspeople, who were in a pathetic situation, started gathering in groups, finding places safe enough for them to stand on.

Activities of the city of Lhasa started returning to normal. Excited, some started gathering at the premises of the main monastery. The main Lama, the religious authority of the region, was scheduled to address them. Standing on a raised pedestal, the Lama said, "My brothers and sisters in Lhasa are enduring through many painful outcomes of a natural calamity. I am also bearing the same. I am deeply saddened by this fact. So I announced in front of you all: anyone that has been rendered homeless in this city, that has lost business and or is a victim of this natural mishap shall receive food, clothes, homes and treatment from the side of the monastery. Right from today, we shall start our search for those that have gone missing. We shall also manage the last rites of those who are yet to receive it. All these activities shall be launched now, and shall proceed at war footing."

Taking a brief pause, he added, "There has been a huge loss of livestock. The loss shall be compensated. We must remove dead human and animal bodies from the ruin and save the town's air from getting contaminated. For this, I expect the help of the town people."

He continued, "I also appeal the rich men, businessmen, industrialists and traders in Lhasa for help. I believe they are also keen in the reconstruction of the devastated Lhasa. I am confident that they will take initiatives with pity and compassion for their brethren in peril.

"The departments concerned will undertake rescue operations with alertness, having in mind the feelings of goodwill. I must get immediate information on what thing is needed where, which thing is more in demand and what has to be done. I must also get the report on the loss outside the city of Lhasa, and the condition of the people there at present. I also need your help in that avenue.

"If any individual or a philanthropist wants to offer any type of help, a record of the same should be made available to the monastery after the task is executed." He opened up further: "If you are interested to render any help or take up a welfare initiative, you don't need permissions. Instead, if anyone tries to pose any impediment on such tasks, let me know. I shall make all attempts to make it easy for you. I shall find a way out."

He paused again, albeit for a brief time, and said, "Finally, I express my sympathy for the bereaved families. My thoughts are always with them at this hour of grief and pain. The monastery shall make all arrangements for the cremation of the dead ones."

Making a slight change in the fashion of his delivery, he said, "At the time when we had guests from our neighboring country, nature enacted its havoc. I express my heart-felt pain at the inconvenience and terror it caused to them. I express my embarrassment, and pray for their comfortable journey ahead. May their goal be achieved and lead to wonderful fruition."

He raised his palm and said, *Bhawatu sarva mangalam*"—May welfare shower on everyone!

Of the dwellers of Lhasa present there, some remained safe inside the monastery premises.

The significance of the Nepalese guests reaching Lhasa from Kantipur was quite high for the dwellers of Lhasa. The guests, coming from a neighboring country received a lot of honor and respect owing to the fact that Nepal and Tibet had friendly relations in one hand, and on the other, the travelers were there at the invitation of the Emperor of another neighboring country, China and were therefore subject to higher measure of respect. So, as long as they stayed in the royal city of Lhasa, they received a lot of honor, each one receiving separate and complete reception. In other words, the hosts didn't discriminate anyone as leader or valets. One didn't see any division between a commander and followers. This was, in itself, a unique thing.

The capital city of Lhasa considered the presence of eleven guests a happy occasion, and shared its joy with everyone. It considered the huge loss from a natural calamity ordinary, and thought it merely the continuation of events that took place from time to time. It took it as something that could be mended easily through reconstruction. So other things were considered trivial in front of these eleven guests for the dwellers of Lhasa.

***

Mounted on horses decorated in royal elegance, Panchashar and his friends left Lhasa in the fashion of royal guests and moved north, aiming to reach the capital city of China.

Lhasa now was desolate, wearing grimy looks of a dry water-tap, of barn after the grains have been cleared, of a shed devoid of cattle or of a tree with no fruit at all. It looked like a yard after a *yagya*, a home after the nuptial procession has departed, or like a garden after the flowers have been removed. Lhasa was lost in dilemma for a while, in the interface of the thrill of meeting and the grief of parting. At such a moment, tears had simmered in the eyes of the Buddha, who was leaving his family, palace and the kingdom to look for a fourth path. Even as their hearts were gripped by the pain of separation, the people of Lhasa recalled the eyes of the Buddha at the time of valediction and consoled themselves.

Seeing them move on horsebacks in such a large number, the people of Lhasa revered the guests as distinguished people, honored that in the same footing, and treasured them in their hearts. Some young men and women felt that their hearts had been hooked to those of some of the guests, and were now being snapped. Mauni, more than others, had mesmerized many with the folk tunes he played on his flute and *murchunga*. Therefore, many felt their hearts falling for Mauni while a few others at the guest house felt crush for Panchashar. In fact, leaving his admirers in grief, Mauni took his steps forward, not caring to stand and look back even for once. Panchashar didn't know that Mauni had conquered many hearts with the power of his flute and *murchunga*. It's true that every language and feeling can be tuned to the symphony of music, and no element can pose itself as an impediment, and once music mounts, the empire of the heart and feelings becomes even more comprehensive.

The Tibetan Plateau is considered a matchless example of a highland among all creations of nature. Neither life there, nor a journey through it is easy. It seems, comfort and life are limited to the periphery of the city of Lhasa. It perhaps was true that the real heaven was located here, and perhaps the most comfortable and beautiful life rested here.

The swagger of the royal guests mounted on the horses exquisitely decorated, and the glory of the one leading the journey were quite spectacular—glorious and unusual. Dozens of horses would be at the front and back, whenever a special guest traveled. On seeing a caravan of horses, the villagers would stand on two sides of the roads to welcome the guests and informed one another of their presence there.

After one or two stops on the way, the number of horse-ridden travelers decreased. The mules carrying their stuff lagged behind. They perhaps were not in as much hurry as the horses carrying the travelers. Yet, this trip had a specialty: the horses were changed in every two days, while the mules were changed every day.

For the travelers coming from a bigger country into Tibet—a smaller country—anything the soldiers of bigger kings, or their employees did on the way or in their stays would be tolerable. Food, accommodation and luxuries never posed as impediments and issues of decorum for these royal people. They always needed to have maidens by their sides. The hosts had to tender food and drinks prodigally, and the maidens had to bear the way the coarse and loathsome hands and fingers of the royal men touching their cheeks and clasping them hard. They also had to endure the carnal attack that followed, after the twig-lamp of pine splinter was doused off. The evenings with such hues often went silent, painful and devoid of reactions.

Even in such a situation, Mauni continued to stay silent, and Panchashar feigned not to see him. Others wondered what it was, but for the royal man, it was an ordinary thing. Since Mauni was both romantic and a patron of art, he had kept himself a pure vegetarian. More, his looks and his sign language and gestures were extremely attractive. In a true sense, they were seductive. If he were to be considered a flower, why should those hovering around him be named bumblebees? The maidens fell for his smiles and gestures. This was not, at any rate, an exaggeration. But then, the nature of Panchashar was taking an altogether different turn.

One stop, after they had left Lhasa, had got into Panchashar's nerves. The atmosphere of the stop had turned depressing mainly because of the mishandling a member of the royal trip had shown against a man, who was overseeing their accommodation, his rough demeanors and bragging, his neglect of foods and drinks and his violent gestures against a maiden, and the wrong and untimely demands he placed forth. More, some members of his team had grown tired and sickly because of arduous and long horse-ride. Since they were not used to, their travel by horse was proving cumbersome. As they progressed, neither the horse-ride, nor a journey on foot seemed easy. Even standing straight had become a task. They were soon reaching a condition wherein tossing from one side to another in bed, or getting up from a sitting position too would become impossible. This made Panchashar disheartened from time to time.

Mauni ate, drank and pleased himself. He often sat on one side and played his *binayo*. Other members of his troupe often pressed close to him. At the place they sheltered in, maidens and children surrounded him. He left an impression at every stop, before moving.

Nine other friends they had spent their time, talking about their village affairs, carnivals, fairs and love. On their first stop after leaving Lhasa, they played a *madal*[36] and sang to its beat. This way, they amused themselves. But with time, their travel made them fatigued beyond telling and thus they lost interest in entertainment. In summary, traveling on horsebacks along the hilly terrain was proving a rigorous punishment for them. Yet, each one of them had their own mental consolations to keep going. They rested their minds in various resorts of their memories, engaged in self-consolation and satisfied themselves, before launching yet another segment of their journey. They slept deep so that they could gather optimum amount of mental energy to resume their journey the following day.

According to a scientific arrangement, separate accommodations were managed for the Nepali troupe, and it could cook its own meal, if wanted. Since their clothes and much of their food were left on the mules that lagged much behind, they could not make any use of them during the trip, but they didn't regret much about it. That moment, they were driven by a singular goal: reaching the Chinese capital as soon as possible. They wondered how far it still was.

Panchashar could not manage any sleep in the stop of that night. He remembered the way Mauni mounted on a horse from time to time and showed him a slate with something scribbled on it. He thought that he had done so many a time, and had drawn his attention to many serious issues. He recalled how, at different points in times, Mauni had jotted various sentences and shown him:

"Do you remember the miracles Siddha Kirat man had shown?"

"How thrilling was our stay at Sattal?"

"Did you understand the song Teejhang sang?"

"Inside the guesthouse in Lhasa, did you become Sage Vishwamitra or Arjun?"

---

[36] a cylindrical leather drum played typically in Nepal, especially to folk tunes

This last question from Mauni deeply moved Panchashar. He went to bed, recalling his night-rest inside the guesthouse in Lhasa, and remembering the thrill.

Panchashar could not sleep. He sat up on his bed sometimes, and some other time stood up and went around his bed, moving in a circle. He sometimes peeked at the light coming from the blue sapphire gemstone on the ceiling with strange looks, like those of a man in abnormal mental condition. Again, he reclined on the bed, only to get up abruptly before long. In fact, he was sick both in body and mind.

The maidens couched in the room next-doors were observing and experiencing the restlessness of their guest. One of the maidens walked close to the guest, feigning to sneak into a different room. In fact, she had pressed there with the expectation that the guest would tell her something. As soon as he saw her, the guest said, "Excuse me!"

The maiden walked close to the guest and said, "You had no sleep, did you?"

"Not at all. It has never been so."

"Wait for a while."

She went out, making him wait.

The guest appeared like a monkey attacked by cowitch. He scratched his body with his own fingernails, making nail lines appear like bruises everywhere. The condition was both pathetic and heart-rending.

A special meeting of the four attendants decided to help the guest sleep under special arrangements. Accordingly, two maidens entered the guest's room, took him out, and made him dive into a ditch of hot water, mixed with fragrance. The pool was inside the premises of the guest house. But then, he was under compulsion to enter the pool only as instructed by the maiden that escorted him hither. The maiden feigned of looking in the other direction and closing her eyes. Soon, all the maidens entered the pool in order to entertain the guest. The help of these maidens was crucial for the guest inside the pool, because there were slippery stones with algal growth, and stepping on them in balance was quite a task, and he needed something to hold on.

That is why all three of the maidens entered the pool. They knew that if they did not lend him support, their guest would fall, get hurt, invite a disaster and thus face a calamity. So, two of the maidens held him tight, and made him dive into the warm water in the incensed pool, making him drown ear-deep and nose-deep for quite a long time. In fact, this was a sort of therapy, a nature cure for sleeplessness. This way, they accomplished their first step of diving into an incensed pool of lukewarm water.

The second step included massaging. For a massage with wild herbal extracts, two maidens came forward. They took him to one corner of the infirmary and started their massaging. When they started massaging him from top to toes, the guest experienced unprecedented pleasure and divine peace. Instead of shame or treatment, the guest felt a touch of love and affection entering his existence. After the massage, they made the guest clean and tidy, and making him recline on a bed, the two maidens went out.

In fact, after the dive into the fragrant pool, the guest had started sedating. Now, after the spell of mesmerizing massage, he could hardly hold himself in place, and before long, he was numb.

In the third phase, two new maidens came near, and lifted him to the make-up room. There, they made him weak *chinagsuk*—a highly acclaimed silken wear—and helped him lie on a bed, supporting him from two sides.

The bedroom was a new one, not the previous one. So was the bed in it. Two maidens, who had been sleeping there, had warmed it. The escorting maidens made the guest lie between the two sleeping maidens and left, patting all the three from outside their quilt, and wishing them a sound sleep. The atmosphere outside the bedroom was harsh and appallingly cold. Once inside this fourth stage, the guest even forgot himself.

The guest was entranced by the maidens' seductiveness, enhanced by their fragrance and warmth. His mind started hovering in an altogether different world. He could not, therefore,

HARI RAJ BHATTARAI

reject the youthful sleeping arrangement, given the freezing chill outside. He thus slept a sleep of comfort, adopting the sleeping pattern decked by the youthful company of the two maidens.

"Oh," uttered Panchashar, waking up. He said to himself, 'What a beautiful dream I had, even in such a torturous sleep! What more I would have dreamt of and felt if I had not woken up so soon?'

Recalling yet another incident, he thought, 'we did not even happen to know the right way of sleeping. We did not understand the need of our bodies, either. We happened to be living cheating ourselves or keeping ourselves deprived of many things. It is true that having the knowledge of sleeping is an art. Who would stay happy, living a life detached from its physical aspect?'

Panchashar considered that day's sleep a blessing from God because the sleep had driven him to an unforgettable realm of dreams. In fact, he could not tell if it was a dream or reality, or a part of heaven. Expressing his wish, he sighed, 'Let similar dreams occur to me at every stop.'

"But two at every step." Panchashar expressed himself.

"What two?" asked Mauni, writing on the slate.

"Nothing; I will tell you later." Panchashar tried to divert the issue.

"True. You and I are two." Mauni showed his slate again.

"Sanjhang and Teejhang were two as well," he added.

"Siddha Kirat and the public representative—they were two as well." Mauni showed his slate once again.

Aiming directly at Mauni, Panchashar said, "I told you it's a long story. I shall tell you later, shouldn't I?"

Mauni tendered a formal smile and chose to stay silent. Most of the things continued to stay mysterious. Yet, musing of many indelible impressions laden with youthful cravings, Panchashar said to himself, 'These beauties in the Kinnar's land happened to be odorless, like the rhododendron. They played with whispering winds, and lived in a storehouse of kasturi bina—the glandular sac of the musk deer. With exuberant feelings of youthfulness, Panchashar wanted to drown himself again and again in the sentiments communicated by romantic transference of unfailing beauty and carnal comfort.

After a romantic show-off of love business, Panchashar had just woken up, following a long repose. So, at any rate, he was unwilling to darken, forget or slice the context of his dream and the series of incidents he envisioned inside it. He talked little fearing that if his mind drifted away, he could lose the playfulness of his dream and the romantic images it sent forth.

He thought over and analyzed the dream issues in solitude. In fact, he was no longer alone; he was with many in the world of dreams. He was rich, and now, he often reaped robust, strong and healthy sensations.

There was yet another context: that of the hearts! The consciousness of morality and culture often force a man to lag behind, while there are moments when the same accord him honor and safety. Its outcomes could be benefitting, but the future tells it. But the present time, caught in the agony of self-restraint, caught between the high walls of morality and culture. Could such a thing sound dear to a grown-up man, that too in a foreign land?

This was the last stop before the end of their current trip. After walking one more morning, the royal troupe coming from Kantipur in Nepal would land at its destination. So, the members of this 'construction group' got together and started talking among themselves. There still was some time left before sunset. Mauni drew the lines for *bagh-chal*, the tiger-and-goats game, and showed it to others. The troupe got busy in it. On his part, he started playing his *murchunga*. Someone started beating a *madal*, while others partook in the entertainment with their cheers. Soon the team glued to the game of *bagh-chal* joined the musical company, only to stop soon because everyone was extremely tired. Two maidens came forward and said, "We are listening and enjoying. Please go on. Why did you stop?"

To keep the maidens' words, the troupe sang:

Hajar thaun ukali chadhyoun, hajar orali
Chinko desh ramailo bato rasilo sangati
Timilai dekhen yo man nachyo mujura bhayera
Hami chhaun dherai timi chhau thorai ke hunchha
herera

[At a thousand places, we walked uphill; descended a thousand comedowns. The path in the country of China was quite beautiful, and the company was enjoyable too. When I saw you, my heart leaped up and danced as a peacock does. We are many and you are a few; what does mere staring do?]

One of them sang, signaling that she already had a lover:

Mero ta aafnai tanneri
Gaunma baschha khelera
Parkhera baschha mailai
Pharkera aaija bhanera

[I have my lover, a young man, who stays in the village, playing. He is waiting for me and sends me words to return soon.]

Another one sang, opening up her heart:

Gaunma basne man chhaina
Sahara? Basne thaun chhaina
Dauntari arko khojdai chhu
Tungoma aafno mann chhaina

[I have no willingness to stay in the village. In town, I have no place to live in. I am looking for a lover; my mind is not in peace.]

The Nepalese troupe clapped, boosting up the singers. Both the maidens were delighted. In fact, they had come there to assist the travelers, but had taken part in the entertainment, cashing the opportunity to express themselves in guiltless moods.

"We have come here to invite you. Let's go for lunch; the food is ready," said one.

The members of the touring team hesitated a little.

Finding an apt opportunity, Mauni showed his slate: "If only we could bathe."

Deciphering the essence of Mauni's words, Panchashar said, "It will be better if we take bath first. What shall we do?"

"We have made arrangements for that too. First meal; shower next. Our practices here are rather different. Maybe you will find it rather strange," said the other one.

The inner hearts of the travelers exclaimed: "We are witnessing many strange things."

The travelers approved of this local practice. They decided to bathe after lunch.

In fact, their stay for the day was at one of the four entrances leading to the capital city. The travelers were tested for their layers and capabilities, before making any arrangement for them. For state guests, their residence, time and work were decided beforehand. During their stay at such entrances, the travelers were trained for special qualifications to enter the royal city. After that, the visiting guests found it easy to enter the royal city without any hassle.

The guests coming from Kantipur got to rest there for one day and two nights. A direct dialogue was conducted with them from the side of the state administration. They were also informed that the state took full responsibility of their comfort and facilities.

The royal team of trip instructors that had come up to this entry leading from Lhasa to Beijing returned. The travelers got a bonus opportunity to read and entertain for one more day. They also received the food of their choice. They rested, freeing themselves of all types of worries.

Soon they got into talking—about languages, facilities, state objectives and viewpoints.

"We didn't face language problem no matter wherever we reached, did we?"

"That is what makes a country developed and well-cultured."

"That's true. No matter which country a guest comes from, he won't face language problems here. Speakers of all languages get ready to mix with these people."

This way, this troupe of travelers coming from Kantipur started engrossing in its own conversation, enjoying and resting.

Soon a new day broke. It was a bright day, quite scintillating. The morning sun had spread everywhere. The plains and the small, green hill ranges appeared pristine. The birds had started soaring in the clear sky. The young fawns had come out of the safe groves to bask in the sun in the velvety lawn, frolicking with their mothers. This must be the reason why their minds were quite exuberant, as were their bodies. Yet, they had started feeling a lack, an absence. Filling the void among them, the same pair of maidens entered their room and said, "Let's move into another room. Someone has come to meet you. They say they want to have their breakfast together with you. They are waiting. Come please; let's go."

The maiden guided the guests into a different room.

On the gate stood yet another beauty, standing with her hands folded together to receive the guests. As soon as she saw the guest, she uttered, "Tarémam, Tasidilé, Sewaro, Namaste, Hai Mero to all of you." [37]

With ease, she added, "Come in. You all are welcome here. I have come to meet you and talk with you. In fact, I am here to help you." She added further, "Let's take the snacks too, even as we take our seats."

Welcoming the royal guests, she joined them in the breakfast.

There was naturalness and heartiness in the way the maiden welcomed the guest. It seemed simple and light-hearted. There

---

[37] Words for greeting in various Nepali dialects

was intimacy and a sense of responsibility. The royal guests were overwhelmed with happiness on seeing her speak so well in their language. They were even more elated on finding snacks of their tastes. The troupe tendered a natural smile. One could easily read their inner minds from looks and smiles.

"For those who are not used to it, traveling on horsebacks along a long route is quite cumbersome. I don't know how you all felt," said the maiden, making a natural statement.

A few of them stared at one another a couple of times.

"I had never ridden a horse before. I held myself from crying out by a narrow margin," one of them said.

"I rode the horse, granted. But the body aches so much that I could not sleep," said another one.

"I could not even take my meal properly," yet another one added.

"What to talk of sleeping! I could not even take turns from left to right."

"At one point of time, I even thought I had come on such a troublesome trip."

"If I knew that it was thus far, I would not have come for sure."

Mauni showed his slate to the friends. It read: "It's enough. Why should we bother the poor maiden by telling her our sad stories? Let's not lament now. Let's talk of good things. Please change the context."

Sundari stared at Panchashar with inquisitive looks. He was silent. In fact, to whom should his friends narrate their on-the-way troubles, if not to him? Once asked, they would obviously narrate their own tales. Panchashar thus stayed silent, thinking that this was the only day they had the opportunity to open up their minds, for they were not sure if anyone asked them about their plight again.

The maiden turned toward Mauni with interrogative looks. On being aware of that, Mauni appeared quite uncomfortable. Other friends stared at one another. In the meantime, Mauni showed his slate: "I enjoyed the trip. I have gathered both bliss and experience."

Panchashar turned even more serious. He was experiencing a sort of uneasiness on having no opportunity to explain Mauni's case to the maiden. But he consoled himself, 'We have had joint introduction so far. I shall tell about Mauni, when there is individual introduction again.'

"I cannot read the script on your slate. I think I should learn it first from you and then read," said the maiden, winding up the issue.

"If that is the case, I should read this one out to you," said Panchashar, taking in hand the paper that contained the names of the eleven members in his group.

The maiden stretched her hand. Panchashar handed over the name list to the maiden. She scanned it thoroughly and said, "You read the names yourself, and introduce the person alongside the name."

He started reading.

"Panchashar Gorkha. This is my name. I will read the rest of the list now."

"Mauni. His full name is Manthan. He is speechless." While he was being introduced, Mauni stood up and folded his hands.

Panchashar added, "He is a highly skilled artist. It's his specialty to stay happy all the time. It is his natural habit to rejoice and enjoy everywhere he goes. He doesn't even know how to get engaged. He has a hypnotizing tool with him. Whenever he smiles, every onlooker gets mesmerized. He thus conquers everyone. For us, he is both a guru and a secretary."

He paused for a while and resumed, "Though God took back his voice, He has spared him the power of hearing. His looks also befit the name 'Manthan' — contemplation. We call him Mauni. He is identified with this name."

The maiden said, "I can see that you in this group are people with different qualifications and specialties. I shall take more information later." Signaling toward the name list, she added, "If you give that paper to me, I will send it to the palace. If you need too, you can keep a copy of the same."

Panchashar said, "Alongside the name, the expertise and area of interest of each member has been mentioned. This had been prepared for the palace and handed over to us. You can keep it with you for the palace." He thus explained the context.

The maiden said, "Let's do like this. You are still not done with resting. I can clearly understand that. I am always rather busy today with my shopping. After breakfast, you should move from here, targeting to reach there by afternoon tomorrow. That way, you can reach in time, enjoy various sights on the way. How about that?" she said.

All the travelers nodded in agreement.

In a mode of commandment, the maiden said to two other girls beside her, "Take measurement for their clothes and make arrangements to make them rest. Also arrange foods and drinks that can be consumed in a free and easy way. I shall be here; so shall you all be. I leave it to you to decide if you would sing and dance on your own, or invite some more friends. Here I go. I am in a hurry. I shall be back before long. You have the responsibility to oversee all the arraignments for today."

The maiden exited from there.

Two maidens came forward giggling and frolicking, took the measurement of the travelers' bodies, and left. The travelers enjoyed the touch and the fragrance of the maidens.

The contingent of the travelers coming from Kantipur left the city on a carriage after a stay of two days. Those days, those who moved on carriages were considered prominent people. The people in that part of the world believed that such people were different from the ordinary laities. The villagers had gazed at this troupe of horse-ridden travelers with equal reverence since the time it entered the city from one of the passes leading into it. Those glimpses were still fresh in the eyes of the travelers.

As soon as they heard the sound of the hoofs, the local people rushed out of home and gathered at places to see the people move on carriages. Many of them stood barring the way to enjoy the show. There were many who rated the carriage-ride very high.

But the movement of the carriages was quite ordinary that day. Whenever the king had such a travel, his men and courtiers dressed in royal outfit would stand out from a long distance, and that required the people to stay alert. They had to both suspect and stay frightened. But the carriage-ride today had none of those effects, as it looked quite ordinary. Those on the carriage appeared simple, plain and informal, as viewed from the eyes of the locals.

Each of the travelers was on a carriage. There were no lone horse-riders before and after. The carriages were only three. In other words, all the travelers were on the carriages. Remarkably, men and women sat evenly distributed in the carriages. Even more remarkable was the fact that each of them looked smiling and happy. They talked a lot among themselves. Those overseeing the passage of the carriages seldom got to see such a spectacle.

The original food and clothes of a place are elements that introduce the dwellers or society of a place. The costumes introduce a nation and a community. They also inform about culture and geography. Dresses are also used differently in accordance with religions and ages. They also give a glimpse of special occasions, gender and professions. But those mounted on the carriages had not put any dress that could introduce any strange country or community. So, in the eyes of the local onlookers, they appeared to be people belonging to the same place. If watched from a close distance, one could see pigtails on the head of some left uncovered out of carelessness. If the friends sitting nearby noticed it, he or she immediately cautioned. That was not a matter of concern, therefore. The shape of their faces and the tinge of their skin faintly suggested that they were outsiders coming from far-off places. The way they looked out, and the manners in which they accepted or sent forth impressions through gestures clearly set them apart from the local inhabitants. However, in order to make such minute observation and make such fine comments, one was required to come into carriage and observe. The context, therefore, was a non-issue.

In fact, these newcomers, who otherwise reeked of horses and sweats and were rubbed, crushed, folded and facially deformed, had thrown off their usual clothes and were dressed in the outfits of the royal guests. Though they were austere, cool and simple, these guests of the Beijing Palace looked quite special. Granted that our body is the first reason that calls for clothes, the second reason is honor we need to safeguard, while the third one is cultural nourishment, fourth one a celebration of aesthetics while the fifth reason is the identification of class distinction. Yet the members of this group of travelers appeared in mixed dresses. For this reason, the outfit of the carriage riders did not become an issue of discussion among the onlookers. Instead, the onlookers speculated, though in an expressed way, that young girls were lending leadership to this troupe of men. But then, this also failed to become an issue of criticism or commentary.

There were three grown-up maidens in the first carriage. The second had five experts of architecture while the third one had six such experts. The driver of the carriage used to be alone, lost in his own world. This was the arrangement, more or less.

A discussion erupted in the first carriage about the accommodation and food for the guests. Those in the second carriage started discussing about the sights one saw during a trip, the enjoyment, mystery and excitement it was entailed with. The men in the third were caught up in their own mental conflict. They discussed about their shelters, their trips abroad, and their own joys and sorrows. Yet they were in a huge country as the king's guests, and were thrilled by the way they were being received and welcomed in this new land. On top of that the honor they received in Lhasa and the type of hospitality they were accorded the previous night made them hopeful that they would be entitled to enjoy similar privileges all through the trip.

In short, this group of architects was contented, cherishing such positive thoughts. Memory and day-dreaming, however, tormented them from time to time, stealing chances, and they deeply pined for the company of youthful maidens to befit their youthful mentalities. There is a huge difference between the mentalities of young men who have had a taste of the feminine fragrance, and those who had not yet had such privilege, but are deeply lusty. Life abroad is probably easier for those whose minds are not cleft and they perhaps find it easier to hold themselves in place, as long as they are single. But for those whose minds settle nowhere, is not finding any resort or has not yet been hit by anyone's hook, no place on earth is likely to be uncomfortable.

Each one of them was enjoying. Every heart was serenely moon-blenched. They were all enraptured by the newness of each passing moment. From the last stop they left until the arrival of the final stop thereafter, the travelers on the carriage rejoiced themselves in the surrounding landscape, while a few of them were tickled by a sense of curiosity and partial apprehension. One could easily read such complexities from their faces. However, they all took pride in the fact that soon they would be reaching China with a mission, and would be received as royal guests. It can be safely said the troupe reached Beijing without any hassle and got settled at the place set aside for it.

***

China is the centre of an ancient and glorious civilization. At the present time, China is necessarily mentioned whenever other human civilizations are talked about. In fact, China is in itself a complete and a vast world. Owing to its cultural heterogeneity and topographical diversity, the country is not that easy for outsiders to understand easily. The society and literature of China has remained obscure and inaccessible to the rest of the world even today. In simple words, it can be referred to as the fourth world.

China seems to be moving in tunes with ancient to modern times, in three waves, three stands and three streams. It is a structure that can be conceived as a union of several states and is a matchless example of a human sea. For that reason, the developments it has registered in art, culture, history and physical sciences have made it glorious and commendable.

After taking a round of various places inside Beijing City, Mauni wrote on his slate: "China is an incomprehensible scripture. It's an inaccessible museum."

Panchashar added, "If we loiter this way and that, we can get lost. We need to do nothing but take our way straight."

The visiting artists shared their impressions about China among themselves. During their leisure and moments of joy, they engaged themselves in a myriad of discussions and deliberations. But when they had to wind up the issue, Mauni made it a point to play his *murchunga*. Whenever he had the desire to enjoy on his own, he picked up his *binayo*, and stepped two steps backward. At this, they wound up one issue and picked up another for discussion. The group, glued together in a circle, soon disintegrated in an easy and natural fashion.

The group of the artists rested for two full weeks in Beijing. In the meantime, it visited some of the important places in the city, and got to know about them. They moved around ordinary market areas, centers of entertainment, ale houses, theaters, casinos, gardens and parks, travelers' rests, religious shrines and places that abounded in nymphets and gathered as much information as they could, until they were greatly pleased. This opportunity to move around in carriages driven by four horses and guided by maidens that could speak their language and understand their feelings had nourished their minds in a balanced way.

Materially, this was an experience that brought home a feeling of specialty on their parts. This way, the atmosphere of the city of Beijing and a few people and place they knew turned out to be indelible memories for them to anchor their hearts on, and grounds to remember.

The occasion for which they had come to Beijing was approaching. Melamchi came forward with orders from the government. She was the same maiden, who had welcomed them at the spot in Lhasa where they had left their horses and had ridden on the carriages, and had arranged their breakfast.

But none of the artists could recognize her. She had appeared in a different form, and had welcomed them in a different manner of courtesy when they had met first. This time, she looked completely different from her make-up. Her wears were quite different too. The jewelries and cosmetics too were new. Moreover, she had not found time to tell them her name in their first meeting, nor had they cared to ask. In such ordinary issues, there perhaps is an influence of graver civilization and culture, and a lack of them. But then, she had become familiar albeit in a state of strangeness.

"*Sewaro, taremam, tasidile, namaste!* Didn't you recognize me? Why are you looking at me with strange eyes as though I am unknown to you?"

"Oh, it's you?"

"Oh God.."

"You look so different."

"You were different then. Here you look different."

"I am left gawking."

"I was wondering where such a beautiful maiden had come from."

"I was confused if it was an angel coming from somewhere."

"I thought a nymphet had come to try our hearts."

Of them, the one most stunned one was Panchashar, but he didn't utter a word. He stayed silent, comparing if she was the same graceful and amicable maiden he had met before.

Mauni showed his slate, where he had written, "Do not get surprised to that extent. Do not flatter her so much."

The maiden considered these words on Mauni's slate the conclusion of their deliberation, and said, "I am Melamchi. How come you didn't recognize me? Did you forget so soon the fact that we breakfasted together and came all the way on the same carriage, talking?" She knew that artists were unable to recognize her as long as he didn't introduce herself in detail. Each of the artists was staring at her vacantly, considering her to be a fairy from a different realm. She was at least aware of this reality.

***

Melanchi was an intellectual maiden deployed by the state. The state had assigned her the task of assisting the construction work, teach the artists Chinese language, coordinate between them and the state, make arrangements for their accommodation and food, take care of other requirements and facilities, help them meet their interests and make arrangements for their medical care. She deployed other human resources as needed.

She said, "I have come here to assist you. Share with me every sort of things, both easy and difficult ones. I shall make all attempts to remove every type of hassle and inconvenience. Feel that your stay, food, sight-seeing and entertainment here should be completely hassle-free. I want to share one more piece of information with you: we shall move to a new residence tomorrow. The construction site is nearer from there. The kitchen is attached to it. A small veranda stands in the middle, connecting the lodge with the kitchen. This house will be used by girls engaged in cooking as their residence. That way, they shall be in one part of the kitchen and you in other."

She added, "As for food, you can avail the items you like. You must teach the cooks to balance the taste, and at times, you must help them as well, at least for a few days."

She paused for a while, scanned the feelings in the eyes and gestures on the faces of all the eleven of her guests and said, "You must also go shopping if there is a shortage of anything in the kitchen. You can buy the things of your choice. At such moments, the girls expect your help. I believe you won't feel uncomfortable."

She paid a look at everyone for a while and said, "We may also run out of woods sometimes. These are ordinary things."

Mauni showed his slate. It read: "How about hot water?"

The troupe made no reaction to it. Melamchi could not decipher the context. She could understand utterances but could not read the script. She looked at the face of all and said, "The main thing is the construction of the building. Even more important is health. You ought to take great care of your health. If a single strand of hair is plucked off, you must let me know. I always expect cooperation from you. If there is any problem, feel free to share it with me. If I am not available at such moments, tell it to any of my girls. They can understand you. They can speak your language, though they are not quite fluent. You must teach them how to speak fluently. She can, however, relay your words to me efficiently in their language. For that reason, the girls shall be of great help to you."

Mauni wrote on his slate, "Befriend the womenfolk, but never make them enemies. If you irk them, they stay ready to bite you any moment like a snake, rife with feelings of revenge. Always keep this fact in your mind."

After reading Mauni's slate, the artisans nodded their heads, expressing their agreement.

Mauni showed his slate once again and asked, "Do we have the facility of bathing and washing clothes in cold water?"

This time as well, his friends were blank, devoid of any response.

Melamchi asked outright, "Read the slate and tell me what he means."

Panchashar explained her the essence of his script.

When she understood Mauni's essence, Melamchi said, "This seems to be a private affair. You discuss with the girls and solve it yourself. Perhaps they will help you out. I can also request them at the most, but cannot force them. Many things shall depend on your mutual help and understanding."

A carriage was sending forth a cloud of dust at a distance. Melamchi turned toward the artisans once again and said, "I will take you to the construction site today. Once you see the spot, you will be able to surmise what the building will look like and where the main entrance will face."

Three carriages drew in and stopped. Everyone present there mounted on the carriages, which then moved toward the construction site.

We often get to hear and read many interesting and impressive things about rulers. Such contexts are often quite influential thought only in the form of a spark. Else they would not have discussed the issue even after several centuries. If we talk about art, it's a very old tradition on the part of the rulers to decorate their royal cities with exquisite and glorious artworks. The royal cities in Europe are beautiful examples of the same.

The storehouse of Mughal art in India has continued to become a subject of research and study even today. Those days, the tendency of creating, developing and conserving art works and cultural artifacts was a matter of healthy competition in many ancient nations of the world.

If we consider Nepal's case, the Malla Kings of all the three towns in the Kantipur Valley had enriched their capital with exquisite art works, and had thus lent climax to the development of art in Kantipur, Lalitpur and Bhadgaon[38] cities. It's obvious that the rulers want to acquire all the best things of the world and make their royal capitals the matchless museums of the best collections from around the world. History has been teaching us such things.

Timur Khan, the king of China, was not an exception. His ancestors had invited artisans from Nepal and got the White Pagoda constructed to glorify their capital. Imitating his ancestors' love for art, he also invited a troupe of artist to build pagoda-style buildings, and the same troupe was taking the initiative with all readiness today. Melamchi was aware of this history.

***

---

[38] Modern day Kantipur, Lalitpur and Bhadgaon cities

HARI RAJ BHATTARAI

CHAPTER FOUR

AFTER THEY MOVED into the new house, the life of the artisans acquired an order. The building where they lodged had enough rooms. They could choose a single room each if they wanted, or could share them. But before they had moved there, Mauni had shown them his slate, writing, "Spare me a room on one corner. It can be at any corner. That will make it easy for me to rehearse music without bothering anyone of you. I should give continuity to my instrumental music. The instruments are my intimate friends. I play and enjoy with them."

Everyone took Mauni's words as natural. They also chose their accommodation with freedom, some opting to share a room between two while others choosing to stay alone. Panchashar stayed alone in the fashion of a ringleader.

The building had a special room, something like a meeting hall. It was located at the centre of the building. One could reach here comfortably from every other room.

The house was a new one and this was the first time people—in the form of these artisans—had entered to live in it. Another part of the building was new as well, and here, grown-up girls stayed, always ready to serve the need of the artisans and oversee their comfort. The kitchen was new too. By cooking for the artisans reaching Beijing from Kantipur for the first time, it had been inaugurated. Therefore, everything here was new, clean, pleasing and intimate. The artisans observed this building keenly from artistic an point of view and silently praised its technical refinements.

Stealing a chance, Mauni wrote on his slate, "If a house meant to lodge workers like us is so grand, what should the house we are going to construct be like? Have you ever thought about it? You must start thinking now."

Everyone nodded with positivity, evincing a positive reception of Mauni's words.

"Whatever Mauni wrote is true. We must think deeply and we should accomplish our work well and completely," said Panchashar, drawing a conclusion out of the present context.

The construction site was not very far. Yet it was not easy for them to walk on foot and attend to their work. So, a carriage was arranged for their transport. Every day, two carriages stood ready to take them to the construction site and back. Once again, it was girls that drove the chariots and took care of the horses. Before their routine had stabilized, they had to tell one hour before so that the carriages would be made ready in time. In this fashion, the artisans studied the natural environment and topography of the construction site for a week. Then they gave final shape to the blue print and thus accomplished their first-phase work.

In celebration of the completion of their first-phase work, they played the *madal* and tambourine, sangs songs. The flute played a folk tune from Nepal Valley. The bevy of girls was drawn toward the entertainment site.

Stealing a chance, Mauni showed his slate. It read, "Kanchha[39], if you are not tired, put on the anklet."

"I find it odd to dance alone. I would, if I had a friend," said Kanchha, without concealing his feelings.

"Jantaré[40], won't you give him your company?" It was Panchashar speaking this time.

They were physically robust now, after having tea and snacks. On top of that, new vigor mounted on them. They got ready with anklets on their feet. Mauni played the Asharé tune on his flute. But he stopped abruptly in the middle.

"Play on. I will also join your entertainment," said Melamchi with a light heart, even as she dragged herself toward this gathering.

---

[39]   The name given to the youngest of the brothers
[40]   The name given to the sixth of the brothers

HARI RAJ BHATTARAI

The young maidens seemingly felt awkward. Melamchi, on her part, looked for a place and sat there.

"You are welcome to this program," said Panchashar.

"You enhanced our honor by visiting us here. It boosted our morale, and made the environment even more thrilling. We are extremely happy." This how Mauni expressed casual formality in writing.

Everyone welcomed Melamchi, folding their hands in the gesture of 'namaste'. She answered them in similar fashion.

Mauni resumed his work, playing yet another folk tune on his flute. The air resounded with the beat of the *madal*. Two of them sang in a sweet, melodious voice.

Some drinks and snacks were also brought in for Melamchi. This way, the thrilling evening, accompanied by singing and dancing, came to an end.

"You don't need to be surprised to see me here. In fact, I was scheduled to be here. It has been almost a week since we met last. I was caught up in some works related with our construction. That has been completed now. I feel that I arrived here at an opportune time; I could partake of the entertainment." She lifted and showed the liquor glass. Both her verbal and physical gestures manifested simplicity and intimacy.

"I will take my dinner and leave. You ask others to eat as well," she said, giving direction to the girls. When the girls had moved toward the kitchen, she turned toward the artisans and said, "I am happy that the first phase has been completed. I want to see the blueprint. If the palace desires to see, I must produce a copy."

"That's fine. We have a draft with us. We will give you a fair copy," said Panchashar in short.

A girl walked in and requested them to join the dinner. Everyone entered the dining room and sat in easy poses in line on the floor, folding their knees. The table in front was quite low; they could sit with ease and eat from it. As for the girls, they kneeled on folded knees and ate like that. They were habituated to such kneeling postures.

On one side of the table, the artisans sat. The girls sat on the other side. The table lay between the two lines. Melamchi sat some yards away. She sat on one end between the lines of the artisans and the girls like Mount Sumeru in a range of several smaller mountains.

"You can rest for two days on Fridays and Saturdays. On other five days, start your work at 8 in the morning. After you are done with your breakfast, the carriages will drop you there at the construction site."

She allocated the times and said, "The snacks will reach at 10 and lunch at 1. At 3 in the afternoon, some light snacks will be served with tea. At 4, the carriage will come to carry you back."

After a brief pause, she resumed, "This is a primary routine. If it creates inconveniences, we can change the eating times."

"What are you planning to do on Fridays and Saturdays, friends?" said one in a rustic tone, giving easy expression to his curiosity.

"I will go to see places, if the girls take me along," said Mauni, writing on his slate.

All of them made their faces bright, reading Mauni's script. Melamchi looked at Panchashar with inquisitiveness, unable to decipher what Mauni meant.

"Mauni wants to go on sight-seeing, if the girls take him along," said Panchashar, explaining the essence of Mauni's writing.

"There's no harm in that. He can go around with the girl of his choice. She will show him the places. You can sit together and set the programs: one spot this week and a different one next week. There is no dearth of visiting places here. It is up to you to decide if you would love to go around alone, or in group," said Melamchi, encouraging everyone.

Mauni wrote on his slate, "It's true that one cannot ask someone moving in one direction to take a turn. He has the right to move according to his will. No one has the right to impede. You said it so well."

Toward the end of their dinner, Melamchi placed forth her conclusion: "It settles the issue if two people sitting face to face make a group. I mean, one who serves the meal helps the one being served."

In a jocular tone she said, "If today's sitting arrangement has been faulty, we can mend it tomorrow and two can feed each other. Such a thing should not be made a matter of discussion."

The artisans and the girls started seeking their mates with their gestures. Melamchi did not wait for any reaction from the ringleader of the artisans. They just started at each other. The leader didn't utter any word. Mauni appeared serious, willing to write something on his slate. Others were engaged in intense search.

"This evening was extremely pleasing. Let such events take place between our work regularly. If you remember me, I shall join you. I shall come even without invitation, the same way as I did today."

Standing from her place, Melamchi said, "I take leave of you now. Thank you all."

She turned toward the maidens and said, "Take good care of our guests. Your inspiration shall be crucial in maintaining their zeal and readiness. Let no complaint come from their side."

Winding up her words, Melamchi said, "They will accomplish the task for which they have come, or the king has invited them. Therefore, you should build up the beautiful, healthy and balanced environment they need. Always keep this fact in your mind."

She stopped for a while and spoke again, "I think personal and psychological care if more effective than collective care."

Having said this, she touched the cheeks of a girl slightly with her forefinger, and disappeared.

Panchashar ran his eyes on the face of everyone and said, "Friends, should we add some pints of liquor?"

No one refuted his proposal. This forced Mauni to write something on his slate. He wrote, "How much of it should be poured into the glass will be determined by the same person who distributed it earlier. If a different hand comes in, that can spoil things."

Panchashar said, "It's not like that. One should have the privilege to serve a person of choice. I mean, one has the freedom to drink from the hands of his chosen one. This should be the rule of the event."

"Oh no. Let's leave this matter to the maidens. Let them serve the man of their choice with their own hands. This seems to be a better arrangement." This is what Mauni wrote.

A wave of joy rippled in the maidens' group. They blushed from this end to that.

Mauni wrote something on the slate and showed it to the girls. It read, "Let's do like this. Let every young man pour some measure of liquor in the cups for the girls. Let the girls pick the cup they like and drink, or feed it to the man of their choice. The night, after all, is ours. Why shouldn't we launch the trend of helping right from this moment?"

One of the maidens openly said, "He is right." She also explained the essence of Mauni's writing to the rest of the maidens.

From the following day, a girl started taking care of a guy, especially in regards to his requirements and comfort. Things done in group were taken as ordinary, and they bore no much meaning. At the construction site, such ordinary tasks took place, and passed as acceptable and fully informal. When it came to the personal residences, their mutual assistances started changing into personal relations and private affairs.

Mauni again wrote, "I could see a number of sons and daughters-in-law gather in this house."

The maidens got the essence of his writing and blushed for once.

Another day, Panchashar picked a sentence Mauni had written and wrote: "I saw a number of daughters-in-law gather in this house." He pasted this sentence on the wall of their kitchen.

As soon as they saw it, the maidens smiled and fussed among themselves. Mauni, on the other hand, appeared apprehensive, lest he should be drawn into a controversy. For that reason, he didn't appear at ease in the dining hall.

But a maiden could read Mauni's eyes. She could decipher his gestures quite well. She discovered why Mauni turned grim as soon as he entered the dining room, and bloomed up as soon as he exited from there. Besides herself, no other soul knew this secret.

Everyone moved toward the common room after breakfast.

Expressing his mind among his friends, Panchashar said, "It's time we dug up the foundation for the new building. When Melamchi was here last time, we forgot to ask if they have any rule about laying the foundation stone, or we can do it our way. What should we do, friends?"

"This building has been ordered by the king. We are mere workers. We must ask," said one.

"Mauni, what do you say?" said Panchashar, turning toward Mauni.

Mauni wrote, "We must ask. We have two things to ask: One about the procedure of digging the foundation, and second, about laying the foundation stone, or inaugurating the construction work."

"To whom should we ask? And how?"

Mauni resorted to writing once again. He wrote, "Let's send a girl with the errand. She will go on a horse and return. As soon as she gets the news, Melamchi will come here. I see no hassle in this." He suggested a solution.

"Who should we send, then? Find a messenger and send her yourself. We leave that up to you."

Mauni displayed a natural smile. Everyone looked happy. If he had to call someone near, Mauni always took out his *murchunga* from his pocket. He took out his *murchunga* for the first time in this building and moved toward the girls' dormitory, playing it. He went past the dining hall and came into the meeting hall. This was the place where their collective discussions took place. On reaching there, he played his *murchunga*. As soon as she heard its tune, a maiden appeared. She shook her wet hair a couple of times and stood beside Mauni. By then, she had come to know that Mauni had no voice.

She looked at Mauni with interrogative looks, and shook her hair again and again, before sending the tresses behind her shoulders. Mauni could feel a sort of art and beauty reflected in that.

"We need to meet Chi once. How can we do that? Can you help us?" wrote Mauni on his slate.

"I will inform her instantly. Here I go," she said in the fashion of a song.

"Will you go alone or with a...?" Mauni could not complete this sentence.

"Not there. We'll go together if we need to go somewhere else, shouldn't we?" said the girl, even as she touched one of Mauni's dimpled cheeks with her forefinger and rushed toward her room in a hurry.

Mauni placed his palm on the spot she had touched on his cheek and experienced an altogether new sensation. He became quite stable following this. After moving ahead by a few steps, the maiden stopped and looked back. Mauni was standing stunned, placing his palm on the spot she had touched. Apparently in a sense of embarrassment, she took a turn and moved ahead, only to disappear before long.

Mauni drew in a long breathe and felt as though he had thrown a heavy load aground. He then moved toward his room, carefully assessing the moment with great pleasure. He allocated works for his fellow artisans. After the foundation had been dug out, other tasks would be left in hand. In works related with stones, wood, soil, cement and concrete, cleanliness, bricks and carrying loads, they would require a hundred and a few more artisans. He was yet to communicate this fact to anyone. Later, with the call of time, they would also need a painter, a gardener and such other tasks and that would require a different chapter to deal with.

After finishing this calculation, Mauni rested and started a deep contemplation. He recalled the beauty of the maiden who was shaking her hair. He also recalled her tender touch on his cheek. He was shaken to remember that his placard bearing the words 'many daughters-in-law' that had been placed on the wall right inside the maidens' room.

In fact, it was the same maiden who had taken out this placard from the kitchen and carried into her own room. She didn't want to see Mauni appear grim. She knew that since the day she removed the placard, Mauni had started cheering up again.

Early next morning, Melamchi turned up early enough to join them in the breakfast.

The workers sat on both sides of the dining table, facing one another.

Talking up the issue carefully, Melamchi said, "Give me two more days. If there is any rule for digging the foundation, I shall arrange for it. You don't need to worry about that. If your digging works, I shall inform you about that too. You can do the best thing that suits."

In yet another context, she said, "I shall also talk about constructing the foundation or laying the foundation stone. These are extremely important tasks, aren't they? If you ask me, I would advise inviting a cultural leader for laying the foundation stone. But my saying won't do. I am also an employee," said Melamchi, expressing herself without any daunt.

After scanning everyone's face, Mauni wrote on his slate, "Work force?"

"Yes. How much work force do you need?" Melamchi asked.

For a while, everyone turned toward Panchashar. He didn't say anything. Perhaps, he did not comprehend the context.

"On working day, we need a hundred people each day," said Mauni, writing on his slate.

"That's fine. I had similar speculations." Melamchi expressed her support. She drew a long breath and said, "We should perhaps divide labor this way: a group will work since sunrise up to midday, and from afternoon until sunset, the second group will take over. The group working in the morning shall return to work next morning, while the group working in the afternoon shall turn up next afternoon."

What next? All appeared inquisitive.

"As for you, you can return to the lodge for afternoon snacks. Or, it depends on whatever you wish. You also take rest, don't you?"

Soon the meeting was over. For the first time, the troupe went to see the construction site. They returned at lunch time.

The meal that day had Nepali items: gunruk, masyaura and soybeans. The items had been prepared following the desire of the artisans. They all tasted a little and appreciated the taste. On finding newness and additional tastiness in the meal, Melamchi praised the cuisine with an open heart. Other workers praised their friends involving in cooking. The environment there was quite free, independent, guiltless and intimate. The maidens also appeared quite pleased in their natural demeanors.

A maiden turned toward Mauni again and again and pointed at the placard on the kitchen wall, making signals. Mauni placed his forefinger from time to time upon his lips, signaling the maidens to stay quiet. In fact, she secretly teased Mauni, saying that the wall was empty and she could bring back and place the placard therein once again. At such moments of indecisiveness, Mauni always took deep sighs, and sought for pretexts to move away from there, apparently trying to recall or forget a thing. This time as well, he did the same.

Two days later, Melamchi reached the construction site, riding a horse. For a while, she inspected the spot from the horseback. She made some analysis and calculation and moved toward the artisans' residence.

The worker boys and the cooking girls sat face-to-face, taking their breakfast. They were alarmed on hearing the gallop of a horse stop outside the dining hall.

It was Melamchi. She entered the hall and started sharing breakfast.

She took an ounce of food, chewed it a little and said, "I am obliged to take your suggtestion about digging the foundation and laying foundation stone. Everything is going to depend on your interest, vision and zeal. I have rushed here to convey this idea and take your opinion."

She sat at her usual place. Everyone else stared at her, seemingly unable to decipher what she meant.

"Can it manage digging the foundation and laying the foundation stone on the same day?" she asked, repealing the context in short.

Panchashar wrinkled his forehead and raised his eyebrows, seemingly unsure how it could happen.

"It's possible," wrote Mauni on his slate.

All the eyes now rested on Mauni.

"Both the tasks can be accomplished on the same day, if we have enough workforces," wrote Mauni on his slate.

Other artisans were surprised. A few of them even thought, 'What does this dumb fellow say? He is sure to put us into problem by talking nonsense.'

"Then you tell how we can do it," said Panchashar, turning toward Mauni.

"But then, why should we hurry?" wrote Mauni and showed the slate to Melamchi. Panchashar read it out and explained it to Melamchi.

"The full moon was approaching. We are thinking about accomplishing both these tasks on the same day. Is that possible? Will that be fine?" said Melamchi, expressing herself openly.

"That's fine. It is possible. We have enough time." Mauni wrote in gist and showed it to everyone.

On reading Mauni's slate, every face lit up with joy. The young maidens displayed smiles seizing the moment and blushed, giving one another a push from this end to that. Melamchi read their gestures and appeared quite pleased.

In the yard outside a carriage drawn by two horses came and stopped. The driver walked in and greeted everyone by lowering his head in Chinese fashion.

"You go and bring a model stone each from the carriage. Let's inspect them here," said Melamchi, aiming at the maidens.

The maidens acted promptly and returned with small bricks, one each. They placed a cloth upon a table and placed the bricks thereon, arraying them in layers.

The Nepali artisans could not understand what this exhibition was for. In a while, Mauni returned from his secluded contemplation and calculated the length of the stones, their breath and width, and their types and color. Melamchi perhaps wanted to know how big the stones should be and what their types should be. These were mere models, showing different shapes and types.

In terms of shapes and size, the big, the middle-sized and the small stones were all considered acceptable. But then, a big stone, when placed on the wall, should be light enough for two people to lift it at the most. If they were wide on the base, that would not be fine. They all expressed their opinions freely.

The carriage driver went out and returned with a bag full of wooden pieces. He removed the stones and placed the woods one after another. They were models of woods needed for the main beam, pole, rafters, door and window frames, etc. They were soft and hard, light and heavy, strong and weak.

The Nepalese artisans lifted them, turned them back and forth and even smelt the wood pieces to ascertain their qualities. But then, for artisans who had not worked with so many variety of wood, choosing the right kind was not an easy task. Perhaps feeling that an unpaved path would be difficult to tread along, Panchashar said, "We are not experts of the woods available here. We would like to use them according to your advice, can we? You can decide which wood is to be placed where, and order for them accordingly. We can suggest the length, breath and width of the woods we need."

He further said, "We have not yet been able to study the seasons and the corresponding energy here. Your support is therefore quite imminent."

"I have a proposal." Mauni showed his slate.

All others appeared keen on Mauni's proposal.

He showed his slate. It read, "Yet, it will be better if we can select the wood considering if it can withstand sun, rain and wind, bear shade and dampness, stand weight and lightness, change with season or resist it, and pick them to befit the place, purpose, condition and time of use. Maybe we also will use wood that emit light and send forth fragrance."

Panchashar explained to Melamchi the meaning of Mauni's words.

She jutted her tongue in astonishment and said, "I like his statistics, classification and analysis. I had never looked at things that way. I am pleased. Yet, I shall assist in deciding which wood should be placed in which part of the house. You give it a shape according to your plans. Won't that work?"

She solved the problem of the wood, placing forth a positive thought.

"Bricks," said Panchashar.

"Bricks of all types and shapes can be prepared. That is a simple task. Please tell us which substance we shall use to join them. That too will be managed. We have all the raw materials with us. You direct us about striking a balance and preparing them. We have workforce ready to do any task." Melamchi summed up everything in brief.

For a while, stillness pervaded.

After a round of tea and snacks, they resumed their talk.

In fact, the nature of their work was quite thrilling.

Some workers got absorbed in stone works. They started to prepare stones of certain shapes and sizes on war footing. Those stones, caressed by hands laden with artistry were not mere stones anymore. It seems, they now had a lining of human consciousness and aesthetics. There was no dearth of skill and workforce.

The readied stone slabs were now collected near the construction site, waiting their placement. The stones were arrayed in such a way that the position, significance and attractiveness of each of them could be felt even from a distance.

The Nepalese artisans didn't know how far the mine was. These stone slabs were brought here on twenty carriages pulled by two mules each. They were arrayed in the fashion of a wall, at different places, in different sections.

In another part of the site, bricks of different sizes arrived on mule-driven carriages, and were arrayed like a wall as people array Teliya bricks.

The task of bringing sliced wooden planks and arranging them in order started.

The Nepalese artisans didn't have to stand the hassle of conversing with their Chinese counterparts in the Chinese language. Melamchi understood the minds of the workers and explained to them in their language. So there was no room for any sort of difficulty or boredom.

Another noteworthy thing was that they availed food and drinks, rest, sight-seeing and entertainment in a balanced measure. So, their life didn't seem cumbersome and depressing though they were in a foreign land and were engaged as workers in construction work. They went on harboring an impressive memory.

On top of that, Melamchi was quite friendly. She became a good friend to them and an able director. Besides being extremely simple, she was intimate and wise too, knew of things in detail and was a sort of patron to all of them. The Nepalese artisans believed that they had a safe refuge under the umbrella of her care, and this group of royal artisans considered itself secure within the purview of her gaze.

***

It was the day of Buddha Poornima[41]. With the brink of the day, a group of Lamas reached the construction site. All those associated with the construction work were present there. There also were those who had support and good-wish for the construction. The density of people there started increasing each moment.

---

[41]   The full-moon night in April, considered to the birthday of the Buddha

The plot where the building had to be constructed had been demarcated with pillars, lines and ropes. The troupe of the Lamas started chanting mantras, moving in circle around the site, and on the four vertices, they performed special prayers. On all the four directions, special worships were performed.

The chief Lama of the central monastery in Beijing has eleven other monks in his team. The chief Lama was himself leading the troupe of the Lamas that was encircling the site in the morning, dotted with light and long, stretched shadows. When the ritual of land worship was conducted in accordance with their religious, cultural, ritualistic and geographical practices, the Lama started the task of digging the soil with a golden spade. The maidens present there made a shower of flower petals. The air turned tantalizing with the fragrance of incense. Several performances were staged and several melodies played, making the spectators thrilling with mesmerizing pleasure. Every task was performed at the stipulated time and moment. When the people had had a holy view of the Lama and had taken his blessings, they all partook in the collective refreshment.

Following this, the task of digging the foundation started at war footing. There was no dearth of workforce, resources, food and onlookers. So, they always met their target before time and waited for another task to start.

The family of the artisans had been informed that the foundation stone of the building will be laid by the chief Lama of Lhasa, Tibet. Melamchi had herself informed the Nepalese artisans and the Chinese maidens, keeping them together. She had also signaled them that the foundation stone will be laid with the rise of the moon.

What a strange coincidence! In one hand, the moon was slowly descending earthward from the sky while the Lama of Lhasa, on the other hand, had just disembarked from his carriage and was now moving toward the construction site. At the spot, thousands of monks and ordinary citizens were arriving on their carriages.

On one side, the full moon in its concrete, spherical, complete, glorious and cool form was shining brilliantly. On the other side, Lama from Lhasa, a city with new radiance of religious, cultural, traditional brilliance glittered with a halo of holy and guiltless personality, radiating with magnanimity, grandeur and a feeling of universal brotherhood.

At the moment of the moonrise, the Lama laid the foundation stone at the moment he had himself stipulated. He also consecrated the blueprint prepared on a paper. All other rituals slated for the Buddha Poornima Day were accomplished at the same spot.

That night turned out to be a special one. All the youthful minds fulfilled their wishes to select the maidens of their choice, meet them, caressed them and held them in their arms. The youthful proximity between the Nepalese artisans and the Chinese maidens grew very intimate. Those who kept themselves at bay were exceptions.

The task of laying the foundation got along, albeit with pauses in between. They had to make it stable, immovable, and capable of withstanding a huge weight. So, when they made good use of patience, contemplation and intellect to make it best, they took twice the length of time an ordinary building would usually take. It was natural for the base of the royal building to appear more special than others. It was therefore natural for the stipulated time to be short, considering the fact that they had to take stock of the length and breadth of the building, the special division of rooms inside, and the access of air, light and temperature depending on the use of the rooms, their conditioning, speed and state.

There also was yet another reason behind such a long time it took. The construction of the foundation was done on alternative days. That helped the foundation become stable, and it appeared perfect on being inspected. It also made the foundation errorless, balanced and reliable. Inspired by this belief, the team of the artisans carried the work in a snail's pace. The open space inside and outside the foundation had to be gradually filled up, and it had to be given a strong support. These two tasks were accomplished with special construction techniques. With the optimal use of water, soil, pebbles and bricks, it was lent strength to withstand a huge weight.

The artisans conversed among themselves and drew their conclusions: "We invested exceptionally long time in the foundation. I think, the progress will be speedier now."

After the foundation was ready, the artisans took rest of an entire month. Yet, they visited the construction site quite frequently and returned after inspecting it for a while. If needed, they instructed the local workers to do this or that before returning. If the weather was favorable, they had no chance of facing obstacles from any other quarters. Since they had no fear of any external element, the artisans were free to move out on carriages with their friends according to their own wishes.

The artisans rejoiced the dinner and the environment in the dining hall in the evening hours. Their minds were relaxed here, and they were invigorated again.

Their second benefit was the conversation, travel and acting with the maidens of their choices. They experienced that the fragrance of womenfolk filled them with ample amount of energy, but they didn't know how to explain and analyze the feeling. At such moments, some went for seeing places, while others went shopping, collecting firewood, roaming about in the garden, washing clothes and take a dive into the pool of lukewarm water. Nothing was behind any screen. Everything there was transparent. Melamchi often turned up and went out along with Panchashar. After having an inspection of the construction site, the two moved toward an unknown place. They returned home, tired to their bones, and partook of the evening meals, enjoying with everyone else. Melamchi returned from there late in the night.

When there was no one around, forlorn Mauni sometimes took out his *murchunga*, and sometimes flute. Whenever the captivating tune from his *murchunga* rippled through the air, a maiden stole a chance and secretly pressed nearer and sat close to him, before he had any tiptoe and got absorbed in the melody. She was the same girl, Omu, with whom Mauni had sent words for Melamchi to visit them.

She was the same girl who had removed the board displaying "Many daughters-in-law have gathered here" from the kitchen and had moved it into her own room. She was the one who could easily understand Mauni's mentality and feelings. On days when the guesthouse was altogether empty, these two used to be the only people left behind, surprisingly engrossed in silent conversation. She was the only maiden there, who looked at Mauni with honor and took special care of him.

"Let's go to see some place as well."

"Someday," Mauni wrote on his slate.

"Why someday? And why for only a day?"

"Our friends went out, picking their partners."

"True. Those who have partners left," the slate read.

"You and I also make a pair, don't we?"

"I don't know that I am considered a partner," read the slate.

"Be agreeable. Do not be stubborn. If you didn't agree to what I say and didn't respect my sentiments, I will force you into a carriage and drive you away from here. No one shall ever know where you have gone."

Mauni displayed a quick, gentle smile and sent forth a ripple of glorious looks in a mysterious way. The maiden kept starting, flabbergasted.

"I am ready to go anywhere, if you would lead me," read Mauni's slate.

He added, "I shall not resist in any way."

The maiden stood silent.

He wrote again, "At least tell where you are taking me."

She again chose to stay mum. But her eyes were moist with tears.

She told to herself, 'Such a lovely, guiltless and suitable man is dear to everyone, granted; but why doesn't he become mine, and only mine?' She thought even deeper, 'Perhaps we lack language and communication between us.'

She concealed her tears and stood abruptly from her place.

Mauni held her by her left arm and made her turn toward him. He then received the drops of fresh tears from her eye into his fingers and showed them to her. He could not, however, ascertain what he made out from it. She also caught hold of Mauni's fingers and pressed herself close to Mauni's breast, concealing the uninvited change mounting on her countenance, following her weep.

Mauni patted her on the bead to console her. He moved two steps closer and showed his slate again. It read, "Do not make yourself pathetic. Life is beautiful. We must live it with sweetness. We should never let it suffer or get tormented."

He further wrote, "I can't stand tears in anyone's eyes. That torments me a lot. Please do not shed tears. I cannot see them sliding down anyone's face."

The month-long vacation was over. They now launched the construction of the part above the foundation. For them, it was difficult to apply their bodies to physical labor, following a month-long Sabbath with good food and luxuries. Yet, they were obliged to engage themselves in the labor. The work with stone and soil was an arduous one. Though their bodies engrossed in the labor, their minds were not bound to the chore. So they were not in a position to anchor their hearts merely to the labor.

The mind, after all, is on unruly thing. It soared amply along the premises of love, and in various manifestations. It imagined innumerable havens and reposed itself therein. It created images of memory and cherished them until it got absorbed in them with self-gratification. On whatever it lacked at the moment, the mind of the adult workers mused of complementing it later, and thus, enacted several optional performances.

For this reason, though the work involving soil and stone was troublesome, they had their mental worlds quite balanced and well-nourished, the workers didn't allow their interest and zeal on the construction work to subside. They let no slackness to overcome them. It seemed, their proximity with the adult maidens had multiplied their energy double. As a result, each worker appeared stronger and more delighted during the work session.

The arrangement of proportional uniformity continued in the construction work. Be it the inner wall of the outer, they erected two lines of walls each day, from one end to another. This mechanism had been adopted to ensure strength and higher resistance capacity. The workers kept themselves busy, inspired by the consideration that the construction work should be beautiful and durable. Materially, their commitment and absorption in the construction work were exemplary.

Soon the doors and windows appeared in their places. The foundation to hold the scaffolding was now firm. The blueprint of the mansion soon changed into a reality. The wall was tall enough for the first ceiling to be laid now. Once again, they had a break for a week. The rest was to ensure strength and durability to the ongoing construction, and this break was considered significant and energizing for the workers. So the workers themselves decided the time of break, and they all stuck to its observation.

In the short break of a week, they decided to go to a picnic, for which they invested two days on shopping and procuring necessary things. For this, every one of them got busy. The maidens took the men of their choices on their carriages and returned with rations together. During such shopping sessions, the working men, and the maidens involved in managing kitchen stuff got closer, letting newer episode appear in their affairs, and thus they exchanged feelings to one another.

As they moved, the young men and women articulated the sparks of their love-laden feelings and inclinations. Later in the evening, after they entered their dormitories, the young men recalled their daytime thrills and appeased themselves, though there were certain things that worried them. Nevertheless, a context that could be considered extraordinary was that Panchashar and Mauni kept themselves away from shopping and journeying through the woods. At such moments, Melamchi appeared and made away, picking Panchashar. Mauni followed as a confidant, acting like Lakshman who guarded Sita and Ram for their safety[42].

Back in the resort, the maiden attending Mauni turned restless as did Urmila at Saket. At such moments, there used to be no one to understand the mental world of Mauni, or the youthful cravings and the trepidations that shot forth inside Omu, Mauni's consort. The atmosphere was bright, pleasing and quite favorable for the patrons of youthful longings, but toward the end of the day, Omu posed like a lark that has just parted from its spouse, waiting for Mauni's return. Usually, all flowers in a garden do not open up in the same degree and fashion. There always are columns of exceptions.

On reaching the picnic spot, each pair took out food items and carpets from its carriage. They left the mules to graze on their own. In the first phase of their picnic, they had light snacks, drinks and fruits. Following this, they divided labor for attending to different tasks related with preparing their lunch. The workers took charge of cooking mutton curry. The maidens offered to oversee the rest. Both the parties got engrossed in preparing meals for their picnic.

For quite a long time, Melamchi had been keeping her vigil on Omu. Turning the table on her, she said, "Omu, get your carriage ready. I want to visit a place and come back soon."

Omu walked a few yards away, anchored the mules on the carriage and started tightening the noose. Reaching there, Melamchi said, "Every face is lit with gladness, but you seem to have lost your smile. What's wrong with you? Aren't you interested in staying in this group and working? If that is the case, I will make an alternative arrangement for you. But you should have interest in it."

Omu listened meekly.

"Everyone plays and rejoices with a favorite friend. But you seem reluctant to utter even a word," Melamchi added.

---

[42] A reference to the *Ramayana*, where Ram and Sita were guarded by Ram's brother Laxman when they were moving through the thick forest during their fourteen-year long exile in the forest

"Everyone is busy in his or her work. Who has time to listen to anyone?" Omu broke her silence.

"Mauni is there. He writes only occasionally. Else, he stays free. You can always talk with him."

Seemingly startled, Melamchi added, "Wait for a while. I beg your pardon. He is speechless."

Melamchi slipped into serious thinking. She said, "To me, that man seems quite noble. I am quite fond of him."

Thinking deeply for a while, she said, "Besides the Gorkhali language, you can also use sign language. You have been posted here to communicate with him and to teach him the sign language. Did you forget that?"

"No," she said, moving her head, suggesting that she had not forgotten her duty.

"If so, put more efforts. This training has been considered necessary for him to attain our goal. Did you get me?"

"I did." She moved her head, signally affirmation.

The picnic spot had been chosen to fulfill multiple goals. The kitchen had been built, considering that too much of sun or rain would do it no harm. One could feel ample degree of scientific consideration in building the kitchen and arranging water and cleaning spot. If the weather condition turned hostile, the small but beautiful cottages could work as the main spots for cooking. In the park, only three other picnic troupes could be seen, putting up at respectable distances.

There was ample area of meadow for the horses and mules to graze in, and many make-shift stables for them to take water and fodder from, and rest. For the entertainment and romance of the picnickers, there were enough bowers, dotted by benches places here and there and low-height swings. During the gay occasion of the picnic, young pairs sneaked into such bowers, making good use of their personal inclinations and rights, exchanging love among themselves. Some pairs, careful enough to prevent their talks from being audible to others, and to let no one else's words fall into their ears, chose spots near the gurgling books, and engaged in conversation in the fashion of the prince and princess in fairy tales. Some other pairs sat near the flower, inhaling their tantalizing fragrance and thus filling their souls with joy. There also were some that sat visibility on benches and had a pleasant pastime. Some of them sat on carpets strewn on green lawns and thus vowed to strengthen the ties of their love, fondly exchanging their amorous inclinations. During such free and pleasurable moments in a picnic, it was considered unusual if no group got lost or strayed, and if that happened, they almost considered it against nature. But the Nepalese young men were not aware of such a practice in the picnic. So, their grown-up companions imparted them trainings of many kinds for the first time, and helped them in many ways. They they all looked at one another with feelings of gratitude, and drowned in a frenzy of thrill.

There are exceptions in every place. Out here, Mauni and Omu proved to be exceptional. In the joyous and free environment of the picnic, these two appeared lonely, though they were together. Omu had been waiting for Mauni. Though Mauni was aware of this fact, he feigned ignorance. He thought that his masculine and cultural awareness made him rather hesitant, but Omu wanted to present herself in natural and easy way. Fishing a *binayo* from her bag and handing it over to Mauni, she said, "Come on; play it. I am quite fond of its tune. I want to listen it to my fill today. I shall listen without hiding anywhere."

'She is waiting for me.'

A flash of thought rippled in Mauni's mind. This made him a little grave. He played his *binayo*. Enchanted, Omu was more and more charmed by its tune. The pairs cuddling in different bowers in the woods sent forth the melody of their hearts, together with the tune of Mauni's *binayo*. The air, light, sky and vegetation there fulfilled their roles and support and witness to it. This made Mauni even more engrossed in his *binayo*. Omu was completely enraptured by its thrill.

Soon they got busy in eating the dishes of their choices and picks. After having a taste of meat, the maidens praised the hands and skills of the cook. The young men also praised Chinese taste and looks. Mauni and Omu expressed gratefulness to others.

They now joined carpets, and sat in a circle to play cards.

After Melamchi picked Panchashar and left, Omu followed suit with Mauni, taking him to the pool of warm water for a swim. Others got glued to cards.

After the picnic, the carriages started returning at different times on their own accords. A notable thing was that no member of these groups gossiped or commented about others. They had no bearing with any of such unhealthy and indecent practice. It was an ideal on their part to bear mutual goodwill, positive thinking, and if needed, helpfulness for one another. That is perhaps the reason why personal interest and freedom were placed first. Discrimination on the grounds of caste, gender, class or race, and the feelings of insiders and outsiders did not exist. Each of the artisans manifested his skills, making the life-style there quite pleasurable and joyful with a tinge of flexibility and practicality in the decorum to befit the atmosphere, actions and objectives therein. By joining the fragments of memories of the different role plays they exhibited in the picnic, they enriched their lives, making it more livable and dynamic.

***

CHAPTER FIVE

AT THE HEART of the city of Beijing, a house modeled on Pagoda style stood up before long, though it was yet to get the finishing touch. It stood in its skeletal form, quite ghastly in look. Therefore, it was not that pleasant to the eyes yet.

The building presently seemed imprisoned inside the scaffolding of the poles and rafters erected here and held in place by wires binding them together. From another vantage, it appeared like a building lifted from somewhere else and placed hereon, because the poles and rafters had peeled the outside lining of the building through fiction, giving it a ghastly and skeletal look. It could be estimated that the building would take some more time to appear complete. Caught inside a scaffolding of poles and rafters, the building appeared complicated, still unable to manifest its real form and structure in a befitting language and expression.

There was no dearth of resources and materials for the construction. The time of two years, including the breaks of a week, a fortnight or even a month in intervals to allow the concrete to settle and harden, was in fact a long time. Though the crude and concrete task was over, the finer work of finishing was yet to be taken up. So, one more year was required to take care of the scrap works of finishing, artistic finery, coloring and painting, and cleaning it up.

The finishing work took pace, divided into different structures and natures. Stairs of three to four steps were laid so that one could reach the main entrance easily. The task of laying the base footing around the building was done at war footing. Around the yard of the building, the task of erecting a wall a little higher than a foot was taken up with priority. A team of workers got fully absorbed in the task of building a toilet and a bathroom at one corner and a kitchen, a store and a closet for the guard at another.

Soon, arrangements for the drainage of roof-water were completed. Before long, the task of fencing the building by an outside wall was over too.

The fine works of the main building also were completed simultaneously. The task of filling the fissures between the joints of stones and bricks with sand-cement mortar, and leveling the wall, including the use of file to smoothen and trim the rough blisters did not take a fairly long time.

They took a long time to fill the ceiling, let it dry, and tamp the cracks twice or thrice with mortar, because they had to wait for one round of plaster to dry, before repeating the same. This way, they could hardly surmise how soon their time elapsed. When they waited for one side to dry up, they continued to work on the other side. For this reason, they finished up the entire construction, the outside wall and the footing simultaneously.

"Mauni, we will return early today. We will come back here. Tell them to prepare dinner early," said Panchashar in a tone of suggestion.

"Should they reach there only to pick us?" his slate read.

"They would come to pick. Else, how can we return?"

"Why return early: for rest or for work?"

"Yes, something like that. Both."

With the slate clasped underneath his armpit, Mauni moved toward Omu's room. Seeing Mauni approach her, Omu drew the curtain on her door halfway, and stood on the door to receive Mauni. Mauni wrote something on his slate. Before he had managed to show it to Omu, she snatched it off his hands and hid it behind her back. Then she said, "Come on. Sit with me for a couple of moments. Be patient. I shall listen to all that you have got to say, shouldn't I? Come."

She held Mauni by hand and led in with honor and said, "I was missing you, and lo, you are here. Lord Buddha has granted my dreams."

Mauni smiled. Flowers bloomed inside Omu's closet. Omu was moved to delight seeing Mauni's smile. Placing some snacks for

Mauni in a plate, she said, "I have prepared this for you. Take it." Her words were laden with feelings of modesty and honor.

He received it. He also drank some water.

Omu read the slate. Then she said, "So you are returning early today. Do come here; I shall be waiting for you. Let's pass our time here. Or, we might as well take a carriage and go somewhere outside."

Mauni smiled again, like an opening flower. His memory started recalling the glimpses of his friends, whose girl friends lovingly gave them things to eat similarly in such little tumblers. He went out of Omu's room, feeling more energized and virile.

A meeting took place in the dining hall, though it did not last too long. They briefly discussed the construction work, especially its progress, planning and cleaning. Of the works to be accomplished now, they had wooden stairs to place between all the floors, apply metal plating on the doors and place two lion statues on two sides of the entrance. Similarly, they adopted a resolution on the skill and utmost care they needed in painting the frames and panes on the doors and windows and the wooden poles on the veranda. The meeting ended, concluding that the construction work would come to a finale after the ultimate cleaning was done.

Before the meeting dispersed, Panchashar announced a break for a week. Yet another proposal was placed forth: they should go for a three-day outing with picnicking.

***

Mauni showed his slate. On it, there was a proposal to organize the picnic tour at the pass at Lhasa, where we had stopped before leaving the city. Calculation of time showed that they would take one day each to go and return, and one day could be spared for picnicking. Roughly, they calculated two days for tour and one day for picnicking, and approved of this proposal unanimously.

Melamchi entered the hall, clapping in support of this proposal.

Soon the preparations for the tour and picnic got underway.

Taking up the issue, Melamchi said, "It seems the picnic this time will be of a different taste. But I am not joining you."

"You all will be with your partners. Why should I go, merely to disturb your happiness?" She presented a taste of humor and satire.

"Melamchi should not miss any of such programs we organize." This was what Mauni's slate read. He showed the slate and turned toward Panchashar.

"True. We cannot spare Melamchi," said Panchashar. He added, "This is a joint organization of we all. It's our joint program. One should attend it necessarily. This cannot be optional. So we request everyone to join us, enjoy with us, exchange intimacy and share love with us. In this case, no one can opt out. One cannot do so, either. This is my humble request."

Mauni showed his slate: "We now need Melamchi's consent. We all are waiting." He blushed like an opening bud. The atmosphere turned harmonious now.

"I must go to boost up someone and lend my help. I am joining." Melamchi broke her silence and gave consent.

"Ha!" said everyone, expressing their joy with applause. In the group, the maidens appeared happier than the guys. But Panchashar could smell some secrecy in Melamchi's decision. He got no time to think about himself, though the maidens took no time to decipher that Melamchi was making the time favorable for them. They understood that Melamchi was willing to go merely in honor of the interest and honor of Panchashar, the group leader.

Eleven carriages, each drawn by two mules, and three spare carriages for emergency, were made ready. Their journey commenced toward the afternoon, and it continued till it was fairly dark.

Their minds were anxious. They could not express who loved to sit with whom, and where.

Melamchi ran her eyes among the maidens and said in Tibetan, "Pick up your friends and sit together."

They did as told. The working men sat in the carriage with the maiden of their choices, appreciating their inclinations. The carriages moved, also carrying their stuff.

"Let's move too," said Melamchi.

There were two mule carriages now, and four people. Who could share the carriage with whom? If Panchashar and Mauni got into one, Melamchi and Omu would be obliged to occupy the other. Such tours become pleasurable, if the accompanying friends are jolly. This is a fact established by experience.

Panchashar found it uneasy to open up with others, not because of any sort of inhibition, but because of his allegiance to a conservative culture. If he opens up, he strips himself naked, and Mauni knew it very well.

So, Mauni made a request in signals, "Melamchi, you get into this mule carriage. Panchu, you also get into the same."

Soon Melamchi and Panchashar were on the move.

Mauni turned toward Omu and smiled. Then he signaled, "Should we return to our rooms and stay there? Or, we should embark on the carriage and follow others?"

This time, Omu blushed with shyness. Her eyes dropped and the head stooped. Mauni pressed closer and alerted her snapping his fingers. Omu came closer, seemingly glued to Mauni's breasts.

Mauni raised Omu's chin with his fingers and signaled jokingly, "Should we mount the mule carriage or return to our room?"

"Our friends are far ahead," said Omu, signaling that their destination was quite far, and added, "We should hurry up."

Their first stop that day was at the home of a merchant from Tibetan side. The maidens were delighted, getting a chance to speak their native language. In view of the Nepalese guys too, the Tibetans were their immediate neighbors on the north and more trustable merchants. Like a woman who dictated everything to her husband at her parental home, these maidens lent the guys thrilling hospitality accordingly to their interest and vigor, and thus gave their loving friends an intimate atmosphere.

The Tibetan merchants welcomed this team with utmost magnanimity. They lent special hospitality to the Nepalese artisans, considering them their daughters' friends, acquaintances from their neighboring countries and guests of their king Timur Khan. Accordingly, they allocated them a free place to roam around. On knowing that it was the team of construction workers engaged in the construction of a royal building, they came to honor them even more. As a result, they got such an environment wherein there was no room or time for fear, shame or hesitation. Instead, the night turned out to be very short. It seemed very obvious that by experience, their stay that night would be extremely memorable.

The next morning, while having breakfast prepared by the Lama woman, the Nepalese guys were flabbergasted to see the maidens in their true beauty and form, having chains and sparkling coins places upon the parting of their hair plaited into two beautiful locks. They took them for angels or young dancers from heaven, or princesses from a distant kingdom. They appeared more joyful and active than on other days, and their verbal and physical actions posed them as maidens different from the ones seen by the Nepalese guys until the previous day. They looked to be highly honored young maidens no doubt. On top of that, they looked like distinguished beauties, embellished by stunning personalities. This made them subjects of more and more curiosity and mystery. The working young men thought such mesmerizing beauties had volunteered to become their attendants at the construction site that was like an open jail, merely for the comfort of the workers; they had positioned themselves to address their interests and inclinations, for their health and mental satisfaction.

Melamchi was in ordinary dress. Taking part in the breakfast, she keenly observed each one present there. On finding Omu missing she asked, "Where is Omu? Isn't she out of her bed yet?"

Her looks were laden not only with questions but also with haste. She asked, "Where is her room?"

HARI RAJ BHATTARAI

All the eyes there were centered on Mauni now. Mauni signaled that it was upstairs and sent that signal that he would go and check. He then stood abruptly from his place and went out.

Everyone was waiting for breakfast. Mauni returned alone and took his place, signaling that Omu was on her way.

Omu arrived after a long time. Melamchi gazed at her from top to toes.

"I had headache. I could not sleep well last night. I happened to doze off at dawn. I am late in waking up," she said in clarification, even before anyone had asked her.

At breakfast, Melamchi kept her vigil over Omu and Mauni from time to time. She drew a conclusion on her own: All others were joyful, like swallows and sparrows. But Omu looked quite serious. She thought, 'Is it because of fatigue after a hard work, or a reaction for some fulfillment? Purge of feelings is necessary for cleanliness of thoughts and for dynamism. Omu seems suffocated. Maybe she has not been able to catch up the aura. So she seems listless."

'Omu's eyes reflect jealousy, rage and dissatisfaction,' said Melamchi in conclusion, but did not announce it to others. She went on analyzing: 'Could this strong derision be directed against her other girl friends? Or, against this accommodation? Against this trip? Or against Mauni?" Further, she said to herself, "Perhaps she got no opportunity to do something she wanted, and that has made her regretful. Perhaps, her zeal has subsided now. Others are happy; perhaps they all got the opportunity, did something and are lax, like after they have purged their repressions. They seem clean. It's true that we must understand others' mental state. These are issues that cannot be learned through teaching. God knows what is wrong with Omu. It's possible that she will fall ill any moment now.' Melamchi was thus a little distressed.

The picnic this time turned out to be quite joyful. It has two reasons. First, the picnickers didn't have to cook anything. A different arrangement had been made for food at the direct involvement and direction from Melamchi. But no one knew of this fact.

Secondly, they had had enough singing and dancing in the picnic, and at its background, the impact of drinks had worked. The picnickers had no information about the same, either. It has made each of the young participants jolly, open and intimate.

There was yet a third thing. Each pair was today focused on keeping each other happy physically and mentally, present themselves with respect to each other, and respect each other's feelings.

There also was a fourth thing. Their night stay was fashioned after a club. The event turned out to be exhilarating. The maidens surprised everyone else with their group dance performed in Tibetan cultural dresses. The men played *madal*, flute and tambourine, and danced with anklets on their feet, even as they sang folk songs to the beat of the instruments.

As long as there was fuel in Chinese *donglong* resembled a sky-lamp, they continued their dance. With time, the adult pairs started getting lost from the gallery, one after another in a secret way, even as the light of the lamp turned dim and faint, like that of a lamp before Samadhi.

Mauni played his *binayo*, breaking the silence of the night. It not only pierced the night, but also ripped the hearts. Those who overheard it conjured some soothing sleep in the tune. That moment, no one cared to see where and how anyone was resting for the night.

For a while, Omu also forgot herself, being carried away by the tune of the *binayo*. She could hardly surmise how much time had elapsed, but the tune had now overflowed into her room, and was ripping her heart. Omu lit up the lamp, walked out and stood close to Mauni. She then placed her palm on his shoulder and signaled her presence. She placed the lamp in the table in front and stood facing Mauni.

Mauni stopped his *binayo* and started staring at Omu. He ran his eyes from top to toes. Omu was dressed in Tibetan outfits.

Before this, Mauni had never seen Omu in that dress, and had never imagined how she would look in such a dress.

The lamp was not that bright, but Mauni took no time to see the tears simmering in Omu's eyes. Omu chose to stay silent. Her presence was telling many things, and was signaling that they needed to do next. The situation was such that neither Mauni had to write anything on his slate, nor had Omu to speak anything. The two studied each other, taking care of the time, situation and need, but could not land on any conclusion.

One had been rendered quite conceited by his sickly masculine awareness while the other one feared that if she made open advancement, it would belittle her position and might be neglected. Mauni could understand that Omu's tears were waiting for someone. He knew, she had been waiting for him, forgoing her sleep. He was aware that Omu had spared her time for him, and for no one else.

Even as the drops of tears were about to roll down the eyes, Omu took a turn, her eyes still simmering. Mauni stood up from his place, walked to the back side of Omu and stood. In the dim light of the lamp, Omu could ascertain that Mauni was not at a long distance from her. So she made an abrupt turn, walked close to Mauni. She folded both her palms, ran them over Mauni's cheeks and signaled, "Shouldn't we sleep now? Come."

Mauni moved his head in a gesture of acceptance and wound up the context, displaying a smile in honor of Omu's sentiments. This time, Omu held him by his shoulders and pulled him in from there.

After this picnic break, the construction work did not pick up the expected pace. But they maintained their balance, because they had adopted better alertness this time. Whenever they had leisure, they talked about Bekha and Gola with priority. They were all apprehensive, and were sad, unable to tell what would come up next.

Bekha and Gola got lost somewhere in the afternoon on the picnic day. They had probably taken their own ways from the picnic spot. Others wasted an entire week, hoping they would return today or tomorrow. But Bekha and Gola did not return. When they were assured that they would not return, the Nepalese workers were deeply saddened. Those at Bekha's family expressed deep sorrow.

"What should we say if anyone asked where our companion had gone? Should we say he eloped with a girl? Or else, the girl took him away? How should we answer if the king asks? Could it be that a wild beast had captured them from a corner of the bower near the picnic spot and devoured? Only Melamchi can tell us if such an incident could take place there."

Such were the issues the workers discussed among themselves.

Thinking that the workers should not be panicked and should stay free of fear while working and should bear no doubt and apprehension, Melamchi said, "The two liked each other, and went away with agreement. That is an ordinary thing. We will take time to find out where they are. On my part, I think Gola and her mate took the path leading toward Tibet. It's also possible that they moved toward Nepal. If they were bound to a distant place, they probably took horses or mules."

Considering it relevant, she said with ease, "These are simple things. They must have moved in agreement, but I sense Gola's initiative more than that of Bekha. Because, Gola is familiar with the geography and culture of this place." Boosting up the workers, she said, "If you anticipate any question or problem from the side of the state, leave that to me. I will take care of that. You don't need to be bothered by that. You concentrate on your missions. You have my best wishes. Do not allow your minds to get disturbed. Do not get panicked at any rate. Leave all worries to me. We should make this incident ordinary, remembering and talking about it from time to time now, and making it commonplace slowly. Every day, two to four of such incidents take place here. For that reason, you don't need to consider it surprising or new."

Announcing her conclusion, Melamchi said, "Let them stay in joy wherever they are, and let them live long. Let Buddha give them his protection. That's all."

HARI RAJ BHATTARAI

Every one present there looked at Panchashar and Mauni anticipating their reactions to Melamchi's words. Panchashar, however, made no remark.

Mauni wrote on his slate, "I second Melamchi's opinion. Let's assign Melamchi to handle the administrative or social problem that rises out of this incident. Let's imagine problems that befall on our countries and look at them from various angles. The problem will get solved on its own."

"How?" asked Panchashar, firing an immediate query.

Mauni wrote again, "We came together, stayed together, and are glued to the same mission. We have almost finished our work. This is a transparent thing. There comes no question of curtailing anyone's personal freedom. That is not possible either."

He looked all around and wrote again, "We all get lost for some time; we have been doing that. We get lost in the marketplace, in the woods, in our hunt for firewood and water, in warm-water pool, and at times in picnic, and in the garden or in our own closets shortly after dinner. We get lost in the way that pleases us, don't we? Bekha is likely to get lost for a longer time; so is Gola. Had they gone missing alone, it would be proper for us to worry much. But then, if they are lost together, they are showing their victory, leaving us defeated."

Driving his words toward a conclusion, he wrote, "I don't think they are dead. Let such news never come. Let them live long. Let's us send our best wishes, and hope, they will return soon, winding up their tour."

They took look breathes. Realizing that the thoughts of everyone present there were taking a different turn, Mauni wrote, "I was the one who desperately wished to get lost, but I didn't know how to do it. I wanted to run away, but no one picked me. They won out. I lagged. They opened up; they didn't choose to live smothered. I send them best wishes from the core of my heart."

"Oh no! They could have stayed together with all of us here. There was no way we would disturb them. No one poses any untoward question to anyone here. Nor does anyone have such a right. Moreover, why were they obliged to leave us and run away, leaving all of us in worry? I would rather say—Bekha betrayed us. What should we say, when we reach back to our villages? How could we show our face therein? It's shameful," said Panchashar, articulating his anguish and complaint at the same time.

Running his eyes on the face of everyone sitting around him, Mauni wrote, "None of us should emulate Bekha and Gola now. One can ask for leave for a few days with due information and go. One can return late, or not ever return. But we should be informed."

Mauni turned his slate toward Melamchi with the same script. Before she had uttered any word, Panchashar said, "It's true that we can frame our own standpoints. That also makes it easy for us to arrange alternative workforce."

Mauni further wrote, "We are done with heavy and difficult works. All that's left now is minor and fine work. So, the lack of one or two worker will not make much difference now."

"True. But the work left in hand now demands extra carefulness. Bekha was a skilled painter, and an assistant of Mauni," said Panchashar, presenting a reality.

In fact, Mauni had the knowledge to decorate woods used in a building by carving different art works on them. He was the one who taught others as to where a particular color was to be used. Bekha always followed his instructions and his hands were blessed with the magic of luster. Now that he was gone, Mauni had to handle the task alone. Therefore, considering the nature of his work, Mauni considered the loss of Bekha as the loss of his own half.

In fact, Mauni was caught between joy and anxiety. In one hand, he was happy that Bekha had embarked on an invisible path of love. He wondered how far he would reach, walking along such an impassable earth! He thought, 'This very place is the destination he would ultimately reach and so, he will certainly come back to this spot. He cannot forget us. He is not an ungrateful man, nor can he ever become one. In absence of Bekha, the artistic dimension of the mansion cannot bloom in its totality, and cannot attain its optimal attractiveness.'

Mauni knew it very well that the lack of his artistic touch would certainly be reflected somewhere. So, he viewed the incident from a vantage of his personal inclination and interest and therefore considered Bekha's absence unfortunate. This made him grave from deep within. Materially, Mauni was caught in a conflict between joy and frustration due to which, we got lost in his own thoughts at times. He grew happy for a while considering Bekha's journey of love, only to return to distress, considering the artistic dimension on the mansion.

***

CHAPTER SIX

MELAMCHI WICKED DOWN the *donglong*[43] burning in her room. 'It will douse on its own,' she thought and reclined on the bed. The noise of a mule neighing fell into Melamchi's ears. She got alert. Her eyes, and not merely ears, longed for many things.

She rushed and wicked up the lamp. 'It had almost died out,' she thought, and gathered happiness. The mule neighed again. She peeped out from the crack in the door.

A *donglong* was approaching her door. She stayed alert. Someone knocked on her door. She opened it. She was chilled by some degree of fear.

The newcomer said, "I am Gola. Bakha also is with me."

She raised the *donglong* to a height so that Melamchi could see her face clearly. Bekha's face was still in the dark. Yet, he didn't appear to be in dilemma.

"Come in."

After they were in, Gola spoke before she had taken a seat, "In the first place, please forgive us." She then got up abruptly and lowered her head in a gesture of apology. Bekha followed suit, facing Melamchi with folded hands.

Seeing that the two were expressing utmost respect for her, Melamchi reciprocated in a befitting way and made them sit beside her. She stroked Gola's cheeks with love. Looking at her with moist eyes, she expressed the feelings on gratitude on their safe return. Bekha, on his part, felt immense love and compassion Melamchi was expressing for him. That moment, a mother's dutifulness and a master's magnanimity were being expressed simultaneously.

"Is there any food left? We are awfully hungry. We also ran out of the mules' food and fodder; we have fed them nothing. I am

---

43   A Chinese lantern

extremely tired. After eating, I want to take a dive into warm water before going to bed," said Gola. She seemed to be in a hurry.

"That's fine. Make it quick. Set something aside for the mules and take your meal. You can go for the dive thereafter. On my part, I want to sleep. You sleep according to your convenience. Come and see your bed first. I think a single bed will do for both of you now, won't it?" said Melamchi, giving expression to a reality. Gola expressed a partial 'yes', partly shy, and partly mindful of Melamchi's honor.

A view of a pair of ducks swimming didn't feel their eyes, nor did it satiate their minds. This pair, planned by the Creator, did not become a sore to any eye. This came to be a mysterious incident.

A strange curiosity besieged Melamchi's heart. She could not keep it tamed within. Seizing a chance, she pressed close to Gola and said, "I am interested to know a few things. Tell if you can quench my curiosity."

"What's it? I will tell if I know anything about it."

"How did you find a man's company?"

"Fie! What a question you are asking! This is a thing one should experience and feel. Others' experiences will rather pain you. So, it is better not to hear about such a thing."

"I agree. But I am impatient to know it. So I am asking. Tell me, how did you find a man's company?"

Gola was trapped in dilemma, unable to decide where she should start and what things she should include.

"Tell me, how did you find a man: fearful, loathsome, complicated, jolly, lovable, interesting...? Tell," she added.

Gola said with openness, "Initially, a feeling started tickling me all through with fluidity and lucidness. I was then struck by currents that seemed sweet but painful. I could not control myself alone, no matter how much I wanted to. At such a moment, the man proved to me the sorcerer, faith-healer, doctor, or whatever you might call him. He came closer. The desire to touch him besieged my entire self. That was perhaps the only treatment for the body and mind."

"And then?" asked Melamchi and kept staring at her.

"I found a man extremely interesting."

"Tell more."

"If I have to tell in a nutshell, I would say women can do nothing for men, but they can grip a man and use him for their convenience, happiness and contentment. For that, a man is not in advantage from any angle; he is always at the losing end. But a woman is always on the winning side."

"How can you claim that with confidence?"

"It's plain. The element of masculinity is merely a means. All his actions are for the elements of femininity. But he has no advantage in this. He holds the illusion of making an attainment, but in turn, it is the woman's interest that is fulfilled. But the masculine element is unable to see this reality."

"How is that possible? Aren't the male and female elements equal?"

"No, they are not. The masculine element can be on the rise, even if the feminine element is missing. But if the masculine element is missing, the feminine element is disturbed and gets strayed; it cannot have a healthy development of its existence. It can be on the rise."

"What do you mean by that?"

"What we need to think about is that the masculine element is inevitable for the feminine element, but the feminine element is dispensable for its male counterpart. It's merely optional."

After a slight pause, she resumed, "Look! We should have the skill to use and hone the male folks. If that happens, we can put them to ample use according to our desire and needs. For that reason, we should safeguard them strongly in a reliable manner. The reserved energy can be of a great use at the time of need."

"Then?"

"Then, my conclusion is, the libidinal strength of the males is the cause of a female's healthy life and entire development. For that reason, proximity with the males becomes useful for the purgation of physical and psychological pollution. This is what I feel."

"If your realization after cohabitation with a man is interesting, pleasing and result-oriented, so share."

"Oh yes, it is."

She told in brief, "Everything appears quite interesting. Only positive vibes emanate. A new light get added up on life. The world appears more loving and lucid. There is an ample enhancement in interest, appetite and sleep. The mind becomes stable. When we walk, the body seems to be extremely light as though we were walking on the sky and not on the earth. Joy mounts on an individual, and she gets filled with satisfaction and self-confidence. Are you listening? I have the experience that all these positive impacts are results of one's cohabitation with a male."

"How is your man in your opinion?"

"He is tireless, placid, obedient and healthy. This is all I know and need. Everyone else knows he has skills. What more should I say?"

"Did you also learn any art from him?"

"Are you talking about the art of sex?"

"Something like that."

"He first drew pictures about postures; I had to pose accordingly. That was interesting but tiresome. The methods, dose and sequence happened to be crucial. The body becomes agile and fit like that of a mare."

She added yet another episode, "Look! My body has become slimmer, hasn't it? All the toxins have flown out, and I have become healthy."

"It's true that after cohabitation with the men folk, a woman's body exhibits seductive changes. The beauty also multiplies."

Seeing the glow and satisfaction on Gola's countenance, Melamchi added, "How nicely you bloom up! What a halo has mounted on your entire personality! Our Gola has in fact become healthy and lively now."

"Gola, they say, the men there put the women below. What did you experience?"

"When we are below, many things become easy. The one on the top has to be more responsible. He has to bear the role of an umbrella. The joy of lying underneath is untellable. One doesn't have to do anything; giving company from time to time suffices. On my part, I feel lying underneath makes it easier for us to reap the pleasure of life. One on the top has to labor harder, until he sweats. Such things should be understood emotionally, not materially. Who can surmise the height of those who lie underneath?"

"Oh, how many things our Gola knows! How articulate she is!" said Melamchi and asked, "Does a man always become yours? Doesn't he get dispersed? What is your opinion?"

"I have a clear opinion on that. A man belongs to the one who knows how to drive him, and possess the capacity to do so. To make him yours, you must have the skill to dance, to play and to open up in the front-yard of a season, an age and an environment."

In the meantime, some birds chirped. The cocks started crowing in duet. Life started perking at the brink of the daybreak, as darkness started darting away.

Rosiness started spilling over the eastern horizon. Melamchi's sleepiness subsided gradually.

The neighing of a horse fell sharply into her ears. She alerted her listening capacity. The horses continued their neighing. She told herself, 'Maybe a new horse has walked in from somewhere. The horses seem to be fighting. How could I separate them?'

Melamchi alighted from the world of dreams and bumped into reality. She opened the main door of the house. Bright sunlight entered. She came out of the house. Two adult bodies could be seen standing on one side of the yard. She watched with care; one was a young woman and another young man of similar age. It was not easy to tell the sex of these two people, clad in Tibetan outfits. So she had to watch with keenness.

Before she had uttered anything, one of them walked closer and said, "Our mare ran in here, looking for a horse. We let loose your horse; we could not help that. This is where we made a mistake. We

HARI RAJ BHATTARAI

had been waiting outside for a long time just to communicate this fact. We waited for your door to open…"

Melamchi listened to their report with care and stared at both with a feeling of interrogation.

"It's enough now. We would like to tie and pull your horse back to the stable, but it doesn't recognize us. Maybe it would allow us to tie it back. What can we do?"

"Do not worry about that. I will do it myself."

She then scanned the faces of both with a sense of gratitude and thought, 'This young man and woman are very simple.'

The pair of youngsters left, showing their gratefulness toward Melamchi.

'How difficult it is for me to tell where the dream ended and reality started,' thought Melamchi. She further thought, 'The pair of Tibetan youngsters that just left, and the episode of the horses' mating is no less interesting than my dream.'

'But I can never forget the things Gola told me in my dream. I should be able to mix her experiences and mine, and reap the pleasure of life. I had people say they wish certain dreams to continue forever, stay intact, pop up again and again in episodes, segments and fragments. If a beautiful dream gets snapped in the middle, they say, it leads to dissatisfaction. As I see it now, that's true.'

Laying stress on the subject, she said, 'That dream, and the dream following the dream are of equal significance for me. Was the reality after the dream less interesting and thrilling than the dream?'

Melamchi smiled to herself alongside her soliloquy, and reclined back on the bed, rather ashamed. Remembering her conversation with Gola in the dream, she started concentrating on the same. For her, that became a subject with which she could color herself. She started rejoicing the same, even as she coiled in her bed.

She suddenly got up with vigor, and talked to herself in an unclear accent, 'If Gola comes back, I will ask her every single thing. If I do, she won't conceal anything from me. Let her come back soon, at least for my sake.'

She was mum now.

Panchashar, on his part, made a calculation and inferred: the workers were not as enthused as they used to be before. He analyzed Mauni's case rather deeply and said, 'Mauni also doesn't seem that energetic and stable. He seemingly wishes the time to linger and Bekha to return as early as possible.

Mauni, however, was clear in this issue. More than Bekha, he was in need of his skill and artistry. In Mauni's view, these things were crucial for the overall completeness and virtuous beauty of the royal pagoda to be completed by the Nepalese artisans.

Breaking Panchashar's silence, Mauni stole a chance and wrote, "Let the task of painting be left for now. I am somehow convinced that Bekha would turn up any moment soon. I have premonitions of his presence. Maybe he is also calculating the time for painting."

"So you have that much trust in him," said Panchashar.

"There's no question why he shouldn't come back. You just watch; the same girl…what's her name? Yes, Gola…Gola will herself bring him back," Mauni's slate read again.

Astounded, Panchashar chose to stay silent.

"There is no reason to be astounded here. He will certainly return and handle the task of painting the building. This is what my conscience says."

Having shown this, Mauni rubbed off his slate. Then he said to himself, 'Bekha will not leave me alone, and never force me to labor alone in our work. I can read his innermost heart.'

Mauni stared somewhere in the distance with moist eyes.

"What should we do now? How long should we wait for him. Moreover, there is no guarantee of his return."

"No. We don't need to wait. He will show up even as we are working."

"I didn't get you," said Panchashar curiously.

"Except for painting, we shall complete all other works. By then we will be here."

HARI RAJ BHATTARAI

"If he doesn't come?"

"I shall handle it alone. What more should I say?" wrote Mauni on his slate.

Panchashar once ran his eyes among other fellow workers. He looked blank, unable to decide what he should say.

"We shall start the remaining work on Monday, day-after-tomorrow and finish up everything," Mauni wrote.

In fact, all the workers had become impatient to finish the task now. Their minds were besieged by the desire to see the completion of the task as soon as possible so that they could return home. The result was that the work progressed in a speed and readiness never seen before. The kitchen and the store also were made ready before long. The construction of the bathroom and other parts attached to it were also accomplished without any ado.

Metal paint was applied to the frames of the main door. This enhances its attractiveness. On the left and right sides of the doors, two lion statues were placed, and a concrete road was paved from the main entrance of the building to the entrance at the outside wall of the premises. The road was big enough for horses and carriages to move on two lanes.

The task of constructing a garden in the space between the inside and outside walls of the building was now undertaken at war footing. They gave continuity to the task of planting trees and flowers of different species and colors and making a nursery of flowers with different kinds of fragrance.

"Friends, do not forget to give some geometric touch to the garden. We all must stay committed to that," Mauni wrote. He ran his eyes far and wide for a while and wrote again, "Who could be coming in that carriage that sends for such a cloud of dust? Could it be Bekha?"

All the workers turned their eyes in that direction. On seeing Gola and Bekha simultaneously, they were left gawking, besieged by curiosity. The countenance of Panchashar showed the glory of the sun.

Melamchi got down from her horse.

In the dinner that evening, they sat in the same order as they used to do before. The spaces that had remained vacant for quite a long time got filled. A sweet zeal and satisfaction could be seen rippling among friends. Everyone of them felt a surge of joy.

At the mealtime, Melamchi spoke from the high-raised pedestal, "I want to take Gola with me tonight. She will come back tomorrow."

Having completed her sentence, she once stared on the faces of Panchashar and Mauni.

Panchashar could not utter any word. But Mauni showed his slate that read, "Bekha himself or Gola should speak on that. All we can do is clap, isn't it?"

Mauni raised his eyebrows. Gola was pricked deep inside her heart. Bekha's heart was crushed by a heavy burden.

***

Soon the season of flowers rushed in, and the rains went away. The clouds appeared brighter now; the sky started appearing neat and blotless. At one end of the sky, the sun at times appeared preparing for rest following a tiresome toil, while at another, the moon could be seen launching its journey across the blues just now.

It was the playtime of the aerials, the season of flowers, the time for the exhilaration of the terrestrial, and the green season of youthfulness. In the living world, it was the season when the females enchanted the males to follow the former. The living world appeared elated all over the sky and the earth at this time of joy, just before the advent of the fall. Excitement and joy could be felt spilled everywhere.

The Nepali artisans, at times, felt forlorn on being away from their homes and families for such a long time. At times, they deeply missed festive times from the New Year to the Shivaratri Festival. Granted that it was now the season of flowers, of fruits, of rice lush in bunches, but all they could do was get lost in reminiscence and regret in this foreign land. But the melody of the tune 'tumutumu chhyan' they had heard over these years started reverberating in their ears. They had been deeply touched by the monotone music of several flutes that played the classical tunes and folk, cultural melodies, and the music emanating from several instruments they played in their valley. How could such a thing stay away from them? But then, the memory attached to incoming season moved them much more than the years gone by. The panacea to their forlorn mind was either the memory of the bygone days or the autumnal beauty of the adult maidens therein.

We have no idea how such artisans are viewed or treated in other countries. But the Nepalese artisans invited into the great land of China always received high honor and great hospitality. During cultural days of the national scale and historical occasions, and during social and entertainment games at the local social levels, Melamchi herself came and took the Nepalese artisans, and made arrangements for them to take part and entertain themselves. In Melamchi's treatment, they could never sense any feeling of discrimination on account of their being foreigners, aliens, workers, poor or pathetic. She always bore high feelings of honor and cooperation for these artisans.

She dealt every difficult and impractical problem with ease and in a practical manner. She negotiated every conversation with the state of the palace with her own proactive initiation, and worked as patron, director, friend and guide for the artisans and the maidens. Though she was still in a minor age, she had become mature in actions. So she did not let any inconvenience befall any of them. As soon as there was any prblem, she would volunteer with ease and with special readiness to sort things out. Therefore, on the question who and what Melamchi was, she was like a scripture that was mysterious, incomprehensible and inaccessible. She never posed as a special being, but she lived in her own world with many mysteries surrounding her. That is, however, a different chapter.

People who watch from a long distance perhaps think Melamchi was a youthful and active girl, skilled at work and quite nimble. She was laced with capability, was aware of her obligations and was faithful to the palace. She also was beautiful, attractive, fragrant and captivating. She had a dashing personality indeed. In the world led by men, she was recognized as an able and courageous lady, but she was there, among the workers, with an aim and firm commitment to giving the royal interest a national height, and the construction had become a good pretext for her to anchor herself to the royal interest. By some means, she had kept herself occupied and restrained. Materially, she had no attachment with the royal obligations and the construction work. They were mere bases that gave her an atmosphere. She was nowhere in them, yet she was everywhere.

In order to address others' curiosity about Melamchi, Mauni once wrote, "Though Melamchi prioritizes personal comfort and individual freedom, she is a maiden that loves to live a high order but simple life in the society."

"Mauni, does it mean a single sentence can exhaustively capsulate Melamchi's entire life?" someone abruptly asked.

"That's the crux. The rest of the things can be incorporated in its explanation. I don't think further interpretation is necessary. If there is a need, can't I do it some other day?" he wrote.

It's human nature to get attracted to one's own creation. Soon the building was ready. But Panchashar was not still ready to assert that everything was over now.

The team of artisans coming from Nepal declared that its task was over now. All the maidens praised the grandeur and divinity of the mansion. The local Chinese artisans also felt that nothing was now left to be done on the building.

But Panchashar initiated a new episode. The pagoda was, for him, something like a shrine. He visited it every morning, made a note of things it was short of, and worked for its improvement, perfection and exquisiteness. The troupe of artisans followed his suggestions and instructions. Such a task, however, was extremely minute, and people with ordinary outlook or non-artistic background would seldom notice.

Panchashar, in reality reached to the mansion to make several circles around it. Even in a state of half-sleepiness, he started haunting the mansion.

As soon he entered the structure today, he heard a woman's voice echoing. Alert, he followed the sound. He concentrated all his senses to catch the voice. Soon, he could make out these sentences falling into his ears: "Pan, I can fight any war for your sake, but I need your support in it. Your interest should be connected to it." He could sense that it was Melamchi's voice.

He further listened to her with a pure heart. The voice said, "Pan, love dotted by trepidation shall never be acceptable to me. So I want to stay out of his boundary. Do please help me. Deliver me out of this suffocating situation."

Panchashar moved further ahead, moving his feet slowly. His ears caught Melamchi's voice again: "I can no longer stay alive, keeping Pan away from me. But how should I express to him the love I bear in my heart?"

In this delivery fashioned after a verbal echo, there was no streamlined coherence of content. The voice reverberated again. Panchashar held this breath for a while not to miss the words. It said, "He can now communicate very well in our language. Or, should I write in his language and show him the message of my heart? For want to a reliable medium, what if my love for him spills in the middle, before reaching up to him?"

Following the source of the sound, Panchashar moved one floor up.

"Pan, I want to live inside you. Give me a place in your heart. Do not mention word of non-acceptance or inability. That shall be intolerably painful for me. It suffices for me if you merely understand my feelings. There is nothing more I expect."

He heard a clear voice.

"I shall never pose an impediment on your interest and goal. Instead, I shall assist you, help you, and wish you all success." Melamchi added in yet another line.

Panchashar got up from his dream. 'Fie on me! How come I happened to dream in siesta? This means, she has crept deep into my heart unconsciously' he said to himself.

Mauni was beside him. On hearing his utterances, he wrote on his slate, "How big is your heart? Two have already made their entry on our way. I am at least aware of that. Weren't there a few in the village too? Yet another one is likely to besiege your heart here." He further added, "What a piece of man you are! Even without speaking a word, you win deep love. And a wide one."

He showed it to Panchashar and wiped out the slate.

In his view, the building was complete. But Panchashar took far longer a time to complete it as he wished. Yet, that day still seemed quite far when he would satisfy himself. The building continued to involve more of their time. Panchashar often visited Melamchi and said there still were rooms for improvement. This impatience and concentration apparent in Panchashar soon became a cause of headache for Mauni. For two days, he did not even come out of the guest house.

One day, stealing the right chance, Mauni showed his slate to Panchashar. Panchashar read, "The building is complete. Shouldn't we move homeward now?"

Mauni wrote yet another sentence, "Five years have passed since we left our homes. Our friends have become impatient. Tell me your plans now."

Panchashar appeared alert, seemingly retuning to senses. Instantly, he remembered his world, and scaled it with his mind. Again, he read the feelings on Mauni's eyes. Then he said to himself, 'How can I abandon the friends that came together? After showing the mansion to the king, maybe we will have to return.'

But Mauni failed to extract any answer from Panchashar.

***

CHAPTER SEVEN

STANDING AT THE centre of the pagoda, Panchashar today ran his eyes on every part of Melamchi's body. Melamchi didn't consider his gaze awkward, either. Considering that the time and context was opportune, Panchashar said, "Melamchi, if my wish would be granted, I would build and place a stone statue of yours inside this mansion, at this sport, at this particular part of it. Only then you would know how beautiful you appear from my eyes. More, you would yourself be enraptured by seeing your own beauty."

She chose silence after staring at him with a sense of enquiry and interrogation.

"If your statue is built and placed at this spot here, the beauty and glory of this mansion would multiply by four times."

Melamchi pulled her locks forward and caressed them gently.

"The same tress shall find a place in your statue," he said, giving a gentle touch to her tresses.

He ran his fingers over Melamchi's eyebrows and said, "These eyebrows that constantly radiate guiltless and pure feelings would find a place on the statue."

She concealed her eyes, lowering her head ground-ward. She had started blushing, seeing Panchashar's artistic description and intense passion.

"On the statue, I would transplant those very eyes, laden with the image of strength, good-will and commitment."

Melamchi wanted to conceal her eyes altogether, but failed to do so. Before this, she had not heard any comment about her beauty from anyone else. Though rather shy, she continued to listen to Panchashar.

Panchashar gently touched her fleshy neck and shoulder. Following this, he touched the slender and thin wrists of her with his fingers and gave her a hint of excitement. But Melamchi stayed unmoved, displaying an immeasurable degree of patience.

Her fingers were the most attractive parts of Melamchi's physical personality. They were long, slender, soft and round, and the harmony of the nails on them with their shapes made the combination a rare thing. This must be the reason why Panchashar ran his hands over her tender fingers and said, "The beauty that ripples in your body will perhaps never appear again in the human kind."

Melamchi considered that she was caught in an exaggerated rhetorical snare and got impatient, seeing that her awkwardness was not finding an outlet. Panchashar moved two steps back, and gazed at her from top to toes. His looks were potently laced with the awareness of her beauty. Mindful of the limits that did not temper with the honor and dignity of the womenfolk, he once again started at each part of her body with looks of softness and love, and stopped his eyes around the navel area. Though she was aware of this, she feigned ignorance. In fact, her navel had become the climax of a person's physical perfection. It was spherical and grave, and on top of that, the spiral pattern of fine, slender and glistening hairs that ran down to it from the top were seductive enough to arrest an onlooker's gaze, and his masculinity would be overwhelmed and benumbed.

Panchashar moved two steps forward, held Melamchi gently by her waist with his hands and lifted her into the air, and said, "I would make your statue as tall as this."

For a moment, she expressed astonishment, enjoyed another moment and soon found herself wondering at the mystery.

He lowered her a little and planted a hot kiss on Melamchi's round and grave navel. He then pressed her against his chest, and gradually let her stand on the ground. Then he said to himself, 'I respected her beauty.'

The kiss on the navel and her landing on the ground together with a frictional touch against Panchashar's chest drove Melamchi to astonishment, curiosity and pleasure at the same time, and she got lost in it.

He sat in front of Melamchi in *veerasan*[44] posture. He then rubbed his palm against the lower half of Melamchi's body and said, "Melamchi, as for the thighs, ankles and feet, I cannot make them equally fleshy, slender and attractive on the statue." In a more modest voice, he added, "I call the one who make you, and ask him to make your statue, OK?" This time, he tried to add an admixture of humor.

Until some moments ago, Melamchi was bent on reading Panchashar's feelings, but his words, action and touch were so strong that she forgot herself even more that moment. When the long dialogue of Panchashar ended, she started reading herself. She could feel that passionate love had gradually started moving her to excitement. She thought she needed rest or repose, albeit for the immediate time. Therefore, exercise full control over her and making use of her inclination and personal freedom, she said, "I am extremely tired. Can I rest for a while?"

Lending her his support, Panchashar led Melamchi to the pedestal inside a room. Making Panchashar's lap her pillow, Melamchi rested. Panchashar, on his part, played fondly with her long, soft, dark and seductive hair, wishing her a happy repose. Whenever Panchashar's fingers slithered into Melamchi's hair unimpeded, Melamchi experienced unprecedented pleasure, but she could not avail such untellable ecstasy for more than a moment.

Startled, Panchashar rose up from his place and stood straight. Melamchi could hardly surmise its reason. He had woken up in the fashion of a frightened man, abruptly as though something had bitten him. He had stood with panic, apparently quite impatient.

That was, however a thing miles away from the reach of Melamchi's imaginations. But she also rose carefully from her place. She cuffed Panchashar in her arms to help him compose himself and said, "Pan, what's with you, suddenly? Why did you

---

44   Literally meaning the 'hero's posture', it is a posture in the modern yoga

panic? Your panicking has made me frightened. My heartbeat is still so fast."

Instead of showing any verbal or physical reaction, Panchashar kept standing still like a machine. He forgot to exhibit the natural and formal action expected of him at such a moment, or didn't want to do so. The situation there turned quite unusual.

Melamchi deeply pined to get caught inside the robust, firm and loving arms of Panchashar, wanted to see her arms welcomed by that of Panchashar and thus paying back for his favor, and these expectations, she considered, were without options. But then, she didn't allow expression to the acrid experience of being deprived from such inevitable and natural privilege that moment. Her patience, that moment, turned out to be commendable.

After all, why was she drowned in commendation for a hot yet distressed statue standing erect in front of her in loving, amorous action and in symbolic expression of its embracement? What was its primacy in the first place? Such a question rose in her heart. To some extent, she loosened the hold of her arms that embraced Panchashar, and stood face to face with her eyes meeting his, seemingly trying to make an advent into her.

In a while, yet another layer of her heart got peeled off. With her cheeks pressed against the furry bosom of Panchashar she contemplated, 'My Pan appears like a youthful lover who stands between two different environment and cultures of love, and has lost his destination. He might be passionate, but he is not distressed; he can never be so. I cannot stand to see him slip into a path of forlornness and thus become inactive.'

In reality, Panchashar was trying to stay non-aligned. It also was true that he was trying to contain his amorous drives and himself. But how could he express that? How could he explain his efforts to save himself from the touch of hot, energetic and seductive fragrance emanating from a woman's body? He was unable to tell that the incensed breath of Melamchi was driving him mad and that he had abruptly stood up with impatience, unable to keep himself under restrain. Can anyone express the climax of sexual inclination without the partner's interest and consent? How could such an issue be pulled in, there?

Panchashar fixed his eyes on that of Melamchi and observed with looks of love. He could see tears simmering in her eyes. He then remembered a slate of Mauni, where he had written, "Let no tear simmer in anyone's eyes. Else, the same tears will torment you."

He again thought, 'Could it be that I had caused tears in Melamchi's eyes? Did I make any mistake unconsciously?"

The sentences Mauni had written on his slate from time to time on befitting occasions started unfolding in Panchashar's memory one after another. One of them read this way: "Never bear enmity with the womenfolk." He explained this formulaic expression from Mauni in his own way: "True. As soon as there is enmity, all womenfolk, except Mother, become adversaries. In that case, they await for a moment and occasion to bite like and poisonous snake. This is what the experts say."

"Give women love and honor. They remain hungry for the same. After this, they become ready to tender everything they have to you. They will lend their help to you from all quarters."

He remembered yet another slate of Mauni: "Your inactiveness and listlessness can also hurt, ignore or belittle someone unconsciously. The noble men stay alert in this matter, and carefully move their steps."

'People earlier said, embarking in a journey of love entails fear. But then, it is a natural weakness. Maybe this is the nature of pure, simple and complete love.' Melamchi contemplated on her own and thus bore a feeling of warmth toward Panchashar.

'I failed to appreciate the worth of life, love, time and place. But I must present myself to women with honor from all these four quarters' thought Panchashar, moving close to practical reality.

'There's no crime in the field of love. It qualifies to the rank of a crime, if it is executed against someone's will. We are not on such a path of crime. Panchashar must be aware of this fact.' Melamchi consoled herself, expressing her firmness with confidence.

Mauni's slate read, "Morality, conscience and cultural awareness can prove impediments and unhealthy intrusions along the path of love. It becomes imminent to keep them at bay."

Panchashar tried to derive positive energy from this statement.

"If one fails to embark on a balanced journey along the path of love, some lovers often become victims of unhealthy mental conditions including sudden guilt and self-torment. At the moment, we both are not the victims of such a mental state. Nor is the atmosphere around us so inhospitable. Still, some invisible limit of bondage seems to be deterring us. Else, what can be the reason why Panchashar has not been able to conjure the degree of flexibility expected of a passionate lover?' Melamchi tried to trace a way out.

'The highway of love is located at a formidable height. The temporary streams of caste, culture, language and location do not impede it.'

Panchashar recalled Mauni's writing even as he was engrossed in self-contemplation. He erected four pillars of love, belief, sacrifice and honor, and mused of erecting a loving, warm mansion of love on their foundation, in which, Melamchi could be given an honorable space.

'My Pan has not yet been able to transgress his cultural limitations and come out. He is perhaps cursed by the consciousness of some moral or ethical code.'

While she was musing on herself, Melamchi happened to recall a script on Mauni's slate: "He is raw mud. You can give him the shape you want."

She accepted this expression as a talisman to find a way out from the present predicament. Lending liquidity and coolness in her thoughts, she said, "What's wrong with you, Pan? Why have you become so listless? Come down to reality; land on the present."

She said to herself, 'Instead of treasuring someone in the heart and deriving self-amusement, appeasing the mind for a while by embracing someone as soon as the chance permits, erecting an imaginary pleasure dome and embarking on an oblique path toward fulfillment of repressed amorous desires even in dreams, why can't a youth today live in joy, without falling into the trap of remorse?' This time, Melamchi appeared really serious.

Giving his thoughts a slightly philosophical touch, Panchashar contemplated, 'I am not pure anymore mentally, verbally and physically. I might be pure in action, though. That is but a different thing.'

'Unconsciously, I happened to build for myself a retreat inside the pure sacrifice, guiltless behavior and high honor of Melamchi. I should no longer deceive myself now on.' Picking up words from Melamchi, he said, "I have settled down on real grounds."

Letting the crimson sunrays of autumn paint her countenance, Melamchi said, "If that is the case, listen to me. The tendency of self-exaltation through external specialties can never be a garb to one's personality. A person known through a country, time, caste, class, gender, religion and color doesn't take much time to fade and perish, because these are common embellishments for everyone. We must maintain our identity in our own ways, through our own strength."

Panchashar looked with a sense of enquiry, seemingly unable to understand her words.

"We'll stay alive now. Did you get me?"

Melamchi held Panchashar strongly by his shoulders shook him all through and said, "Where are you, Pan?"

From whatever Melamchi had learnt about Panchashar through their cooperation, mutual journey and mutual achievements, there was no room left on her part to be hesitant to say anything to Panchashar. So she conjured strength and said with authority, "Pan, I am here. Where are you?"

Panchashar scanned the feelings in Melamchi's eyes. There, he saw the ripples of new strength, unfathomable love, uninterrupted dedication, unprecedented excitement, and unseen agility. These feelings moved him to emotion, and thus, he turned introvert. He then caught Melamchi by her slender and soft arms with love.

In his touch, Melamchi could feel a masculine touch and commitment. She then concentrated her mind to decipher the feelings in his eyes.

Panchashar received both her cheeks in his palms, seemingly aware of the feelings of her eyes. The scene that moment appeared as though he had received a sunflower in full blooms in his palm.

Melamchi, out of embarrassment, concealed her eyes and felt her face drawn very near to that of Panchashar. This time, under the spell not only of his desire but also of his indomitable lust, Panchashar tried to plant a prolonged kiss on Melamchi's cheek. He cared little how favorable that spot and moment would be for him.

In tune with Melamchi's silent acceptance, Panchashar launched his first step along the journey of love, exercising love, art, virility and intellect in a balanced way. Considering the methods and rules of love undertaken before his time, he gave them a practical continuity. The tantalizing touch of Melamchi's fragrant breath and the high-order incense of the ripple of vapor emanating from her body made him glorious, haloed and virile.

The two went on presenting each other according to their interest and comfort. As a result, they went on immersing into a mysterious journey of unity in the midst of curiosity, fear, bliss and pain. Pride and doubt had no place here.

It was morning time. The tantalizing earth, drenched in a downpour of fresh and bright sunrays from the sky just cleared off the clouds following a nightlong rain, looked extremely scintillating. Some soldiers of the king happened to be watching the amorous playfulness of Panchashar and Melamchi in their privacy. But the two were unaware of this vigil. When the horse neighed nearby, Melamchi was shaken, apprehending some untoward thing to happen, but did not fear any harm upon themselves. Yet, she was surrounded by apprehensions of some calamity, in the meantime, sympathizing with Panchashar.

The incidents informing rigorous punishment and death penalty sentenced by the Mughals, especially Mughal men, rulers and kings, and the visual imageries built thereof and settled permanently in their minds started haunting Melamchi again and again. She started experiencing laxness besieged by the apprehension of the imminent death penalty and said to herself, 'If anything happens to Panchashar, I shall be its cause. And if there comes a moment when I will be obliged to punish myself, I should not falter.'

At this moment, she turned quite emotional and rather worried as well.

Melamchi and Panchashar looked at each other with feelings of dedication. They were face-to-face with a possibility that their meeting, and their lives as well, could end any moment now. A flash of such a thought rose in the minds of both.

The soldiers of the king informed Panchashar that he had been summoned by the king. Having delivered this message, the soldiers returned on their horses in a fleeting speed. The neighing and hoofing of the horses became dimmer with the passage of each moment.

The two looked at each other with feelings of love and got caught up in each other's arms as mutual refuge. They even apprehended that this was going to be their last wish.

Binding Panchashar tightly in her bosoms, Melamchi prayed secretly, 'I am ready to take any sort of punishment, but this guest of ours should be harmless. Oh God, save the newcomer. Oh Buddha, have mercy on Panchashar! My Panchashar should be safe under your security.'

She was pathetic.

Melamchi woke up from her dream. The birds were crooning their daybreak numbers. Oh what a beautiful love and a dangerous suspicion she had in her dream! She thought about it secretly. In fact, she could surmise a higher degree of doubt and fear. Soon she started feeling her heavy head lighter. She woke up, opened the window and started watching sunrise. She watched the crimson sunrays with all her eyes and mind. She deeply pined to get connected to the dream that had been snapped just now, and so, she asked herself, 'Can such a thing happen with Panchashar in reality too? What happens if the king's men really see us at such a moment? This way, she gave birth to a small but prickly trepidation inside her heart and carried it herself.

She grew more and more impatient to relay her dream to Panchashar.

***

Emperor Timur had heard about the completion of the building from informal sources, and he was impatient to have a look of it.

"Mauni, I think we should formally inform the Emperor that the building has been completed," said Panchashar.

"When, do you think, will be the right time to inform him?"

"The information of the progress or completion of a good thing can be delivered any time. For an emperor, information is what matters most, not the time selected for it. If a need arises, they will themselves stipulate a time for the Emperor's visit to the building. That is not a matter of our concern," wrote Mauni, and rubbed it off before long.

When he had seated together for dinner, Panchashar informed his colleagues that they should now inform the palace about the completion of the mansion. The fellow artisans started dancing with joy. Mauni was even happier, considering that Panchashar would now be caught in his own promise and that would benefit every one of them. The environment inside the dining hall turned festive, but the maidens were unable to understand the reason instantly. They came to know it after a while. Following this, some of them appeared quite grave, while a few were happy.

Mauni speculated, 'Maybe those who have pairs are grave, anticipating the incoming separation. Those without a soul-mate or those who failed to pick one, had no reason to regret.'

It was natural that once the palace was informed about the completion of the task, the episode would come to an end and the playground would become empty. Once disbursed, they would be scattered in different directions, though it was difficult to claim that they did not consider this inevitable separation at the moment. But

HARI RAJ BHATTARAI

then, the possibility of many roads forking out from this premise was high. So, they had no option but to consider the imminent separation of the love birds a game of fate or a doing of their karma, and thus appease their bruised minds. However, this aspect was not a serious thing in this part of the world, especially in regard to the diligent beauties. It also was true that fate had some role to play in the lives of the working men who had come here from Kantipur.

As advised by Melamchi, the formal information about the completion of the building under construction was sent to the palace of Emperor Timur. For quite a long time, Timur was impatient to see the new building. When he was given the formal information, his impatience became even more intense. Approving of the information with all his heart, he sent the artisans the word that together with his queen and family, he would be visiting the pagoda very soon.

Melamchi held formal talks with the artisans in an atmosphere of amity and she committed herself to the arrangement of reception and honor they should accord when the royal invitees visited them. The artisans, on their part, were surprised, seeing the skillfulness, contextual awareness, aptness in building the atmosphere and dutifulness.

At the stipulated time, Emperor Timur Khan came to see the pagoda, together with his family. From the side of the pagoda, the Buddhist Lamas chanted the auspicious mantras, played pious melodies and welcomed the royal visitors. Prayer wheels could be seen rotating in the hands of the monks with bald heads. The wheels continued to rotate incessantly.

In the royal visit of Emperor Timur Khan, there also were citizens of the town, prominent people from the society, pioneers of the cultural realm, wise and scholarly people, saints and accomplished personages. The glorious visits of the experts and patrons of art made the pagoda even more embellished.

The visiting members, collected in groups of their own, had a through view of the pagoda. The queens who went around the building together with their attendants praised the building with their open hearts. But the royal visit of the pagoda turned to be historic in the sense that the gentlemen, noble men and the accomplished men, who had a round of the pagoda were those whom the Emperor considered indispensable. But he considered it unwise to bring along the paid employees of the palace, because he believed that they usually had lowly thinking and so they could not give objective observations, as they were adept only on pointing out the flaws and laying impediments. Another order inside their apparent disorder was that the king's inspection pagoda was fully formal and rule-bound but the royal visit and its glory was fully informal. What a nice program it was, having an informal visit for a formal event! Wasn't it thrilling beyond description?

There was a huge turnout of the local inhabitants in this event, and their joy and splendor was worth remembering. The Emperor wanted to see that the excited public could take part in the event without any hassle and each one of them had the opportunity to partake in it. Like his salaried employees, the Emperor also kept his body guards away from the event because he wanted to see the pagoda-style building in complete freedom. He wanted to pass his remark on the building with an open heart. He wanted to laugh naturally and resort to informal conversation.

He was deeply moved by the artistic finery and aesthetic accomplishment of the building. Once inside it, the bliss he experienced left him speechless. It was a real bliss granted, but it was something inexpressible in words. In fact, the beauty of the building was expressive from both concrete and abstract ways.

Emperor Timur Khan was elated on seeing the building in a new and unprecedented way. He lavishly praised the artisans present there for their knowledge and skill.

When the Emperor started praising the grandeur of the building and the skills of the artisans and thus expressed his joy, Panchashar grew impatient, and his eyes grew even more restless, intensely looking for someone there. On one hand, the Emperor was delivering his speech; on the other, Panchashar's mind and eyes were roaming in a different world. Mauni, as a witness, was able to comprehend both these situations. Melamchi could understand it even better. Therefore, she considered it wise to keep herself neutral, considering the situation therein.

She sat at one corner of the building and heard the Emperor praise the building and its art with joy. To her, the artistic awareness of the artisans and the proportional amalgamation of aesthetic refinement was a vindication of creativity and perfection. Concealing the tears of joy that rolled down her eyes on finding the building endorsed from the social and royal levels, she left the spot.

***

The following day, Melamchi entered the room in the guise of a nurse, carrying treatment tools. She placed the tools in one corner and in a placid environment opened the window on the eastern side. Red sunrays spilled inside the room. The touch of the crispy morning air shook Panchashar up from sleep, though he was still heavy with protracted sleepiness. So his eye lids had not opened yet.

Melamchi walked very close to him and felt Panchashar's forehead, stroked his hair, took the pulse, examined the rate of his breathing and convinced herself that he was fine altogether.

The atmosphere was fully conducive for him to open his eyes. The environment there, and the way he was being addressed were both near to the royal order.

Panchashar woke up fully. His first view fell upon the face of Melamchi. This was the first incident of this kind in his life. This startled and amazed him.

Melamchi's countenance that looked fresh, clean, austere and stunning, and the red-yellowish admixture of the falling runways made her even more seductive. For a while, Panchashar thought, 'Who is this lady that looks exactly like Melamchi? Why is she here? Am I in a dream or in reality?'

After scanning the feelings on Panchashar's eyes and face, Melamchi said, "You were lying unconscious inside the pagoda yesterday. I brought you here in the night. Consider it my own home. You need not feel uncomfortable here."

Melamchi was a girl of patience and grave nature. Whenever she talked, she did it only after displaying a smile. Her eyes did most of the talking and heard most of the things that were spoken around. That must be why she spoke very little. At the moment, she looked like an epitome of a complete and matchless woman. In fact, the liberal thinking, liberal viewpoint, liberal behavior and guiltless words of love emanated effortlessly from her feelings of helpfulness and dutifulness.

The artisans coming from Nepal could never recognize her as an expert of architecture and sculpture. Nor did they ever surmise that she was a distinguished official of the Department of Construction. But Mauni was aware of certain aspects of her personality. At this moment, Panchashar considered Melamchi a combination of soft and hard elements arrayed to make a glorious personality, but was still unable to fully recognize Melamchi made of several invaluable and heterogeneous elements. The layers of Melamchi's personality unsheathed one after another, but Panchashar seldom recognized this fact instantly but when he did and comprehended, most of the things would have fleeted away. He used to learn many a thing, and they used to stay compiled as a collage of recollected memories in historic forms.

"Pan, how are you feeling now?" asked Melamchi in a voice laden with compassion and good-will.

Panchashar could feel an unexpressed curiosity emanate from his heart stirred by Melamchi's question. So he just said, "What was wrong with me in the first place?" His counter question was laced with an admixture of wonder.

'Could it be that this man has become stiff due to the sense of pride resulting from bad practices, lack of interest, ignorance and self repression, or the sense of inferiority that barred him from opening up with womenfolk? What is there so mysterious and wonderful in it? What is there to be concealed? And why?' Melamchi was engaged in self-contemplation.

HARI RAJ BHATTARAI

Panchashar asked with a request, "Tell how I reached here."

"Hwangdi (Emperor) liked the pagoda very much, and praised it profusely. He praised you and also praised Mauni, who was nearby. He also praised all other artisans. They had all been standing in a row. He looked at each of them and thanked them. Your Nepalese friends had appeared as bright as the sun. I was watching from a distance."

"Why did he abruptly leave the ceremony?" Panchashar asked.

"That is a personal matter of mine. I considered it wise to leave, and so I did. But why do you keep asking me questions?"

"Still."

"I considered it unwise to register my presence there. That moment, at that place, you, Mauni and your friends were the central people. And that was what befitted the occasion. You won't understand this fact; Mauni perhaps does. I had signaled Mauni before leaving from there."

Mauni knew well why Melamchi had left the spot. Also considering the background, he thought, 'They say, the king has a thousand eyes, and they use their ears even for the task of seeing. So they sometimes invite havoc by doing untoward things. They get blind with intoxication, get excited and thus get dethroned sometimes, as history vindicates. In formation and deterioration of a personality, the role of time, context, inspiration and mentality are crucial, but no one can explain this fact to a ruler. These people, who consider themselves omniscient and omnipotent might not be counted among the commoners, but they considered themselves the lords of the people. What a big paradox it is! Melamchi perhaps moved away from there, in a secret way, being aware of this fact.'

Mauni had such considerate thoughts for Melamchi. Then he added, 'Perhaps, Melamchi thought for the need to hide and save herself from the rulers and their kinsmen, who, like a lion that picked a prey and lumbered toward the woods, had bestial feelings, seeing her blooming beauty and artistic awareness. Else, could any powerful man tame his potent amorous inclination toward such maidens in the full bloom of their youth? This is a fact everyone usually thinks about and contemplates. Maybe Melamchi was in dilemma considering the same, had been disturbed and thus concealed herself.'

Melamchi wanted to keep herself safe by staying away from the heathen Mughal rulers, who practiced an atrocious tradition and followed an evil culture of accumulating many wives. Beauty sometimes becomes a curse for the bearer; youth can sometimes become a source of agony forever. The youthful maidens and their well-wishers cannot help but bear such apprehensive thoughts. Melamchi herself thought of such things in seriousness and contemplated on them, but never expressed any glimpse of such thoughts through her words and actions. In fact, Melamchi always kept herself under great restraint and wise balance, though she always stayed dynamic in action. So, Mauni considered it a wise decision on her part to stay away from the ceremony and to leave the spot after a while. He supported her decision and exercised silence but Panchashar continued to stoop in a pensive mood.

Panchashar was not aware of such a background. He stayed glued to a single issue all the time and raised the same repeatedly.

"You were not present in the ceremony. Tell me why."

"I considered my absence more relevant there."

"That moment, I also wished to share my happiness with you and with my near ones."

"Your conviction is right in its own place. But that spot was not meant for us to share our happiness. Nor was the occasion proper. Hwangdi's happiness was more important there."

Panchashar was shocked to see Melamchi's practical shrewdness. He got no chance to ask a question or make a comment.

Giving continuity to her explanation, Melamchi said, "Our happiness is trivial considering the Emperor's happiness. We can share his happiness and take our parts, can't we?"

This proposal from Melamchi had the feeling of request.

"Then?"

"What then? That's all. I returned to the guesthouse and waited for you for a long time. Everyone else arrived, but you did not. I asked Mauni. He wrote on his slate that you had been brooding in a pensive mood. I reached the pagoda immediately with some girls. You were lying there, almost unconscious. We then lifted you on a carriage and brought you here. When you came round in the morning, you didn't find yourself in your room, and I was here. That's all. Nothing has remained hidden. Nothing has gone wrong, either."

Panchashar rested for four complete days. It was Melamchi's request that he should rest at least for four days.

A short deliberation was held on the fifth day. The issues of discussion were Kerung and Dhancha. The two were in mutual love, and Kerung was pregnant. The discussion slipped to a conclusion at once. After explaining everyone the context, Melamchi said, "I wish them to stay together. I never support separation. You discuss it yourself and let me know."

Mauni listened with care. Panchashar looked even more listless.

At this moment, Kerung remembered a suggestion from Melamchi that while staying with men, the girls should use yao—a medicine—and keep themselves on the top. She said to herself, 'At such moments, who remembers *yao* or a method? One is seldom mindful.'

This moment, Kerung was rather bashful, and one could notice a change on her countenance. But she was extremely beautiful and glittering. It seemed, she was lit with the glory of motherhood.

On hearing Kerung, Mauni raised his eyebrows. But Panchashar appeared listless.

"What do we need to do now?" Mauni showed his slate.

"There are ways. Dhancha should either take Kerung to his country, or Kerung should take Dhancha to her own home. Or else, the two can look for jobs here and stay back. But it is not that easy to stay here," said Melamchi, making things plain.

The others stared at one another's face. There also was a spell of whispers in the group. Melamchi said, "There also is another help I can lend from my side. Both of you can move to my home and stay there. But you must work to keep going. You can work, considering it your own home and my field and your business yours own."

After a brief pause, she resumed, "These are the four solutions at your disposal. You must choose one. It will be even better, if you have a plan of your own."

Mauni was extremely pleased to see Melamchi's helpfulness. Panchashar, on his part, was unhappy considering what a mess the boys had invited.

"You now decide what you want to do. You can also take others' suggestions. If you opt to move anywhere else, I will make arrangements for that." Having said this, Melamchi stood from her place.

Kerung also stood. Dhancha was with her. He also stood and followed Kerung.

Melamchi started at them and said to herself, 'What a stunning pair they make! Kerung was smart in choosing her man.'

Mauni thought, 'Though Dhancha looks like a muddle-head, the girl he chose is smart.'

Others said in a voice, "Let such a matching pair live long."

"They are with us till now, under our care. They now need a base to enter social life formally, and that has a process. They need social approval. Only then can they exercise duty and right upon each other. How can we leave them alone? How can we tell them to go?"

Mauni contemplated on his own and wrote on his slate, "Let's complete the marriage ritual. That has now become our responsibility. That will make it easy for them to move their steps in the society, no matter where they go and stay."

Everyone clapped after reading Mauni's slate. The girls blushed, pushing themselves on the seats they occupied from this end to that.

Considering everyone's mentality, Mauni again wrote, "Let's sit now, every one of us, and have a collective feast in approval of this new couple's marriage."

The snacks were quickly brought in and placed on the tables. As bride and bridegroom, Kerung and Mauni took the initiatives in serving the dishes. The methods of serving and eating, one could feel an admixture of Newari and Tibetan styles.

Melamchi was deeply moved to see Mauni's wise thoughts and decisions. Reading the glimpses on the countenances of her friends engaged in feasting and merry-making, she said, "I am inspired to say something to you all today. Shall I?"

"Do tell. This is how democracy inside this guesthouse works. At this moment, even the Emperor can be denied an entry here. The moment now is no less significant. Do speak out your mind, without any hesitation. Add things and tell; share a lot of things," said Mauni's script on the slate.

All eyes were now centered on Panchashar. He was firm like a rock.

Before speaking, Melamchi sent forth a wave of sweet smile and said, "To my friends on both sides, I would say that if you are also willing to get married, place *yao* beside you and lie on the lower side."

All those on the boys' side did not understand her signals. So they looked at Mauni for explanation. Without ado, Mauni wrote on his slate, "I shall explain you later after I understand what it is. For now, it will be wise to wind up."

"Bekha, play the *madal*."

"Dhancha, put the anklets around your feet."

"Give Mauni his flute."

"*Murchunga, murchunga, murchunga*…who, did you say, I should give to?"

This entertainment, enjoyment and merry-making of the day time turned out to a substitution for *rateuli*[45] staged on the night of someone's marriage. The maidens also presented dance in their own ways, exhibiting the romantic, Tibetan art. Soon the collage dance ended, and everyone appeared in tired faces.

***

---

[45] Singing and dancing that takes place at the boy's home, after he has departed to bring his bride on the wedding day

A week passed since the Emperor inspected the pagoda and returned to the palace. In the meantime, Panchashar also rested for half a week considering his health, under the special goodwill and direction of Melamchi. Moreover, they withheld their work in order to celebrate the return of Bekha and Gola. The pair of Dhancha and Kerung aggravated the problem even more. It became necessary for the group to engage in mental and ideational deliberation to solve the problem. By mentioning four possible solutions to it, Melamchi made it easy for everyone. All that was left now was to formalize the marriage of Dhancha and Kerung according to religious and cultural procedure. Feeling a sort of relief, Panchashar moved toward the pagoda. Melamchi also was with him, and was driving the horse carriage.

In the eyes of Melamchi, Panchashar appeared thoughtless, completely devoid of any idea. Causing a ripple in the pacific, stable pool, Melamchi said, "Pan, Why had you looked for me at the pagoda the day Hwangdi had visited?"

Panchashar remembered the context, contemplated on it and said, "You have played a crucial role in making the pagoda stand in that form. The reflection of your artistic awareness is manifest till the very core of the building. I wanted to explain this to the Emperor in your presence. But I failed; I did not get the opportunity."

Overtaking him, Melamchi said, "It was good that you did not get the opportunity. You know or not: my coming into their eye is like experiencing death while standing alive. It's like being in house-arrest. It would mean end of freedom and living in a state of paralysis."

Panchashar didn't listen to Melamchi though he feigned to be doing so, and listened, feigning not be doing so.

Melamchi took a long breath and added, "Do not give so much importance to post and power, Panchashar. Those are trivial things. Anyone can acquire position and power, and anyone can fall from them. Thousands of strong, prominent and great people have perished with the passage of time. The ones to perish are those who did nothing for the welfare of the society."

Elaborating further, she said, "There is not much difference between such rulers and violent, wild beasts. It is always to maintain a respectable distance from them. Thank God, you did not take my name there and I was safe. That is a great and remarkable achievement of my life. Another episode will start now." After giving her sentence a stop, she drew a long breath and took rest.

"Melamchi, people choose to wait all their life to have an audience with kings and emperors. They consider their life blessed the day they meet them. But you…"

"I give no importance to that," she said, overtaking Panchashar. With an added excitement, she added, "The beggars go there to beg. The robbers go there to collect strength, and become successful in big acts of banditry. The wise and the enlightened ones, pursuers, recluses and scholars stay away from such people."

She added, "Their worlds are often very small and cramped. We cannot be accommodated in those worlds; we cannot enjoy there. If we pay more importance to them, we will be risking our freedom. I don't want to lose my path, but you are free in your decision. I don't want to influence your thoughts. If, as a friend, you seek my opinion, I will be happy to share." She said all these things in a single breath.

Laying some background, Panchashar said in a modest tone, "If the kings and emperors offer anything to anyone, the receivers consider their heights enhanced and they eulogize the formers' magnanimity. In that case, if the king knew of your knowledge, artistic awareness and aesthetics, you would be benefitted. They are on look for such opportunities so that they could have mercy on others and thus show off their magnanimity. These are worldly things and quite natural as well. But at any rate, you didn't allow the Emperor to add up to his height. I am fond of your sense of dignity and rational analysis. I respect your convictions."

"The thing is plain and simple," Melamchi said. "They give even wealth and honor to bring people in their favor. If there is a need, they don't hesitate to concede even some power. This, they think, pleases an individual, but that it not an absolute truth. This doesn't always happen."

"How did you learn such a thing?"

"I am an exception to that."

Panchashar gazed Melamchi with curiosity.

Melamchi said, "I am not a subject that could be pleased with wealth and honor. Nor can I ever be."

Giving her words a tinge of self-respect, she said, "I embark on karma, the right action, and try to be happy with that is there at my disposal. So I can never push my happiness and peace underneath anyone's control. Wealth and honor are nowhere above my personal happiness."

Panchashar continued to stare at her and listen to her with utmost curiosity.

"No other thing can equate my happiness. I don't consider strength and honor more valuable than you." Laying more stress on her words, she said, "As for now, you are my joy, my success."

"Tell on; I am listening," said Panchashar in a casual way.

"Pan, I think my wish to move about you will be limited to my dream alone."

"Why so? Aren't we moving together right now?"

"We are not; we are merely acting. In reality, we don't have that much of time at our disposal. So after having a look of the outer part of the pagoda, let's come back and stay here in the garden. We can see the inner part some other day later."

"As you say," said Panchashar, paving the path to her in a neutral way.

The pagoda had been erected at the center of a royal garden. So, from the pedestrian lane along the circumference of the garden, one could see the outer part of the pagoda. Panchashar and Melamchi made two circles around the pagoda. They enjoyed the external beauty of the pagoda with all their eyes and treasured it in their hearts. They also looked at each other with feelings of gratitude on being able to erect such a grand building. They looked in the way husband and wife look at each other with a feeling of gratefulness after a child is born. It seemed the pagoda was a child of Melamchi and Panchashar. So, it was logical and natural for them to look at each other with such outlook.

Even as they were walking, Melamchi sat down on a chair kept by the side of the garden and took a long sigh, as though she were extremely tired. Panchashar sat beside her, giving his action natural formality. Melamchi appeared stupefied. She feigned thoughtless, giving Panchashar an inarticulate invitation to touch her body. Panchashar did make mental efforts to decipher Melamchi's inclinations but could find no entry into her heart, because Melamchi's mental make-up was nourished by Chinese society, culture and geography and influenced by Tibetan atmosphere, and it was not that easy to Panchashar to fully comprehend it.

Panchashar's eyes got stuck to Melamchi's hands and her fingers. Only a painter or a sculpture could ever create fingers with such extraordinary form; Melamchi posed her fingers as third wonder for Panchashar. She became aware of the fall of Panchashar's eyes on her fingers, and so, she blushed a little trying to conceal her shyness. But then, finding no point in concealing them, she said, "Why are you staring at my hands like that, Pan? What did you see there?"

"Your hands and fingers are artistic and fleshy; that makes them extremely beautiful. I had never thought you had such beautiful fingers. We have passed such a long time together, but I had not noticed it so far."

Melamchi observed the beauty of her hands and fingers rolling them back and forth, and tried to decipher the beauty emanating from them. In her bid to digress from the issue, she said in a tone of satire, "Do not consider these fingers merely beautiful and artistic. If even you and I quarrel, I will use them to catch hold of your pigtail." Melamchi ran her finger through Panchashar's hairs, caught them fondly, and started caressing them with love. Panchashar showed no reaction instantly, but she considered herself a winner. Thus, she fulfilled her craving to play with his dark, glistering and curly hair.

After a while, Panchashar drew Melamchi's hands—that were roving through his tresses—to the front side and watch them, rolling up and down, until he was satisfied, and hummed a segment of a *ghazal* he could remember:

Ma timra haatka aunlaharuma khoob khelethen
Najanejhain garyou pyari, yahi nai yaad rakhen hai

[I had freely played with the fingers on your hand.
You acted innocence. My love, keep at least this much
in your mind.]

Melamchi tried to read the feelings on Panchashar's eyes once, but could not. In her bid to disturb Panchashar's concentration centered on her hands, she clasped both her palms in the space between her thighs. But he showed no reaction to that. She thought, 'Pan has not come back to normalcy yet. Couldn't it mean that I have removed the bridge along our journey of love toward its climax, merely by concealing my fingers? How if he took it that way?'

This consideration made Melamchi serious.

The time was late afternoon. The natural environment was scintillating. Sometimes the cloud cloaked the sun, and some time, the air turned sunny again. In this play between shade and light, Melamchi tried to discover the reflection of her own mind.

On seeing a pair of birds in the round sky just above the garden, she thought, 'Could they be flying with an agreement? If that was the case, shouldn't they be flying in the same speed and distance? Why is one ahead of the other? Even if the free flight across the wide and unimpeded sky, should one follow another? Which could be the follower in the bird pair flying this way: the male or the female?"

Then she asked expressly, "Pan, which in this pair of birds is leading and which following: the male or the female?

"Your question has inspired me to recall a song," said Panchashar and sang:

Agadi timi thyo agadi-agadi
Ma hunthen pachhadi timi nai agadi
Pachhadi pachhadi timi thyou pachhadi
Ma hunthen agadi timi nai pachhadi

[You used to lead; I used to follow. Whenever you were following, I used to be on the lead.]

In a natural environment that balanced heat and cold, Melamchi stood agape, posing herself several questions. With an unknown drive, she covered her eyes gently with her eyelids and leaned gradually toward Panchashar, resting her head against his shoulders.

'Melamchi is tired. Let her dose off for some time. I should not, at any cost, temper with her heartfelt honor and a bright belief in me even in such a secluded spot.' This is what Panchashar's soul said.

Materially, this repose in such a secluded place was a moment of test. It was time to measure their mentalities and actions. It was also a time of action in the articulation of their love.

Melamchi was lying in a relaxed mood, experiencing the bliss of fine, internal thrills. She had herself fallen asleep in the way the ants sleep. The warm touch of the intoxicating fragrance emanating from her body, had not, however, been able to drive Panchashar enraptured, nor had the conscious, amorous drive of manhood inside him had conjured enough courage to touch her. He didn't have the internal guts to grasp her within his bosoms, either. In response to Melamchi's silent invitation, he could neither shower prolonged kisses, nor take the first step of love in consonance with any sort of love, artistry, masculinity or intellect. All he did was wished for Melamchi's unimpeded rest.

In fact, this occasion was a background for trust and liberality as well. It was not, however, a man's cowardice and negligence of femininity. No. This also was not an undeclared invitation of a grown-up woman to a male counterpart, nor an estimation of a man's character. This much was however true: At this moment when the man was incomplete in his study of a woman and vice-versa, both the lovers were new in identifying their initial inclinations and trust. Their destinations were new to them.

Melamchi opened her eyes. It was dusk now. She took a breath of relief. She came to know that she had dozed off, reclining on Panchashar's chest. When she realized this, a rosy hue of embarrassment spilled over her face. In her bid to normalize the situation that otherwise seemed odd, she ran her eyes all around. In a grove of deer at a distance, the stags were fighting among themselves and winners were formally impregnating the females. She watched this play of the deer and with the same eyes looked at Panchashar without a wink, and chose the path of silence. Her silent eyes were articulating many a thing, and Panchashar was trying to decipher them. Drawing his mouth close to her ears, he said in a voice as low as a whisper, "Shouldn't we enter the pagoda now?"

"Not today. Outside is better for now. We shall enter some other day," said Melamchi fondly, letting her voice bear the tinge of affection. She also mixed some nasal sound in it. She then ran her eyes on the outgrowth of dark, thick hair on Panchashar's chest and sat, pressing herself against his bosom. Panchashar tried to make her pressing posture as comfortable and natural as possible. Melamchi tried to drag Panchashar toward the path of tenderness by running her fingers over the hair on his chest through her fondling advances, but Panchashar did not let his patience stoop. For the first time, they shared some moments of their life in a resort of love.

Recalling and analyzing the event they saw from dawn to dusk that day, including the amorous playfulness and games of birds and deer, and deriving untold pleasure from the same, Melamchi dozed off in her room.

***

This building, constructed for the first time in China, was a little different from the pagoda-style building in Kantipur, Lalitpur and Bhadgaon. Its style was pagoda no doubt, but it stood with a difference in its structure, and only the artisans knew about this reality. They also knew that the pagoda had stood in its present form as a result of scholarly Melamchi's touch, love-laden goodwill and liberal outlook. For these reasons, this pagoda in the central part of the city of Beijing stood as an instance of a new and rectified edition of pagoda architecture.

At the request of Panchashar, Melamchi had drawn a picture of the pagoda. When Emperor Timur Khan visited the building, the Nepalese artisans jointly gifted the painting to the Emperor during the formal program. The painting was extremely attractive and realistic, but the building was even more attractive. Timur Khan praised the building by showing its painting, and spoke highly of the artistic sense of the artists.

The apex of the pagoda was longer than the usual length of the pagoda-style buildings, like the hump of a heifer that stoops when she stretches her body all through. Since the apices of all the four vertices had been raised a little, making it look like a huge rooster preparing to soar and take a hen by brooding her all through with his finger, and engaging her in coitus. The very structure and painting of this building held the power to spur the latent romantic drives of a man and a woman. In fact, the building seems psychologically expressive and provoking. The lusty people look for sexual expressions in every object. This is natural too and possibly, this building had become a centre of energy for people's mental world from many angles.

Today, a short meeting was convened at the palace. It was almost like an emergency meeting. The agenda to be discussed was single, too: "What should we do with the pagoda?"

Only selected people were present in the meeting. So the number of attendees was quite small. The meeting had representations from sociologists, culturists, experts of politics, academia and architecture, and historians.

People from far and near had heard, through oral sources that there had been changes in the objective with which the building had been decreed initially. So the members attending the meeting that speculated that the meeting would end with a resolution, deciding that the pagoda 'will not be used by the palace'. They also had surmised that it would be left to the discretion of the Emperor Timur to decide as to what use the building would be put to. So, instead of getting stuck in discussion, they thought it wise to move to the conclusion directly and so, deciding to hear the decision from the Emperor himself, the members turned to him.

Emperor Timur was quite contented, and its reason was the pagoda. He never missed a chance to praise the structure with people who came to meet him formally or informally, and said, "See it once if you can. It's worth seeing."

His queens also had visited the pagoda several times together with their relatives. The presence of the pagoda in the royal city of Beijing had made it especially embellished, and all denizens living there had got a feel of it.

The people had the general belief that Emperor Timur's inertest, vision and commitments were reasons behind the emergence of the pagoda inside the royal city of Beijing. In addition to that, the artistry of the workers coming from a foreign country and the newness they gave in its structure also found ample discussion among the people. So the citizens said they were the real builders, whose skills and creations would ever remain immortal.

The pagoda looked so neat, clean and pure that even the touch of human breath was thought to tarnish to defile its luster. This must be why the Emperor, during a meeting with his family said, "The people in this city are not yet qualified to stay inside that building."

Those who heard the king took his words seriously, but did not consider it ordinary. Interpreting the same, they said, "Even the shadow and reek of the human beings can spoil its brilliance. So the Hwangdi has himself been reluctant to use the building."

The meeting hall now turned silent and tranquil, building and environment for Emperor Timur to speak. Seizing the moment, the Emperor said, "I dedicate the newly constructed pagoda building as a gift to our people from the side of the state administration. Let the people accept this gift. I have taken this decision in honor of the people. Let the building always stay worth seeing."

Taking two breaths in the interval, Emperor Timur said, "The state, on behalf of the people, shall itself take care of its maintenance, repairing and management so that the pagoda doesn't become a 'white elephant' for our people. Let the pagoda become an invaluable treasure of the entire subjects of China. This is my desire."

After a break, the Emperor added, "Our guests artisans from our neighboring country came and constructed this building according to our sentiments by coming here. We highly appreciate their enthusiasm, skill, sense of art and aesthetic brilliance. They all deserve thanks from us. In this context, I also extend my sincere thanks to Nepal, our friendly neighbor."

He further added, "I also thank our people, who lent their support in this task. I thank those who have been involved in the construction of the building directly or indirectly.

Addressing the people present in the meeting, Timur said, "I also thank the members present in this meeting."

The Emperor left. The meeting ended.

***

CHAPTER EIGHT

IT WAS PRAYER time in the morning.

The sunrays had not yet reached the garden in the eastern side of the guesthouse. For a while, someone ran a sickle there, followed by a spade, mowed the grass therein and broke up the divots. The spade was run at all places, turn by turn. The sods were broken and the land was leveled. There were no rooms for illusion now. The context was obscure; no one could surmise what was happening. Was it a dream, or an instance of cooperation from the soul of the dead? For, it was not an act of destruction, but of construction.

Soon, they could hear the flow of water falling from the tap. A tapping was heard at the main entrance of the building, followed by steps on its wooden floor and a door leading into the building opened. Somke of the hearers, with raised hair on the heads and the parts, consoled themselves, for they could see the door leading to Mauni's room opening. Soon their breathing returned to normal.

The sunrays had now entered from the windows and the doors. Mauni came into Panchashar's room, but the latter was not there. He had been to the tap; Mauni met him on his way back. He instantly showed him his slate that read, "Clean yourself and bring everyone to the garden immediately. We must seize the most propitious time. Send words to the girls as well."

He then lumbered away to Gola's room. By then, Gola had finished her exquisite make-up, as always. She asked, "Why? Do I need to do anything?"

"Bring Kerung after make-up. Also ask your friends to quickly come out to the garden after make-up."

The group of the girls came out to into the garden and stood on one side in a line. The group of the boys reached next, and stood on another side, making a similar line. The girls were standing on the northern side, and the boys occupied the line opposite to theirs. In fact, the two groups were standing in the direction that befitted the locations of their respective countries.

The girls were dressed in Tibetan dresses and jewelries. So, all of them appeared similar and in identical faces. The well-made hairs in two plaits had cylindrical caps gently placed upon them with silver chains a singer coins tucked at the part rendered partially cleft at one end. When these started to move, the eyes of the onlookers would naturally get glued to them. For a while, Mauni stood gawking and said to himself, 'The make-up of the girls happens to suggest their sexes, ages and marital status. All these girls must be unmarried ones.'

Kerung appeared slightly different from others. Mauni thought, 'Today, she is rather different from others, and special too.' He then ran his eyes toward the boys. All of them were in Tibetan dresses. But Dhancha looked different, for he had put a Bhadgaonlé cap upon the Tibetan dress and had tucked a *khukuri* in his girdle laced with a girdle cloth. The *khukuri* was tucked upside down, its hilt tilting slightly on the right.

Mauni was obliged to write on his slate, "Adjust his *khukuri*."

Everyone there gazed one another. Maybe none of them knew what was to be adjusted.

"The *khukuri* is upside down." He wrote again.

One of them went and righted the *khukuri*. Still, he didn't do it perfectly. Feeling quite uncomfortable, Mauni rose from the pedestal, wiped his hands and corrected the position of the *khukuri*.

Then he wrote, "Do not forget it now." He thought, 'Louts! They all are same.'

All the eyes were glued to Dhancha's *khukuri*. The *khukuri*, inside the scabbard, was upside down, and the hilt was tilting left from inside the tightly placed girdle cloth. But no one wanted to think about the rationale behind tucking the *khukuri* upside down with a tilt on the left-hand side.

Mauni signaled Kerung and directed her to sit at the stipulated place. Kerung came out of her girl friends and sat as directed.

Mauni now glanced at Dhancha and signaled him to go and sit next to Kerung.

His eyes were not centered on Gola. Gola pushed forth the basket containing garlands. She also pushed another basket containing flowers separated into petals, in order to shower upon the wedding pair.

Mauni now turned toward Panchashar. The latter got startled, seemingly coming back to senses. He gazed at everyone for once and said, "We have gathered here to solemnize the marriage of Kerung and brother Dhancha. They are not formally entering social and marital relation as man and wife. Come; let's pray for their happy married life. Let Lord Ganesh shower his blessings upon both of them."

Mauni showed his slate to Lyanduké. It read, "If you have a different procedure for marriage, mix it. Come forward; help me accomplish the procedure."

"On my part, I am a pure Limboo breed, a Kirat. In the first place, our marriage cannot take place in such a small space. We need to run, chase, hide and search. At times, we also use clubs and *khukuris*. We need a lot of space around the woods, bamboo groves, banana fields, rivers and brooks etc. There are separate arrangements for singing, dancing and feasting. There also are many rituals to be done before and after marriage. At the marriage spot, we cannot show the dearth of space and time. We ought not do that. The Bahuns and Chhetris finish their marriage even in a small, cramped space. Ha ha ha…" He laughed.

"And another thing," he added, "is that, our marriages are supervised by Bijuwa Phedangma. These are traditional things. So I don't know any rule and procedure. If other friends know, they may tell." Lyanduké finished his words in an instant and moved a few steps back.

Mauni turned his eyes toward Guindé and thought, 'He is member of a special class in our country. He has extraordinary talent and high-order artistry with him. He has skills and vigor too. He always thinks of new things and adopts a dynamic lifestyle accordingly. In spite of all these skills, he has not been able to open up. We don't know if hesitation, inferiority, pride or sense of specialty has been inhibiting him.' Adding yet another clause to his contemplation, Mauni thought, 'In what a big space his creation pervades!'

'This class, which can give novelty to every construction and lend it an original hue befitting every caste, gender, class, religion, business, age, color, physical structure, place, season, occasion and objective, has not been able to progress optimally or receive the recognition it deserves. After all, there was no dearth of anything.'

Mauni again added, 'If they bore clean thoughts, simple behavior, refinement in language and honor for others and move ahead with these, they would certainly progress. But their objectives are not easily understandable. As for mere living, even the crows do. They also beget children. What can I say to that?'

Brining slight alternation to his thoughts, Mauni showed Guindé the same slate he had shown to Lyanduké.

Guindé said in clear terms, "I am a Damai man. I will present myself if there is a need to sing and dance in this marriage. I have no idea what the marriage procedures are. But in a marriage, we are always on the lead, together with the auspicious melody. For that, tell me what I ought to do. I am ready." He added, "I shall sew a blouse and a cap for them."

Having said this, Guindé stepped back.

With his slate, Mauni now walked close to Jokhé. Jokhé said, "Mauni, You sometimes drive us to embarrassment. What should I say to you? If you need household tools or weapons for battles, tell me. I am ready for that." After taking a long breath, he said, "A battle is marriage in itself. We would know procedures, if the brides won in a battle needed them. Why do we need procedures for that? Isn't a battle always done by abiding with procedures?"

The listeners found Jokhé's words interesting.

Moving around, the slate now came to Birasé. He said outright, "Mauni, do not stage a show. Tell who is needed to do what at which moment. Or, if you need shoes, jackets, caps, bags or belt according to age, gender, place, work, reason or occasion, let me know. I can prepare one for each. That is the only skill I have. This is my procedure; this is my rule."

He said with a tinge of pride, "Even if we don't follow the right rules, we beget worthy children. Why do we need a procedure none of us knows?" With added excitement, he said in mockery, "I am a person that rejoices in flesh. I know the procedure of begetting kids. That's all."

Birasé's words left everyone else laughing. Mauni also burst into laughter. This time, Gola and Kerung laughed for quite a long time. Omu subdued her laughter and leaned on one side.

Mauni reached next to Namché. He rubbed off the script he had shown to others, and showed a new one. It read, "Namché, I hope you certainly know some procedures of marriage. Whatever you know would suffice. Come forward."

"Namché is a youth belonging to a community rich in culture. So, he certainly knows some procedure." This is what the onlookers calculated softly in their minds.

Breaking the pervading silence, Namché said, "Fearing that my family would send me away to become a monk, I ran away from the village. Had I studied the same, I would supervise the ceremony today. At the moment, I don't have any trace of knowledge about marriage. More, if I chant like a Lama in front of these girls, they will take me for a different man and maintain distance with me. Even if I knew the ways of a Lama, I could not dare to profess the same here."

Namché was in excitement; he spoke further, "Mauni, If only one of these three girls falls for me, I shall pose as a Lama for my own marriage. That will make no difference." Trying to strike humor, he added, "If I stay bachelor and move about solemnizing others' marriage, people can call me Hanuman. How can I myself provoke people to call me Hanuman? Tell me."

Finally, Mauni came near to Dhancha and wrote on his slate, "Dhancha, you tell it yourself if there is any way out."

Dhancha said in a high tone, "I am a princely man from Magarat region. I am also a member of a community wherein others observe the procedures and we reap its fruits. More, members of the royal families do not wait for such procedures. If they like someone, they pick up and elope, and make procedures on their own. The acceptances by the society will follow later, gradually. The Kshetris and the Thakuris also followed our ways. Later, as they tilted toward the Aryans, they started appearing different from us. I respect the procedures and make others supervise them, but for myself, I do not do."

"Then?" said Panchashar curiously.

"I picked her from among these many maidens. That way, I have finished the procedure. At the moment, you are my society here. These friends of Kerung, for me, are similar now. I mean, you make what my society is. You are my elders and youngsters. You are my refuge."

He paused for a while and resumed modestly in a different tone, "Please do certain procedures. This is what I expect. That shall make me mentally settled, and Kerung shall feel you have endorsed her marriage. That shall make her happier, and she shall consider herself a member of our community."

He took a short break and said, "My friends said whatever they feel. Maybe the remaining friends have similar things to say. The sayings of everyone are true and rational in their own places. They have enough places to prove them right. On my part, I lack time. So, let not the occasion we have in hand slip off. I lay this request with you all,"

Dhancha stood with his hands folded. Kerung followed suit.

Kerung looked really like a princess, even as tinge of coyness bedecked her countenance. In reality, she was clad in a bride's attire and make-up. Early that morning, she had been summoned with honor, in a well-made form, near the spot where fresh, raw mud had been dug out in the garden to complete some rituals. Kerung was aware of this, and Dhancha too was ready to become an actor in this drama directed by Mauni.

"Do you have anything to say?" wrote Mauni, showing the slate to Panchashar.

"Enough of entertainment now! Maybe these friends pine for the scene to change now. We have smelt many mouths; resolved it yourself now," said Panchashar, easing the issue.

"Just a moment." Signaling with his hands, Mauni walked close to Bekha and showed his slate that read, "Bekha, come forward if you want to perform a part or enact a fragment of the marriage procedure. Tell your girl if she has any idea. This is an opportunity at our hands. This is also an occasion of joy. Else..."

"No 'else...' There is no need to ask anyone anymore. Everything is ready, and the hero and his heroine are with us. Finish the procedure in the way you can and let's move toward feasting," the mouths therein said.

Mauni signaled everyone to be silent. Then he turned toward Bekha and asked him to concentrate.

Bekha said, "We could not ensure the presence of Gubhaju or Dyaubhaju here. Else, our marriages are interesting. Our procedures are equally thrilling. On my part, I know none of them. All I know is how to cue her. The only procedure I followed is that. Ha ha ha..."

Bekha wound up his sentence, laughing like a fool.

Mauni came forward, bringing a change in his form and action. He closed his eyes and invoked the big-bellied god considered the common son of two mothers. Then he bowed to Brahman, the chief god of creation, Vishnu, the chief god of the department of preservation and Rudra, the chief god of the department of destruction with reverence.

Mauni also mentally prayed to Sun, the eye of the world, and Moon, the god of the heart. Members of both the communities carefully watched the concentration and deep engagement of Mauni, who sat in the ritual pedestal built at the garden.

Mauni also invoked the seven planets. He spelt the names of the *dikpals*, the guards of all the ten directions[46]. He also did honorary invocation of the gods in other realms, not sparing the chance to

---

[46]   four major directions, the interstitial directions between them, the up and the down in the vertical axis make the direction ten

show his reverence to the Yaksha, Kinnar, Badi and Gandarvas' personality. He also mentally prayed to the earth, water, heat, wind, sky, the local deities, nature and Goddess Pathivara and worshipped them all. He then opened his eyes and gave a sign instruction to Omu. Omu immediately unrolled a painting of the Buddha and showed it to everyone. Mauni bowed to the painting. All those present their followed Mauni in showing their reverence to the Buddha.

After having completed the marriage ritual in minute and detailed way, Mauni took two long breaths, inhaling cool air. Then he wrote on the slate, "Prepare *charu*[47] in the basket there. You follow whatever I do. Also ask the girls to do the same."

He signaled something to Omu again. Omu explained in Tibetan the process the girls were expected to follow.

He wrote, "Om swaha[48]!" and made some incantations.

All others followed, "Om swaha!"

Offering the *charu* in the fireplace, Mauni again changed, "Om swaha!"

Others said the same, offering *charu* to the ritual fire.

Mauni said something to Omu in sign language. Omu said to her friends, "He is going to chant the blessings now; let's maintain silence."

Kerung and Dhancha were still standing. Mauni signaled Omu about something again. Omu said, "Kerung, hold the hand of your man and lead, and you two move around the fireplace three times. After that, present yourself before Mauni to take his blessings."

Mauni kept writing his blessing on the slate, and explain its essence to Omu in sign language. Omu repeated the same in Tibetan, translating it. The context turned out to be really interesting.

Everyone present there sang the phrase '*barasya badhya bitanoni bhutim*[49]' collectively, wishing the new couple all happiness. Getting

---

[47]   *charu* is the mixture of cereals, incense, lentils, jawar seeds, ghee etc. offered to the fire in a religious Hindu ritual

[48]   This is a Sanskrit segment that means, "Here we offer to the ritual fire."

[49]   Let God, through this bride, ensure the progress of the bridegroom (in Sanskrit)

a signal from Mauni, Omu spoke in the middle, "Mauni would explain its meaning later in the dining hall."

"The marriage is over!" wrote Mauni on his slate. He added, "Visit the monastery some time later and take blessings from the Lama there. Also complete the procedure there. Also take Kerung's consent; see what she has got to say."

"We all will go," said Dhancha.

"That's right; we all will go," said others in a single voice.

Mauni added, "Now onwards, we are bound by the relations of *solta* and *solti*[50] and the feelings of goodwill and love that entail these relations. In that case, we can see one another, albeit with some degree of obstinacy and some right. However, let there be alertness toward this rationale. We are in a foreign country." This way, he sowed the seeds of romance.

Standing form the wedding pavilion in the garden, Mauni wrote, "This marriage was accomplished in the presence of fire, scriptures and the society as witness. I now request the deities, invited here for that purpose, to kindly return to their rightful abodes. I thus wind up this ritual."

Omu interpreted the things he had said in sign language: "The bride and bridegroom shall dine with us in the same dress they are in."

Mauni sent a signal again. Omu explained it again, "Since now, you shall stay together in the adjacent room"

While explaining, Omu stopped for a while. Seemingly remembering a forgotten thing, she said, "I shall make a room ready for you. You don't need to worry about it."

Having said this, she pressed close to Kerung and pushed her away from there, catching hold of her by her shoulders. Her eyes were simmering with crystal drops of tears.

"We are done with the construction as well as wedding. If we could return home now, I would also get married. What is left for us to do here now?" said Tyanduké in a compact language.

---

50   brothers and sisters of spouses are one another's *solta* and *solti*

HARI RAJ BHATTARAI

"We await the feast now," said Melamchi, even as she arrived at the marriage pavilion on the garden. She added, "I shall partake of the marriage feast here today. Day after tomorrow, I shall throw a party to celebrate the wedding between Dhancha and Kerung, right here in this guesthouse. None of you should miss it." As she said this with a gesture of happiness, the atmosphere turned lively.

She scanned at the nuptial gathering thoroughly and brightened up her face. Everyone was there in Tibetan cultural dress. Kerung and Dhancha looked special. Melamchi's looks were such that she was perhaps trying to derive ample degree of visual energy from the environment. From the garden, the nuptial gathering moved toward the erstwhile dining hall and sat down to eat. Melamchi sat down at her usual place like before. Kerung, like before, sat in the line of the maidens. Dhancha occupied a place among men as before, but the two sat across each other like lovers in the first stage of their affairs. Kerung had a pervasive gaze upon Dhancha, seemingly unwilling to see him eclipsed from her eyes even for a moment, but Dhancha, out of shyness, tried his best to stay away from the immediate present. He wanted to free himself from a sort of obscure and unexpressed awkwardness. Was this uneasiness coming from the atmosphere? Was his marriage itself its cause? Or Kerung's youthfulness? Or his own hasty decision? He was himself unaware.

The feast organized by Melamchi had arrangements for everything from food to their servers, from drinks to their distributers, from dancers to those who made others dance, from those who laughed to those who amused others. That night, Lhotse came to become the apple of the maidens' eye through the Sherpa dance he performed. Yet, no girl had been able to win his heart till date. Having four girls on his left and right hand sides each, he amused everyone with his Sherpa dance.

Following this, they could notice private conversations, gestures of love and glimpses of love proposals. The members started getting lost from the site one after another, until only three people were left in the dining hall: Melamchi, Mauni and Panchashar. Omu peeped in from a distance from time to time.

"Oh God, I happened to forget handing over your letter. It's one a horse-riding errand from the palace had left. When he had come in, I had received it on your behalf. He returned. Open it; see what it says," said Melamchi, making calculation of the context.

"If it's in Tibetan or Chinese, I won't be able to read."

"Open it. If you need help, I am there," Melamchi said.

"If it's in Tibetan, even I will be able to understand," wrote Mauni.

"How did you learn Tibetan?" Panchashar aired his curiosity.

"Omu is my teacher. She taught me," wrote Mauni, explaining the fact.

Panchashar unrolled the letter that had been rolled in a cylindrical form. Melamchi ran her eyes over the Tibetan script. Mauni glued his eyes to the Devanagari letters while Panchashar concentrated on the Ranjana script. All three of them understood: The palace had invited them.

On the stipulated day, Panchashar and Mauni, along with their friends, presented themselves at the palace meeting hall. They were on time. Soon Emperor Timur Khan arrived in the meeting hall. The meeting hall had been waiting for the same. All the faces there lit up. The meeting started.

When the formal words of starting were over, the conductor of the meeting said, "The artisans coming from our neighboring country have completed the building according to the wish of our Hwangdi. The building is in pagoda style. In our part of the world, this is the first building of this type. Hwangdi has had its inspection and our experts of different sectors of knowledge have also examined it. All these things have been made public formally."

He added, "May I remind you they have come here at the invitation of Hwangdi. They are eleven in the team."

The speaker looked at Timur Khan once and continued with his speech, "We heartily thank them from the side of Hwangdi, from the side of this meeting, from the side of our country China, and from the side of the people of China. We also extend heartfelt thanks to Nepal, our friendly nation."

There was some whisper, some low murmur, extension of some gaze, and delivery of some silent smiles.

The group of the artisans thought, 'Maybe they are still unaware who among us is the main person.'

Emperor Timur said, "By building such a beautiful building, you have enhanced my glory. That way, you gave me a chance to celebrate this grandeur. For this, I thank you on my personal behalf and also on behalf of the royal palace."

Adding to his speech, he said, "I dedicated this newly constructed building to the people of China as a gift to them from the side of the nation. I think you are aware of that."

The workers nodded suggesting that they knew of it, and said, "Yes."

"Build yet another well-furnished building for me now. I shall make it my personal residence or the palace," said Timur Khan in such a way that there were no options.

Panchashar and Mauni shook their heads silently. Other members of the team stared at them, quite stupefied. They even pinched one another, for they were packing up their stuff to leave China. In fact, they had made all preparations to move homeward.

"You should yourself select the construction site. Move around and see."

Timur Khan expressed his mind in a clear way.

On hearing this proposal from the Emperor, Panchashar just shook his head without uttering any word.

Mauni immediately showed his slate: "Speak carefully when you speak for your friends. Do not say anything against their interest and welfare. Let not their freedom be curtailed. Let no wall erect in front of their freedom."

"Majesty, we have not yet been able to acquaint ourselves with the topography and nature here," said Panchashar, seemingly neglecting Mauni's slate though he read it, or acting not to have seen it. He continued, "For such a building, we need to have a good study of the productivity and seasonal cycles of fruits, leaves, wood, herbs and trees that give shade and fragrance."

The fellow artisans who sat in line were now worried, apprehending that Panchashar would yoke them again to labor, and were thus in a state of restlessness. They started talking among themselves. Mauni also bore similar worry for all his friends, doubting that Panchashar would drag them into a hassle.

Besides the high officials of the palace, the meeting also had the presence of senior citizens, social workers, businessmen, religious leaders, tantrics, folklorists, experts of art, historians, meteorologists, archeologists, experts of architecture and other scholars. In the same way, on one side of the meeting hall were the queens, prominent women from the town and their attendants, while on the other, there were writers, monks and professors. With such people, this meeting of Emperor Timur Khan was really graceful and august, but the Nepalese artisans appeared mum, beset by their own personal problems. For these reasons, though they were all present there, they were unaware of the significance and specialty of the meeting.

In other words that sounded simpler and more direct, Panchashar articulated his conclusion: "For constructing a spectacular building, we need to have a thorough inspection of the nature of water, soil, air, positions of planets and stars, etc. More, the royal construction undertaking should not be detrimental to any unit of the society, culture and natural environment. Only then do we look for the auspicious moment to start the work and determined the placement of the main entrance. For these reasons, we need a long time to materialize our commitment."

Inspired by his ignorance and pride, Timur Khan said to himself, 'Had I pointed a spot and asked him to construct the building, he would start straightaway as before; this time, he is annulling my entire thoughts by bringing up a myriad of issues. By job, he is an artisan but by words he is like Brahma…"

Mauni went on listening to each and every word of Panchashar. Other friends were physically there, granted; but none could tell what their minds were up to. Some among the members present in the meeting considered Panchashar's words and thoughts wise and useful, because the meeting had the presence of experts from different disciplines. By reading the gestures on Hwangdi's face, they would instantly tell that he was not happy with what Panchashar had been telling.

"He is an artist of extraordinary talent. It's indubitable that the work of construction has its bearing with many things. This man is not an artisan; or say, he is not just an artisan. He deserves to be a guru to each one of us here. His knowledge can be an energizer for all of us.' With such thoughts, many patrons praised Panchashar secretly.

"Isn't he trying to escape, citing unnecessary complexities and explaining the task as impossible?' Timur Khan thought.

Mauni took no time in comprehending that Timur Khan was impatient, and at times quite cross with untoward rage and evil thoughts rising inside his mind. He concluded internally, "Hangdi, by this token, is an Emperor only for a name's sake. He doesn't, at all, have the wisdom, patience and farsightedness worthy of a king. Can we ever imagine a king without intellect and knowledge?' He started concentrating on the personality of Timur Khan even deeper.

With utmost patience, Panchashar explained further, drawing in other contexts: "Majesty, if I had a scholar and an expertise of art who had mastery over different subjects and places, my task would be easier in finding the right place for the construction. He has to take me to different places and show various locations."

'God, he is killing us…' said all other Nepalese artisans in a voice only they could hear.

With crimson eyes, Panchashar glared at his friends. Then he gave continuity to his plea: "Otherwise, a building as willed by Your Majesty can come up at any location, but if the climatic condition and nature become unmatched, the building shall have no significance, nor will it be suitable for use by the humans."

The attendees of the meeting were both impressed and satisfied with the classical, pragmatic and multidimensional explanation about the site of a building. They had nothing to say on it from their sides. They had no opportunity to play any role other than filling up the meeting hall, resorting to silence, according assent, sitting stupefied and fulfilling a ritualistic obligation while coming and going, because, those days, the Emperor was their biggest hurdle. He had got a tiptoe about Panchashar's intellect and farsightedness. He had discovered that he was a matchless artisan, filled with genuine self-confidence.

In the meeting hall, even those senior honorary members from the days of Emperor Kublai Khan were present. One could see them weary due to sickness and old age at times. Seeing their condition, other attendees wanted to see the meeting ended very soon.

"Don't prolong the issue," wrote Mauni on his slate, and showed it to Panchashar. Acting to pause, Panchashar moved two steps backward. The members were impatient to hear the resolution of the meeting from the mouth of Timur Khan himself. In the fashion of a close confidante, a man pressed close to the Emperor and spoke something in his ear. Timur thought for a while, looked all around and discussed the meeting. Then he stood from his place. Others followed suit and moved toward their destinations. Panchashar was left stupefied.

Mauni wrote, "The palace always wants to make itself a mystery. That is not a big thing, but a trait. Do not be panicked."

While coming out of the meeting hall, Panchashar appeared gloomy, while Mauni was listless. Others criticized, taking it for an absurd show. The environment appeared dull. They felt as though they had lost their destination.

Melamchi was alone in the guesthouse. She was waiting for the artisans to return. The day had waned into dusk. So she lit a huge, spherical Chinese lamp '*donglong*' and hung it at its usual place in the dining hall.

The neighing of the horse outside could be heard from inside too. Melamchi stood from her place and walked up to the door, apparently impatient to welcome the newcomer. The artisans entered the guesthouse in quick paces; she scanned the face of each of them. She could not trace the type of gracefulness she was expecting on any of their faces.

She went in and sat near the dining table, the same place she usually occupied. The maidens entered after tying the horses in their stables and presented themselves in front of Melamchi, having cleaned their faces and limbs.

Melamchi said, "I have made the food ready. Make some hot drink or soup and serve."

Some girls started serving meal, while others got busy lighting the lamps. Kerung didn't show much interest. Gola came forward with added agility. Omu started inspecting things in the fashion of an experienced teacher.

"Omu, let me tell it to you: go and tell every artisan that dinner will be ready some time earlier this evening," said Melamchi with respect. She then drew a long breath and added, "Ask all the girls to come to me immediately for a while."

Melamchi could not see the usual grace on the countenance of Panchashar and Mauni that evening. So she herself appeared partially grave. She speculated that something adverse to their interest had happened. She let the bevy of girls sit in front of her and said, "I don't really know the context, but all the workers appear appalled. It seems they are in deep mental anxiety. They are all in gloom. Therefore, my only request with you is this: Do whatever that pleases them. They must appear in mirth like the one they had before. Devour the distaste and lethargy in their minds and fill them with joy."

Gola said, "You happened to be gnawed by such a trivial thing. Making them happy is not a big thing, you know. If we all get together, there is nothing that cannot happen."

"Come on, Omu. You also share your hand. What to talk of Gola; she is always ready. You all volunteer, giving everyone equal importance, and make them happy."

"Put the board of 'Festive Night' on the dining table and move this one to a distance, there. It's rather too big," said Melamchi, giving directions. The board was in Tibetan language.

The artisans gathered in the dining hall. Omu said 'Festive Night' in sign language. Mauni also presented himself there, letting a flowery smile mount on his lips.

The maidens were in informal and free dresses that evening. They looked plain and simple. Their natural beauty opened up in such unexaggerated dresses, without any make-up. On top of that, they had the beauty of their age, the charm of their speech, gestures and bantering, the culture of their service and goodwill and their guiltless, simple and liberal thoughts, and the beauty of the processional motion drove always the gloom and dejection that had lingered since the time they left the palace. Materially, at this hour, the presence of the grown-up girls had become an unfailing weapon to vanquish all sorts of hassles and impediments, and restlessness and dejection in a dramatic manner. In this regard, these dancing Tibetan maidens had upheld the meaning and primacy of the word '*Trivishtakam*[51]' at this moment.

It's true that except in a few exceptional cases, the number people who do not accept the seductive invitations of fairy-like maidens as soon as they come in front of their eyes is negligible. All of them gave up their worries and sorrows; doubts and trepidations. They all landed on the present and concentrated for collective amusement. The maidens themselves fed the foods and drinks to the artisans. By then, the boys also had learnt that they should pay back for the favors. So, they also fed the maidens accordingly, requesting them, pleading to them and pleasing them. The feelings of friendliness and belief became even more profound.

Guindé took out his *sahnai* and played a short folk tune based on a song. Then he wiped the end of the *sahnai* and handed it over the Mauni, apparently making a plea. Mauni played the same tune on it. Birasé joined with his song. Guindé started dancing. Others

---

[51]   Ancient name of Tibet, which envisions Tibet as a part of heaven

clapped accordingly. One played the tambourine; another played the *madal*. The song resounded in their throats and *sahnai*:

*Lhasa ramro bainsaka thitile, bainsa ramro haubhau
ra bolile
Aaune gara barpeepal chautari, gasaun maya dohori
khelera
Sanjhatirai deurali kataunla, godulima paila sarera
Nalau taka aankhama ainale, bhagai lanchhu soltiko
natale
Tibbatako gham-pani ramro chha, maya timra mann
sarai chamro chha
Kasko jodi kasto chha jandina, mero jodi kamti ta
mandina
Hunchha bhane mai aajai laijanchhu, natra bhane
ghumba mai roidinchhu*

[The youthful maidens make Lhasa a beautiful place, while gestures and voice make one's youth lovable. Do come to the *peepal* and banyan mound at times; let's play duet and fall in love. Toward the evening, we can cross *deurali*[52], if we set in motion our first step at dusk. Do not let the sun's reflection in a mirror fall into my eyes; I shall lift you away, calling you *soltini* by relation. The weather in Tibet is beautiful, but your heart, my love, is extremely stubborn. I don't know how others' partners are, but my partner is no less anyway. If you say yes, I will elope with you straightaway. If not, I will weep right here at the monastery.]

The program ended joyfully.

---

[52] a wayside shrine, usually an erected stone, where the travelers offer flowers and leaves to the forest deity, wishing for themselves a safe journey

Early next morning, the group of girls got ready to visit a monastery, together with the bride and the bridegroom. Omu also proposed the boys to join them. The boys got ready to accompany them to the monastery. But Melamchi decided to stay out.

On reaching the monastery, they first completed the ritual: lighted the wick-lamp, whirled the prayer wheel and made several rounds of the monastery chanting '*Om mane peme hum…Om mani padme hum…*'

All the faces appeared contented. The chief Lama of the monastery blessed the newlywed couple formally with scriptural procedures. He sprinkled holy water on them and blessed them for happiness and prosperity. More, in the feast organized by the monastery in their honor, the chief Lama himself took part, enhancing the glory of the event. This event turned out to be a significant one in their community, and people talked about it till a long time later. People believed that the monastery and Lord Buddha himself had great blessings and mercy upon the newlywed couple. This must be reason why everyone appeared extremely pleased. They enjoyed a lot, and returned before it was late.

***

Panchashar was shocked to see Melamchi in the outfit of a special horse-rider. Several thoughts started rising and falling in his mind.

Melamchi picked two of the best horses from the stable and ordered to get them ready in such a way that it would reflect a formal royal event. She mounted on a pure black horse with a white spot on the forehead and reached the guesthouse, leading a mare, brown in color. This was the only role she played for the day.

Melamchi alighted from the horse and hooked the harness nearby. Panchashar watched her repeatedly from top to toes, and from toes to top again. He could recognize her not from her dress but merely from her face. When he had had a glance for her, he had failed to tell her. In the outfit of a formal horseman, she looked like the chief commander of an army.

He lightly thought, 'This means, our days here are numbered. What could be the mystery behind sending up away to Kantipur without prior notice? I would return to my homeland with all joy, but they are forcibly trying to justify themselves. They should ask for my opinion at least once; at least a hint should have been given.'

Panchashar was a man who neither bore any ill-feeling toward anyone, nor saw any blot on others' personalities. His mind, however, had become mean today. He thought low, and on seeing Melamchi said, 'She is a tricky magician. She knows why I am returning home in such haste. It would suffice, if she had hinted that we would be obliged to return. That would make us mentally ready. Isn't it an extremity of unhealthy behavior and selfishness on the part of her community to bear not even a trace of goodwill for us, even after such a long stay and prolonged friendship?'

Panchashar's mind was totally turbulent. He turned introvert and extrovert, turn by turn. The glimpses of Kantipur, Lalitpur and Bhadgaon started flashing in the mirror of his mind.

He started remembering his village and neighbors. He briefly recalled the sylvan route from Kantipur to Koshi bank, and the segment up to Menchyayem, via an ashram to Budhasubba Temple. He remembered Siddha Kirat, Limboo culture, loving Kirat people and the guiltless, pure, warm and intimate love of Sanjhang and Teejhang, and analyses their disinterested sacrifices. He was moved to emotions, when he thought, 'They must be waiting for my return till this day.'

Melamchi took no time to comprehend Panchashar's feelings and the mentality they concealed. Today, she didn't see the type of excitement and joy Panchashar used to exhibit on seeing her before. She surmised that Panchashar was trying to stay inert, taking her presence as mysterious or being unable to explain its purpose. Knowing that Panchashar was caught up in a snare of fear, doubt and mystery, she ended up the prolonged stillness, speaking with ease as always, "Listen to me, Pan! The dreams sometimes signal straight things, and sometimes reverse."

The sentence left Panchashar disturbed. He grew frantic. He concluded that he had never been pained to this extent before. Panchashar chose patience in order to keep himself safe from this inauspicious trap.

Seeing that some coolness had mounted on his personality, Melamchi said in her bid to assure him further, "I came here ready, because the state administration assigned me to accompany you in field visit and inspection."

With this, Panchashar returned to his previous state of mind altogether, and appeared cool. It appeared as though a man, who had lost his way in the forest, had just come out into a human village safe, and was fully at rest. After they had usual conversation for a while, the feeling of intimacy and belief between the two returned to its previous state. The dilemma and doubts that had brewed up a while ago disappeared. Both changed the pace of their respiration and got engaged in exchanging deep love.

Melamchi helped Panchashar to put on a horseman's dress and shoes. She had brought all those things with her. Without his notice, she planted a quick kiss on the horseman, clad beautifully in the chivalric dress. Though the kiss was beyond description, it was undoubtedly loving, quick, brief and fondly. It also was like a game, more like the advertisement of ease and intimacy. Maybe it contained invitation and welcome to a certain moment later, or invocation to the pool of love! Or, was it a hearty communication of amorous drives, or a lip profession without contentment, or else a valedictory gesture? If not a complete signal of a rightful act, how could the context ever be explainable?

"Pan, you look so stunning today that it seems I will have hard times bringing you safe home from others' eyes." Once again, Melamchi stared at Panchashar, running her eyes from his head to feet.

"All these games are yours; yours are the entire plans," he said in brief. Melamchi did not pass any remark. That was the most beautiful thing at the moment. She accepted Panchashar's comment in a healthy manner and said with a stunning smile, "You should pay me back. Else, it will go on mounting, and one day, stop altogether."

"Fine," he said, without trying to understand what he was supposed to pay back and why.

Though they would take two complete months to visit spots that could be surveyed on a single day, they made a plan only for a month. The spots thus inspected lay inside Beijing only. Yet, they could not find a satisfactory plot.

The same horses that had been used on the first day came back today. Thinking of reaching out to spots rather far-off, Melamchi had brought them out. She also had a mule that carried the necessary stuff. She anchored the horses outside, and entering the guest house said, "We shall go a little far today to see the sites. Pan, you get ready."

Looking at the maidens, she said, "Also set my breakfast for me. I will eat here and go."

The breakfast was almost ready. All the artisans had occupied their places for breakfast. She also sat in her usual place.

"What do you mean by far? How far? How many miles?" asked Panchashar, facing Melamchi.

"We can reach in one day, if we move fast. There are many places to inspect. So we might take around a week to find the right spot for the construction." Melamchi made it clear.

Mauni immediately showed his slate: "One day each to go and come; one day for rest; three days for seeing the sites. This must be the arithmetic of a week."

He showed it to everyone and erased. Everyone stared at one another vacantly.

"I won't go alone, leaving my friends behind. We can always return here in the evening. Let's not go with plans to stay out. In fact, I am not at all interested to go." Panchashar ended the context by polling in his friends.

"Friends, what do you say to it? If they are taking all of us, shall we go out to see places? That way, we both see villages, and refresh ourselves. What's wrong in that?" Birasé said.

"Do not mention of going anywhere out."

"True. It's better to stay home instead of moving out anywhere."

"What should we be doing here?"

"It has been so long since we left home."

"Jokhé, you said it so well. Guindé also aired his grievances. We could also sense that Birasé is frustrated. Let's now allow Tyanduké Subba to speak." This time, it was Bhalé who broke the silence.

"Look; we came here after the kings talked among themselves. Actually, we were sent here; we didn't come on our own. Did we have the guts to land here on our own? So when you speak, do so, considering its pros and cons. We should talk for everyone's welfare. No one should be pushed in any sort of fix. Melamchi has come here; she is our protector at the moment. She should listen to us; she can understand our minds." Thus, Tyanduké put forward his view.

"Lhotsé, why don't you speak out your view?" Panchashar said.

"What should I say? I have no complaint. Jethi and Kanchhi are very much here with us. They are happy and so am I. I am not in a hurry to return home, nor do I have any difficulty staying here more. I enjoy wherever I go. This is what makes my philosophy." Lhotsé made his position clear.

Lhotsé and two maidens he loved had been leading yet another romantic context, because all the artisans there had been aware of the affairs among them, and each of the maidens had given a nod to his romantic advances and pragmatic strength. In brief, a maiden could rarely find a robust man like him. In reality, Lhotsé was such a man in that age and time, who could be termed the full and perfect incarnation of Kamdev[53].

The Sherpas are one of the most distinguished communities of Nepal with a history of their own. So the members of this

---

[53]   Kamdev, according to Hindu mythologies, is the God of sex

HARI RAJ BHATTARAI

community were not inferior to others from any angle. Lhoté was a living instance of this claim.

"What does Sainla say? Let's listen to his mind as well. Brother Ghalé, truly speaking, we have heard you utter no word ever since we landed on Beijing."

This time, it was Bekha who provoked Ghalé.

What could Ghalé say? He was a young man, and was the most attractive and handsome of all men therein. Yet, he had been rendered a loner. No one knew if he didn't want to pick anyone, or the girls didn't like him, finding no virility in him. The only truth everyone knew was that he was rather shy of nature and kept to himself most of the time, singing folk songs or playing on his flute at times. When he started dancing, he continued until the program ended. He always stayed ready to respect the feelings of his friends.

But he said it openly today, "I also need a retreat. But I could not find one. That must be why my friends think I have been left alone. My mind is drawn homeward looking for such a refuge." He was precise in his opinion.

Mauni wrote on his slate, "Speak openly whatever is there in your mind. You are clean of thoughts. Speak, for you can do so."

"Listen to me. The building is one of the central resorts. But that is common to all. But then, our minds no longer reach out to it. So, it can no longer be our purlieu. It has moved away from everyone's mind now."

"Tell more. Your style of storytelling is captivating, and your perspective is objective. Tell us whatever you have seen." This was Mauni's writing.

"For Panchu, Melamchi is another sancturary. He rests his mind in her. Contemplation is where Mauni finds a resting place for his mind. He reaches there to rest." He paused for a while, turned to a different direction and said, "Dhané and Kerung have become each other's comfort. Bekha and Gola have also found the consolations of their hearts."

He now turned his eyes toward Lhotsé and Namché and said, "Culturally and linguistically, Lhotsé appears more enriched. That must be the reason why no one else appears as contented as he is. Namché, on his part, appears happy from without, but has been crushed between two cultures within. Yet, as long as is here, he has been dancing the way it suits, thus spending his time."

"Brother Ghalé, I want to say something out of humor. Hope you won't mind," said Panchashar.

"I won't. I also bantered against some friends a while ago; hope they are not upset. This is a jolly pastime, after all." Ghalé first announced the limits, and gave an outlet.

"It would have been better, had you also found a resort for your heart as long as you lived here."

"That would have been wonderful. But I lagged behind in picking one. But my friends did. They not only built the building, but also showed the guts to bear other major responsibilities. Some developed wonderful love relations. I am satisfied with all these things. I won't fret and regret."

"And?"

"And, the maidens here happened to play to the game of marriage with other maidens. My share was forfeited…"

Ghalé laughed all his heart out.

Mauni wrote, "Brother Ghalé! What is your opinion about Guindé, Jokhé and Birasé?"

"What opinion would I have? Truly speaking, theirs is an altogether different world. So I didn't choose to enter that domain and disturb my mind to get lost in an obscure path. But their opinions mysteriously match, in belittling others and aggrandizing themselves. Beyond that, I didn't find them making any intellectual progress. I consider that my ignorance. Usually, I love to keep myself away from obscene conservations. That is perhaps a weakness on my part."

"I don't consider your estimation wrong," Mauni wrote.

"The talks were not only good but interesting as well. But the context digressed elsewhere. That made the issue stuck. Melamchi has been waiting. What shall we do now?" Panchashar said.

"You go, planning to return in two weeks. Melamchi will also approve of your plans, if you promise to be back in two weeks. Till then we shall be here. We shall eat whatever is cooked and move out to see places whenever we want. Two weeks will pass in a trice. We shall also visit the pagoda at times. Why worry?" said Ghalé, giving the problem an outlet. Drawing his conclusions, he said, "I still have desire to see the White Pagoda constructed by Balbahu, Brother Araniko. Considering it a pilgrimage site, I propose that we all should visit it once."

"True. We have spent these many years. Why not spare two more weeks?" someone said.

"No. Let's listen to what Melamchi says. We should follow whatever she instructs. That will be in our benefit," Tyanduké said.

Melamchi was taking part in a prolonged discussion. Announcing her decision, she said, "I ask for one month's time at the most from you. Till then you stay here and enjoy. The girls shall take good care of you. I shall instruct them before I leave." After a short break she said, "If there is a need, I will call Mauni somewhere, or we will ourselves return."

Tyanduké said, "I am satisfied with Melamchi's proposal. Allow Panchashar to go, but let him return within a month. Maybe she won't elope with him."

After a hearty laughter, he added, "In our practice, a girl doesn't take a boy away; the boy does. Keep Subba's words in mind. Ha ha ha…"

Panchashar and Melamchi left.

They could not, however, find a proper site for construction, even after a thorough survey of lands in the north and south.

Panchashar was firm in his commitments. So, there was no slash, even of a small degree, in his morale. But Melamchi had started feeling physical exertion. But she never allowed her zeal to slash in assisting Melamchi's aim and Panchashar's construction plans. She was not expected to look tired."

"I have understood what sort of a plot you are looking for," said Melamchi, carefully finding a gap.

"What sort? Tell me where such a plot is," said Panchashar curiously, lending special care to her words. With a background, he further said, "You are not merely my supporter and co-traveler; you are also a part of the royal authority, a unit of it. After such a long time of friendship and cooperation, you have fully understood what my interest and perspectives are. This is what I believe."

Melamchi was quite elated, listening to what Panchashar was saying. Yet, she stayed quiet, allowing Panchashar to speak.

Panchashar drew in a long breath and stayed quiet. Then he resumed, "At this moment, I am impatient to listen to you. Tell me where such a spot is. Where did you consider is the best place? I want to release by burden at the very spot. Let's fix it wherever it is. Do take me to that very spot now. Will you?"

"That's fine; we shall hold the night tomorrow at that spot. We shall be happy to construct the building in the direction you suggest."

"That's a matter of joy for me. But Melamchi, how can you claim that I shall like that spot?"

"From your interest and psychology, I have ascertained this. And this is an ordinary thing. We don't need to consider it anything special and lay high stress on it," she said, without hankering after options.

In reality, Panchashar's interest was, at the moment, more important for Melamchi than the Emperor's mansion. This could as well be a matter of joy for herself. Yet, she could feel a gradual but mild pain flowing inside her unknowingly, mainly because of uncertainties rising out of the awareness of social and regional differences.

Her conviction was that if a royal mansion was erected, the people of that region would be in utter distress. Many of them will be obliged to leave the place, leaving behind their land and property. They would be forced to leave their houses and homestead for a nominal cost. It was predictable that they would be forced to vacate with no worthy return. Who knew they could as well be forced to run in order to save their lives?"

With such thoughts tormenting her mind, Melamchi grew restless and asked herself, 'How, if going to that very place turned out detrimental?' She looked quite distressed. She again thought, 'If I myself invite misfortune to the people here, I won't be able to pardon myself.'

Consoling herself, she thought, 'Yet, I have spoken about it. I should not retract from my promise. I should not embrace defeat.'

She treated her mind herself. She returned to her earlier state and mindset, and looked elated.

Panchashar, on his part, did not have any idea of the rise and fall of turbulences inside Melamchi.

***

CHAPTER NINE

T HE HORSEMEN REACHED near the outside wall of a building that appeared miles away from them, a few hours before sunset. They rested in a nearby *chautari* for a while. The premises of the mansion were very wide. From the entrance on the wall, the horsemen took about half an hour to reach the main building.

A matter of surprise was that, the Great Wall of China, one of the Seven Wonders of the World, had been modeled after this wall. Like the Shah kings of Nepal who ignored the Buddha's birthplace and indirectly supported a plan to build a replica of the Buddha's birthplace in a foreign land, the rulers in China had also been making this wall—historically the oldest, and materially an example and ideal for the upcoming age—equally neglected.

The clear, blue sky, the tantalizing touch of the slanted sunrays, the rapturous chirp of the birds, and the deep and light greenness over the sylvan plants and crops are invaluable assets of this plant for its people. One is never satiated watching them; no one ever wants to return from here. It has a hypnotizing attraction, as far as one's eyes can notice.

There were freshly cultivated crops somewhere, while some other places, one could see extensive meadows for grazing cattle. The placid and classical humming of the serpentine brooks, and the gradual darkness of the evening mounting on the sky above were sights too spectacular for human experiences to describe. At this moment, human language fell short of the capacity to describe this miracle.

Panchashar looked everywhere, contemplated deeply and said to himself, 'If heaven is not merely happiness but also beauty, this place is perhaps heaven. And the people living here are gods.'

He paused for some time and said emotionally, 'How beautiful is this part of the world! If it were possible, I would lift and carry it with me.'

Melamchi concentrated to reading the joy spilling over Panchashar's eyes and the thrill in his heart.

"Melamchi, shall I tell you about a thing I like most?"

"Do tell. I doubted if you have lost your voice. Come on; speak. Do not maintain such long silence. That makes me feel awkward."

This, she said, amidst a different sort of smile.

"The changing hue of time, when light gradually gives way to darkness is a sight I love to watch without blinking my eyes. In the same way, I also love to watch, without the wink of my eyes, the slippage of the night to make a way for daylight. I attempt to make it my daily routine, but in vain. For that reason, I often feel I have been deprived of a rare bliss. How do you feel about that?"

"Your words are attached to my feelings. As long as we stay here, we will be able to derive such bliss from nature. We have enough time in our hands here. We also have enough space. There also is a chance that we ourselves will get lost in the spectacular beauty."

She stopped. Bringing a slight change in the rate of her breath, she said, "The beauty of life in the countryside is of a different sort. We are free of the urban complexities here. Look at ourselves; aren't we carefree, independent and self-governed?"

Winding up the issue, she said, "Let's go. We must find a shelter in time."

The horsemen reached the main entrance on the wall, riding along a serpentine trail. This way, they left the main trail. When they were though half the path inside the wall, they were stopped by two manacing dogs. The horses were disturbed. The riders found it difficult to keep themselves in place on the horses. Melamchi shouted at the dogs, calling them names. They were silent. For a while, they showed off their self-respect, and started leading the horsemen ahead.

Panchashar was now reassured. Melamchi appeared at peace. Toward the end of that dusk, they came to the courtyard of the building, asking for shelter for the night.

It was evening, and everywhere people were lighting spherical Chinese lamps. The scripts on the outer surface of these lamps hung equidistant from one another were hieroglyphic, each letter consisting of a picture and communicating an idea. Panchashar interpreted them in his own way: 'The four parts of the lamps, perhaps represent life, struggle, power and achievement. They cannot be meaningless things."

There were lamps of a bigger size on the outer side of the building, while those in the inner parts were smaller. The sight of these luminous lamps made an onlooker think that there are little Buddha and his mentor monks, meditating for world peace.

Inside the mansion, Panchashar followed the ways of the dogs. He entered a decent room, where his eyes fell on a carpet that had been spread there. He internally praised the embroidery on the carpet that bore a meaningful combination of paintings and colors. The type of artistic carving he saw on the panes of the doors and windows and on the beams and rafters were types he had not seen even in the Emperor's palace. He had not seen it in any other part of the royal city, either. He could see no metal stuff there that had not been embellished with one kind of art or another. Be it the art worked on wooden vases or on the hard stones, these timeless art works were, naturally unimaginable at the present time. Panchashar drew inferences from his own side: 'This house must be that of patron or art of a great artist himself. This doesn't seem to be the handiwork of a single generation."

He then ran eyes on the huge paintings of men and women clad in attractive dresses and ornaments. Then he concluded, 'This house is, in itself, a museum of the Tibetan art. On seeing the cultural affluence of the house, he felt, that was the resident of the old settlers of that place. The house was a grand manifestation of the micro-history of the cultural grandeur of the whole of China. In fact, China is itself rich in art and cultural excellence. Still, why does the Emperor keep on inviting artisans from a foreign land to build buildings?'

Melamchi was busy in her own world. Two young maidens had been deployed for attending to evening needs. The two brother-like dogs of the same color kept guard.

Panchashar was in complete leisure. He was thinking, 'The subjects and the rulers have completely different views about artwork. Most of the people are patriotic; they are lovers of their culture too. When it comes to the rulers, even one fourth of them are not. A ruler's patriotism becomes manifest for his selfish cause. But the people's patriotism becomes manifest for their land, life, culture, belongingness, freedom and rights.'

"Melamchi, are you understanding me? The rulers consider domestic, traditional and ethnic art and culture trivial. So they act to appear different from their subjects by accumulating, consuming and exhibiting foreign material objects. Only a handful of rulers and statesmen are really patriotic, pro-public and supporters of culture. Most of the rulers and leaders are found embarking on wrong trade of things, merely to make their personal treasuries richer. What a swindling behavior. Fie!"

In the meantime, Melamchi showed up. She said, "I beg your pardon; I had been to the stable."

Changing the context, she said, "What new thing did you think of? Tell me. But you have to be brief; not too long."

"I had been speaking for you so long. Weren't you here?"

"I was not."

"You heard my words then?"

"They."

"Who?"

"Who do you mean?"

"These: Norbu and Torbu," she said, signaling at the brother dogs.

For the first time, he sensed that Melamchi was being jocular.

"Now that I am here, I will listen. Tell what you thought."

"I was thinking—the rulers export the glory of their country to foreign lands. The subjects, on the other hand, earn elsewhere and bring it to their countries. What a big difference lies between the two, doesn't it? In fact, the property the rulers or leaders export also rightfully belongs to the public. This is what we can see, if we analyze."

"Why?" she asked, abruptly.

"As soon as there is a slight tremor in their country, they sneak to another country. They had one leg on their land, and the other one in the air ready to land abroad in case there is likelihood of any calamity. There are only a few rulers or leaders, whose both feet are on their own countries. There also are very few that do not sell their souls."

"Go on; I am listening."

"A nation is not merely the soil inside a boundary. It entails life, culture, nature, natural resources, language, art, wealth of all sorts, entire life, underground wealth, and many of such things. If a character or action that oppresses life can be termed 'nationalistic', it must hold good in some other realms. I shall today tell you openly about my view on nation, nationality, national character and perspectives."

Panchashar took a long breath after completing his sentence.

Melamchi said in a formulaic manner, "Conspiracy, oppression, exploitation and revenge are other names of politics. It also entails selfishness and crime. It's itself a shield and a saber too." She added, "Let your statement end there for now. I am extremely tired. Let's first have dinner; we can talk of other things later. Come."

She closed the issue there.

Melamchi didn't pose like a strange guest there. She was not. Everything could have been easy and comfortable for her, by dint of her being a royal employee. Panchashar didn't try to understand this, nor did he try to do it. But in his view, Melamchi was an employee at the palace of Emperor Timur Khan, and a close friend deployed to take care of him, as she had been appearing in the past. But this was only half of the truth; the other half was different.

Panchashar was quite grateful, receiving simple, gentle and easy treatment from her in an intimate way. He had not even imagined that people in China accorded such love to their guests.

This site of construction was cool, like a plan on a river bank in winter. It was in a way moderate in temperature. So they did not need any extra preparation to deal with weather. Such is perhaps the nature of naturally-bestowed comfort.

The oldest man of the house spoke, aiming at Melamchi, "Make good arrangements for our guests. These days, we live in the adjacent house. But don't have a fireplace there. We cook and eat here."

Having said this, the Lama gazed at his wife and children one after another, and got up slowly from his tool, pressing his palm against his knee.

Standing from the side of the fireplace with the help of a stick, his wife said, "If you need anything, tell it to Jimu and Yangsila."

The Lama man and wife went out of the room, coughing like old folks. Jimu and Yangsila posed at the front and back sides with lamps in their hands. The dogs followed.

"This house has a different story. Had you been a writer, you would have written a long fiction about it," said Melamchi, placing her eyes against those of Panchashar and concealed herself. She didn't let her simmering tears expose.

For a while, the words were frozen inside a dictionary. The eyes of their hearts started roaming unimpeded in their worlds of imagination. All that was left there now was a look laden with scintillating, trustful and romantic kind. Albeit for a short time, the environment there turned quite refreshining and joyous.

In the meantime, they heard the paws of the dogs scratched against the floor. The dogs entered panting, with their long tongues tucked out, and sat near the fireplace. Jimu and Yangsila also came in, together with the lamps in their hands. They placed the lamps in their due places and sat near the fire.

On the fur of the dogs that sat vertically, the hue of the flame added its polish.

"Shoo the dog away. Look how he sits; shamelessly," Melamchi said. Rising from her seat, she said, "Pan, I will visit the other house and return soon. Yang, you come with me carrying a lamp."

Melamchi and Yangsila exited.

Making the dog's posture a reason, Jimu giggled for a while. Controlling herself, she said, "You happened to come from Nepal. It has been long since I met anyone coming from there. You are the one I am meeting after a long gap."

"I was wondering how this place had a person speaking such fluent Nepali. You happened to be a Nepali yourself. I was initially surprised. I am happy to find you speak English. You have a sweet voice," said Panchashar, carefully crafting his words.

She was startled.

"Isn't your name Jimu? Where is your home in Nepal?"

Panchashar used the informal pronoun 'timi'—equivalent to English 'you'—not in the language of his mind, but of his soul. But the listener could easily feel the intimacy dissolved in his words.

"My home is at Olangchunggola. I think you came here along that route."

"We did. But the trail was both difficult and appalling."

"Did you also pass through Phungling? We also have some business there."

"I came along Tamor bank. I didn't mount up."

Again she laughed aloud and spoke in mirthful words, "Didn't you *mount up*? Don't you even know how to do it?"

This time, Jimu rendered Panchashar's decent and gentle personality quite weightless. She said, "Also take me along on your way back. I have not found a companion for my return journey."

She was now quite simple and practical.

"How did you reach this place?"

"This is the home of our aunt, my father's sister. I came, because she was alone. Now that Yangsila has come back, she won't be lonely anymore. I can leave." She added, "Let's go together, for we are in good terms. Do not go alone, please."

HARI RAJ BHATTARAI

She laughed out for a while. Composing herself, she then said, "It would do, if I could reach up to Lhasa. Beyond that, most of traders are people we know. I can go with them up to Gola."

In Jimu, Panchashar saw the glimpses of a matchless personality. She said with confidence, "Do not abandon me when you leave. Let this become a deal."

"That's fine. We'll return after I am done with my work."

Jimu brooded for a while and said, "What kind of a friend is Melamchi to you? Will you please tell me?" This time, she looked rather grave.

"She is a good friend. The palace sent her to me. But why do you want to know that?"

"Just!"

She laughed quite high and said, "I want to know if she is a friend who minds if I come close to you." She laughed again.

Melamchi returned together with a dog, a lamp and Yangsila. Even as she rushed in, she said, "What a high laughter it is, Jimu! You can be heard next-door too. Fie!"

"Look at me, Mister Stranger! I happened to be junior to Melamchi by a few seconds. That's why she exercises power upon me. Had I been elder even by a few seconds, I would not have abused or belittle anyone. This much is sure. I would not have boasted that way. I would first make juniors happy and take rest of the happiness for myself. But that doesn't happen with everyone."

Directing her words are Panchashar, Melamchi said, "She is a chatterbox, but as a person, she is quite jolly. Once you start listening to her, you never feel bored. Nor do you realize that you are running out of time for your work. The worth of time, however, depends on how one things about it."

Jimu said in a jocular way, "Melamchi, shall we take a little? We also have a guest today."

"Of what? If it is of millet, I can take one shot, just to respect your request."

"How about our foreign guest?"

"Go and ask him yourself."

Yangsila was starting without blinking her eyes. She fixed her eyes on those of the guest and tried to allure him. She then acted of scratching her own ear, signaling that she was unwilling to ask. Then she shook her head, albeit for a while.

"You all take from the same container. You also take. As for me, I shall only taste. You are the one who shall drink. Come on; hurry up." Melamchi appeared to be in a hurry.

'Does our foreign guest drink? If he declines?' With this thought in her mind, Yangsila disappeared.

With great interest, Jimu started readying the drink.

The bedroom on the third floor of a four-story building looked neat with a befitting carpet on the floor. Inside this special room, one could simultaneously feel excitation and support, mainly because of an environment that could easily arouse the fragrance of a seductive curiosity and romantic fervor. In fact, this room was spared for special guests.

It was a night in the bright fortnight—quite near to the full moon—and so the atmosphere was one that could easily chant one's emotional surge. It was a cool place with veranda on all its sides, constantly guarded by the acute vigil of Norbu and Torbu. It was their duty to give an incoming guest security, trust and assurance of fearlessness. Once inside this house under the refuge of its master, the guests were understood to have glorified their personalities twofold. Melamchi was well aware of this fact.

Targeting at Jimu, Melamchi asked, "Where's Yangsila?"

Placing the drinking water on the table and covering it with a lid, she said, "She has gone to the other house to give Grandpa his pills."

"Call her. You also come with us to the water pool."

Jimu looked at Panchashar once with sharp eyes, and bit both her folded lips once. Panchashar could feel electric current shake his heart. She exited form there in a flash. Panchashar felt he was somehow assured.

The act of taking a dive inside the pool of lukewarm water and rested there for a while had become a part of culture in many places, many countries. A dive into the pool before sleeping had become a part of daily routine for Jimu and Yangsila as well. But then, on the proposal of all four of them going for the dive today, Jimu shot for mysterious sensations in dramatic ethos. In reality, she was most interested in the act, especially at that moment, that particular day.

"Jimu, we will go ahead of you. You come together with Yang."

The way from home to the pool and back home was a wooden trail inside a tunnel. One could not go anywhere else from there. The length of the tunnel road was not very long; it was merely around forty to fifty yards. On both its sides, there were lamps glowing in a myriad of colors. Near to the mouth of the pool, arrangements had been made for closets to change clothes and put cosmetics and ornaments, and for a mound to take rest on.

According to the pool culture, one had no permission to enter with clothes other than a small handkerchief or a patch on the head. It was used to be if there were sweats, though people often used it to conceal their privacy before entering the pool.

For entering the pool, one had to be acquainted with spatial, aerial, photonic and aquatic dresses. Melamchi was adept in them; she didn't have to think of anything. Panchashar made use of all those four attires for the first time and dived in, concealing his groins with the patch of cloth meant for the head.

Jimu and Yangsila also entered, giggling. That moment, Panchashar was so nervous that he could not see them while they were making their entry into the pool. This was not, perhaps, his self-censorship; it perhaps was an act of destiny that didn't let him concentrate on them. But the eyes of Jimu and Yangsila fell again and again on the thick, dark hair on his chest. But he was not aware of that.

Sweating inside the pool is considered success in the bath culture here. In order to sweat, the swimmers dove neck-depth in the pool. In the faint light of the sky-lamp, the faces of the maidens looked like white lotuses blooming in the sky.

The bedroom was adequately wide. One of the beds was beside the larger window, and the other beside the smaller window. The beds were always the same. All they changed were bedspreads.

"Where is my bed," asked Melamchi, directing her question to Jimu.

"I haven't arranged one for you. This one is for our guest. I was willing to ask you and manage one according to your interest. I didn't get time earlier. I rushed to the pool. I will quickly arrange it now. Where do you want it?"

"Make it ready next-doors. Leave it; I will do it myself. Where will you all sleep?"

"There, in the other house. Aunt needs a companion. There's no smoke there. Yang also loves to sleep there."

"From tomorrow, one of you sleep here, if possible. Will you?"

Jimu nodded. Stealing a chance, she had a glance at Panchashar. Then she took a few steps backward, showed her back, and exited. This, Panchashar considered, was an expression of romantic advance, and responded to her looks in a natural way.

Yangsila entered with two pairs of night dresses. Melamchi picked one pair from her hand and said, "Pan, you wear these. I will also change and come."

She went out together with Yangsila.

Jimu returned with a jug of water and said, "Our foreign guest at the moment looks like a bridegroom on honeymoon night. How well the dress suits him! He looks stunning. As for me…"

Melamchi entered in sleeping dress. Even as she was entering, she overheard Jimu's last words. She said, "What were you saying, Jimu? Will you say it again? I also want to hear you."

"I was saying I am very tired. After returning from the pool, I often have no interest to do anything."

Jimu shielded the thing she actually wanted to say. Panchashar had got a hint of her presence of mind.

'I would play the game of marriage all night…' She said this to herself secretly. She could not say it openly due to the presence of Melamchi there. She placed down the water, and paid a killing glance at Panchashar. Whenever Jimu peeked at Panchashar, he could feel electric currents running through him. This time, she left, having fired an even more intense current.

In her imagination, she caught the image of a tree and a climber. At the stroke of a potent wind, the tree fell, crushing the green, adult and soft climber there and then. She conjured this mental image herself and tried to brush it aside before long. But she failed. Immediately, she started imagining another scene to veil the former.

She was a tender spinster, slim and slender. Panchashar, on the other hand was as robust, agile and gaudy bull, though not much of a mismatch. At time, Jimu imagined herself at Melamchi's place and considered herself qualified from all quarters at such occasions. An imagination, sometimes, remains a mere imagination though it occasionally becomes a reality. She partially knew this fact; yet she had not been able to convince herself. Deferring her internal desire to stay close to strong men with thick body hair all over, Jimu started keeping herself away. Practically, this was both natural and necessary, and this had no choice.

"Pan, I want to hear something about our trip today. I am free; I am independent. I can express my mind, and act out my will. You share your experiences, will you? I am also yet to hear the things you told to Norbu and Torbu, aren't I?" said Melamchi, squeezing into her bed.

"What should I share with you? I have become sedated, like someone charmed with bliss. At the time, there is no thought in my mind and heart. I have become peaceful, like a disinterested man in a state of thoughtlessness. I am in an ecstatic state, experiencing the bliss of a different world. You rather share something. I long to hear you speak today."

"What is the secret behind China's decision to invite artisans from a foreign country and get buildings constructed? What is its rationale? Perhaps, it's not merely done to address the king's madness, passion or pride. This seems to have engendered credit as well as trepidation on both sides. Won't you ask how this becomes justified?"

"Those things were there in my mind. I analyzed them on my own; contemplated alone. It would be unwise for me to ask any question. I have my own limitations. Carrying out the director's advice was my own work. But then, once the issue has been raised, let me ask you: had you invited artisans from Nepal merely to get a building constructed? I am sure, this was just a pretext. The goal is different; the accomplishment is somewhere else. Isn't it? You can tell me openly today. Open if there is any veil."

"Certainly. The decoration of the royal city is both transparent and objective, which can be felt by everyone. But underneath the surface, there are secret and far-reaching objectives. Things like bilateral trade relations between the two countries, social, familial, religious and cultural relations and the far-reaching political relations will become solid and stronger. Through mutual trust and help, we can shape a ground and atmosphere from where we can easily vanquish a common enemy. The construction of the building is merely a symbolic bridge to bind our relationship. From here, we will not be able to attain several objectives. They shall also give protection to each other, shan't they? To put it in other words, the construction of the building was an apt plan to bring you and me together. Else, how could we have met? Tell me."

She laughed.

"Chi, I liked your analysis."

She stretched herself.

As for him, he yawned.

***

The house was distinct, and located away from the settlement area. They used horses to reach there, or move away from there. The guests also commuted by horses most often. Since the entire house had a compound of huge walls, it was not easy for it to establish links with the country life in its vicinity. One had to put great efforts for it; a chance had to be awaited. A moment had to be caught.

Once or twice a year, during cultural occasions or social events, collective gatherings were organized. On that occasion, solutions to many issues were sought. For many, such occasions turned out to be beneficial, and so, many people waited for such a moment. The adults considered such occasion a festival of love. They always stayed impatient to partake of the event and get their cravings fulfilled. It's true the adults were in need of matching partners. A youthful heart longs to get exchanged; to get clung to someone. If the longings of the bodies and minds go unfulfilled, they can distract one's musings and conducts, leading to delinquencies. For such reasons, these events organized once or twice a year, turned out to be of great importance for the young ones. The youths appeared waiting for such occasions to reap some gain in order to attain the harvest of their significant attempts and desired goals.

The celibate youths organized competitions on adventurous sports. The unmarried maidens competed among themselves to own the valorous young men. There were times when maidens got kidnapped on such occasions. Materially, during such occasions, many cases of maidens being kidnapped came to limelight.

Those days, many incidents considered unusual these days also took place. But people always sought the goodwill and consent of the most honored and eldest members of the society to seek appropriate and logical solutions to such unhealthy incidents. So, everyone was free to exercise personal interest and right, staying within the purview of social rules and decorum. From the same elders, the youngsters had received the ideal education that they could rise without belittling others.

Melamchi drove away with Panchashar to show the latter a cultural show in her locality. With them was Jimu as well. That was the day of Baishakh Poornima, the full-moon day in the month of April.

Only Panchashar and Jimu came back from the fair. On finding Melamchi missing, the Lama old man speculated she was fell into the clutches of boys. When Jimu confirmed, the old man's speculation came true. Even the Lama's wife heard of Melamchi's absence. The information made her even more anxious.

The old man was obliged to set out in search of Melamchi, at least to appease his wife if nothing else. He made his horse ready. Then he turned to Panchashar and said, "She is a daughter with seamless self-confidence and enough. She doesn't opt to lose in matters that do not concern her, or to take part in such things. She is not even familiar with the word 'losing'. I belief she will show up soon; perhaps she is on the way home. My inner convictions say no one can stop her; she is unstoppable.

Panchashar nodded, seconding the old man's statement.

Mounting up the horse, the old man said, "Jimu, tell your aunt I shall come back with Melamchi.

Making Jimu even more alert, he said, "Take good care of the guests. We can be late in returning."

He whipped the horse with the sole of his boot, and pulled the reins.

***

Melamchi and Panchashar moved toward the forest of Chuli.

The Green Hill, having a medium height, had a sharp apex, like the triangular pile of grains in a container. A meandering road moved up to the top spirally like a serpent. There also was an alternative pathway paved with stones, made especially for those who wanted to make their travel fun. The serpentine road passing midway through the forest was steep uphill, and was meant for those who could walk fast up and down the hill, and were strong. This forest, a reserved area and a park in itself, was the hood and the emblem of consciousness for the inhabitants of this countryside. In fact, it was a place every inhabitant considered a piece of heart. The forest of Chuli appeared eternal and young, nourished by the love, compassionate and considerate conservation from the inhabitants of that part of the world in order to enhance its stability and beauty.

Truly speaking, it was both a significant tourist spot, and the self-respect and existence of the dwellers.

Besides that, it was also a pristine picnic spot. There were stone spouts at places preserved in a natural way. There were simply made fireplaces for cooking, small closets for resting, and wooden benches underneath tree shades here and there. There also were wooden mounts for resting, made with artistic carving, while the spot was also dotted with small playgrounds here and there. For first-time visitors, it was no doubt a seductive place, besides being a romantic and a reserved forest area. The natural balance of flowers, leaves, creepers, shade, light and air made this place optimally warm and cool.

The third sector in the forest of Chuli was a highland, beyond which, there was a stone spout and a wooden bench placed beside that in a bend. From there, one could see an extensive plain, far and wide. So Panchashar dismounted from his horse and asked Melamchi to dismount as well.

The sun was on the descent, just past midway now. The entire earth dazzled in broad daylight. No other thing save a few birds could be seen in the sky. So the earth appeared rich and mature across long distances. The cultivated lands and natural forest gave the landscape a concrete look, like that of a rainbow in seven colors in the fashion of a collage. This made the onlookers stare without a blink, or with eyes wide stretched. In fact, Panchashar was mesmerized by this spectacle one could see from that spot inside the forest of Chuli.

"Melamchi, come and look from here how beautiful that plain there looks!" said Panchashar, resorted to a monologue on his own accords. He added, "That sunlit slope, the river valley there, the top of the hill yonder and the vast plain below! Any spot would do, if the building is constructed on the top of this thick forest, making it face east."

Melamchi was expecting that Panchashar would select that spot. So, on hearing him say so, she returned to senses as though she had just had an electric shock. Her countenance glowed up for a while, only to catch back its pervasive gloom, and she looked listless and dejected again. Panchashar, on his part, looked elated.

"Melamchi, shall I really express you my mind, the thing I really long for?" Panchashar moved two steps forward and added, "The place we have put up presently is no less tantalizing."

Melamchi didn't say anything. In fact, a worry was bothering her mind. And now, she sensed her worry escalating. Then she turned left and right, seemingly looking for a spot she could rest at.

Panchashar walked farther away and said, "Look at the sunlit plain yonder there! Can you see two houses standing together? We shall reach there for resting tomorrow. If you have no objection, we can finalize that spot."

He went on expressing him mind in a monolithic manner. He said, "You are now aware of my interest. Tell how you found my choice. You cannot possibly consider my pick unusual. What do you say?" He articulated his mind in a guiltless and straight manner.

Since the pain in her was mounting, Melamchi sat on an wooden bench nearby, stooping.

Panchashar, on his part, was still gazing at the same flat land with eyes wide open, even as his countenance glowed with brightness. He didn't see Melamchi throw herself on the bench out of acute pain. In fact, he was unaware of it.

Melamchi's horse neighed. It's neighing was strange; it had the admixture of pain. There was restlessness and haste in it. But Panchashar was unaware of all these things.

The horse walked closed to Melamchi and neighed again, expressing some dissent. It stood on its two hind limbs and made utterances of utter dissatisfaction, forcing Panchashar to turn toward itself.

Panchashar made a turn, as though he were waking up from a nap. With alertness, he turned toward the horse. The horse, on which Melamchi mounted before, was making strange gestures through the movement of its neck, mane and head, suggesting that things were not normal around. Once again, it stood on two legs and neighed. Panchashar started running his eyes here and there in search of Melamchi. She was there on the wooden bench, bending. Panchashar took a leap and went near. His heart grew heavy, and his mind quite panicked.

Making himself composed and patient, Panchashar sprinkled water on Melamchi with heartfelt sympathy and goodwill, wiped her face, fed her some water and said to himself, 'It must be some spell. It can even be Sikari casting his spell on her in such a desolate forest. Could it be Budheni casting her shadow on her? Or, did she lose her senses seeing a *sokpa*?' He made several calculations in himself.

Panchashar felt her pulses and checked her forehead though he didn't have much knowledge of pluses and nerves. Yet he could read psychology, though he didn't think on that line. He was unaware how he should exhibit his intimacy and warmth toward Melamchi at such an odd hour. Yet he considered Melamchi's health and decided to return, along with her, to the house they were sheltering in.

He wound the rein of Melamchi's horse around its neck making it loose enough not to strangle the horse. He made the rein of his horse a little longer to encompass himself, and lifted and placed Melamchi on his back side. Thus he started riding downhill.

On reaching the foot of the hill, he rested on a *chautari*. The horses were freed for a brief rest.

Melamchi was now in full senses, though still quite frail. This incident, wherein she was frail though in full consciousness was not an ordinary happening. Its reason was internal gash and ailment, which could be deciphered only through psychological and intimate path. But Panchashar in no way thought along this route.

After a long rest, Melamchi recovered. She washed her limbs and face and drank water. The horses that were alarmed until a while ago now looked fresh. They started enjoying between themselves, playing.

Time glided on its own track. Panchashar and Melamchi mounted on their respective horses and reached their shelter at a time when people had started lighting the evening lamps.

The two brother dogs didn't come out to receive them that evening. On their way back, Panchashar and Melamchi didn't engage in any sort of conversation either, though the horsemen that walked in equal distance embarked on continuous conversation and exchange.

On getting the news of their return, Jimu started yelling, making the entire house shake. Yangsila turned more and more mute. The dogs came out to hail them, wagging their tails. Everything seemed quite simple and ordinary.

Tired to her bones, Melamchi entered the guest room to rest. The dogs duo surrounded and started sniffing her as though she were a stuff meant for sniffing. From there, she moved near to the fireplace and sat there. Then they climbed a stair where the bedroom was, only to climb down again and moved toward the other house where the Lama's wife had her stay.

Panchashar carefully studied Melamchi's face that was fast growing listless and devoid of any glow. But his study was not directed toward exploring the reason for Melamchi's condition. Lama, the owner of the house, had read her face, and was restless from the core of his heart.

After Melamchi left the fireplace, the Lama old man narrated an incident to Panchashar: "Stranger! Melamchi is my granddaughter. We also call her Shangri-la. As we were moving on our business trips, her mother bore her on midway. Her mother had to bear a lot of hardship that time."

He added, "When she left home for study, her name was changed. We don't find it easy to call her Melamchi. We don't love that too."

"I see," said Panchashar, suggesting that he was getting the gist of the story.

The old man alerted himself, as his story was getting digressed. Pulling him back to the gist, he said, "Though Melamchi is our granddaughter, we call her 'daughter' to make her feel closer." Calling up some compassion on his face, he added, "I cannot quite tell if she has any glimpse of her parents. She was quite small. But everything has fallen into her ears."

The old man got his throat choked with emotions, even as he was narrating. He stopped, thinking if he should narrate everything or let it go.

"He parents herded four thousand sheep. Their business of meat and wool flourished quite well. They specially traded in carpets, blankets, *chutuk*, *chhara* and *radi*. The range of their trade encompassed Lhasa, Olangchunggola, Mauwa Khola Thum and Bhojpur on one side and Bhutan, Sikkim, Khasa, Kantipur, extending further to the Western Himalayas, reaching as far as Tinkar."

Panchashar went on listening to his story in utter silence.

"They were hardworking people; quite young too," the Lama resumed his story. "While she was going after their flock, Melamchi's mother was attacked by a bear one day. When her father rushed in to save her, the beast attacked him too, and the two engaged each other for a long time in a terrible fight. Finally, the bear won out, and both of them were left dead."

The old man turned his face away from Panchashar and let a few big drops of tears fall from his eyes. Returning to normalcy, he said, "Since that day, this daughter became an orphan. Her grandmother and I stay weeping all the time."

Panchashar listened on in deep concentration, his face all soaked in tears.

"She is the only child of my daughter. So whenever I see her face grip, I am deeply pricked."

The old man let down tears once again, forcing a pause in his story.

He drew in a long breath and said, "To console her grandmother, I often go to meet her. It takes me two days to reach there and two more days to return. If I choose to stay there for two days, it becomes a weeklong trip. There are times when the horse falls sick."

Again he took a long sigh and said, "I now find mounting and dismounting a horse quite a task. I have aged. That must be the reason. It's time her parents will call me up now. This is the rule of the world, you know."

Panchashar grew even more eager to listen to the old man's story. His looks reflected curiosity, while his mind rippled with waves of compassion.

Breaking the impending silence, the Lama continued, "I had hoped my daughter to be quite lucky, but I see her depressed all the time. Else, there is no girl in this part of the world more graceful than her."

Drinking his share of Tibetan tea dry, the old man kept his cup aside and said, "I am very tired today; let me rest."

Turning toward Yangsila, he said, "Yang, take good care of our guest. Don't leave it to Melamchi today."

The old man left. Yangsila showed him the light. The dogs followed.

Sitting close to the fireplace, Panchashar said to himself, 'Why could Melamchi be crying in the fair last day? Who could have moved her to tears? How then did he recuperate? Is the conclusion doubtful or satisfactory?'

His mind was poked by such questions rising frequently. He wanted to ask the old man directly, but didn't find the right opportunity. He took time before deciding if it was proper for him to ask someone a personal issue. So his questions were confined to his mind only.

'Maybe she met a friend, or was stopped by a relative. Maybe she had conversations with a peer. She is an employee of the palace, and it's possible, she had to attend to an important work.'

One after another, Panchashar tried to address the questions that had risen in his mind.

He recalled the face of Melamchi who was sitting near the fireplace a while ago and thought, 'It was quite depressed; completely graceless. She looked grim, utterly forlorn. Memories of the time he met Melamchi first, up to the day they were together in the forest of Chuli started criss-crossing his mind. Melamchi, who was always excited, satisfied and graceful in every turn, work, commitment and success she had a bearing with, had now turned so dejected that the mysterious change, Panchashar felt, she was sure to push him into grief. So he said to himself, 'It's not without reasons that such a jolly young girl has turned so much distressed. There certainly is a mystery there. If chances favor, I will certainly ask the old man. Maybe Jimu also knows a lot of things.' This way, he made himself assured.

Panchashar sat on the mat and in dim lamp light, started drawing the blueprint of the planned building. In the meantime, he had a sensation that someone was making an entry from the door. The situation was calm, completely still. Panchashar did feel that someone had entered, but didn't feel it important to raise his head and look, for it was not a matter of any significance for him. He merely thought, 'If anyone had entered, there would have been a voice. Maybe no one has come in; it was perhaps a dog that came and went out.'

This way, he sought an easy answer to all mysteries.

Without caring to see if the doorsteps had any glimpse of an intruder, Panchashar got absorbed in his work as before. The incomer perhaps considered his or her presence insignificant, worthless, or more, belittled and so, chose to return even without letting the footsteps make any sound.

Panchashar was besieged by cold fear. He merely rolled his eyes, but didn't dare to raise his hood and look around. From a lowered state, he raised his head from the blueprint. He looked rather disturbed. The atmosphere was grave; the lamp glowed incessantly. In the fashion of an electric current shaking him, Panchashar thought, 'Could it be a mermaid…?'

He tried to raise his eyes and look out, but could gather no guts. His heart shuddered and body gathered heat. Still, he could not change his stopping position and continued to face the blueprint. He could not look above the intruder's toes.

"Stranger!"

It was a voice he had not heard before. He was sure that it was a human voice. He drew a long breath and felt cooler. Then he gathered some courage and raised his eyes above the stranger's toes and made them fall on the cloth just above the knees.

The incomer stepped two steps back and stood making it easy for Panchashar to see.

"Yangsila, you?"

She smiled, still standing where she was.

"Why didn't you speak so long?" Panchashar asked, brushing aside every bit of fear. He added, "I couldn't speak out for a long time, not knowing who or what it was. I was really feeling that some mermaid was trying to attack me today."

With a changed air, he said, "You could have given me a voice while coming. That would have made things easier. My thoughts went blank for a while."

"What would have become easier?"

"Everything."

"Everything is easy, you know. Come; let's go to the pool. I have come to take you."

She gave him her hand; he got up, taking support from her. Then he stared at her from top to toes in a strange fashion.

This gaze touched Yangsila somewhere deep inside, and she grew nimble. It irked her somewhere or tickled her, and she grew impatient. She let her eyes meet Panchashar's once and hid them again. Drawing his attention to her mission she said, "It has been long since I came here. Let's move."

Panchashar's eyes feel on the neck and the fleshy shoulders of Yangsila. He paid repeated looks on her arms, shoulders wrists. Addressing her by name for the first time that day, he said, "Yang, turn here."

His voice had both request and attraction. Yangsila didn't herself turn; Panchashar held her by her shoulders and made her turn slowly. That is what Yangsila wanted too. He turned, slightly bending her head and blushing in the fashion of a new bride.

The yellowish complexion of Yangsila, her beautiful body, her coy and nimble looks were matters of attraction. On top of that, the fragrance emanating from her body was far superior to the usual fragrance that came from virgin's bodies. Panchashar was charmed by the fragrance and he stood enraptured, caught by the indescribable attraction of the perfume.

Yangsila drew Panchashar, as does a magical force, and took him to the pool of water. Pulling him together with her, she made a sudden dive into the water with a splash!

Panchashar woke up with a start. "Oh God, I happened to be dreaming," he exclaimed. He balanced his position and smiled to himself, secretly. Then he made a brief remark, 'This means, Yangsila has started hovering around my mind now. Else, why would she appear in my dreams without any reason?'

With Yangsila housed in his heart, he reverted to deep contemplation.

Yangsila was a maiden of a unique nature. For her, nothing was quite loathsome or attractive. Nor was anything indispensable to her. In a way, she was far from things like passion or indifference. In all occasions, ordinary or extraordinary, formal or informal, she mostly kept herself non-aligned. In ordinary contexts of conversation, or in moments that expected her complements, she chose to stay silent, and took most of the things as ordinary. Such a nature in Yangsila made Panchashar quite serious. This drew him more and more toward studying the mystery of Yangsila's nature.

Yangsila was quite talkative, sweet of words and precise in message, but talked only when required. It seemed, her life had nothing to compete about, no object to gain or lose as though goodwill, equal treatment, and disinterested contemplations were the highest ideals of her life.

In realty, Yangsila was a maiden of introvert nature. She placed life on highest priority and always sided with its lucid sides. She sided neither with competition, nor with any desire for power. Abusing and acridity were not her cups of tea, either. She took life as something lively, grew with reality and lived with self-confidence. Helping others, and contributing to their happiness seemed to be her prime responsibilities. No storm could bring about any rebellion in her life. It seemed she still had the vestige of her childhood days, or the soul of high profile and guiltless saint who has risen from the highest degree of ideational excellence. She took all hindrances and unexpected and unwanted jerks in life as short pauses, and as far as she could, considered others' vices and weaknesses as lessons contributing to her own evolution. Patience, tolerance, positive thinking and dynamism were embellishments to her personality. The Lama's wife, by dint of her experience, knew about Yangsila's external and internal personalities to a great extent. Others were largely ignorant on this issue. As for Melamchi, she had had no opportunity to get mixed up with Yangsila.

Granted that Yangsila was a maiden, and youthfulness was her first beauty, but that beauty was common to all, and everyone possessed the beauty of youthfulness. So, such beauty was not worth considering special or additional; it was a part of the 'ordinary'. However, Yangsila's beauty was something that could not be merely confined within the limits of such ordinary beauty.

The complete energy flowing in from the morning sunlight, the twilight in the evening, the moon-blenched night in the full-moon nights and the fragrance in autumn made Yangsila's beauty even more pronounced, even more nourished. Her eyes were same like those of others, but the looks in them reflected beauty of a higher order. Her speech too was ordinary too, but the beauty in her tone and choice of words were matchless. Whoever saw her stayed glued to her looks and voice, and thought, making her a close friend would be a thrilling experience.

It's true that only patrons of aesthetics could feel such beauty, but the beauty in Yangsila was something immeasurable. It was sovereign, and nowhere like any issue of advertisement. Beauty is perhaps a sensation, a matter of self-contemplation, an experience, a realization. In every turn, every meeting, every gaze, every smile and every observation, beauty becomes more enhanced than its previous manifestation. In that case, how can it be called an ordinary thing? Can an onlooker change perspectives in each gaze? If it is real beauty, it appears in a different manifestation in the next moment, in the next waiting.

Though Panchashar was not a great patron of aesthetics, he started brooding in seclusion, receiving in the canvas of his minds that pictorial forms and gestures of the glory of beauty. Compared to concrete manifestation of beauty, its abstract counterpart sends forth hypnotism that results into an inexpressible attraction. Panchashar started feeling that he was lulled from deep within.

Yangsila now charted out a different routine for herself. For her personal time and interest, she made use of beautiful ideas. Inside her domestic routine whereby she had to abide by what others demanded of her, she mixed her personal routine and rejoiced. Others had no idea about it, and so they never raised any finger against her conduct. This developed as an open philosophy with time.

The path now ran from a close vicinity of Panchashar without any hassle. Though it was a serpentine path, it looked quite comfortable and proper. Through certain means, pretexts and paths, Yangsila now started getting into Panchashar's view, and on her own part, make it a point to have a look of him, before leaving. This sent currents of mental excitement down the spine of Panchashar, and unknowingly, he was being drawn toward Yangsila in a strong way.

Once he thought, 'It seems I was not the only one to have a dream. Maybe she also dreamt of the same thing. Else, why should the impact of my dream fall on her? Or, wasn't that a mere dream? If it was not, what was it, after all?'

He went piling question upon question, albeit to himself.

***

CHAPTER TEN

'MELAMCHI IS NOT feeling very well. She has been running quite upset ever since she returned from the fair a few days ago. When she was in the forest of Chuli with the stranger, she returned home quite sick. What could be the matter? What has gone wrong with our daughter?' the Lama old man, thought sitting on his bed in the morning. Then he resolved to himself, 'I will myself take the guest out to see places a couple of days.'

The Lama and Panchashar set out at sunrise. The shadows of horses and their riders followed them from the rear. The two moved close, maintaining a distance of only a few yards between them. Most of the time, the Lama's white horse was on the lead. At one point in time, the old man took out a beaded garland from the pocket of his inside cloth and started counting the beads, one for every round of the song he sang. The horse was familiar with his musical high tones. It moved on, twisting its ears, whirling them, and shaking them frantically at times. Panchashar's brown horse followed whatever the Lama's horse did.

After a long walk, they came inside the premises of a monastery. There, at a stipulated place, they gave their horses their feeds. Then they sprinkled water to make themselves holy and entered the monastery. Inside the monks were busy in their routine enchantments. They lit lamps, lowered their heads in reverence and sat in the line of other monks, taking part in their prayers. The fragrance from the tantalizing incense was new to Panchashar. In the forms of the local monks, he could see the reflection of the Buddha. He tried to interpret this, saying, 'It's true that a seeker can find the reflection of the object of his pursuit on the face of someone he likes.'

He started concentrating on the Buddha's eyes. He realized peace, trust, firmness and stability emanating from there. He said to himself, 'Before this, my conscience had not even got a hint of such feelings.' He expressed a high degree of trust and said, 'It's true that the Buddha is the exponential personage from the last chapter of human history. There is no alternative to this.'

After a pause, he said to himself with pure feelings, 'There is no denying that the Buddha was a mahatma, but I find in him a hero and would love to call him one, more than a mahatma.' He continued to murmur to himself, 'It's a matter of victory to vanquish and altogether relinquish all social relations, cravings of the bodily organs, attachments of the mind and luxuries of intellect. Besides calling him a superhuman, I would love to call the Buddha a victor. But the human today is not ready to call him the best of the humans. He is trying to make him a god and thus belittle his worth. The Buddha was a yogi way far from divinity; he was a seeker and an accomplished man. It's altogether unwise to make him a god and lock him within limits. He is a great soul venerable to the entire world; he is a timeless man indeed, the pioneer of a new philosophy. He is an apostle of emancipation and freedom. This aspect should not be shadowed. The selfish men are today making him their shield and promoting their business. That's is a gross crime.'

Unknowingly, Panchashar had reached very near to the Buddha's statue, in fact very near to it. His heart was filled with emotions.

Ya veera banchhan vasudaiba bhogi
Ya bandachhan jeevanamukta yogi

[The brave ones either become consumers of the universe or become yogis free from attachments.]

— Madhav Ghimire, national poet of Nepal

The Lama old man walked close to Panchashar in no time and said, "He is a guest of mine. He has come from Nepal, the land of the Buddha. He is our neighbor as well. He came at the invitation of our Emperor. He came here, to our land, to work for the Emperor."

In fact, the Lama was worried if the presence of a foreigner would disrupt the decorum and order of the monastery. Yet, he considered his age, his social prestige and his relation with the monastery, and chose to stay quiet.

Tears trickled form the eyes of Panchashar. He appeared extremely emotional. The Lamas prayed for him, and blessed him to attain accomplishment. But he could not fully comprehend the dramatic incident that took place there and the outcome thereof. Finally, he made only a guess: his singing of the brave's song had made an impact in the atmosphere there.

He appeared in a state of embarrassment, down with shame and hesitation. The senior monk of that monastery, the disciple monks and other dignitaries there accorded him their honor, considering his highly cultured personality.

The old Lama now appeared satisfied, feeling that his honors had been saved. He felt sort of pride. Giving a whirl to the artistic prayer wheels, the two moved out of the monastery. On reaching the top of a hill of moderate height some distance away, the Lama's horse stopped still all of a sudden, and started shaking. It appeared like a routine task on his part whenever he moved along this route. Showing Panchashar the flat land on the north-western direction from there, the Lama said, "Look; that is my ancestral land."

Panchashar's horse stopped when it stood on the same line with the old man's horse, as though it too was interested in watching nature's panorama. The mountain range extended in a lavish way, decked by extensive plains in between. In between were natural meadows of various shapes that looked like valleys and *doons* separated by water bodies. On the fringe of each of these landforms, there were thick forests and fertile farmlands. Running his eyes on each of them, Panchashar said, 'The Lama happened to be a rich landlord.'

HARI RAJ BHATTARAI

After they had moved a short distance making a bend, the Lama made his horse stop again. He raised the same hand that had his prayer garland and said, "Stranger! This land belongs to my daughter and her husband."

Trying further to show him the boundaries, he said, "The whole plot from this end—see here!—to that one—over there!—is theirs. They also have similar plots, equally wide, in other places."

After running his eyes in every direction, Panchashar thought, 'Oh what a beautiful place, inviting to roll over her surface! How beautiful is nature's doing, ah!' The last sentence was the only utterance he made in response to the Lama's long description.

That part of the earth that always appeared young, fertile and beautiful had crooning brooks, gurgling canals, water outlets in serpentine shapes and moderate-size rivulets and creeks, making the land seem a high quality gift from nature to the humankind.

"From now, the ownership of these plots have passed into the hands of Melamchi. But she lays no importance on them. I have been personally taking care of them now; I also have the income from these lands for her," said the Lama with a sense of responsibility.

As they moved seeing places, they arrived at yet another plain. They eyes now fell on thousands of yaks, *naks*, horses and mules grazing together in an extensive meadow. The livestock seemed fully nourished, growing in the plain with enough greenery in it. The eyes of the Lama reflected excitement and satisfaction.

On another side of this plain was yet another meadow, full of sheep flocks. The horse-ridden shepherds were seen in the company of Tibetan dogs that looked like bears. They were alert every second and mobile every moment, and this, for them, was the code of conduct.

"Grandpa, there perhaps is the fear of wild animals entering the animal farm."

"Yes. And the sheep farm runs a higher risk."

"Maybe the wild animals also get into the herds of domestic animals."

"That happens around yak farms."

Panchashar went on listening. The Lama added, "We can see wild cows, wild horses and wild dogs getting mixed with our animals. They also mate and bear cross-breed kids. Our domestic animals sometimes get lost in the forest for a few days and return home later. They cannot stay in the forest and in the dark for long. They need the love of their own flocks and the company of the human beings."

"Maybe some return home pregnant."

"They do. We have seen that happen. Some of our yaks, mares and bitches return with the kids of their wild mates. Maybe the wild beasts also beget from our animals. Maybe the children of our animals are also living in the forest."

"Maybe they also sometimes fight."

"They do, and when they fight, it is fierce. Many times, animals return home with wounds and bruises. Some come having their horns broken, or they come limping. The wild animals are naturally stronger and nimbler than the domestic ones. In front of them, ours appear pathetic," said the Lama, sharing his experience.

In the meantime, someone whistled. The Lama turned his horse and looked backward. Four to five horsemen were coming toward them. The Lama was soon surrounded by the horsemen. The sight made Panchashar quite stressful.

The dogs in the yak farm started barking, signaling of a danger in the offing. They continued to yelp incessantly in a harsh manner. The horsemen retired, leaving the Lama old man to himself. Lama took a deep sigh of relief. The surrounding and retreat lasted for a short time, and disappeared like a gush of wind that comes and goes.

Panchashar had been observing all these developments from a distance. Seeing the Lama somehow throw his tired body atop the horse and come toward him, he considered himself safe and felt himself again.

The Lama man walked close to him. Panchashar could not look direct on his face. He hesitated, but the old man read Panchashar's countenance instantly. He appeared disturbed, helpless and seemingly terror-stricken. So, before he had asked or uttered anything, he said in the fashion of a clarification, "They all are my family members, workers or cowherds. They have come to meet me on seeing me here. They are all trustworthy and intimate." The Lama had opened up in his bid to console Panchashar and erase his fear.

"Ye Ye…"

"Ye Ye…!"

It meant 'Grandpa!'

After they had moved a little, they heard someone's voice again. The Lama made his horse turn. Panchashar also stopped his horse and made it turn.

Two men drove close to them on horsebacks and said, "Ye Ye, we are here. If anything untoward happens, please tell us."

"Fine, but nothing like that will happen. Yet, I respect your feelings."

Assured, both the horsemen returned the same way as they had come, and in the same speed.

***

'There certainly is a problem, but it's a secret.' Many questions rose and fell in Panchashar's mind. Questions concerning Melamchi's behavior at the fair a few days ago stated poking his mind again. He was willing to ask the Lama many more things, but hesitated seeing the old man make his face quite grim. Trying to draw this context to a closure, he said, "'This is not the time I asked question to the Lama.' He gathered self-confidence and said, 'If there is any problem, the Lama should raise the issue for discussion in the domestic parliament. Maybe he will do that, and I will be able to know. Time is powerful. I think I must wait. If these are seasonal sores, they come and disappear on their own. That might not be a much awaited time.'

This way, Panchashar tried to console himself.

In fact, the world Panchashar saw during his outing with the Lama was a different one. One finds such an opportunity once in a while. With time, context, incident and outcome seen or experienced, one can embellish the diary of life with different episodes and sections. Whenever new, unprecedented and mysterious things occurred to them, they remained worth contemplating and archiving. The trivial hassles were both imaginary and short-lived ones. As for the bigger ones, they did not face or experience any. So the trip turned out to be joyous and effective. This is what Panchashar experienced after the trip.

This outing was neither ordered, nor systematically planned. Their conducts, experiences and outing were all abrupt, unplanned and unbalanced. Whatever it was, the trip had been planned solely for Panchashar. So it was not altogether absurd. The trip could be considered a pleasant confluence of time, nature, goodwill and cooperation. It deserved archiving as a memoir. Yet, there lay a question: is such a trip more pleasing with a senior guardian or a peer of one's own age? Had the trip been undertaken in order to maintain an archive or to excavate something? Or anything else?

It was morning, on the third day of their outing. The Lama stopped his horse at a sunlit spot on a hill of a moderate height. That way, he allowed his horse some time to rest. He also fed it some fodder, served it some green grass from the tree and gave it leaves of the mountain bamboo. The horse shook, giving expression to their happiness.

The spot was fit to be a resting place. A wooden bench had been kept underneath the shade of a tree, and trickling tap ran some four yards away from there. It was a sunlit spot with slightly red and sticky soil. Though a bright sun was shining above a cool breeze fanned the spot.

After eating their fodder, the horse peed. As always, the Lama derived the conclusion that the horses were healthy. He coughed once or twice and said in a sensitive manner, "Stranger! Can you tell Mount Chuli from here?"

The Lama asked this in casual interest. It was a question he had just asked for fun, and Panchashar's answer would make no difference at all. Yet, drawing a thread of conversation, he again asked, "You saw a lot of places. Which of them did you like the most?"

"There is no spot I don't like this part of the world. I like whichever place my eyes fall on. Sometime before, from the top of Mount Chuli, I had showed Melamchi a sunlit spot with two houses to the south-east of the mountain. I didn't know she had been lying sick on a bench some distance away since an unknown time. Much later, it occurred to me that I had been babbling to myself."

The Lama chose silence, and went on listening to Panchashar's thoughts.

"I found that spot suitable, plain, moderate in temperature, and quite fertile. We could see even winter crops equally verdant, playfully swaying to the winter wind. This entire belt is quite rare."

"What then is your decision?"

"My decision won't work; Melamchi or the palace should take the final decision."

At this, the Lama's face turned quite sour. His face wrinkled, and the looks in his eyes changed. He turned grave, and appeared drowned in some sort of shock. Panchashar took no time in reading the change in the old man. But he didn't consider the reason for such an immediate change.

The Lama sat where he was, seemingly listening to Panchashar. Panchashar said, "The Emperor shall love this place very much. The weather here is always pleasant. If Melamchi says, the palace won't deny. This is what I believe."

The Lama got up from the bench with a start. He took two quick steps and urinated. Then he walked up to the tap and washed his hands. Then he mounted on the horse, this time appearing comparatively more energetic. He drew the rein with a great force. The horse galloped away.

Since the Lama had come back from the tap wiping his face, Panchashar could not read his gestures.

Panchashar's horse followed the steps of the old man's horse. Since the horses have a great sense of memory, there was no fear that Panchashar might lose his way. The horse didn't keep the same speed as that of the Lama.

Their way meandered and moved toward a river. The Lama happened to tie his horse at a distance; maybe he had nature's call. The horse found a mate, and started shaking.

When the old man returned, Panchashar tried to read his face. He could not. The old man said, "I am relieved now."

Having said this, the old man mounted on the horse.

Panchashar wondered if it was stomachache alone that had made the old man so willful to run away alone.

'Thank God, the stranger didn't notice me run away in a fit of anger. Even if he did, I can now assure him that it was my stomach that made the mess. I can look like before now,' thought the old man.

Though it was a meandering route, the way along the riverbank was far easier and enjoyable. Houses could be seen standing thinly on the plains along both the banks. At places where the gurgling of the water grew fainter, they could hear the barking of dogs. Usually, the sound from the river eclipsed conversation along that route, and so the passerby walked without talking. At the moment, it seemed the two had no interest in any conversation with each other. For that reason perhaps, the two travelers walked without exchanging any word for a long time.

The horses moved on their usual speeds.

The Lama thought about Melamchi, 'She is the ancestral souvenir of my daughter and son-in-law. How can I submit her in a king's hand. While I am still alive, how can I see her getting stripped? Hwangdi will also devastate us. Where can we go then? I think the issue of this land shocked Melamchi; she fell sick. She doesn't at all like Hwangdi.'

The Lama was busy in his own contemplations.

Allowing the horse to keep his own usual pace, he thought, 'Why did Melamchi come here to see a spot for Hwangdi's

HARI RAJ BHATTARAI

house? Could it be that Melamchi wants to hand over our world to Hwangdi? Is she disenchanted with her ancestral land? Does one's mind change when she starts working in the palace? Doesn't she need the rest of the world again? Does one grow that much powerful or non-attached?'

Panchashar, on his part, started a conversation with himself. He thought, 'That day too, when we started talking about a piece of land, Melamchi lost interest and before long appeared terrified. Today too, as soon as the old man pointed at a spot and started talking, his mentality changed and his face turned grim. There certainly is a story here. Else, why should both be affected by the same context?'

'Melamchi is grown up now. Could it be that she is unwilling to stay in her ancestral land? Maybe she wants to sell this one and get settled elsewhere,' thought the Lama. 'But this daughter not the type that would covet such a thing.'

'Perhaps, instead of getting troubled all the time with this spot that reminds her of her dead parents, Melamchi wants to hand it over to the palace and free herself from the painful memory for ever. She could also have considered that this place could develop rapidly if that happened,' though Panchashar. After a pause, he again thought, 'She could also be thinking that the royal palace should stand at the earth's most beautiful location. If she took the initiative with the inspiration that this could prove her heartfelt loyalty to the Emperor, that is not unusual. These things seem obvious because she is in extremely good terms with the palace.'

This way, thinking on the same issue from different perspectives, the two incessantly moved toward their shelters. The Lama and Panchashar entered the house they had made their shelter for this trip from its easternmost end, through an entrance on its outside wall, the small wall that mothered the Great Wall of China.

The harsh, monotonous cadence of the river gradually grew fainter, and finally became inaudible. All they could hear now were the sweet chirping of birds and the sound of dog barks coming from afar. The place had no impact of adverse heat or coldness; the weather was pleasant and completely thrilling.

They were now on the road inside the wall of the house. The horses appeared in romantic moods. Their hoofs were separated from each other's by a short distance. The fragrance of nature around and the ditty of the birds flying freely in the air sent a new wave of ecstasy inside them. Yet, the Lama old man appeared rather disturbed. Panchashar, on his part, was in high elation.

They still had to walk some yards, and the time was dusk. Panchashar let himself rest on the horseback while his mind flew away. He soared together with his mind, in the speed of the mind, in a wave-like fleet. His mind picked up pace, called Melamchi in his memory and reached the fair where she was.

"I have a piece of work here; I will come later," Melamchi had said, asking him to move homeward. She had also told Jimu, "You return with him." This way, she expressed her will to stay back, and from there, she moved elsewhere.

Once she had left, Panchashar asked Jimu, "Won't Melamchi be in any sort of problems?"

"Oh, no. The youthful boys showed many types of games there. Those who liked them made them their partners, chose them, accepted them. Melamchi didn't pick anyone; maybe she was not here for that. Her only mission was to bring you here, show you the places and entertain you. Though she didn't lay her eye on any young man, it seems someone has fallen for her."

"And?" asked Panchashar, tickled by curiosity.

"If a boy likes a girl, one has to wait until the issue is settled. That's why, she held herself back."

"How is the issue settled? Who does that and when?"

"There's such a big society here. There are seniors and the wise ones. We have a custom, a law; we have our own decorum, practices and tradition. One can do nothing against the will of the other. So we don't need to be concerned about her. Let's take our way."

After a brief pause she said again, "She might take time. But that is different thing."

HARI RAJ BHATTARAI

Jimu continued, "The boy that stopped Melamchi hadn't won any game. But this is my speculation, and my speculation seldom goes wrong." She stopped for a while and resumed, "No girl picks that loser boy. Mad at his defeat, he must have come to stop Melamchi."

"What will happen now?"

"We must follow the practices of our society and the rule of the fair. Melamchi is a staff of the palace and was here on a royal errand. So, it's possible that she had to attend to a work here. If any member of the place had come to the fair, he or she could have engaged Melamchi for a while."

Bringing some change in her tone, she said, "Anything is possible in a fair. It's a fair, after all. We don't need to worry; she will be back soon."

Jimu opened herself up further, "Mind my words; she will be back this very evening. Who knows she must be following us right now! If she is, she will soon meet us. Her horse moves faster than ours."

Picking up yet another issue, she said, "The people in this part of the world have not been able to recognize her fully. She is an expert of many things, you know. No one can abuse her taking her for a girl. Melamchi is far different than us."

The conversation didn't quite please Panchashar. He quickly wound up the issue connected with the fair and steered his mind elsewhere: toward the hot water pool. He then concentrated on his efforts to allow his imagination to make the spot as lively as he could.

He contemplated with a telescoping vision. He could see Melamchi, the Lama's wife, Jimu and Yangsila taking bath together in the pond. He made himself alert to see the thrilling spectacle and to overhear their conversation.

"If you say no, no boy can stop or bar you, against your will. Who's that crossing the limits and pestering? Do you know him?" asked the Lama woman, expressing her obvious love and goodwill to Melamchi. Her voice had compassion, love, and a slight tremor. Her eyes were moist, while her voice appeared elated. She stopped.

Jimu looked quite graceful. She wanted to reap joy from everyone's words. Such words used to prove healthy and nourishing to her. She was impatient to hear Melamchi's words.

Yangsila's mentality too was quite vibrant. Yet, she was busy trying to red Melamchi's mind. She was quite alert in her attempt to decipher Melamchi's looks, the gestures of her eyes, the admixture of compassion and pathos in her voice.

From the neck-deep pool, Melamchi rose higher—up to the chest to be precise—and said, "I am not familiar with any aspect of his life. Nor is he a character I am bound to know about. I know him only casually, the way others know him."

The Lama woman had never before heard Melamchi talk this way. She appeared quite curious to hear more from Melamchi. Jimu and Yangsila kept quiet, respecting the old woman's curiosity.

"His mother's brother also works in the palace. He is in the department of animal husbandry. Since he needs horses for his work, he sometimes comes to meet me," said Melamchi, narrating them the truth she knew. She added, "One day, he introduced a boy to me, saying that he was his sister's son. I took no time to know he was trying to bring him close to me. But that didn't interest me. There was no way he would come along my way."

After a short pause she said, "Another day, he introduced the boy to me. The introduction took place there, and it ended there itself. Everything was a mere formality. The episode ended there."

In a light fashion she added, "He is like any stranger for me. I neither fell for him, nor ignored him. I always keep myself occupied in my own world. In fact, I have no time to care about others."

Melamchi presented herself in a grim way and said, making others feel the futility of the boy's advances, "He happened to be the one stopping me. I don't even know his name. I think he told me once, but I forgot. I didn't have any business to remember his name."

Seeming irritated, Melamchi added, "A thing worthy of forgetting need not be forced into our memory, you know."

"Auntie, Melamchi has no right to engage two young men. We also need one," said Jimu in a jocular way, and burst into a loud laughter herself, before diving into the pool. The issue entertained Yangsila very much, but by habit, she didn't burst into similar laughter. Instead, she acted of having caught water in her nostrils and so, she cupped her face with both her palms and delivered a subdued laughter.

"How then did you escape from there?" Jimu asked.

"One who loses always has weak morale. He was already in a low estimation from himself."

Melamchi reiterated her own saying, "I told him, 'Do not bar my way this time. I am not interested in a game with win-or-lose arrangement. This is my healthy proposal to you. We must act with wisdom. Allow me to leave.'"

"And then?" This time, it was Yangsila. The Lama woman got even more curious to hear Melamchi. Jimu smiled.

"When he declined, I placed forth a condition to escape from there. All others surrounded us and clapped."

"What was your condition?"

"One that wins me can only stop me."

"Was that your condition?"

"Yes, it was."

"What happened next?"

"I was reading the gestures on his face. I looked into his eyes, face to face. I could easily read a kind of weakness, guilt or inferiority concealed therein. This made me even more confident and I easily said, 'That's OK; defeat me in the foil. I will stay back.'"

"And?"

"Mom, look at this. Jimu and Yang are after me."

"Oh now. The story of your wits makes me even more interested. Go on; I am listening too. They also seem interested," said the Lama's wife, provoking her even more.

"He hesitated on hearing my proposal."

"And then?"

"I knew that I was winning. Finally, I won him out. And I returned." She took a victor's sigh and felt proud of herself.

The moon spilled over the faces of the Lama woman, Jimu and Yangsila.

"There were some people who looked like palace staff in their dresses. When you sent us away you held back, we thought the palace staff had stopped you for some work. But it happened to be a different game. Isn't it, Auntie?" said Jimu and burst into laughter as soon as she was done with her last sentence.

With a lingering laughter she added, "Did you get it, Auntie? I had imaged, Melamchi would be held back there, and I will be able to woo our guest from Nepal. But everything has turned into thin air now," she said without any reservation and laughed out again. The water in the pond started splashing out of the border walls.

"What a thing this Jimu speaks! Oh, how many things you know! You don't seem to get tired," said Melamchi. Then she said to herself, 'The stranger belongs to no one. He belongs to anyone who has the art to win his heart.'

Sprinkling some water drops into the mouth of Yangsila, Jimu said, "Yang, what are you thinking about? When mine is settled, it's your turn now. Till now, we both were single."

She laughed out before completing her sentence.

Yangsila, a graceful and sharp girl with a yellowish tinge on her skin, glittered even more inside the pool of warm water. On top of that, Jimu's words had driven her all but crimson. Her bright eyes were filled with innumerable questions and curiosities. Inside the pool of warm water, she started drawing a translucent collage of the romantic playfulness of young men and women on her mental canvas made out of her own imaginations. No one around her knew how safe her imaginary pictures were. From time to time, the articulate nature of Jimu and the ripples of her trebling sound fragmented the imaginary pictures of her youthful musings, and they fell apart into pieces. They came to get integrated once again in tranquility and become one.

Yangsila was quite lonely, though she was always in a group. She often reaped satisfaction by musing with herself. With time, she prioritized this part of self amusement even more. When there were romantic talks about youths, she sometimes partook of them and amused herself, while some other time, she imagined others' youthful times and got thrilled.

In the imaginative firmament of Yangsila's youthfulness, the man of her choice was only externally near to others. But in mental proximity, and in permissible physical proximity for youthful luxury, he was only with her, and with no one else. At such moments, he was only hers, and besides herself, no one was present therein. So she continued to derive self-satisfaction in herself, rippling together with the sensational forms of place, method, implementation and satisfaction. Though she appeared among others while in a group, she was always lost in her own musings. She always executed all actions of love without feeling fatigued, or without feeling any hesitation. She owned those actions, and after each of them, got benumbed with exhaustion following untold satisfaction.

With such imaginary contexts, incidents and spectacles fabricated by his imagination, Panchashar moved on his horse, letting characters he loved and the dialogues he longed to hear tune up with them. The Lama was caught up in his own worldly concerns. He bumped into the external and the real world only when the dogs came and started barking. Panchashar told to himself, 'Perhaps, people who are engaged in such imaginations, dreams and internal forage, and embark on a journey along a new path become true seers and successful writers.'

At dusk, they reached their destination. The lamps were being lit. With a deep sigh, the old man dismounted from his horse. The sigh was the patent signal of his arrival.

***

Melamchi was a girl who considered time and context secondary, and moved ahead with the force of age and self-confidence, not allowing herself to accept defeat at any cost. Yet, the factors she ignored also make differences. Their amount and the way they are approved of do have an impact. Time and context also affect one's mind, as they influence the body.

It's time and context that dictate the form and measure of hardship and the nature and form of loss. External or physical hardship is perhaps inevitable, whereas mental hardship is optional. This is because wise men take philosophy as the surest remedy for both physical and mental hardship, and profess the same. That way, they try to keep themselves free from all sorts of ailments. This is how we understand this fact.

It's true that its second remedy is one's self-confidence. It has direct relationship with one's psychology. The context also leads to the development of a special state of mind, and time and age contribute to it from their ends. The health of the physical body and the trust from the members of the society add to one's energy to a huge degree. So time and context pose to the human beings as mere stages to show the plays of age and mental fabrications. Man goes on acting; he goes on performing a drama.

Panchashar sought for sweetness and joy on the face of Melamchi as always, but didn't find any. He speculated that she had been running sick since the day they had an outing to Mount Chuli.

It seemed, Melamchi was deeply hurt by the fact that she was not only losing her ancestral land, but the settlers of that part of the world were also being forsaken of their land property. On the basis of his experience and capacity, the Lama, in himself, drew an inference that Melamchi was sick owning to the issue of the same land.

'If there were also people from the palace attending the fair, they must be the cause behind Melamchi's dejection since that day. They could even have plotted from a distance. By all means, they try to make people helpless. For their selfish interest, the people from the palace can make any move, no matter how heinous and vile act it is. It seems, the courtiers want to use Melamchi as they will,' thought the old Lama's wife.

"Melamchi's inaction, her gloom and her disenchantment suggested that her mind was disturbed, dispersed and had gone astray. It seemed, her mind had glued to something; was running away from a certain thing, and so, she was nowhere. Life is but for one time; why should anyone squeeze it? Why should one char it? Why should anyone torture herself? There are numerous ways to live life. Why does Melamchi stay brooding like this?"

This way, Jimu expressed her observations. After a short pause she said, "One's body doesn't get defiled. It suffices, if one doesn't defile the mind."

She added, "Her face has been overcast with clouds since the day she returned from the fair. I am sure she is beating eaten by her self-incurred worry. We know nothing about it; she only knows. Why then is she trying to tell us through her face and condition? Does one always have the same issue, same place, same friend and same interest always? On a journey, one should stop at shades and resting places, sing and dance, drink water from the tap of one's choice if hungry and quench it. If one does anything unwanted, it suffices to tell it to the heart. Is one's mind too recalcitrant to get consoled by its owner? Small sores and bruises keep coming and going. The balm of time clears all aliments and diseases. What a girl is Melamchi, behaving this way?"

She paused for a while and said, "I had heard people say, the educated ones argue in various ways and hatch various plots, only to get themselves caught. Melamchi turns out to be one of such people.

In a trice, Jimu made such serious remarks about Melamchi. She appeared serious for the first time. She reverted to self-inquiry again.

"One should live for his or her own happiness. Who can always live for others' happiness? Could it be that a person tries to carry an unnecessary burden with increase in age? Instead of caring what others say and what future says, one should mind what her mind says. If you ask me, I do what my mind tells; I do it at all cost. If I cannot, I seek an alternative but I never choose to get tricked, oppressed or manacled. I cannot live that way, with any sort of pain concealed in me. Is it true that when one attains an age of twenty, problems and hassle arrive on their own? If that is the case, I don't want to be twenty; I want to get stuck at nineteen."

Yangsila expressed her dissent.

In that zero hour, Yangsila called up several episodes of her contemplation and lamented. Then she said to herself, 'No one has the right to do anything to others against their interest. One should move according to his or her own interest. Who stops anyone from doing so? Sister Melamchi works at the palace. She must be under restrain. But I am not. I shall set no foot on a place where my freedom will be curtailed."

"Palace?" Yangsila recalled a word she spoke herself, and shuddered. For a while her internal universe shook frantically, and her heart grew heavy. She was, in a way, utterly stunned. The word 'palace' started presenting to her mind the stories and incidents she had heard about. Several thoughts and images competed to make their appearance in her mind. She recalled what she had heard: a palace is a museum of queens; here, women are brought in from all directions, and made an object of museum."

She had heard: the queens stay divided in several units, big and small. They are divided as married and unmarried, as classed and classless, as people with positions and without positions, as manifest and latent. There also are uncountable women from home and abroad, including those from other religions, making their entry into the palace as queens through both formal and informal ways.

She had also heard: from religious centers, hunting expeditions, public events, work places, fair and gatherings, they brought maidens into the palace increasing the number of royal wives. Her mind also recalled a few more rumors: they nabbed girls and women from roads, market places, and in some places, right from their homes, besides those picked from schools, hostels, stables, cow farms and sheep farms.

HARI RAJ BHATTARAI

In Yangsila's memory, several of such narrative episodes came up afresh. She had heard: in fields and farms, in gardens and meadows, and not only from desolate graveyards, but also from pilgrimage sites, girls were picked and taken to the palace to fill its collection. It never hesitated to nab others' wives, others' mothers and others' widows to declare them queens and accord them 'high honor'.

Expressing truth in a satirical tone, she said, "In a way, the palace is a legitimate institution to produce a progressive society, which, like a factory, produced human beings with different faces, hearts and bodies, and exports them to the outside world. We might as well say, the palace is not only a seat of untoward actions and crimes, but is also a mysterious unit of a progressive society."

It's good for girls from poor backgrounds to find refuge in a palace, but Yangsila could not think how ready the palace stays in consuming its wives, or if they need to bear nothing but protracted craving, repression and delinquency inside the palace.

Yangsila shuddered on recalling things she had heard as a child. She had heard: the courtiers rejoice in nightly luxury accompanied by rape. After they fully satisfy themselves from sex in assaulting manner, they haunt for newer victims for similar pleasure. They consider it a matter of valor on their part to mutilate others' bodies and leave them unattended, devastate them, making them useless and abandon them. Going for abortion, robbing someone of her joy beyond repair, and finish off someone's life by feeding slow poison are new episodes for the royalties to please themselves. They entertain themselves by stabbing others with knives, throwing them down from a height or by plotting deliberated accidents. In such a place, who would listen to the helpless ones?

She paused for a while and thought, 'Justice? That is something others give in mercy; it's not a thing one is entitled to. Melamchi is perhaps being gnawed by such things from within.'

All of a sudden, she yelled out in a loud voice, "If she asked, I would give Melamchi my advice."

On hearing indisputable words from Yangsila, Melamchi pressed close to her. She shuddered to see Melamchi approach, and tried to stay calm as though she was trying to recall a forgotten thing, or was trying to forget a thing that was bothering her mind.

"Yang, continue with what you were saying. I want to hear you today," said Melamchi in love-filled words in an inspiring fashion.

Yangsila could read ample degree of compassion in Melamchi's eyes that day. Melamchi appeared quite attentive, seemingly to ready to hear something. But Yangsila was frozen right at the spot where she had stopped before. All she did was lower her eyes and accord her honor to Melamchi's seniority, but spoke not a single word.

"Darling, I have to ask you many things. I have to hear you a lot." With intense love, Melamchi read Yangsila's eyes and face, raised her chin with one palm and with the other, showered love upon her head. After that, she left the spot.

Melamchi could read patience and simplicity in Yangsila. Before this, she had never got an opportunity to get so close and talk. She was not familiar with her past and present, either. They held superficial and informal conversations sometimes. They both were not in need to reach each other's birth charts and study every detail. In fact, Melamchi had placed Jimu and Yangsila on the same footing and understood both in the same way. She thought, 'They both are my cousins—daughters of my mother's brother, and daughters of my grandmother's nephews. She also knew they were not born sisters; their fathers were brothers. Melamchi had spent some of her childhood days in Olangchunggola with her mother, at the home of latter's maternal uncles. That was the only thing she knew about her family background in relation with those girls.

The glimpses of her childhood days started flashing afresh in her mind as memory. She thought deep for a while, 'I think I played with Jimu as a child. I can recall some faint memories. She has now become so unruly, like a horse that cannot be tamed.'

She also thought about Yangsila, but could not remember seeing her at Olangchunggola. She arrived at an inference: 'We all were quite young those days. Yang is, after all, much younger than us. Maybe she was just born. But then, she appears to be of my age, though she is younger, and of my height.'

She abandoned this context at this point and started thinking of something else. 'She also happens to read Kirat scripts. There is no Kirat village in Olangchunggola. Where could she have learned that?'

Yangsila, from the very beginning, had a different reading of Melamchi's personality. On an ordinary and insignificant issue, she neither made a judgment, nor gave a thought. But then, much earlier than coming here, it was in Olangchunggola itself that she had heard about Melamchi, and had inferred that her personality would be a matter of glory and veneration for her. That's why, she was quite eager to know many things about Melamchi. Her thoughts were quite healthy; she was not at all prejudiced. The Goa and Ukyap families in Olangchunggola knew that Yangsila's views and estimations were always healthy, balanced and trustworthy. This fame had spread across the Kirat Kingdom, the place of her maternal parents. But the Lama couple, who lived confined in such a walled house, was not aware of Yangsila's entire personality. To every girl visiting them from Olangchunggola, they accorded an honor of a family member or one from the in-laws' family and treated as children. Yangsila, especially, stayed with everyone with guiltless and spotless feelings, and presented herself to everyone with simplicity. That must be why she never became a matter of discussion for anyone. Instead, she became an ordinary onlooker or a dear member in every family.

On the day Melamchi entered that house with a stranger, she looked extremely happy. Her face glimmered with the type of joy women have when they reach their maternal parents' homes, parents' home or their own homes after a visit. She had seen on her eyes the glory of twelve suns, and on her face there was the type of coolness that emanates when sixteen moons shine together. But as her stay in that part of the world lingered and her visits increased, and as incidents went piling one upon another, their shadows made Melamchi appear grimmer and grimmer. Yangsila, herself remaining an introvert, was making a detailed study of this change in Melamchi.

Melamchi, a girl who loved to live a joyful life, had gone to the fair with a lot of excitement, but was down with dejection while returning home. Shadows had mounted upon her usual countenance. When Yangsila closely studied Melamchi's personality, she took no time to infer that she was in a sort of mental trauma. After this, she contemplated on the second point and concluded: Melamchi's visit of Mount Chuli with the stranger and her return from that very spot had some bearing with Melamchi's illness.

An incident from the recent past started rippling in Yangsila's eyes: when the Lama old man and Panchashar had moved toward the meadows, a pair of king's men had come from the palace to meet Melamchi on horsebacks, and held a long conversation with Melamchi in the court yard. But they didn't rest for even a while, though Melamchi requested them a lot. That was perhaps the way a royal order worked. They returned immediately on their horses. She also recalled how, while they were leaving, they suddenly remembered a thing, and came back to hand a letter over to Melamchi.

Yangsila had especially noted how, after that, Melamchi's mind had become invigorated. She had made a special note of the fact that for some time, the monologue from the side of the horsemen had been like a command, and not anything like a cordial conversation. Rather it was like an interrogation and grilling. She had seen grimness mount upon Melamchi's face after this.

Explaining the possible reasons for Melamchi's mental imbalance, Yangsila dwelt upon yet another factor. In her view, the letter the horsemen handed over to Melamchi was another cause of her trauma. This is because, as many times as Yangsila saw Melamchi alone in her room, she was always brooding with the same letter in her hand. She found Melamchi having a dialogue with the sealed envelope.

Yangsila, in spite of such deep studies about Melamchi, forgot to inquire that fact that the austere image of the stranger was tightening its grip in her own mind, while Jimu, on her part, was looking for an opportunity to engage him romantically.

***

CHAPTER ELEVEN

MELAMCHI WAS PRIZED gem of that place, that family. She was a star in herself, a new myth, and an instance completely different from others. Age, education, art, realms of services and her circumstances had contributed in making her personality developed and optimally nourished to befit the changing times.

She kept herself within the bounds of her responsibilities and discipline, and fulfilled her duties. In the roles of a good friend, an ideal teacher, a good administrator, a skilled horse-rider and a successful director, she always faired extremely well. She knew many a thing, but didn't pose herself as a teacher unless someone asked her help. While she was not engaged in any physical or external assignment, she stayed in her own internal world, busy in herself. At such moments, she appeared completely different to others' eyes, as though she was not the Melamchi they were familiar with, or she had changed dramatically.

On seeing Melamchi lost in herself, Panchashar thought the incident at Mount Chuli, and the atmosphere therein, was behind her dejection. He summarily rejected the possibility of any other factor being the cause of Melamchi's illness. He could not convince himself that factors like evil spirits, Budhyani, Jungali and spells— things a culture superstitiously believes in—were possible causes, and so, he didn't lose his time in investigating along that line. He stuck to a single opinion.

But Jimu, this time, thought rather differently: 'People said, beauty, youth and knowledge, sometimes, pose as one's own enemy. Could anything like that have happened with Melamchi? Who tempers with an ugly one? Who trusts such a person? But then, how can I cross the limits of decorum and counsel Melamchi, who is elder to me albeit by a few moments?'

He thought further harder: 'Fie! How pathetic has Melamchi made herself with that self-incurred dejection? Is this an age one stays defeated? On my part, I cannot even think so.'

The reality was that, the letter or anything like that were not the factors that had driven Melamchi into dilemma. After all, she was not such a weak girl. Yet, she appeared brooding, her eyes fixed on the same sealed letter.

Melamchi herself forwarded a weak argument: "If the letter contained any unwanted news, he would return to his home anytime, and if he does, the plans for constructing a new building would be aborted or postponed. If he decides to return, would it be wise for us to stop? Can we stop him?"

She analyzed it herself: 'If this letter is likely to pose any discomfort on the path of construction, how about hiding this letter from him? Can't we do without giving him this letter? Can a state be so unjust to Pan? Can it trick him so badly? Doesn't that prove to be a violation of his human rights and freedom?"

She further thought, 'Why am I so much attracted toward this letter? Because, Pan is dear to me? Or, is it because, being an employee of the state, I am in a position to set him free? No. He is an accomplished artist. The state administration should fail nowhere in ensuring him all comfort and satisfaction. So, it's a duty on our part to offer him a balanced environment. He must also be aware of this. After all, wasn't it the state that gave him the opportunity to visit our place and families, roam about, and get mixed with people?

According a lot of honor to the entire personality of Panchashar, she thought, 'He is, first of all, a labor; an artist. Second, he is a stranger. Third, he is a state guest, and a close friend of mine.'

She turned toward herself and said, 'For him, I am merely a guide and a helper, moving at the state orders.'

In relation to the letter, she made a self-contemplation: 'If this letter is meant for him, he must receive it. I do have the right to study its gist and decide whether I should give it to him or not, but when it comes to this letter, I will withhold my right.'

'I can also get the gist of the letter by making Jimu or Yangsila read it. That's not a big deal. But why should I do a thing the palace didn't do?'

Giving a twist to her soliloquy, she said, 'Am I bound to follow the orders of the king's horsemen? If the king had such a thought, he would certainly write to me. But I won't listen to them in order to make an estimation of this letter. I will hand this letter over to the stranger as it is, and use my rights according to my intellect. I am not obliged to follow the horsemen's words.'

Melamchi ended her musings, and took a long breath.

"Yang, come here for a while," she said, in order to make her thoughts lighter and to find a new subject to think about.

Yangsila walked in. Jimu came too, walking side by side.

"Yang, you read this letter. I could not make it out," said Melamchi, handing over to her a sealed letter.

"It's still sealed. Oh, it's the stranger's letter," said Yangsila, carefully crafting her words.

"Bring here; I will read. You didn't even read the address," said Jimu, snatching the letter from Yangsila's hand. "It happens to come from Mauwa Khola Thum. The sender is a Kirat."

Having said this, Jimu started reading the letter, albeit with difficulty.

"Bring; I will read it myself." Yangsila snatched it back from Jimu's hand. He looked closely at it and said, "This name in the new ink is in Chinese. The one before that is in Tibetan, and even before that, in Kirat script—Srijanga." After having scanned the outside cover of the letter, she said, "The first stamp on it is from Lhasa. Maybe traders traveling along that route posted this letter from Lhasa. That is what people in our part also do," Yangsila said, passing her comment and remark simultaneously.

"Fine; let's first give letter to the stranger. We can then borrow and read: you and I, can't we?" said Melamchi in a loving tone, and took the letter back from Yangsila's hand.

After Jimu and Yangsila had left, Melamchi said to herself, 'God, let this letter contain a good thing. Let the stranger have nothing to worry about. Let him not move away from us. I would rather go to stay in the monastery for some days. Please listen to my prayers.'

This way, she started making attempts to keep herself assured.

When the letter was handed over to Panchashar, he tore the envelop and started reading it silently. Melamchi was sitting next to him, albeit in a different mood. Calculating that Panchashar had read the letter twice, she asked, "I don't think the letter has any bad news."

"No; everything is fine."

"Why then did your face change?"

"Old memories! Their impact, perhaps."

She considered Panchashar's answer a fact, and said, "If it's something I can also hear, read it out to me. I want to know. If they are private affairs, leave them."

Displaying a brief smile, Melamchi said, "You can also read out, omitting the portion I should not hear."

After running his eyes on every nook and corner of the letter, he said, "There is no portion you may not listen to. Come; I will read it out to you. After that, you can as well read it yourself. Or else, you might ask Jimu or Yangsila to read it to you. Listen; I am reading it to you first."

Mauwa Khola Thum, Taplejung
Limbuwan, Kingdom of Kirat

Dear traveler Panchashar
Sewaro! Namaskar!

Ever since you left us, we have got no news from you. That has made us deeply anxious. Take the same route when you return. Sanjhang and Teejhang have been waiting for you. By now, the hill where they keep waiting for you, have been named Menchhyayem.

The village of Sanghu has been waiting for you, assigning Sanjhang and Teejhang the responsibility to build a beautiful garden at Milke, where sixty-six varieties of rhododendrons bloom. As you know, we are Limbu Kirats. We believe in others' words, and stick to our promises ourselves.

We have sent this letter in the hand of traders moving to Lhasa. We have asked them to post it, also by writing your address in the local scripts from there. We hope the letter will reach you. If you have time, do write back to us.

Let Goddess Pathibhara fulfill all your wishes.

Yours
Siddha Kirat, Sanjhang, Teejhang
People's representatives and the village folks

The doubt that had gripped Melamchi before reading the letter existed no more now. She came at peace and the waves of joy started tickling her body. She recalled her promise to visit the monastery and said, "I shall certainly come to stay in the monastery. My mind is at peace now." Again she said in a decisive way, "Panchashar will not go away now. He won't face any trouble here."

For general courtesy, she turned toward the letter and said, "Pan, who are Sanjhang and Teejhang, after all?"

"They are little Kirat maidens. They are Devis."

"And who is this Kirat?"

"He is an enlightened man, a powerful pursuer. He has strange powers to create a different world. He can do miracles in a trice."

"Why would Sanjhang and Teejhang wait for you?"

"I had promised I would return along the same way. That must be the reason."

"Why that issue of trust and mistrust?"

"I have promised to reach there again. I had assured them."

Now she was quiet. Panchashar said with ease, "What a difficult test you put me to?" He took a short break and said, "Do you have any more questions?" This time, he laughed out himself, thought guiltlessly.

"No, I don't. Come; let's go for a dive in the pool. We can wash our minds of all malice there," she said, putting a stop on their dialogue.

Handing over a vial of medicine into Panchashar's hand before diving into the pool, Melamchi said, "You take this medicine. It will relieve you of fatigue."

She placed some water on another hand of Panchashar and said, "Drink this too. You have slept at many uncouth and uncomfortable places. If you have caught any sort of wound, sore or itching, or any sort of disease for that matter, you will be relieved."

Making acute calculations of time, she took out yet another vial of medicine and said, "This is a different sort of medicine. It will generate new vigor and new zeal in your body. You will start considering yourself strong, enthusiastic and dauntless. Take it."

Whenever he got up in the morning, Panchashar always considered the water-play and collage-like memories of the previous evening mere dreams. For him, all these things belonged to the dream world, for he believed that such things could never take place in the real world. Materially, such thoughts and contemplations were figurations of his mental world built on his culture and environment. It was his life-view, an objective truth in which a shield could eclipse the entire solar system. In reality, it was a mere dream for him.

A thing that was true for one was a mere dream for another, maybe because they had come from different cultures and different environments. They were half mysteries! Half truths!

***

"Pan, I want to tell you my thoughts before listening to your decision today."

"I am waiting for that. Everyone welcomes a good thought."

They finished one round of breakfast in the morning. Waiting for additional cup of tea, Melamchi said, "I don't have much experience in this regard, but I have heard certain things. I know a few things. Yet, I am unable to make good estimation of it. I shall propose to you something on the basis of whatever experience and knowledge I have."

"Come on; tell."

Putting aside her cup after a sip of tea, Melamchi said, "State buildings should not be constructed in the rural areas, in agricultural fields, orchards and farming areas. A royal office should never be established in the countryside."

She took a break and said, "If it's a health centre, we must accept it. It's an obligation, you know."

Panchashar started at her with interrogative looks.

"Because," she said, giving continuity to her statement, "the soldiers, the policemen, the employees, and the henchmen that grow under their refuge and patronage will make the countryside their fray, and destroy it, making it their playground."

"The rural folks do not like the state bulls, buffaloes and horses devastating their area. If they get looted, oppressed and neglected, it will be a matter of pain for us too. That will disrupt the balance in the nation. We should never plant the seeds of crimes in the easy, simple and pristine life in the countryside. That will be regrettable. We should never force our people to tolerate state-sponsored crime and oppression. Let's not even open a door to that. It's not yet time we must be doing that." She said all these things in a trice.

Melamchi paused for some time and spoke, after taking a long breath, "A palace is always quite dangerous. Those who have stayed close to the palace turn out to be fiercer demons. At such times, the ordinary people find no one to listen to their grievances. They are recklessly looted; they are abused. For that reason, let's not open a track for the palace to enter the country."

Halting for a while, she resumed, "When the people gather enough power to challenge oppression and atrocities, or say, when justice becomes strong, opening of such tracks will not make much difference. But if we do it now, that will be a direct injustice upon the rural life. So, we must refrain from initiating such an untoward act. This is my proposal. I too was quite afraid on knowing about the king's character and his henchmen's conducts and crimes."

She raised yet another context and said, "I have heard and understood many stories about a wicked ruler torturing his subjects. The kings are, by nature, cruel and ruthless. Our king is no exception. Our grandfather often says, the wicked rulers might as well peel off their subjects' skin and make shoes out of it. There are really few rulers that were wise and merciful; most of them are cruel and blood-sucking. This is what history tells us. So if one wills to live a healthy life, it is always good to stay away from their eyes"

Panchashar found Melamchi's analysis and experience quite logical. So he said, "If we have a construction site there, we had better use that. This place is a bit too far from the palace. Isn't it?" He wanted to take Melamchi's opinion once again.

"True; it's rather too far. Who will come here and go back, riding a horse for two days? After all, a building will be used more, if it is nearer to the palace."

Panchashar drew the gist and said, "If that is the case, neither will the rural folks suffer, nor will we be in a position to harm them."

He turned toward Melamchi and added, "You opened my eyes and also showed me a way out. The intellect and perspectives you have in you are highly commendable. They are high. I have great honors for them. In reality, your thoughts are very logical. They are timely too."

The spot Melamchi suggested for constructing the royal building was on the top of a stunted hill on the eastern side the existing royal palace. There was a beautiful and wide flat land on its top, surrounded by a green forest from all its sides. In fact, there was no other place as suitable as this one in the vicinity of the palace. Panchashar considered it proper from many quarters. So he looked at Melamchi with eyes of contentment, and expressed his satisfaction.

Seeing that the task of selecting the site was finally over, Melamchi felt relieved from a huge burden. So she thanked

Panchashar silently. Then she said to herself, 'I will take some more measure of rice tonight, and will sleep longer."

From the royal palace, one took one full morning on horseback to reach that spot. The road along the bank of a river was easy, though a crooked one. The only difficult portion was a short segment up the hill just before reaching the spot. So, it was not very far from the palace.

The plain on the hilltop saw sunlight all through the day, from sunrise to sunset. The Himalayan ranges visible from east to west fell on the back side of this spot, and appeared quite near in the background, though it was fairly far.

This land, flanked by two glaciers flowing from north to south, looked extremely exhilarating and fertile. After a detailed study of the trees that gave wood, the shrubs that gave leaves, the plants that gave fruits, the bushes that gave flowers, and the plants that gave fragrance and medicines, Panchashar opined that such a spot might be rare elsewhere. Melamchi was left wonderstruck by Panchashar's original view and brilliant talent. She was truly pushed into stupefaction, and turned mute.

They were in a great hurry. Much of their time had slipped off before they had started anything. The haste had gripped both of them very badly. So, Melamchi took the blueprint of the house painted by Panchashar dramatically, and added on it a natural background, making it more realistic, concrete and permanent. Then she gave it a finishing, adding the pictures of dragons here and there. These two patrons of art, through their habit of nourishing each other's interest and intellect, and promoting the same, stayed grateful to each other and expressed their gratefulness without any words. In fact, both were overflowing with a sense of liberality and greatness.

They now committed to the task of identifying the most auspicious moment to kick-start the construction of the building, and returned to their erstwhile shelter.

***

HARI RAJ BHATTARAI

Back in the guest house, a new episode sprang up.

One evening, five horsemen dressed in formal attires showed up. They had spears in their hands and swords in their girdles. They seemed to be moving toward a battlefield.

It was time they lit lamps in the evening. Someone blew a strange type of whistle. Alarmed, the Nepali artisans came out of their rooms.

Panchashar had been away from there for a few days. Melamchi had taken him away in her bid to find a site for constructing the planned royal building. If only Melamchi were there, she would work as a shield against the invaders.

Mauni could do some question-answer even by writing. Omu could lend him enough support. But then, both were missing at the moment. Since Mauni was running sick, Omu occasionally took him on a carriage for treatment. That evening, they had not been back to the guest house yet. So, those who were present there came out, one after another, gathered on the western side of the veranda.

The horsemen gathered on the yard. The yard was rather low. The artisans stared at one another. They had no issue to talk about. Each of their minds was tickled by the same question: Why have the horseman come? What will they do now? What will happen next?

The first horseman said in a commanding manner, "You ought to vacate the guest house immediately. Leave it within seven days."

Another one said, "Get your things packed within five days."

The third one said, "There's no time; it won't be extended."

The fourth one said, "We'll take care of your transport and food on the way. You don't need to worry about that."

There was stillness in the air for a while.

"One of our friends is out on work to find a spot for building a new palace for the king. We won't leave this place before he is back here. We can't go, leaving him alone," said one of the artisans.

"He is our leader," said another.

"True. We will wait for him," said the third one.

The horsemen paid them deaf ears and turned their horses and moved toward the girls' yard. They conveyed the message they had brought, and returned.

From among the artisans, one placed forth an argument: "I don't think they have come from the side of the palace. For, a king's decision cannot be so harsh and impracticable."

"Maybe they are here to defame the palace, or are on the move to stop Melamchi and Panchashar's path," another one added.

"That's possible. They were supposed to inform, which they did. It's for us to think now," said another one, suggesting a solution.

Coughing, Mauni entered the guest house. Omu was with him, helping him with his steps.

"Our friends didn't happen to light lamps even by this hour," Omu said.

"May be they are somewhere. Let's do that, instead," wrote Mauni, striking a solution.

"It seems our friends are out," said Omu in a voice dotted with dissatisfaction.

"We are here. Come here. There was earthquake a while ago. There were hailstones; there was an earthquake. The wind and storm didn't allow us to light the lamps," said someone from the kitchen.

Time to light the lamps was fast elapsing. Omu came into the dining room, leading with her hand. Everyone was brooding in his or her own place, letting a small lamp throw a dim light from the mantelpiece.

A group of girls came from the other side lighting the lamps and got mixed with the boys. They could now notice one another better in the light of the lamps. But then, no one could tell if the lamp light was faint or something was wrong with the onlooker, each face inside the dining hall appeared grim and dejected.

After dinner, the girls initiated the issue. They informed that the artisans would be escorted up to the monastery of Lhasa. They said this, quoting the source of the horsemen.

Another day, this issue was openly raised and discussed before Mauni. At the end of the discussion, Mauni wrote, "I want to meet the king myself once. I will rest for two days and recuperate. I will go there and talk to him, not after three, but after four days from today. I assure you of this."

It was a matter of gladness that they were returning to their home country. After all, every traveler remains impatient to get back home. The native soil keeps pulling. But the abruptness of the notice that was forcing them out was a matter of pain for them.

Everyone seconded Mauni's idea. Yet, no heart appeared happy there. They had no option but to wait for the fourth day in the midst of dejection and dishonor. There was no other resort at their disposal.

But the fourth day never came. Because Mauni, who had gone for treatment on the second day, didn't come back. He didn't return on the third day either. Omu returned and told the artisans that Mauni was seriously sick. Then she returned. The third day too slipped off this way. On the fourth day passed in the midst of hope, dejection, frustration and dilemma.

No one had any interest to do anything or listen to anyone. They spent their time in utter silence and frustration. But the girls continued to feed them their snacks and meals in time, and continued with their conservation, cleanliness, smiles and compassionate actions—though forced ones—without allowing any change in their usual ways. They gave continuity to their excellent management, though deep in their hearts, they were sad about the approaching moment of separation.

The Nepali artisans were seen divided in two mindsets. One that could speak Tibeto-Burman language didn't appear that weak, mentally. The members of this group, in intervals, appeared conscious, awakened, enthusiastic and glorious. The words of the horsemen left them dejected, like others, for a brief time, but later, they accepted the reality and the destiny of life. Like a glorious young man, each member later said, "After all, we are returning to our own homes, to our own land. Why should we lament? We are still young and strong; we still have dreams to do a lot of things. We ought to become someone's consorts; we need to make someone our own. I console myself; I won't be lamenting anymore. Thank God, I can finally return home. I will go back happily, singing and dancing."

There was yet another group that spoke the language of the Aryan family. It was in deep gloom, for having a different mentality. It world was perhaps narrower, confined to its own margins. It could not perhaps make its thought magnanimous, for the ken of its contemplation was small. "What will happen of us if we die? If we cannot lift a single step homeward? Everything has gone wrong; our ship is in wreck. We came here with high hopes; everything has been shattered."

This group, with such thoughts, was mentally very weak. It started torturing itself with loneliness, dragging, trampling and dangling its life-history on the crutches of hatred and inferiority. The result was that, Director of the department of garments, Dean of the faculty of arms invention, and Professors from the department of skin development continued to be dejected like employees that had lost their jobs after the change of guard. They returned, considering it a game of destiny of gods.

One group returned in full enthusiasm and excitement, carrying home a commitment to live life to its fullest. It returned, deciding not to hold back at any cost, even if there was an earnest request, committed to making no compromise with anyone. It returned happy, and set out happy.

The other group returned in the fashion of a patient being carrying on a stretcher. It was beset by a dejected mindset as though it was returning, having left its family members buried at a graveyard. It seemed like someone returning home from a hospital with a chronic disease and losing his way in the middle of the journey. It is gripped by the feeling of 'I', but has no trace of 'we' feeling. This is why it's alone; it's lost.

Mauni came back after a weeklong stay at the clinic. Omu never forgot her responsibility. The guest house was silent. Omu left Mauni at the dining hall for a while and rushed toward the girls' dormitory. She found her belongings in her room as they were before. From there, she rushed to inspect the men's dormitory. Mauni's room had his stuffs; other rooms were all vacant. She controlled her cry by force and rushed to embrace Mauni, in whose arms, she burst into real tears. Mauni gradually understood the cause of her cry. He allowed her to cry all her heart out. She cried to her fill, and relived herself.

***

Irrationality, abuse, foolishness and absence of dignity, at times, push a person into a difficult fix. A person can resort to annoying acts due to the absence of self control. In such cases, he not only harms himself, but also pushes others into difficulties.

The result of the incident that took place there was that they had to return home dishonored. Many still didn't know why they had been packed off so abruptly. It was a case in which the wrongdoing of one person was harming an entire contingent.

Jokhé was rather vicious by nature. He gossiped about others and pleased himself. He presented himself in one way while in group and behaved differently when he was alone. He was young, granted, but was stronger than others. He was good looking no doubt, but his excessive pride and stubbornness had made him rather delinquent. The habit, which developed into an addition, was the cause behind their abrupt departure from there.

Birasé was too gullible to understand his ways. He was a man of a different nature, but was quick in making speculations. So Guindé feared him, thinking that he was aware of their under-table story.

In this issue, however, Birasé knew nothing. He had only kept his doors of doubt and suspicion open.

'Jokhé has risked his life from his own doings. I am sure he is in the snare of one of those girls. An unruly, bullheaded man! He is a Kami man no doubt, but his heart also happened to befit a vigorous

Kami. It now seems, he is reaping his harvest as a Kami does,' said Guindé to himself regretfully.

He suddenly remembered: Jokhé had caught his hands and showed him a scene outside his window. Guindé didn't follow the sight again. But Jokhé failed to control himself. His engagement with the scene increased with time. His stubbornness and pride made him even more unruly.

Birasé had had a quick glance of the collaboration between Guindé and Jokhé. But he didn't care, for he was not a follower of that path, by nature. But at the moment, Guindé and Birasé merely stared at each other. Birasé stared at Guindé knowing that he was a witness, but of what? He didn't think it wise to speak anything, though.

'Birasé perhaps knows many things. If he breaks his silences, things can go wrong. Oh, God, make him seal his mouth,' said Guindé to himself, making a silent prayer.

Tyanduké, Namché and Lhotsé were in slight gloom on finding some of their friends gone.

Dhané got absorbed in Kerung's happiness and facilities. Gola continued to move around as the partner of Bekha.

But everyone was prickled by the same fear: Jokhé was the one who had become victim to a wild beast! What would they tell to his family and relatives? How would they console themselves? They lumbered on, trying to find answers to several of such questions rising in their minds.

***

An unbelievable incident happened to take place in the background. Most of the members of the artisans' contingent didn't even know of such a thing. Omu had the tiptoe, but had chosen to stay aloof, considering it someone's private affair. She had controlled herself in honor of someone's personality, interest and freedom. She believed that trying to counsel or stop someone at such moments would futile.

This was a tale of the guest house. Two girls, Sang and Sinja, were engaged in prolonged, lesbian relations. One day, incidentally, the sound of ecstatic contentment emanating from their relations, at the peak of their mutual engagement for physical pleasure, happened to fall into the ears of Jokhé. He had been passing along the path through the garden at the back side of the garden. Considering it an appeal for help at an hour of emergency, he moved a few steps ahead toward the bush, from where he watched the show for a while, without a blink, holding his breath. He watched them until they were done with their coitus. Since that day, he started following their routine and peep at their game. These were external things. Omu knew every detail of this, but kept the fact with herself.

Once Jokhé's blind masculinity was aroused. It was an uncontrollable excitation. He transgressed every limit of decorum, and rushed into the dormitory of the two girls. As always, the two were engaged in physical pleasure in the dim light of *donglong*. As soon as he was inside, the girls shuddered with fear, and were shocked, gripped by intense fear.

Jokhé played with both, turn by turn, until he was fully satisfied. That was not, however a healthy cohabitation. It cannot be termed cohabitation at all. That was a hunt for pleasure. It was one directional. That was a hateful drab they had been compelled to wear though it was against their will.

And this act started recurring. He used to enter, poke them, sway with them, pour himself and come out, exhausted. Jokhé had no idea if the girls had interest in sex with men, or if they got any pleasure in it or not. He put his labor one way, but the girls didn't welcome his moves. He played alone, and thought he had won a big battle. He didn't bother to know if the girls had their involvement in it. Still he considered himself a victor. He might have been successful in the way one had to play, or use his partner. But incidentally, the girls never went against his will whenever he was at the peak of excitement. At his comfort, they got kneaded like flour, allowed to be twisted or rolled like a ball in the form of a fresh corpse. He was the sole player, proving for every hole in their bodies. He had no idea of the loving acts of sex, its healthy methods and procedures, its rise and fall, and its pace, pause and final stop. All he knew was how to attack. That was not, however, everything. That would not suffice.

Omu knew all these things, for Sang and Sinjha had told her every detail about those incidents, word by word. So she thought from her friends' perspective: they considered a man's reckless intrusion into their territory an unforgivable crime. In their regular, well-managed and lively play, they considered his intrusion and attack not only unwanted but also incompatible and dangerous. They thought that his masculine ego had abused them beyond toleration, taking them for nothing but mere playthings. They tolerated their own dishonor and slight to a great extent, but when they thought their secrecy and mystery had been exposed, their pain was beyond telling. This, they considered was a big blow to their self-respect and dignity. As a consequence, they considered such a beast, in the guise of a man, incorrigible and thus, like a ferocious lion or a snake, they were not bent on giving him the most rigorous punishment they could imagine. They have been living with commitments to fulfill this vow.

Omu made a short analysis of the situation and said to herself, 'I have to take Mauni for treatment. Let not any untoward incident take place until we return. God, let no hardship befall in between!'

She then bowed to the Buddha and said, "Lord, grant intellect and patience to rivals on both the ends. Save them from calamities."

She dropped a few drops of tears and said, "Have compassion, my Lord! Forgive all. Make all of us filled with compassion; filled with forgiveness." Omu spread her palms, cupped together, and prayed for the Buddha's mercy.

Sanga and Sinja opened up their bodies before Omu. They bore many marks of pinching, gnawing, trampling, strangling and clawing. There was no part on their body that had not been mutilated. Their cheeks, lips and even eyebrows had been rendered ghastly. Omu thought her friends' bodies had changed into a collage painting and remembered the way they had cried their hearts out, letting down torrents of tears.

She thought about Jokhé, "He is a devil, out and out. A fearful sinner! People make others happy; he robbed them of happiness. Others accord honor; he accords dishonor. People establish happy love relations and go, leaving behind memorable examples of love for the world. But this beast happened to drag himself far below the level of a rapist demon. Fie!"

She drew in a gush of cold breath and released it. In a state of dejection, she thought, 'People expect friendship; he exhibited slight. Is cohabitation devoid of consent, cooperation, harmony, trust, intimacy and dedication copulation at all? But then, how can I tell them to forget such a devil and leave him alone? No, I cannot tell them so. Both their mental injuries and physical bruises are beyond toleration. How long could they stay, bearing all those wounds? Poor things! How could they console themselves?"

Soon, the news about the incident fell into Melamchi's ears too. She came grumbling, "Whatever was most unwanted finally happened. Can one man fulfill the sexual desires of many women? The sexual power of man can never fulfill the physical craving of a girl. One woman, at the least, needs two men, if she is to be completely satisfied. Only then can one derive healthy and complete contentment in sex."

With added anguish and hatred, she said, "Jokhé is a mad man, out and out. If I were there, I would stab him with a sword there and then. Can anyone be so bestial and cruel? Doesn't such a young man know anything about rationality and decorum?"

Melamchi turned dark with rage. She took a brief pause and resumed, "If it's true that they got him wiped by a wild animal, I don't consider that a big deal. But I don't believe anything like that happened."

She entered the guest while, still grumbling.

"What, did you say, is not a big deal? What, you were saying, you don't believe?" said Panchashar, directing his question at Melamchi.

He looked at Melamchi in silence. Melamchi was not in her usual gait that moment. She didn't look calm and composed as before. He thought hard, calling up some wrinkles on his forehead. He saw Melamchi quite vigorous that moment; she looked quite enraged, as he could make it out from her looks. So he kept quiet fearing that if his words missed a balance, it would be like adding oil on fire.

"Did you know how many things took place?" she said to Panchashar, sitting at her usual place.

For a while, he stared at Melamchi with strange eyes. Then he said, "Oh no; I have no idea," before returning to his erstwhile position.

"Didn't Mauni tell you anything?"

"He doesn't have chalk with him. More, he is seriously ill. It seems, he doesn't have enthusiasm left in him. Maybe he will tell when he recuperates."

"Didn't Omu tell you what took place here?"

"It seems Omu has no time. She is busy attending to the sick man. Maybe she also has no idea; else she would find time to tell me."

In a usual tempo, Panchashar added, "You rather tell it yourself what went wrong here."

"It seems your Jokhé has been eaten up by wild beasts. The entire town is buzzing with the rumor."

"Jokhé must have returned home with other friends. How could a beast eat him?"

"He has been devoured. I don't have any complaint though. I think you won't have any, either."

"I didn't quite get you, Melamchi. You are in emotions; do tell me clearly. We have enough time; we can talk at ease. Cool down first; I will listen to each of your words."

In the meantime, Omu prepared tea and breakfast for them. Mauni also showed up, dragging his sagged and frail body. Their discussion got continuity.

"Jokhé happened to quarrel with our girls. It was not a quarrel actually; he happened to rape them turn by turn. They were girls who would not enjoy with men. They didn't like Jokhé's action. They had revenge motifs; they threw him before wild animals."

"Could it be an incidental happening?"

"No. It was deliberated. It was well-planned."

"But why?"

"For revenge. It was a capital punishment."

"Are you sure? You have no doubts? Isn't it still a matter of mystery?"

"No. When Omu told me, I went to inquire. The torn clothes procured form the site were his. I made a bundle of the clothes left tattered by the animal, and have brought home. They are in the carriage; go and see it for yourself once, and assure yourself. Also decide what should be told to his family. I thank that is equally important."

Panchashar did the tears that were simmering in his eyes.

Omu inclined on one side, hiding her face.

Melamchi drew in a long gush of breath and said, "It was a well deliberated plan—one that had no option. Because they first bound his limbs and rendered him like a log so that the beasts didn't spare him. Then they made him stand against a tree, on which, he was bound with strong ropes. They thrust cotton into his mouth. They also left some chicken clasped underneath his armpit and a few piglets in a bamboo basket kept nearby. The smell was enough to allure a beast. All the three preys were finished in a trice."

Seizing an opportunity, Omu said, "While going, Sang and Sinja asked him to join them to the forest, where firewood had been piled waiting to be carried home. He was still high on booze. He had added more, and was almost senseless. The mule-carriage held only three of them. On seeing them leave, no one could guess such a thing would happen. His life happened to perish in a matter of one night."

She burst into tears.

"Such a big incident happened to take place while we were away." This is all Melamchi could utter, collected all the courage she could.

"We have been away for treatment. I think, they did it cashing on the absence of Mauni and me," said Omu, revealing the truth.

"That must be the reason others were sent home immediately, Panchashar," Melamchi said, breaking the secret.

"Yes, that's the case. But the plan appears to be sequentially maneuvered," said Omu, reiterating what Mauni had said in his sign language in the past two days.

After a pause she added, "His friends said, Jokhé had eloped two girls at once seeing all three of them missing. Later, it came out to be this."

"Let's all take the balm of philosophy to treat the bruises in our hearts. That is the only remedy at hand. We have no other way out here," wrote Mauni, but didn't erase it.

Mauni and Panchashar did the posthumous rituals for Jokhé formally. Melamchi and Omu were quite generous in their help. The local artisans also attended the ritual in a good number.

Though they had their own understanding and interpretation of the event, they were all quite edgy. Gradually, the incident slipped into oblivion.

***

CHAPTER TWELVE

TIMUR KHAN ENTERED the royal meeting hall with his new queen. He was welcomed by the courtiers present their in a traditional fashion. When the king and the queen had taken their seats, the courtiers sat down.

An ordinary girl from an ordinary family in the countryside had entered Timur's royal meeting hall in the capacity of a queen. Though the regal swagger and show had always been the same, the queen found it quite extraordinary and mysterious. She started observing the gestures and smiles there, and the physical, verbal and artificial expression therein. For her, this world was altogether a different one, and beyond her imaginations.

Timur Khan appeared especially excited, owing to the arrangement that soon after the dissolution of the meeting, he would directly move with his queen to a new closet. His face glimmered with a new glow and feelings of victory.

Seeing two distinguished people—a man and a women—standing on one side of the meeting hall that day, Timur asked, "They?"

"Hwangdi! One of them is a member of the contingent of artisans we had invited."

"Why is he standing? Ask him to take a seat."

A man walked close to Mauni and asked him to take a seat. Mauni sat down, but Omu continued to stand.

The man also requested Omu to take a seat. She also sat down.

Reiterating his sentence, Timur Khan asked, "Do we have any special agenda to discuss in today's meeting?"

"The artisan has come to make a request."

"Tell what you have got to share."

Mauni rose from his place, stood aright and greeted King Timur in his own ways. He folded both his hands and genuflected with respect, lowering his head slightly forward. Then he returned to his former position.

He signaled Omu, who was sitting next to him. She also rose from her place and stood next to Mauni.

Mauni took the bundle of papers from underneath his armpit into his hand. He sorted out one page from the bundle and showed it toward the royal couple. It read:

"I am speechless."

The sentence had been written both in Tibetan and Chinese Mandarin languages.

He showed another page that read, "I need someone who can read for me Tibetan, Devnagari, Ranjana and Maithili scripts."

The courtiers faced one another once again. There was more curiosity in the hall.

Mauni waited for a while and showed yet another paper. It read, "If there is no one, I will take help of my own friend."

He got the signal that his request had been granted. He checked if the write-ups were in right order and kept his slate, chalk and eraser ready.

'What a fool this king is! He has picked a man tired of working and forced him to move around the earth. If I were in his place, I would build the new building at Cheng Du in Sichuan. I would rejoice around Nyingchi and Menaling even more. He has four sons; he could spare one building to each of them. Does kingdom a thing one should avail alone? Development is something that is directed to a new place that needs it best. A state should also learn to expand itself,' said Mauni to himself.

Breaking the silence that pervaded for a long time, Omu whispered to Mauni, "Mauni, you seem to be lost in yourself. Where have you reached?"

Mauni clarified in sign language, "It has been long since our leader left us. We don't know where he is, and what he has been doing. Poor thing! How long should he wander?"

"He is with Shang. Shang will keep him clasped. You don't need to worry," said Omu, making him reassured.

"Who is Shang by the way?" asked Mauni in signals.

"Oh yes, you don't know that her name is Shang," she said in signs, carefully making herself seem non-aligned.

"Is her full name Shang Melamchi?" wrote Mauni on his slate.

"Her real name is Shangri-la. She was born on the way, while her parents were traveling. On being born at a valley—locally called 'Shangri-la' on the high Himalayas, she was named Shangri-la. We always use that name for her. At Gola as well, people recognize her with that name. When she came here and started attending school, she was renamed Melamchi," said Omu, revealing the history in sign language.

"If that is the case, my guess is right: Shang Melamchi," Mauni wrote in short. Omu read it, and burst into a loud laughter.

Mauni turned mute again. He was thinking, 'I see the need to give the king a third eye. I will tell him all my feelings today. I *must* speak. Else, why would I be so impatient to express myself? It's possible that my dream will materialize some day in future.' He found himself even more resolved.

Disrupting Mauni's silence, Omu said in signals, "Where are you at the moment, Mauni? Every eye is turned on us."

Mauni turned attentive, turned toward Omu and said in signals, "Instead of reading out my written texts, you first tell the king about my opinions."

At this moment, Mauni's silent expression was laden with feelings of modesty and request.

Omu approved of Mauni's request with the gestures of her eyes. He articulated the trepidations of his mind in signals. Omu translated them in the local Mandarin language and spoke aloud:

"These many days have passed, but our friends have not returned. It seems, they have not been able to finalize the spot yet. It would do, if we constructed the building at Cheng Du or anywhere near. That would perhaps benefit Great China in many ways in future."

"In future? asked the king, who appeared excited and vigorous. He added, "Tell how?"

"Hwangdi! The plain land around Yarlung in Jangbo Jiang, the flat land around it and the marshy land around it is extremely fertile and nourishing. The underground soil too is quite rich there. However, it has not been peopled yet; no human village has come up yet. The produce from that region will be enough to feed half of China. For that, water ways should be developed to reach Yarlung Jangbo Jiang. Tunnels along the mountains also will be necessary for the development of the region. The place is quite near to Cheng Du. It's a square land, like a backyard garden or a meadow. So if the construction site has not yet been finalized, we might as well consider that place. But then, this is merely a proposal from a fool like me."

King Timur Khan thought, 'Yarlung Jangbo Jiyang! And the marshy land around it. The land falls under the territory of China, no doubt. That region should now be fully utilized.'

Elated, the king said in a high voice, "Wow, artisan! I commend your vision and contemplation."

He added, "The proposal you have placed is highly inspiring for me and for all rulers of China. It's a mantra of awakening for us. If I cannot, the great descendents will surely materialize this dream. I am confident in that."

Giving his voice a short pause, he yawned, and gave his twenty-seven-strand moustache a twist.

Mauni now stated giving his write-ups, one after another, to Omu.

Omu continued to read them to the king. She picked one sheet and read, "We got orders to vacate the guest house within seven days. I think Your Majesty is informed about this fact."

After having read it, Omu placed this sheet on another side.

The king made some signals. Another man sent his signals of yet another direction. A third man acted as though he was making notes of things being discussed there.

Mauni forwarded yet another sheet. Omu read it out in a loud voice, "We the artisans were given commands to return home. I believe, this was Your Majesty's decision."

Omu took a long breath after reading out the sheet.

Yet another peal of signals commenced. There again was some acting.

"We have been invited in service of Your Majesty. We were sent for that purpose. That's why, we are not that free. I don't think Your Majesty ever desired to see us dishonored and ignored. But under the patronage of Your Majesty, we faced both dishonor and indifference. I think Your Majesty has no information about this."

Omu read the sheet in a decent manner and placed it aside dramatically.

"We also got threats. We should be given security. We are artisans; we also deserve our wage. This is a plain demand from our part."

"Your Majesty! These are our mere grievances. Now I want to raise some questions. My questions are directed to the palace, to the state, to the state employees, to their assistants and to the entire planning of the state.

"If the royal staffs, and all the units of the royal power do not get deployed in the interest of the state, how can the state survive?"

Someone sent forth a signal from a distance. The signal traveled, until it reached Mauni. A messenger walked close to him and said, "It's time for His Majesty to go back. Give me all the papers; Hwangdi will himself read them. This is both a request and order from the new queen."

Omu felt the significance of the words used in the said request and command and said to Mauni in Nepali—a language only Mauni could understand, "Mauni, how many write-ups are left now?"

Mauni counted the sheets and said, there were four more now. Omu took them in her hand ran her eyes cursorily once. She caught the gist of all four of them and rolled them into coils before storing them back into a garment cylinder. The messenger was still standing nearby. She handed over the cylinder to Mauni, asking him to hand it over to the royal messenger. Mauni handed it over to the messenger with his own hands.

Finally he wrote something on his slate and showed it to all. It read, "I have presented all these things in writing to His Majesty after seeing and experiencing those things. If Your Majesty needs any help or information from our side, we are ready."

This was Omu reading out his writing in a high voice.

The messenger returned with the write-ups. Mauni erased his slate and gave it to Omu to help him hold it.

There was dead silence for a while.

The king rose from his seat. The queen followed suit. The courtiers left their positions. The king moved into a special hall, where a pre-scheduled program was taking place soon. But the king didn't appear quite happy. On the eve of his latest honeymoon, the gloom and listlessness that appeared on his face was read as a bad omen.

As the dusk gave way into night, Mauni and Omu reached the guest house. Omu lit up the lamps and got absorbed in preparing dinner. Mauni reclined in the dining room itself, utterly tired.

A horse shook outside. It was a signal that someone had come there on horseback.

"It all glitters with light, but there is no sign of human presence here," said Panchashar, as he walked into the house.

"Maybe they are outside, and are coming. It's time the birds should be returning to their nests," said Melamchi, tuning up with Panchashar.

After dinner, Melamchi and Omu got into talking.

Melamchi both listened to Omu and took stalk of Mauni's complaint. She also comprehended Panchashar's concerns. She took no time to have an estimation of the situation therein. She analyzed the incidents in a sequence and moved toward a conclusion. The night slipped, even as they were busy sharing the thrill of meeting friends, the pain of separation and the several other discussions and contemplations."

Based on proofs and speculations, she started analyzing the first incident. Who was responsible for stopping her way in the fair and forcing her to pose the challenge of foils? She started her analysis from there.

She took no time to know who was behind the arrival of horsemen at her residence, who wrangled with her on a wrong issue and left, spewing their entire rage on her.

Through keen analysis, she also inferred that the unhealthy and loathsome plot to send the girls from the guest house to the monastery in the name of getting it vacated, to command the artisans to pack up and more homeward, was a part of the same sequence of three serial incidents, like three stands in the same rope.

***

It was breakfast time. All four of them sat together to have their breakfast. Melamchi was in deep thoughts. She appeared lost in contemplation.

"Melamchi, what are you thinking? Take your breakfast," Omu said.

Panchashar was trying to say something, but Melamchi overtook him: "The impish plan of sending people to the fair, to my home and to the guest house and foiling all our plans are the handiworks of the same devil."

Omu and Panchashar stared at each other.

"One more incident is in the offing. After that, the imp will disappear on its own, or we will have to change our way," said Melamchi, seemingly foreseeing the future.

"This means, he has the royal backing. Doesn't he? He must be someone in close relation to the king," said Panchashar, breaking his silence.

"I cannot tell it for sure, but I cannot claim that the king is unaware of some employees taking bribes and torturing the public. More, it is the royal power that shields a rogue's crimes by registering it in someone else's name and preaching the same. Isn't it? When did the country fall short of people who did such things themselves and made others do so? All such acts are planned very well; they are organized and are sponsored. It takes not much time to discover who the mastermind was, and why was the incident planned and for whom. How long can a mystery remain a mystery? Once, maybe in your part of the world, the king's mother and brother had themselves approved of a plan to kill the king as willed by their neighbors. Those days, people didn't take such things otherwise. Such issues were considered common in politics. Our mythical stories and characters also affirm the same thing. Don't they?" Melamchi explained the incident, giving it a different interpretation.

"That's right. Melamchi said it so well. Behind the decline of every great personage, there have been the hands of his own close relatives and confidantes. Several pages of history are filled with examples of such incidents." This was what Mauni's slate read.

"Maybe," said Panchashar, making himself brief.

"But in most of the cases, decline and fall have some bearing with women and dishonor," wrote Mauni on his slate. As soon as Panchashar had had his eyes on the slate, Mauni erased his sentence and packed up the slate. Panchashar giggled a little and acted to be serious again.

Omu served them Tibetan tea for the second time.

"I will take my lunch here. Omu, prepare lunch for me as well. I will stay here for a few days, until the construction is launched," said Melamchi.

She said in a while, "But I will visit the palace once and come back. I must settle if the work should be started or not."

Panchashar appeared dejected. Mauni chose to stay silent. Omu went on reading everyone's face.

"Shall I frankly open up my mind to you? On seeing, experiencing and hearing about all these things, I have lost interest in starting the construction work again. I am utterly down," Melamchi said.

Others faced one another, seconding Melamchi's thoughts. Whatever she spoke had been poking their minds in the same way for quite some time.

HARI RAJ BHATTARAI

She added, "I accept that I have some degree of obligation, because I took the initiative myself. So I cannot easily pull my hands back from the work. I think we shall decide it very soon what we are doing next. Let me go; I will be back in the evening."

Melamchi ended her sentence.

***

CHAPTER THIRTEEN

THE BLUEPRINT WAS the same though they changed the location and direction, added newer objectives and commitments. After a few days, a contingent of masons and artisans left for Cheng Du in Sichuan, under Melamchi's leadership.

The construction commenced. There was no dearth of workforce; so there was no problem of any kind to produce the construction materials and fetch them to the construction site. There was neither any hassle, nor any need for anyone to stop the work.

Mauni used to remain at a certain place like a director or an advisor. If needed, he used to move around the construction site with a stick in his hand. At times, Omu walked together with him, boosting his morale. Everyone around there knew that Mauni had just recuperated from a serious ailment. Like before, the workers had been divided into two groups that took turns in their works. So the construction progressed in a smooth pace.

The working pattern was both objective and scientific. So the first group of workers always came early in the morning and rested in the afternoon while the one taking the second turn came in the afternoon and worked till the end of the day.

The workers' quarters had been built inside the construction premises temporarily. There was no dearth of firewood, water or other facilities.

The group charged with the arrangement of bricks, stones and wood did its work, changing its shelter as required. The people in charge of the horses, mules and carriages also executed its works, changing location as needed. But those who had direct hands in the task stayed at makeshift shelters built beside the site. For Panchashar, Mauni and Omu, separate cottages, like those of the meditating ascetics, had been built. And they were all connected to the dining hall.

There was yet another cottage, built especially for Melamchi. It has an office for her and a bedroom too. But she stayed there only occasionally, especially if there was any important task, or she was late in returning.

The construction work was yet to see its completion. The use of matchless art carved on the woods and the depiction of various aspects of life through them soon collected fame, and from mouth to mouth spread even to the neighboring countries. With this, the curiosity of the hearers about the building intensified. The fourth floor was going to be the last one, and its construction too was almost toward the end. All that left now was its roofing, screwing the rafters on the top, and cleaning it all through. In the meantime, Melamchi discontinued her visit. Five to seven days passed by, looking for her way, expecting that she would show up any time.

'Why isn't Melamchi showing up,' thought Panchashar, as a sort of chill passed down his spine.

Who could tell why she had stopped coming! All the workers seemed perplexed by the same question. In this regard, neither Panchashar wanted to talk with anyone, nor did anyone else want to raise the issue. Mauni and Omu had their own worries plaguing their minds. But they did not discuss the issue of Melamchi's discontinued visits between them.

But Panchashar embarked on a flashback at this point in time. Ever since she visited the palace and returned, Melamchi's countenance had changed altogether, and there was no glow like before. He could feel that there was a slight change in her looks, voice and interests. He further contemplated to infer that Melamchi had been gradually turning forlorn, annoyed and listless. Reaching a conclusion, he said, 'I don't know if there has been any mistake from our or my side. She must not have any grudge against us. It's possible that the palace had certain objections. How could we tell anything about the policy and the internal affairs here?"

He stopped for a while and said again, 'Mauni and Omu were saying they were at the palace. Maybe they have some clues. I think I must ask Omu; she might be able to tell something.'

One evening, Panchashar asked Omu, "What did you say when you were inside the palace? What happened there? Could it be that your visit created some problem? How can we know that?"

Omu said candidly, "I read Mauni's paper in front of the king. Later, a messenger came and took away all those papers. That was what the king had wanted."

"I think we have their copies with us."

"We do," wrote Mauni, and erased immediately.

"If you do give me all: both the ones you read out to the king, and the ones you could not. I want to see them once," Panchashar said.

"Omu; go and bring them all. I will sort them out and give him," wrote Mauni on the slate and showed it to Omu.

"Can the state employees go against the nation's policy and the king's interest to the extent of misusing and overusing state power to discourage the national plans for their personal interests? How did such devastating thoughts occur to them?" Panchashar read.

"What is the motive behind packing off our contingent so abruptly in the fashion of extraditing prisoners? Are we deprived of the right to timely information? Even the most ferocious animals inform in advance; it gives signals before attacking. But here…" He read yet another sheet.

"Can one deprive a man of the right to information, in case there has been any crime, and of the ways to redeem or clarify?

"The ears always do not do what the eyes are supposed to do. Access of anything can prove detrimental. It was not in vain that the scholars said, it's better to live in the forest than to live in the kingdom of an irrational king."

Panchashar drew a conclusion: "It means, Mauni told the king whatever was needed. I am satisfied. But if the king can make out, the content of the last two sheets is quite acrid. But if his concentration is elsewhere, he won't understand. Let's see whatever comes about."

Two months passed since Melamchi visited them last. The second month passed without a single visit from her. The worry in Panchashar's mind multiplied. Yet, he continued to drag the work along, like a sick traveler. After all, this was his obligation. He soon grew used to living in pain. He grew habitual to keeping by himself, engaged in silent soliloquies.

Mauni and Omu now turned out to be his equally formidable assistants. Mauni was yet to regain his health completely. He started expecting Omu's help most of the time. In a way, Omu turned out to be like a personal assistant to Mauni. It could safely be said that Omu was Mauni's speech and vision.

One evening, an old body came sauntering at the construction site, looking for Panchashar. He stood at the doorstep of Panchashar's cottage. Panchashar guessed that this man coming from the direction opposite to the source of light was dressed like a horseman. When he saw the newcomer clearly in the light of a *donglong*, he shuddered, raising his brows quite high.

He could instantly tell he was the Lama old man, Melamchi's grandfather. After usual courtesies, he said, "Melamchi is presently at home. It has been many days she's there. But she is not interested there."

Panchashar listened on. He didn't have the habit of talking in the middle and interfering, if anyone was speaking in a tempo. That must be why he didn't think it wise to speak back. He continued listening to the Lama patiently.

"The king's men dropped her at home and returned." Even as he was speaking, the Lama's emotions gave way to compassion and helplessness.

After pausing for a while, he added, "Her face suggests that she is unwell. But she doesn't tell us about her problem. It would do well, if she at least told her grandmother."

"Where's his maternal uncle?"

"He is away too. Had he been there, the problem would have been sorted out in a trice. Melamchi goes quite well with him. I have heard that he is in Lhasa, engaged in the task of constructing the main monastery. He has reportedly married a girl there. What can I say about someone who hasn't returned home? But Melamchi exchanges letters with him."

Panchashar went on listening to the Lama's words.

"Melamchi does share important things with us, but she doesn't share the trivial ones. She told us about her uncle getting married, and having a daughter before long. She also told about the progress he made in business. It's always like that…"

The mention of the uncle, his marriage and his daughter didn't move Panchashar. For him, the most intriguing thing was the fact that the king's men had left Melamchi as her grandfather's, and returned. So he turned quite serious, trying to decode these riddles.

The Lama said, "Stranger, I have come to meet you in order to discuss her case. She has been waiting for you. I have come here as her emissary; I have brought you her invitations. Please come after you are done with your work here."

Panchashar went on listening.

"Melamchi has asked me take a word from you, that you would surely come. Please give me your word."

Panchashar appeared even more serious.

"When she hears about your coming, she will brighten up. I cannot stand to see her face in gloom."

The Lama continued to speak all his feelings out: "Stranger! I think you got me. I don't know how well I explained the things to you."

He drew in a long breath and said, "I also request you with all my heart. Please come; I am eager to welcome you there. I shall be waiting for you. My wife shall also be waiting."

The Lama's voice was accompanied by tears. His voice reflected utmost modesty and heartfelt goodwill.

Panchashar remembered the face of Melamchi he had seen last. She looked lost and quite forlorn, like someone who has run out of blood. It seemed like she was beset by a deep shock. Like someone terrified by a ferocious beast. She appeared as though she had been appalled by an attacking spirit. She no longer had her usual smile; she showed no interest in talking.

Panchashar brooded deeply and thought, 'What forced Melamchi to leave this place so suddenly? Whatever the Lama old man told me is only superficial; just a cursory report. It seems even he had no knowledge of the underlying secrecy. It's only Melamchi who knows everything. She has experience; she has see things. Could it be that her own beauty and youth turned out to be her enemy?'

Even as several unhealthy and appalling thoughts gripped his mind, Panchashar stood from his place to escape from them. He wiped his sweats clean and drank water from a goblet. At peace now, he thought, 'The palace is in itself a pool of mysteries. One can never know what happens there, nor is there any point in trying to know.'

Panchashar know became articulate. He turned toward the old man and said, "We need two more months to finish the outer structure of the building. The internal construction and finishing will also take a fairly long time. The finer works are yet to be picked up. Moreover, the garden, outer wall and the main gate are only half done. It seems, we will take two more months to pack up everything."

He added, "If Melamchi was here, it would all have ended by now. Yet, I shall try to speed up. I also need some respite. I have been tired to my bones. I'll tell the king and go on rest."

"Come at ours to take rest. We shall be waiting for you. If I can help, I will visit you at intervals," said the Lama, opening up his heart.

The old man returned, after sharing some more intimacy. Before he did, Panchashar introduced his friends Mauni and Omu to the old man. Omu welcomed him according to their Tibetan traditional practice and thus gratified the guest.

The Lama man returned after having his dinner together with Panchashar and others. Before he left, he said, "Omu, you happened to be the granddaughter of one of my relatives. I am happy to know that. We shall talk more when I'm here again."

"That's fine. Please tell Melamchi I am missing her. Ye Ye," said Omu, expressing all her good wishes.

The old man pulled the reins and galloped away. He had a home to take shelter in at the suburb, outside the busy city area. That's where he rested whenever he was traveling along this route. This time as well, he did the same.

The home where the Lama put up also belonged to a Tibetan Lama. Its sole occupant was an old Lama woman, who was quite old now. Her workers returned to their own homes in the evening with their wages. The maidens left after finishing the post-meal chores in the evening. Both the visiting old man and the woman who owned the house had equal participation in building up the atmosphere of freedom and joy there. There were times when the old man stayed there for four to five days. Ever since his wife at home started running sick, the old man frequented this house more, on the pretext of meeting Melamchi. Later, the old man became even more free to travel out when some maidens from his wife's family came and started living with her to care for and help her.

The Lama old man was both romantic and frank. Seizing the moment and opportunity, he used to say, "If you want to stay healthy and live longer, play with maidens junior to you. They are the best therapies for your body and mind. If that happens, you will become energetic, and you will be on the winner's end always."

Whenever he kept that route, the old man stopped her for snacks. On his way back home, he spent the night here. This was his usual routine during the travels. He always left this place with renewed zeal, enthusiasm and self-confidence, having his entire body thoroughly massaged. The snacks used to be a promotion for their cohabitation later in the night. Accordingly, the old man managed for the man's night stay with special care in a special style.

Such a thing is perhaps scientific, logical and interesting. It can be interpreted and explained in both abstract and concrete ways. This is what its experts say.

Once he was back to his own home, his wife used to examine her husband minutely. Every time he returned home from a journey, she found him more satisfied, happier and zealous. In a way she thought, 'Once out of home, a man becomes freer and carefree. That's what makes my husband brighter and happier."

But there were times she suspected the old man's loyalty. She thought, 'I'm physically sick. Could it be that the old man has found a healthier body elsewhere? These traders have various ways and various eyes, and I know that quite well. As they move, they take shelter at any place they like. What can I do or say? I don't even know what the matter is.'

She had told her husband once, "I have become like an invalid woman. It's difficult for me to fulfill your physical needs. What should I do?"

In reply, the old man had said, "You are not that sick; you don't have any chronic disease. You took the death of our daughter and her husband as a big shock, and made yourself inactive. That is what I feel about it."

She also remembered another thing the old man had said: "We should not always engage these young girls in our works. That doesn't suit us. They want to have to fun with guys of their age. They will have to return to Olangchunggola any time, early or late. Thank God, people on your parents' side are so considerate; they sent their daughter here to attend on you. The girls also have high respect for you. My honor for them is mainly because of you."

She remembered him say, "And now, let me tell you the main thing. You feign innocence in many matters though you know about them very well, and keep yourself contented. If that is the case, why don't you give me the freedom to go on outing or picnic to please myself?"

She drew a conclusion secretly and said to herself, 'This must be the secret behind his healthy and fresh looks. Perhaps he goes to open up his heart at some place, sometimes. If I cannot always be a part of his entertainment, why should I object? Why should I grudge? No, I don't have a question anymore. Nor do I have any complaint.'

The Lama woman came out of her musing and took a long sigh, drawing in a cold waft of air.

The seniors, by dint of their memory and imagination, make an ordinary thing seem extraordinary and a distinguished thing quite simple. They easily make an impossible thing feasible. They push time to the moment of their choice, and use it again at their convenience.

Panchashar used to daydream very often. Though alone, he was not altogether alone. It seemed, he always had Melamchi with him in each of his steps, actions and breaths. Though she was away, Melamchi, in practice had become for Panchashar an entity like Kamadhenu[54], who would always be by his side at one call from his imagination. She has become the magnanimous goddess, who would stand with him for every necessary, logical and sought-of thing.

While at work, Panchashar could feel the presence of Melamchi at any place he liked. Magically, he used to put her imagined suggestions and inspirations into his art and apply the same to embellish the building he was working on.

The Lama old man showed up at times, stayed for a night and returned. He was the messenger and the official spokesperson for both the sides. The relation of love and passion between Panchashar and Melamchi that was fading away now, was coming to life again, regaining its lost stability and charm, thanks to the old man's goodwill and cooperation.

Adapting the architectural skills he had brought from Kantipur to the local geography and culture, Panchashar finished the

---

[54] a mythical cow, the mother of all other cows, who is believe not only to give plenty of milk, but also to fulfill whatever her master wishes

construction of a concrete and hale pagoda-style building for Timur Khan, furnished with every imaginable facility.

People say, behind the success of every man, there is his mother's hand, pouring her blessing on his head. There's his wife's penance and his lover's goodwill. The dead ancestors have their blessings, and gods always have their mercy. But in Panchashar's case, who was the real inspirer: Melamchi, or the Kirat maidens? How was that to be ascertained?

Mauni said to himself, 'Could Melamchi's friendliness be stronger than the blessings from Siddha Kirat and the penance and dedication of the Kirat maidens?' His analysis had an admixture of folk beliefs from the Eastern world. More than objectivity, it has the energy derived from feelings. When he considered Melamchi's presence, he was not sure if her conduct and goodwill contributed fifty-fifty in their progress. For quite a long time, he kept himself busy in this calculation as well.

This time, there was no chance of any dialogue with the palace. Yet, Panchashar and Mauni both moved toward the palace. Omu drove the carriage. They presented themselves before Emperor Timur and informed him about the completion of the building. This made them feel relieved.

Timur Khan expressed his heartfelt happiness to Panchashar and Mauni and thanked their entire team profusely. Then he announced, "This has made me the richest king today. I have something which other kings do not. I can feel my height increased by many folds. From my personal side and from the side of my nation, I extend heartfelt thankfulness to you the artists, and to our friendly nation."

With a prodigal heart, he added, "Blessed is your country for begetting such citizens. It's highly venerable! I extend my high honor to our friendly neighbor Nepal, and this honor from the side of China shall always remain intact."

In silence, Panchashar and Mauni studied the moods of Timur Khan. Seizing a moment, Panchashar ran his eyes around all the courtiers present there and said in a balanced manner, "I don't have much idea as to what sort of trees and fruits best suit the building premises? For that, Your Majesty will surely get suggestions from the botanists, environmentalists, aestheticians and cultural spokespersons from here."

"Well said. I shall consult the scholars here for that. Thank you for your suggestion. I am thankful to you."

The hall resounded with applause. It was time the meeting was dissolved. But Timur Khan stopped them short and said, "When, do you think, will be the most auspicious time to inaugurate the building?"

Panchashar started counting on his fingers. Mauni scribbled on his slate. Before long, Mauni came up with a solution. He nudged Panchashar and drew his attention toward his slate.

Panchashar read out, "Your Majesty, it will be best if you enter the building only after having tour of the south for some days."

Timur Khan was in deep thoughts for a while. He ran his eyes on the courtiers sitting on the first row and said, "If that is the case, arrange for my tour of your own country Kantipur to see its artistic elegance."

The hall resounded with yet another round of applause. All the people around looked joyous.

Giving them orders to arrange his tour of Kantipur as soon as possible, Timur Khan rose from his seat.

The Nepal wing of China's foreign affairs department sent a letter to Kantipur without delay. For that, a messenger set on a horse early in the morning and took rest at midday. Another horseman received the letter and continued the relay race, and reached his shelter by evening. Another morning, yet another horseman would take over and move in the same fashion for half a day, handing over the letter to his successor. This way, the message was carried on. This way, in a great speed, the letter of Chinese Emperor Timur Khan reached Nepal through its postal system. Once inside the territory of Nepal, the message had to embark on an on-foot journey, and after walking for many days, he was able to deliver the letter to its due recipient in Nepal.

After three weeks of the receipt of this letter, a reply, which was actually a letter of invitation and welcome, was sent from Nepal to the palace of Emperor Timur Khan through an on-foot post.

Mauni considered the construction work completed from his side. In the meantime, he heard Omu say, "There's no point in staying here anymore. It doesn't suit, for our work is over. Come; let's move." He also said to himself, 'I'm not ready to stay here anymore and corrode by body. I must return now.'

'My stay seems lingering here. I don't think my departure is destined anytime soon. Before I do, I must meet Melamchi at least once. The Lama old man requested me many a time,' said Panchashar, thinking about himself.

About Mauni, he thought, 'I am not in a position to say anything about Mauni. If he decided to go, I cannot hold him back. If he stays back, that is even better. We can return together.'

He maintained a neutral thought.

He thought again, 'I too am not interested in staying back. But if I opt to move, it can sound a disregard of the royal expectations. It's not as easy for me as it is for Mauni. If the palace asks me about his interest, I think I should tell it to ask it to himself, for it's a matter of his business and I obviously have no knowledge about it. After all, the palace cannot have a face-to-face dialogue with him.'

'Oh, yes,' said Panchashar as he remembered something very crucial. 'We can make Omu take the initiative. He can hold a two-day communication with Omu. She can translate her words in both Chinese and Tibetan."

"If Mauni decides to return, we should ask him to take the remuneration of other friends as well. I hope they will give the labor cost, at least," said Panchashar, drawing a conclusion.

At breakfast that morning, Omu sat where Melamchi used to sit. Mauni and Panchashar sat facing each other, while a low-height table stood in between. The air was quite ordinary. They were not under the grip of any immediate task. So no topic for immediate deliberation sprang up.

"Shouldn't we be returning home now?" Mauni wrote on his slate.

"We should," said Panchashar, briefly.

"We have accomplished our mission here. We must prepare to leave now," wrote Mauni.

"They should know now the work is over, they should see us off. My mind too is in turmoil," said Panchashar with a great ease.

Mauni said to himself, 'He said a superficial thing. He seems interested to linger on, not on returning. He seems to be hooked by Melamchi's message, not by the construction work of the royal decree.'

He also thought from a different quarter: 'But that is natural. We have come at an official order. Unless kings talk and we are sent away or invited back home, we cannot move. How can we return?'

Omu poured another shot of Tibetan tea.

"We want to return now. Let's request them at least once to arrange our return journey," wrote Mauni in tiny letters and rubbed them off immediately.

Omu added, "Well said. You would do better, if you inform them. In that case, it won't appear that you are deliberately lingering."

Mauni now turned toward Omu and started conversing in signals.

Omu translated Mauni's words and said to Panchashar, "If you are reluctant to go to the palace and tell you want to leave, we will do that for you. Should we?"

"OK." This is all Panchashar said.

"Should we tell we are willing to return? Or, should I say, only I am willing to return? I think we must be clear." These were Mauni's words, which Omu translated for Panchashar.

Panchashar displayed a smile, and said in a grim voice, "Oh no; do not leave me alone. I am not in a position to stay alone. But I don't think they will see us both off at once."

He changed the context and said, "If I can go with you, I can visit Sanghu at Mauwa Khola Thum, Milké, Mechhyayem, Jhyaupokhari and Neruwa again. We could also meet those goddesses again. We can also take the blessings of Siddha Kirat. Those four animals must be still waiting for me. We must fulfill the promise we made to them; we must return to them."

He was moved to emotions suddenly. His throat constricted and the eyes got moist. He turned his head in another direction.

Mauni turned grave. Omu scrutinized both and made herself tearful. She rose from her place making some pretext and moved a little away, only to return after getting her tears hidden. Then she reclaimed her seat.

Another day, Mauni and Omu moved toward the palace.

Nature was quite gay since early that morning. As soon as Mauni and Omu were out of the palace gate to return, the weather turned hostile with thunder. The clouds, shaped like dates, started throwing flashes of lightning. The thunder that followed was hair-raising. The gush of the wind grew even more intolerable. The four horses on the carriage were not in a position to take speech, given the inhospitality of the weather.

"Let's rest at this inn for a while. The horses are reluctant to move. Dust had blinded the pathways. We also have the fear of thunderbolt. See, there are drizzles. Let's move when it stops. Only half our way is left now." Omu said all these things in signals.

Mauni was not that familiar with the environment now. So he did not react to whatever Omu said.

Omu stopped the carriage and signaled Mauni to step into the inn and take shelter. Mauni did as instructed. Omu led the horses into the inn and anchored the reins. The cloud laden with wind, rain, light and smoke thundered, following flashes of lightning. They were growing more and more intolerable for ears and hearts. Omu rushed to the carriage and returned with something in her hand.

Such hours of evening, especially with seductive environmental appeals, often turn out to be enticing for young minds. Mauni and Omu started reading the appeals in each other's eyes, and noted the change of color mounting on their bodies. They could feel the change in their breath rates, which was getting faster with the passage of every second. The situation was such that they were inclined to read each other's heart beats. It seemed that though the fluctuation in the outside weather was both unusual and temporary, it was bringing these two people closer, both physically and mentally. The horses anchored to a pole in the inn were witness to this change.

On the fourth day after their return from the palace, Mauni and Omu managed carriages to move homeward. Panchashar and Melamchi saw them off, hiding tears in their eyes.

Panchashar, on the other hand, was in a different state of mind.

Life in loneliness troubles everyone. At such hours, one seems to be punishing himself or herself. Moreover, if the subjects are young, their youthful and enticing conducts and fragrant signals, by nature, give a boost to their amorous cravings. After all, youth is the most thrilling time in one's life, and perhaps the most beautiful. But as soon as the circumstances turn hostile, all these things turn into thin air. Panchashar started experiencing this fact. He started feeling harassed, especially by a surge of emotionality and impatience. In conclusion, he said, 'This time of idleness is proving detrimental to me.'

It was raining torrentially that day since the previous night. Though the sun had come quite high in the morning, the rain was showing no sign of stopping. 'It's not like summer rain in our country. There is no lightning or thunder at all. There's no gush of wind or the commotion of the social alarm; everything is so peaceful and serene this evening. If there is no splendor of agricultural life, how could there be any joyful sound anywhere?'

He made a brief comment on nature.

Whenever he saw horses, he was deeply nostalgic, remembering his travel with Melamchi. Whenever he went out for shower, he remembered Yangsila lovingly fondling his thick chest-hair and communicating her love, and this brought untold satisfaction to his heart. Whenever he was in his bed, he was shocked to remember the way Jimu extracted all his strength, kneading his body all through. And whenever he was all by himself in loneliness, he remembered

HARI RAJ BHATTARAI

the way Melamchi touched him passionately and woke him up. Then he ran his eyes around the world in broad daylight, only to find himself lonely and incomplete.

Granted that the chords of the heart often reverberate, but who hears it all? The feelings of the heart emanate as songs, but who adds art in them? The mind plays the *madal*, flute and *murchunga*, but they seem to lack something. Oomph!

Panchashar went on thinking: 'Let songs have profound feelings. Let there be a matching partner. Let one have a touching melody, and a lucid tune! What more shall I tell or think! Let a romantic group hold a carnival to the intersecting music and dance. Let the carnival have a crowd of people who understand it all and feel it deeper. But in this foreign land, how could I find it all!'

His thoughts were melancholic, and yes, quite banal.

He missed his homeland and its environment, wherein there were plenty of lovers that appeared, signaled their romantic inclinations, developed and communicated their love, welcomed it, and handled it to their utmost satisfaction.

His mind started revolving around *dohori*—the folk duets—and *Asaré* tunes played by his folks in his home country. He remembered the hints his peers sent forth for romantic engagements at fairs, temples and carnivals. He grew more and more impatient to return to his valley, where cloaked underneath its cultural canopy, his mind could imbibe enough of romantic fragrance. His mind also started hovering around the promises, trust, bargaining and intimacy he had shared with the dear ones. In reality, he started drowning himself into youthful musings and ripples of love, in which, he got instantly lost.

The summer rain was running riot without any pause. He remembered how they peeled the terraced ridges, and built them anew. His eyes recalled the sight of paddy turning green, when the newly planted seedlings perked up and stood upright, and the terraces were full of water filling them to the brim and flowing into the other terrace, down the hill, through the outlets called *samaha*. He could hear the *Asaré* songs getting farther away from his ears each moment. He thought of the villagers' tired life going for a short rest, soon after packing up the plantation work with *bethi*, the ritual to conclude the planting session.

He opened his window. The woods were rustling in the heavy rain. He could hear something like a stream gurgling nearby. He remembered how flood and landslide ran havoc in this country.

The heavy rain rendered the day darker. Panchashar's mind was now in worse turmoil. He threw his looks outside the window and got lost in thoughts. At times, the spray of the rain entered through his window and shook him out of reverie. This time, he grew miserable remembering the flight of water spray from the waterfall at Yangmaya resting on the dark, smooth hair of Sanjhang and Teejhang, and the way they saw him off with tearful eyes and heart-rending songs of farewell, their friends posing as witness. He calculated internally and said, 'By now, Sanjhang and Teejhang must have become adults.'

His heart melted with emotions, as these maidens flashed in his memory.

There was no sign that the rain would subside or stop altogether. Soon his ears were filled by the roaring sound of Tamor, swelled by incessant rainwater. A cold waft of wind entered from the window. He remembered how he had almost frozen under the grip of such wind coming from the direction of Tamor, while he was in Olangchunggola.

Panchashar's mind lost its balance. It grew restless, craving for some sort of warmth. The loving hospitality of Lhasa, his sleeplessness there, the healing touch of the warm water pool, and the way maidens clasped him from two sides while in bed flashed back to his memory, making him deeply nostalgic.

The morning hour that day arrived with a scintillating thrill for Panchashar. But then, the maidens felt it better than the guys how detrimental and depressing such a time was, when there was no one around. The rainy weather was proving no less torturous for youthful Panchashar. Memories from three locations, which had three reasons to sensitize him, started moving Panchashar all through. He started seeking Sanjhang and Teejhang in the land much beyond Lhasa, while he tried to locate the beauties from across Lhasa in Yangsila and Melamchi. He also started seeking them in the faces of Sanjhang and Teejhang. He exchanged one's face with another's; sought one's body in another's, and imagined one's gestures in yet another beauty. With the very memory, he was moved to arousal, even as sexual excitements moved him to impatience.

Finally, he rested his thoughts in Yangsila. He had passed full and unimpeded time with her in romantic engagements. No other thing had, till then, been able to surpass her invitations, conduct, blissfulness, complete dedication, and the freshness and excitement that last quite long even after that. Panchashar arrived at a conclusion.

He recalled older incidents and scenes. One day, allowing his entire body to rest upon her breasts, Yangsila had said, "Take me along, when you return home." Her warm breaths had struck his ears. At the moment, Yangsila had bitten the lobe of his left ear gently. As the thought flashed back to his memory, he felt his left ear, and got elated. Everything seemed quite fresh; he thought as though Yangsila was somewhere around him.

'Had Mauni been here, many things would have been easier for me.' Panchashar flipped through yet another page of his memory book and thought, 'He is perhaps enjoying the village at this time.'

He rose from his place, took a long sigh and ran his eyes out of the window. It was still raining, with no sign of stopping anytime soon.

'Why am I so impatient? Why am I divided between two centers? Why is my reason going astray? Why is my mind drifting?' Panchashar gave a thought to the mental conflict within him.

Nature outside and loneliness within had driven his mind restless. He tried to brush aside certain issues; tried to cover certain contexts. He considered some other things ordinary while he neglected a few other things. The result was a shivering in his mind and a distraction in his intellect. He was caught in a whirlwind emanating from the same. His mind was in a turmoil. His feelings, sliced in several streams, were going wild.

'Wisdom is my manliness. It's a path of intellect, embellished with artistic excellence. I cannot change my path anymore. My feelings are secondary things.'

He started losing himself in deep reveries. He thought, 'For an uninterrupted journey, one constantly needs comfortable rests and shelters. I cannot neither shut my intellect and move, nor trample my heart and proceed. I must develop a balanced centre on my own. I must enter a laboratory where the necessity and sensible consumption of both the elements reconcile.'

With confidence, he reached a conclusion: 'In a journey where intellect and the heart travel together, I must keep myself active, assuming the firmness and neutrality of Mount Sumeru.'

Finally, he decided that he must maintain a balance between intellect and feelings, and hone his life ahead toward constructive excellence. After a long spell of self-contemplation, he rested his intellect in Melamchi and his mind in Yangsila.

He rose from his seat and peeped outdoor. The rain had stopped. The birds had started flying joyously in the sky. The world his eyes could glance upon appeared fresh like a maiden that had just come out after a shower. On top of that, the landscape, blushing at the tickling touch of the sunrays appeared stunning in the display of joyful and flamboyant appearance.

Panchashar was thrilled internally.

***

HARI RAJ BHATTARAI

CHAPTER FOURTEEN

Y ANGSILA WAS ALL alone. She was quite introvert. But her mind was playing havoc that day, for she was experiencing strange things, as several thoughts were rising in it. In fact, her body parts fluttered, and as she had heard before, it was a good omen. 'Such quivering signals youthful desire,' she had heard people say, while she was a teenager. She could feel that her own body parts were dribbling with ooze of love, and she was sending forth a romantic fragrance. She felt a new thrill in herself, and blushed a little.

"God, what's wrong with me today?" she said, resorting to soliloquy.

It's said, love-birds have same vision for the living and the nonliving; they have the same perspectives about the consciousness of both human and the non-human world.

Some dogs came panting and entered his room in the fashion of messengers, who are in great rush.

'They have brought home some signals. They had not been here for a long time. Where could they be coming from? It seems they are trying to tell me something in secret. If only they could talk today,' she thought, and contemplated on her own.

She found the dogs' looks quite strange, as though she was a fragrant object and the dogs were attracted to her. The dogs have a great power of smelling; she knew this. She doubted if they had got a glimpse of the romantic ooze in her body. Else, why would they be smelling her, going round and round? Her private organ fluttered more, and some more discharge oozed out. She experienced this, and grew wild with amorous speculations.

'If only I could share this orgasm with someone and harvest ecstasy. If only I could tell how I am feeling today.' She grew more and more introvert, and feeling the organism tickling her, came out on the veranda.

There were horses free in their own world on the lawn. More than grazing, they were busy playing among themselves or competing in fight. It occurred to her that it was the horses' season. A horse pours all the energy accumulated in it on a mare, and waits for the same season to return, resting in utter satisfaction and patience in between. Yangsila saw the game of the horses, and to a great extent, felt quite awkward in herself. She turned her eyes away from there and got them fixed on a house nearby.

The Lama woman was alone there. She was in a good grip of old age. All she needed now was water and medicine. She was never a burden to anyone; her only routine was go share happiness and accord good wishes to others. In the village, her existence was always considered bright and blotless. But now, owing to her old age, she was confined to her own house. She was a housewife, who was now in a long penance, having tamed all her organs. But when she heard that her husband's elder brother was seriously ill, she moved thither, sitting on a palanquin. So her home was desolate at the moment. At this location with two eyes and such wide premises, there were only three living creatures at the moment: the two dogs, and Yangsila. The horses were at a distance, busy in their own carefree world.

'Melamchi has moved away to stay in the monastery. Jimu followed as her companion. Melamchi found it easy to enter the monastery, finding the Lama old man away from home. This occurred to be the most opportune time for her. Maybe Jimu will return; she cannot hold herself in the monastery for long.'

Yangsila made her own speculations. Then she turned toward herself and said, 'Can we make our orgasm more thrilling and satisfying through sexual musings? Why are my organs fluttering as through there has been an earthquake? Could it be that this stillness is trying to goad me away? In stories from distant lands, a prince who has lost his way in the woods often finds a princess waiting. Is anything like that going to happen anytime soon? Why doesn't anyone come inside these walls, seeing a princess in me? After all, isn't this a palace too?'

This way, she deeply signed for youthful pleasure and articulated the feeling of her body: 'Even the season of horses happened to move the humans. Shh....!"

From the veranda, she moved into yet another room. Her eyes fell on the bed where Panchashar used to sleep before. This made him even more impatient. She remembered his chest full of hairs and his robust arms. 'That is the bed where the stranger slept,' she said to her own. She rose on the bed and rolled all over once or twice and let her body rest there. Though it was merely a mental conduct, she experienced relief, and made herself assured, albeit in a small degree.

Toward the end of the day, two long shadows of horses appeared in her front-yard. The shadows of the men mounted on them appeared even longer, as the rays of the setting sun struck them. One of them hushed with fatigue in the fashion of a local settler while the other dismounted from his horse, running his eyes all around. Both her dogs rushed to welcome them in great elation. Yangsila, on her part, experienced a relief.

The door leading out to the veranda from the second story opened by a few inches. The men from the courtyard downstairs looked up. The door slowly opened more, inch by inch, until it was fully ajar. At the doorsteps, the onlookers could now fully see a female figure, standing between the rectangular frames of the door. The female figure, fair like cream and stunningly seductive, now looked at the doorstep glowing in its own glory, highly desirous and dribbling but quite guiltless.

"The Lama old man is at ours, up there. He is stuck for a piece of work. He will be here soon," the guide said.

"He has asked me to tell you to take good care of our foreign guest," he added.

"I leave of you; I'll be late," he said, and took his way.

That man who stood in the direction of the slanting sunrays of the evening time was, naturally, now vividly recognizable to

Yangsila. He conveyed his message in straight sentences, pulled the rein of his horse and left in a great speed, going out of her sight before long. The cloud of dust raised by the galloping hooves of the horses played with the setting rays of the sun for some time.

The scintillating female figure dramatically ran downstairs and came out on the front yard and led the stranger's horse toward the stable. The horseman followed her. Once they were inside the stable, the horse was freed from the reins and the saddle. It purred with happiness for a while and rushed out to join a group of other horses busy grazing in a green lawn nearby.

The season on the lawn was high on heat, enticing the horses to reap the appeals of the reproductive season. Both of them glanced at the overflow of love and action at the peak of the horses' season on display on the lawn. They seemed to be deriving enough excitement form the same, and started feeling ripples of amorous feelings inside their hearts. They could feel their heartbeats escalating in an uncontrollable fashion, though they tried their best to tame and save themselves from anything untoward. But it was natural for the environment of those premises, nature around it and the profuse heat of the horses' season was certain to have its spell on the human thoughts and actions. The result was that they got highly tickled with the color of excitation, fear, pain and pleasure. There was no doubt about that.

It might be natural that with time, fear and pain disappear, and excitement and pleasure contribute to a person's joy. But when the distance in between increases, it's the memory that thrills, and one is beset with urge for more dedication and the gloom of loneliness. After all, when didn't man find himself rich in sweet recollections of the bygone times! Wow!

***

To bring rations and other necessary stuffs, Hwang came down to his home in the plains for one day from the animal farm in the mountains. Yangsila considered his coming a sweet coincidence, and so, she requested him to escort the stranger to his destination, and return.

Hwang could not decline the request of such a beautiful maiden. He said yes, considering that this would please Yangsila or leave himself pleased.

"Hwang, go without any haste. You come back, leaving our guest safely there. On your way back, make it a point to come here before leaving for home. You must convey me the news about our guest." Yangsila said this at the moment of departure, hiding her tears. When he dismounted from the horse to rest for a while on a bench at a wayside mound, Panchashar remembered the last sentence spoken by Yangsila.

Panchashar recalled yet other moments of their togetherness in the past. "Can't you hold back for a few more days?" Yangsila had asked him one day, reclining on his chest. He recalled how her fingers were moving on his chest that moment.

"I will always keep you covered like this. None can see you; nor can you ever leave me." When she spoke bending her head over his face, her long, silky hair had covered his face from all sides.

Hwang could not speak to his fill. He stuck the stone and the knife many a time to make fire on the tinder but his snuff did not catch it. He was despondent. 'Let it; you can do it in some village on the say,' he told himself, inserting his cigar on his ears, and reclining to rest.

The elder brother of the Lama old man was terribly sick and was taken to bed. His relatives from Olangchunggola and Tokpegola had filled his home. The old man was stuck there, to meet his relatives coming from such far-off places, and to take news about his brother's health. Panchashar had information from Hwang.

The Lama old man and his elder brother were quite fond of traveling since their early age. On business trips, they travelled to several places like Manang, Mustang, Kantipur, Kalimpong, Bhutan, Sikkim and Khasi Hills to move beyond them to Nagaland, Manipur, Burma and Thailand, reaching many villages and towns there. By the time they had turned adults, no place was inaccessible and remote for them. Inspired by trade advantages, both the brothers resolved to marry their wives from major trade posts along the border of Nepal. Traders on the Nepalese side did everything they could to build rapports with the brothers, considering their expanding business feats. Finally, the elder Lama married his wife from Tokpagola, while the younger Lama married from Olangchunggola.

A bonus case during the wedding of the younger Lama was that, the senior Lama happened to like a maiden. He was attracted to her the way Rana Bahadur used get attracted to maidens. He was determined to getting the maiden at every cost. The maidens' parents consulted the maiden, and gave their consent. This way, the elder Lama married a girl from the Ukyap Family, while the younger one married a girl from Gowa Family, and they ushered their brides into their home together.

"People say the family of the Lama entered Chinese mainland from Tibet. Their parents moved here many years back, looking for large flat land and fertile fields to sustain their animal farms. That's why their lifestyle is much different from people in the mountainous regions in Nepal. Another reason is that, the later generation in this family established marital relation in China itself. Their number is quite high in this region today."

This way, Hwang narrated to Panchashar a brief history of the Lama families in a short time.

Hwang was not that articulate in nature. But once he started, he was not of the nature to stop until he was done with his story.

"Stranger, it seems you didn't find time to see a lot of places in our country this time. Melamchi was in the monastery; the Lama old man was at his brother's. His wife also joined him there sometime later. Though she was running quite sick, she was compelled to move. Jimu had left them. Yangsila was fully occupied with the household chores." Hwang also narrated the practical issues.

"I also kept myself busy in painting. So I didn't have much leisure too. I moved across short distances on horseback. It seems, this is the horses' season. Whenever I made my horse follow my way, it seemed quite unhappy. I always feared if it would fling me away at some point and go after a mare. But thank God, nothing of the sort happened."

Panchashar was brief.

"If that is the case, Yangsila must find it very difficult, didn't she?" he said, trying to be rather lecherous.

"Why should Yangsila find it difficult?" Panchashar showed his curiosity.

"I wonder how a man fearing to mount a horse mounts a woman." He laughed out again, having spoken this sentence.

Panchashar's mind was fully revolving around Yangsila now. He recalled the intimacy communicated by Yangsila's treatment of him. He remembered the way she communicated in lucid words; he saw in her eyes fathomless curiosity and profounder longing. He also remembered the waves of loving and guiltless dedication rippling inside her heart. Yang's eyes did much of the talking; they listened to many things and comprehended a lot. It always thrilled him to remember her simplicity and ready presence. He thought, 'Yangsila is guiltless, contemplative and wise. In reality, she is a ravenous love-seeker. Let her eyes never show tears."

"Yang is a newcomer to this land. She came to stay here with her aunt for a few days. She will return later. Stranger, I think you are in good terms with her."

"I am. And that has made many things easier."

Panchashar was straight as always. Hwang tried to understand him connotatively.

"But Yang has a different sort of story. Jimu, however, has no story at all."

"What sort of story? Can we hear? I always love to hear you speak."

Hwang said, "Yang's father often went down to the highlands of Nepal, including Letang, Rajarani, Budha Subba and places like that for business. Most of the time, he spent his nights at a place called Yangsila on the way. In due course, he happened to fall for a Kirat maiden there. Yangsila is the proof of their love. She is the living history of her parents. I think you understood me. They named the girl Yangsila after the Kirat maiden, and after that very place."

Drawing his attention further, Hwang said again, "Are you really understanding the story?"

"I am. I'm listening."

"Would you love to know something about Yang's mother?"

"That will be wonderful. In fact, I want to hear everything. I will do, even by forgoing my cigar."

"I'll be brief. Let's smoke after that."

He resumed his story: "She was caught by malaria, when she had been down to the plains in Madhumalla for shopping. She happened to die only from a day's sickness."

Hwang carried on his story. He said, "But then, how beautiful Yang is, isn't she? It's perhaps because she is hybrid."

This time, he laughed out with his heart.

"Hwang, who told you all these things?"

"The Lama Ye Ye's wife narrated this story to many and moved them to tears. It's moving, isn't it?"

"Yes, it's deeply moving. It seems I too will be in tears soon. You are there with me now; so I shouldn't cry. I need to talk with you. When I'm alone, I shall recall and cry. I cannot hold my heart then," said Panchashar, drawing a long waft of breath.

"Jimu is also from that region. I think you know that."

"I came to know that. But this time, I didn't even meet her."

Panchashar turned mute after answering to Hwang. Jimu, as a maiden, was quite agile. She mixed with others very soon. She was quite an extrovert, and outran others in many things. She never fails in what she is supposed to do any moment. More, she doesn't care much about what might happen next. She never fails to cash the moments of youthfulness and opportune times. She is bent on living a life without repression. In reality, she is on look for moments of bliss, and perhaps she had retained a lot of memories of such moments she has lived in the past. It's natural flair on her part to get mixed very soon, open up even with strangers, discharge her part dramatically in a shrewd manner and handle many things beautifully, taking them as ordinary. She has made ample use of her personal inclination and freedom."

Panchashar resorted to a detailed explanation.

"That may be true. Everyone has a unique nature of his or her own." Panchashar was brief this time.

Though quite reserved by nature, Hwang talked freely if the subject was comfortable to him. When his urge to smoke was fulfilled, he would open up even more. He took tobacco for a source of energy. Sometimes he spoke in great details, while at times, he was formulaic. There were times when he communicated merely in signals, while at other moments, he hinted at some mysterious facts. But Panchashar liked the way he analyzed and evaluated others and made his comments. More, he was always new in his way of evaluation. So Panchashar always took great interest in the way Hwang talked.

But Hwang said nothing about Melamchi. Panchashar's curiosity, therefore, remained unaddressed.

"When is Melamchi likely to return from the monastery, Hwang?" said Panchashar, himself initiating the issue.

"She will come after her wish is granted."

"I didn't quite get you," said Panchashar, seeking elaboration.

"Melamchi is a young girl. What could she be looking for at present?"

'Did she move to the monastery with marriage motifs?' Panchashar said to himself. Then he spoke, "Hwang, I think you know why she moved to the monastery."

"Maidens most often concentrate on the issues of friends, wealth, peace and kids. One has to struggle both before and after getting these." Hwang said in points.

"Is Melamchi an ordinary girl like others?" he said, risking himself a conflict.

"She is not. She is starkly different from others," said Hwang, making a judgment.

"I think you and Melamchi have been friends since your childhood."

"We are peers by age. But we weren't friends."

"How's that?"

"She was born in one place and brought up in a different place. For education, she moved to a third place, and later became an employee with the palace. On my part, I didn't move anywhere. So we could not become friends, though we are of the same age. She and I had different stories of our pursuit for place, time and life."

"Perhaps she has a young man in her mind," asked Panchashar, embarking on a straight question for courtesy.

"There are many in this part of the world who like her and are ready to die for her. Even the old ones have their eyes on her. But she doesn't put anyone here on a pin's head. None here can choose or stop her. It's she that has to choose; others' choice doesn't count. I don't know how it is on Nepal's side."

"If that is the case, Melamchi hasn't picked any man till date."

"Oh no; that is not the case. She has chosen one, but I don't know the details."

Hwang chose to be silent again.

"Can there be a thing you don't know?"

This pleased Hwang to some extent. He felt rather proud of himself. Then he face Panchashar eye-to-eye and said, "There's no young man that suits her in this part of the world. If there is one, he should be there, in your land."

"It's a matter of surprise that there's no young man that suits Melamchi in such a huge country. Don't you think so, Hwang?"

"As I can see it now, a match of beauty, age, home and wealth cannot bring two people together. As for these things, all young men here have them. But they are no match to Melamchi."

Hwang tried to reveal the reality. He said, "There is something uniquely different in her. So the youths here cannot easily set their eyes on her."

"Hwang, you never are already there among the most powerful young men here. I think, you didn't pose yourself as a candidate on that account, did you?"

"The interest stayed subdued inside my heart. But now, it has died out."

"Why?" Panchashar asked.

"I told you, beauty, age, home and wealth are not enough to draw girls anymore. I realized that. So I didn't make any efforts to get her, for I didn't want to reap failure. I don't want to fail."

"But Melamchi, on her part, maybe able to get you."

"Yes, that part remains to be seen. If she is willing, there is no question why she should not. She procures anything she wants by any means. She has that caliber."

Hwang added, "But it's not easy to identify what she actually wants."

"It seems she will not stay in the monastery as a nun. If that is the case, why would she need a man?"

He turned grave. Pushing the discussion further, he said, "She went to stay in the monastery to enhance her power and to cleanse her soul. A young man had barred her way in the fair some time ago. After that, she has become rather different. She is not one who can hold herself in the monastery for long. She is one determined to doing something remarkable in life. She is the pride of our land. I am sure she will come back. If she were decided to stay there forever, she would have sent Jimu back. They will return together after some time," said Hwang, speaking like a deciding authority.

"If that is the case, she is not there in the monastery to pray for the man of her choice."

"We might as well think so. But I believe, she has been there to pray so that no other girl sets her eye on her man, and he doesn't get tangled with anyone else.

Hwang opened up a mystery by revealing a secret.

"Hwang, if that is the case, Melamchi has picked her man. And you know him. Don't you?"

"Yang also knows him. Perhaps, Jimu also does." Hwang continued to speak in signals.

"And you?"

"I don't know him quite well. I spent much of time in the sheep farm. So I didn't get to know many things about the outside world," said Hwang, confessing.

"Do you remember where I saw you first?" Panchashar asked Hwang.

"You had come to roam around our sheep farm with Ye Ye on a horseback. That was when I saw you first. Maybe that was the day you also saw me first." Hwang spoke the truth.

This answer helped Panchashar to ascertain many things and to realize facts. He thanked Hwang secretly and spoke, "Your memory power and ability to recognize people is commendable. I am extremely happy with you."

Hwang was elated on hearing such words of praise for himself.

"The village maidens die for shepherds. But how do you talk of love, living in such hinterlands?"

"What shall I say in such an issue? You should think of it on your own. If two people like each other, what is there to stop them? No place, time or distance can ever set them apart. Such things do not matter at all."

Panchashar appeared curious, even as he cast his interrogating eyes on Hwang. With great interest, Hwang continued his words: "The girls sometime come to the mountains with ration items. If the hearts meet, everything can happen. Sometimes, we ourselves enter the village on the pretext of finding a lost sheep, and enjoy. There really are very few in the village, who don't love the shepherds. We sometimes walk down ourselves, while they come up the mountains, looking for *jimmu*, *shilajeet*, honey or medicinal herbs. When there are fairs or carnivals, we ourselves go and enjoy. That's how the life of shepherds like us goes."

There was an admixture of thrill and forlornness in Hwang's account.

HARI RAJ BHATTARAI

Even as he was leaving, he rolled his tobacco and lit it. Drawing a couple of puffs and releasing the smoke in the air, he said, "The best is the time when they come up to take sheep-milk curd, ghee and dry mutton. We churn the buttermilk at such times, and take our butter. They are happy; we are elated too."

He doused the fire on his cigar and added, "The girls love the shepherds and the horse grooms a lot. They find our smell quite intoxicating."

"That may be true. Even I have started liking the horse's smell."

Panchashar raised comparable issue and said, "No girl can reach such a remote place alone, otherwise."

"But that is a simple thing. We bring one to our ranch, promising her all the stuffs from there, and ask others to stay way and prepare snacks. We ask others to wait at some other ranches with food, while retaining the girl of our pick in our own ranch with promises of the sought-of stuffs. They understand our inclination. We send some of them to the woods to pick wild vegetables and firewood, and ask others to manage the loads. This way, they get disbursed. If that happens, we can pick one and pass time with her. There are times when one man has to appease two."

Hwang lit his cigar again, drew a few puffs until he was satisfied and said, "The shepherds' life is apparently very enjoyable. But there is a grimmer part to it. Sometimes the girls pose themselves as burden. There are some who badly abuse us."

"Hwang, you happened to bear strange incidents. If you sit down to write, it can make a long narrative, can't it?" said Panchashar, intending to encourage him further. He added, "Maybe four to five of them come together to stay with you sometimes. You cannot accommodate those many people in a sheep farm. Don't you have problems in such a cold place?"

"That's not a problem at all. When many of them come, they themselves make arrangements, one staying at one ranch each. They get disbursed very easily. That depends on their own interest."

Panchashar went on listening with interest. A wave of enthusiasm was rippling in his eyes.

"Sometimes, we all gather and burn logs, roast things, cook them, eat, feed, drink or make others drink, sing and dance. One never knows how quickly the night wanes. When rosiness appears on the brink of the day, we move to our own farms, taking along the partner of our choices, and sleep in each other's arms. We enjoy; they too are not less thrilled.

Panchashar went on listening as though he was deeply moved.

"If only two of them come up, they refuse to part. At such times, we need to clasp both, one in each arm. Such days are extremely tiresome. Yet, they do all the chores of our farm and also love us a lot. As for ourselves, we sleep away the entire day. When I remember our farm life, I am sort of thrilled."

Hwang paused, lit his cigar again and threw out a curl of smoke.

From the depth of his profound thoughts, Panchashar reverted to reality and made himself composed. Then he said, "Maybe Melamchi, Jimu and Yang also come to the farms, sometimes."

"Oh, no. They have not been to any animal farm till date," said Hwang, and added, "They are very clean girls. They don't like the life in animal farms. More, they are guests who have come to visit their aunt for a brief duration. So there's no question they would be up in our ranches."

Recalling a forgotten fact, he said, "Jimu and Yang have come from a different place. They don't quite know the ways here. Melamchi stayed away from her village since an early age. She can have heard about life in the animal farms, but I am sure she has not seen or experienced one. She looks too strange to be called a daughter of our race. She is markedly different here. And so is Yang. She is so cute and tender; even the wind seems to push her down. Jimu, on the other hands, appears more gregarious; more fun-loving. But then, I don't think she has also ever stepped into an animal farm."

Panchashar very much liked Hwang's observation. Expressing the ground reality in a figurative language, he said, "I found you precise in reading women's mentality and actions. From without, you don't look one with such profound study. Our thinking can never make an estimation of your thoughts. In many of such matters, you can be a guru to me. This is what I think. Your experience will prove a source of knowledge for me."

Hwang didn't consider Panchashar's words an exaggeration. So, in his natural gait, he was elated from within. The joy was apparent on his face.

Hwang was a zealous and romantic young man. For someone, he was an able and honest worker. He had lived his life in the village until he was an adolescent. When he entered his youth, he had to bear the responsibility of an animal farm in the mountain. Once he was in his youth, he didn't take much time to draw himself close to those girls, who were his childhood playmates in the village. On top of that, the scintillating environment around the secluded Mount Kailash and the free atmosphere around it, obviously, acted as powerful stimulant for his emotional exuberance. In the eyes of the maidens as well, he was a romantic, brave, handsome and intimate youth.

He always looked at the womenfolk with eyes of honor, and presented himself before them as a helpful friend. Yet, for certain reasons, he appeared tricky to the eyes of some. The girls latently competed among themselves to draw him near to them.

"Hwang, I want to enjoy a lot in your marriage. Do not forget to invite me." Panchashar looked into his seductive eyes and said, "There must be someone you like."

"There's one. If she comes to the fair this time, I will make her mine, anyhow."

Hwang found it difficult to draw his heart back from many maidens and pour it on one.

"Could she be keeping herself safe only for your sake?"

"I believe so, till now. Unless the girls want, no one can ever own them. If they decide, many things become easier for us."

Hwang continued to send forth romantic feelings, make his eyes dribble with emotions.

"If that is the case, the girl you like is not any of Yangsila, Jimu or Melamchi," said Panchashar, trying to digress the issue and raise a different subject.

"There are really a very few girls like Melamchi. Her thoughts are very different. One can never think of making her his wife and keep with him for long. We cannot be like her; she cannot be like any of us, either. In my view, Melamchi cannot fit into a wife's schema. She is a girl of excellent merits; so it's futile to look at her from that perspective," said Hwang. He added, "I get summarily lost in the glory of her personality. I tagged many of my musings to her, dreamt of her and rejoiced. But that sufficed for me, because such things were not possible in reality. They were nothing but sickly plans, destined to shatter the next moment. I didn't think of treading along that path and making myself sick.

"Jimu, on the other hand is a jolly and carefree girl, who enjoys visiting markets, fairs and gatherings. She doesn't have any place to visit; any goal to attain. She is a maiden who is contented with the status quo, and lives in it, enjoying. She handles many complex predicaments with dramatic ease. She is a nightingale that rejoices in travels, meetings, feasts and festive occasions. She is not one who can look at life from depth, or from a close distance. She is an extremely jolly friend, a true companion and a guiltless pal. This is what I think about her."

Hwang presented such a picture of Jimu.

They were treading along a bare, uphill route, beset by cold wind blowing incessantly. The chill was sending shivers down their hearts. Hwang struck in flint and knife, but the tinder refused to catch fire. It has perhaps turned moist. He prepared fresh tinder and made fire, lighted his tobacco roll, and drew in a few long puffs of smoke. He showed a countenance rendered listless by hunger and fatigue.

Panchashar wanted Hwang to continue with his descriptions. So he was waiting for that with a lot of patience.

"I'm satisfied now. What was that we were talking about?" said Hwang, his interest in the conversation still intact.

"You said, Jimu doesn't suit to be a good wife. What would you say about Yangsila?"

"Oh, do not mention anything about her. Anyone that marries her will lose his own way."

Hwang added, "Stranger, you have perhaps heard of many old tales, haven't you?"

"What sort of tales?"

"Carried away by the looks and seductiveness of girls, many kings and emperors have relinquished their kingdoms. They have forgotten their duties and commitments. They have allowed themselves to be robbed of everything, enthralled by the charms of girls. For abandoning everything else and following them, they have rendered their world utterly worthless," said Hwang. He continued, "Yang, in the same way, is stunningly beautiful. She is sweet and emotional. On top of that, she is quite ravenous, and is filled with dedication. A man who draws close to her cannot live away even for a second. This is not one of Yang's weaknesses; it's a quality she has, a silent weapon that stays concealed most of the time. Some notice it; others fail. So the men drawing close to Yang forget their missions; abandon their duties and responsibilities. They pour all their masculinity at her service. Therefore, such intoxication becomes a misfit for people like me, who sweat in labor, work day in and day out and live a life of simplicity. I don't know if you like my words, but Yang doesn't fall within the bounds of my life. Frankly speaking, a man of my footing cannot hold her for long. We are incomplete for her."

Hwang concluded his narration.

"Hwang, that means one should have a friend like Melamchi if he wants to win the world, and a friend guiltless and dedicated friend like Yangsila for a happy family. Isn't this your conclusion too?" Panchashar asked.

"It is. In a sentence, you concluded whatever I have said so far. That's what I mean too. "Hwang expressed happiness.

'This also means we can have a meaningful wife only if we have a balanced combination of the heart and intellect. But I have to take both along, maintaining a balance, in order to reach my goal,' thought Panchashar, deeply reflecting on the issue.

***

One horse for many mares, one ox for many cows, one bull for many buffaloes, one ram for many sheep is obviously an inadequacy. The females cannot mount among one another and satisfy themselves, nor can they beget offspring. The mounting of a male upon the female and its positive outcome cannot be substituted by homosexual mounting and dismounting.

It's true that if there is lack of satisfaction, there is absence of completeness. From there, malice comes out. The malice erupts as flames of dissatisfaction, hatred, delinquencies and crime. That can lead to a terrible revolt in an uncontrolled condition, devoid of any solution. So the natural physical and mental thirst that appears with age should be properly addressed through love, goodwill, favor and reciprocation.

In case of the human world man and women are the only and the best doctors to treat each other. They can offer each other a befitting and a balanced treatment to each other's mental and physical craving. In case of the animal world, sex drive is limited to procreative activity. That is extremely powerful and untamable. But in case of the human beings, such a drive is more pleasure seeking. The women perhaps know it much more than the men do.

Men who maintain many wives find their love and time sliced into many fragments. The wives are deprived of their rights to receive total love and undivided time. At the time of climax, the exhibition of love often remains extremely potent, as it true in the animal world. The man appears contented, leaving his wife still pining. Here comes the question: don't the unsatisfied wives love to live healthy lives? For that, won't they open the front and the back doors? Won't they embark on other journeys toward fulfilling their sexual desires? Should one necessarily consult reference books to tell that this is a natural and sovereign desire in the human beings? Death and sexual desire do not discriminate. This is a universal fact.

***

CHAPTER FIFTEEN

T HE ROYAL ASSEMBLY of Emperor Timur Khan looked quite forlorn that day. The hall was full; the attendance was total. The courtiers were in their places, quiet. All that lacked was the Emperor's presence. But there was no likelihood that his absence would bring any glory to the assembly that day.

The assembly could not throw its forlornness away even after Emperor Timur Khan came and occupied his seat. There was no problem to be seen; no context or issue expected to be taken up for discussion. After all, one cannot expect thunder without clouds, lightening without collision and thunderbolt without any reason. But the assembly, at the moment, seemed expecting such a thing.

Emperor Timur Khan himself appeared quite despondent. It's possible he was gripped by apprehensions of a revolt for the throne. When his youthful wife told him she was no longer ready for youthful games, he was crestfallen. Rejected by his queen who was still at the prime of her youth, Timur Khan had felt such a bitter sense of defeat that he was retiring into a secret lamentation, when by mistaken, he happened to enter the assembly hall. Or else, the criticism, comment and fiery indignation from his older wives drove him mad, and unknowingly, he walked into the assembly. No one knew the reality thought. No one there had any estimation of his pain, restlessness and trepidation. They were obliged to stay silent, even if they had any inkling of it. This had, in a way, become a part of the palace culture.

It seemed all the courtiers were in meditation, waiting for more information, signals and messages. They were there in full determination and perfect balance of minds. It seemed, a moment was arriving soon, carrying some excellent thought and a wise idea, and the royal assembly was waiting for the same in utter silence.

Inside such a tranquil assembly hall in pin-drop silence, an announcer made a formal entry and said, "Our guest, the great artist from Nepal, Mr. Panchashar is present among us here today after resting for a few days. He has reached here to gift a painting to His Majesty."

The information travelled to every corner of the hall, and got lost in its stillness before long.

The courtiers now appeared resurrected as if elixir was distributed to each one of them. It seemed, the assembly had now come into light from a dark dungeon. It gained life, and it seemed, breath had been instilled into a dead land. The courtiers felt that they had been suddenly delivered from a crisis by an unseen power. At once, a wave of emancipation rippled through their hearts.

Panchashar made a formal entry into the assembly. The courtiers welcomed him with a standing ovation.

Panchashar had a bundle of stalks in one hand and a huge painting, rolled into a coil in the other. He kept them at a proper place for a while and greeted everyone at once, giving a glimpse of his ethnic identity. He paused for a while, had a glimpse of everyone and genuflected in Chinese fashion. This was the first round of actions.

In the second round, he picked up the bundle of stalks he had kept just a while ago and carefully fixed them to make a frame for displaying the painting. Then he turned toward the Emperor for once.

Emperor Timur Khan started watching Panchashar's sequential actions and spotless accomplishments without the blink of his eyes. He nodded his head a little signaling his permissions, apparently understanding Panchashar's appeal.

Panchashar unrolled the big painting and fixed it on the scaffold he had just made from the sticks. He moved two steps back and told the Emperor and the courtiers that it was the picture of the newly constructed royal building.

The area of this four-tire building constructed in pagoda style was fairly wide. Its main gate was on the eastern side, while the other two gates were on its southern and western sides. The picture also had miniature paintings of each corner of the house so that they could see the entire building in piecemeal practically from all the directions.

The glaciers flowing down from snow-capped mountains flanked the building on its eastern and western sides, forming natural forts. At patches, there were thick and thin groves and gardens with trees and flowers, while yaks, deer and sheep could be seen grazing there. From time to time, they could see pairs of birds flying from green, tall mountain ranges. It seemed, the artist had completely captured, without any distortion, the hue of the morning sun spilling its golden paint all over the landscape, and thus, made the painting timeless.

The painting that presented the high mountain ranges on the north-western direction in partially dimmed and distanced background, was felt to be a focus of curiosity and contentment. The spectators inside the royal assembly were feeling that they have looking at the building sitting outside its corridor.

"Wow! The artist has excellent merits, distinguished aesthetics and unique perspectives. We must acknowledge the fact that scholars, philosophers, writers and artists built a world that never ages," said a patron on art, generously expressing his remarks.

"Artist! Stay with us. We shall make every arrangement for your comfort, and you will be highly honored here," said Emperor Timur Khan in great elations. He added, "I shall make for you a culture and fill it with a rich and natural culture."

He ran his eyes among his courtiers once and said, "I will declare you an invaluable asset of this country. Think on my proposal once." Emperor Timur made his intentions public in a careful way.

The wise men, seers, enlightened men, the Buddhas, scholars and the gurus, the writers, artists and the workers and distinguished citizens of the world. They enter their work field with the mantra '*basudaiva kutumbakam*'—meaning, the world is a single family.

They reach a place where their consciousness, wisdom, skill and excellence find due respect. This is something everyone knows.

It's the politicians that need countries. A politician is not hailed in a foreign land. There, they were becoming nothing better than a beggar, and by that token, become refugees—downtrodden, inactive and allowance-dependent. This also is an experienced reality. The great personages that spread figures, letters, service, philosophy and wisdom often vanquish death. That's why things like country, culture and relations are wayside stops; they are like prayer flags that advertise a moment in history. Man, by nature, remains enticed by their intoxicating appeal.

Panchashar took Timur Khan's proposal quite casually. He didn't think it necessary to answer or react. He only thought, 'I must belong to everyone, and live as a domicile to every place. I cannot confine myself to a single location. That is an inadequacy for me. Together with me, I must carry my community and my nation to every corner of the world.'

Time had decreed that the royal meeting be adjourned. The courtiers were impatient to hear the word of adjournment form the Emperor. They also had the natural curiosity to know what the Emperor would say before winding up the meeting.

Emperor Timur Khan ran his eyes in the assembly and said in a trice, expressing himself in an emotional fashion, "Imagine a country like Nepal that gave birth to such an accomplished artist. Imagine the cultural glory of the valleys of Kantipur, Lalitpur and Bhadgaon. Imagine how glorious the royal cities there are, laden with the richness of architecture. How well could they have embellished their entire Kasthamandap valley? I am impatient to go and see.

"I shall certainly go to Kantipur, and will start before long. I no longer need any formal invitation or a green signal."

With some intense feelings, some whims and some uncontrollable excitement, he said, "We also have historical and family relations with Nepal. Our religious and cultural relations were even stronger. In many fronts, Nepal is our guru as well. I

HARI RAJ BHATTARAI

can visit the *gurukul* on my own too. I don't need an invitation anymore. I am not ready to be bound any further. I am leaving soon."

When the Emperor expressed to the assembly his intentions dotted with interest and intense curiosity in a guiltless way, the assembly turned mute for a while, estimating the gravity of the Emperor's declaration. The assembly was immediately adjourned thereafter, following an announcement that the courtiers and Panchashar should be there another day for another meeting.

The meeting commenced on the following day. But the nature of that meeting was something never seen before.

The courtiers got divided into several groups to discuss the management of the Emperor's foreign trip. The Emperor, together with his queen and personal advisors sat on the informal seat. The Emperors mind was astray, recklessly musing about his upcoming trip. When he started musing about a trip passing along different places with indescribable natural panorama and newer glimpses of social life, he forgot the present condition of the assembly and remembered Mauni's advice he had heard from Omu's mouth a few days ago. Then he said to himself, 'The plain land around Yarlung in Jangbo Jiang, the flat land around it and the marshy land around it is also a part of China, but it is in neglect now. We should at any cost make use of it now. It's true that the land there is very rich, and the soil very fertile. Its yield is enough to keep half of China going. There is no question we can forget that place and leave it unused. More, it's a fenced garden in Cheng Du—our own backyard garden. We can also develop waterways, tunnels and ropeways to reach there and make use of the land. On my way back from Kantipur, I will surely visit that rich part of our great China.'

He rose from his place with excitement and clapped, drawing the attention of the assembly. Complete silence filled the assembly hall now. The assembly abandoned its work for a while and concentrated on the Emperor's words.

Breaking the utter silence of the hall, the mild sound of horses' gallop was heard coming from a distance, getting louder and faster each moment. Like a deer that sends the grass it was munching on one side of its gullet and raised its ears to listen to an incoming sound, the courtiers stopped set their works aside and concentrated on the sound of the approaching gallop.

The gallop gradually slowed and stopped outside the assembly hall. Emperor Timur and his relatives also felt the same. The rider walked straight to the gate of the assembly and stopped at the doorsteps.

All eyes from inside turned to the figure standing at the main entrance of the assembly hall. Their eyes were filled with enquiry and curiosity. Leaving the gateman of the hall behind, the human figure appeared running straight toward the hall. It appeared mysterious for a while, for it was coming from the direction opposite to light, only to appear normal again. But the person was not one they could recognize instantly. That must be why the courtiers waited for it with doubt and mystery.

The human silhouette soon turned into a discernible figure mounted on a horse. Even without speaking a word, the person handed over to the gateman a rolled paper coil in a natural way. The paper, passing from hand to hand, finally reached the Emperor.

"What's this? Find out and inform me?" said the Emperor in a serious voice. His words were directed to the assembly. The paper was passed once again, from hand to hand, until it landed in the hand of a senior courtier.

Panchashar took no time in finding out that it was a paper inside a bamboo cylinder, sealed with lids of homemade Nepali paper. He inferred that it must be a letter coming from Kantipur.

The address outside had been written in Chinese and Tibetan scripts. The main body of the letter was in Kirat, Maithili, Ranjana and Devanagari scripts, in different paragraphs.

Scanning the letter with his eyes, the senior courtier said, "Your Majesty, this letter has come from Kantipur. But the body of the letter is in four different scripts. So I hand this letter over to the official from the Ministry of Foreign Affairs. I have no knowledge of these scripts. I am sorry for my ignorance."

Panchashar was sitting quite alert. He thought, 'This means, it's difficult to govern a country if you don't have access to foreign languages. If you have no knowledge of the outside world, the country lags far behind. I can see that one needs scholars and citizens with knowledge of foreign language to best govern a nation.'

The rider who bore the letter was standing outside. They could see no other part of the rider's body except the eyes. It appeared that the figure had covered its entire body, except the eyes, to save itself from dust, wind and chill.

The horse rider with bright, glittering eyes and brave demeanors spoke in a bold voice, "If Emperor Timur Khan's royal assembly has no one that can read these scripts and I am permitted, I am ready to read it." The voice of the rider was filled with abundance of glory and dignity. His voice also reflected modest pride.

"Read out. You have my permissions," said Timur Khan with swaggers. "But the dress you are in doesn't belong to this country. Introduce yourself first," he said.

The horseman hesitated for a while. He gathered guts and said, "Your Majesty, I am a resident of Tibet, and am a monk staying in a monastery."

He ran his eyes among the courtiers and said, "That's a letter coming from Kantipur. The bearer of the letter fell sick and died at our monastery."

The emperor, together with his family members, was shocked. The courtiers were impatient to listen to the horseman.

"Before breathing his last, he requested us to fetch this letter to Beijing, to the palace of Emperor Timur Khan at any cost. The old monk at the monastery also knows this. It was his orders that sent me here with this letter," said the horseman, explaining the cause in brief.

The voice and style of the horseman impressed Panchashar. Quite alert, he pressed close to him and looked into his eyes. He took no time in recognizing them. He also read the feelings in them and returned to his erstwhile seat.

There was stillness inside the hall for a while. Seizing the chance, Panchashar turned toward the rest of the courtiers and said, "People from Lhasa travel to various places in Nepal on business mission, and return. So the people on both the sides do not have much problem with the languages. There are many merchants that know Chinese, Tibetan and many languages from Nepal. It seems he is also a member of one of such merchants' class, and seems to have the knowledge of many languages. The knowledge of many languages happens to be a great asset."

He turned his eyes away from the courtiers and fixed them on the horseman. Then he said, "Mister horseman dear to the palace! Dear patriotic letter-bearer! Dear guest filled with human compassion! I and this assembly believe you will not find it difficult to explain the content of the letter."

"True. Read it. I am impatient to know what's there in the letter," said Emperor Timur, sounding rather soft this time.

The letter returned to the horseman's hand once again. He removed the side lids of a bamboo cylinder and from inside took out the letter rolled like a birth-chart. For once, he turned his agile, curious and thoughtful eyes on all the people present there, and got them fixed on the letter. Then he started reading it.

Shri!

Kantipur, Nepal

Invitation from the King of Kantipur
To His Majesty Timur Khan, the Emperor of China

Your Majesty,

Placing highest priority upon Your Majesty's high curiosity to witness Nepal's art, we hereby send to Your Majesty our due and heartfelt invitation. We are impatient to welcome Your Majesty here.

Your Majesty's kindness to be here shall make our art blessed and the artists proud. We therefore expect Your Majesty's visit here on the full moon day of April. Welcome!

Dated: Kirat Era...Buddha Era...Nepal Era... Bikram Era....

The bearer of the letter read it out, translating into the Chinese language. On knowing the essence of the letter, Timur Khan smiled with happiness.

He said, "That's fine. We must set out for Kantipur without any delay now."

The courtiers were happy, and were smiling to one another. Panchashar turned grave, considering that the emperor would have a chance to see the celebration of many festivals from New Year to Shri Krishnajanmashtami.

"Dear guest Panchashar! Do you have any special advice in regard to my upcoming tour of Kantipur?" said Timur Khan, seeking Panchashar's advice in a pleasant way.

Thinking deeply for a while, Panchashar spoke in a modest language, "Your Majesty, this monk happens to be one who lives in a monastery. He is helpful and a great supporter of Your Majesty, as evidenced by his travel up to this place. In that case how about sending back a letter through him, declaring the dates of our tour and the number of days we would be spending in Kantipur? Can we also request Lhasa to carry to this letter from there up to Kantipur?"

"Whatever our guest says is worth considering. We must think in that line," said Timur Khan in brief and closed the topic. His mind, however, was seemingly busy in a different issue.

He said outright, "Show me your true face. We need to know you."

Great people, sometimes, speak without considering its appropriateness. Something like that happened here.

A shrill feminine voice started echoing in full tides inside the hall. It said, "Emperor Timur Khan, no Mughal Emperor can force an unknown woman to show him his face. Nor is a woman obliged to show her face to a Mughal Emperor. This is a cultural issue of the Muslims. Your Majesty should not invite disruption in the society through this order."

The horse-riding woman composed herself and cooled down. She didn't obey the royal order.

At the Emperor's signal, the leader of the female fighters' squad from the palace ordered her troop: "You take her inside and peel off her mask. We must know who she is."

Three women from the security team did as ordered.

While she was being goaded inside by the guards, the horsewoman expressed her indignation: "How come the Emperor uttered filthy words unworthy of his position? If His Majesty's intentions are evil, his fall is imminent. History is full of episodes that show how willful actions and evil intentions lead to revolt against the regime. I wish nothing of the sort here."

After a short pause, the female voice echoed from inside the veil, "Can a Mughal Emperor transgress the limits of culture and order a woman to take off her veil against her will? Can he force his will in that? Does he have that right?"

'You don't need to teach me what suits me to say and what doesn't,' Timur Khan muttered to himself. With a shudder, he said, "I think she's really a woman."

The courtiers were cuddling into smaller groups inside the assembly hall. Whispers were rife in every group. The degree of monologue increased.

"The horse-rider seems to be brave woman. Whatever she said is right."

"She even yelled to Hwangdi."

"She's also a scholar. There's no doubt about that."

"True; her ways are very logical."

"She is a thoughtful daughter with complete political awareness."

"It seems she knows many languages."

"True. She is aware of her nationality and her national responsibilities as well."

"In fact, Hwangdi invited unnecessary tension by speaking an unnecessary thing. He fell from his own eyes. There's no other person to be blamed in that."

"Experts say willful rulers are delinquent. Their going astray invites their own fall. If Hwangdi blows a lot of air, it can flame out."

There, inside the palace, the horsewoman started wrangling with the female security guards against their leaders' order to take off her veil.

She unsheathed her sword and said, "Be warned; do not try to touch me."

The leader of the female squad inside the palace appeared ready to tackle the horsewoman in sword battle. She signaled her three other assistants to distance themselves from her.

The combat between the two started. The battle of their swords was worth watching. It was difficult for the onlookers to predict who would win the other out.

The sword from the palace fighter suddenly fell aground. Seizing the opportunity, the horsewoman placed her sword on the neck of her rival. The latter raised both her hands, signaling her surrender.

The horsewoman said, "You don't still know two moves; you are yet to learn that. If you fight with me again, you can even lose your life. Keep that in mind."

The leader of the woman fighters' squad in the palace shuddered. Then she said to herself, 'Who is she to know I am yet to finish my sword education?'

She looked on the face of the horsewoman, eye-to-eye. She felt, those eyes were familiar to her. But the tip of her sword was still on her neck.

Elated, she cried out, "Sister Melamchi!"

"Shh…Be warned! If you speak out…" said the horsewoman, sending chills down the guard's spine.

In a soft tone she said, "I'm happy that you recognized me. Help me to move out of this place now."

She paused for a while and said again, "I ask from you a portion of my tuition fee today."

"That's fine. When the day wanes into dusk, let's go lighting *donglong* and reach up to the stable."

The horseman threw herself on one corner and sat, acting of being completely exhausted. This was a mere acting from her part. She was fully convinced now that she was safe here. So she took a long sigh of relief and released it. The neutral spectators inside the palace too were at peace, considering that the horsewoman had now come under their complete control.

It was dusk—time to light the evening lamps. Walking together with the fighter woman of the palace at dusk lighting round globe-like lamps and hanging them from place to place, Melamchi came out to the gate nearest to the stable. She rode on the horse she used to ride before—leaving the one she came on—and galloped out of the palace premises easily but unexpectedly. She was lost.

Nature also played its role in helping Melamchi escape from the palace. There was a storm. The glowing lamps were swaying in the wind. They were going on and off. At such an odd time, the entire human resource inside the palace was engaged in safeguarding the lamps and closing the doors and windows. The birds encaged there started cawing in loud voices. This alacrity, haste and uncontrollable situation in the evening gave Melamchi a golden chance to flee. The fighter from the palace too was mentally quite contented on being able to pay a portion of her fee to Melamchi. She was herself assured that Melamchi was safe now.

Nature soon returned to normalcy from its dramatic show. Pitch darkness unleashed its rein over the living world. The earth was engulfed by stillness everywhere.

The following day, the fighter woman from the palace met Panchashar at the pagoda house and told him everything about the incident of the previous evening. Panchashar, on his part, released

Melamchi's horse with its saddle tied, attaching to it a letter. The horse neighed and left in the dark, following Melamchi's steps.

***

Timur Khan's tour of Nepal had been finalized with two motifs. First, he had to travel south, and second, he wanted to see the artistic elegance of Nepal. So he formally set out on a state visit of Nepal together with his guards.

The tour had been arranged in an extraordinary way. To manage his every stop on the way, different groups had been deployed. From every point the Emperor stopped at, the managing group would come back to the palace. One group could serve the Emperor only once. There would be another group ready for another stop.

Another important aspect of the tour was that, at every stop point, arrangements for food and maidens had to be managed by the inhabitants of that very stop. This, in a way, was an opportunity for the locals, but it also left them pauperized at the same time. In the name of the Emperor, some of his henchmen also ran riots on the villages, and looted the village folks. They plucked off fruits just trying to develop from buds, also in the name of the Emperor. The villagers were bound to bear it all, taking it for God's will.

Those in charge of the bed rooms also changed every day. The horses and mules carrying the loads also changed. The participants of the tour and the body guards of the Emperor also changed. The only team that continued was the medical team. Inside Tibet, after crossing Lhasa, even the medical team would be changed. But once inside the territory of Nepal, the traveling team had made up its mind to use its own materials and things. Timur Khan held the belief that from his side, there should be no damage or disruption in the socio-cultural life of the friendly nation on the other side of the border.

One of their stops was at Lhasa. Its chief, a Lama, had a courtesy meeting with Emperor Timur Khan and made a special request to stop at Lhasa for one more day. Under the Lama's hospitality,

Emperor Timur Khan of China stopped at Lhasa for an additional day, availing the luxury offered to him by the Lama. The first night he spent there gave him an unprecedented thrill. He was fully contented with the ambrosia of heavenly bliss he was offered there. He considered Tibet an altogether different world.

Timur Khan was highly pleased with the cultural elegance of Lhasa, its social courtesy, the stately honor he was duly accorded by its inhabitants and the world-class hospitality during his stay there. He was also fully engrossed in the amorous game next evening. Materially, the specialty of the night luxury offered to him in Lhasa, the capital of Tibet, was for him dreamlike and unimagined.

Tibet's former name is 'Trivistapam', and it stands for heaven. So it can be imagined very well that Tibet was heavenly and the luxury and happiness it offered were befittingly paradisiacal.

Suddenly, at midnight, Timur Khan was besieged by terror, suspicion and restlessness. He decided to return to Beijing palace immediately. His tour of Kantipur was called off.

With a small troop of his army, Emperor Timur Khan returned from Lhasa. Even as they were packing up, he ordered the army to be quick, and not to leave anything behind on the way.

What's possible and what impossible behind an emperor's decision? The number of answers can be as many as the number of questions. It can be read and observed from any angle. It also depends on the context, vision and mission.

The winners and the most powerful ones cannot lift land and carry it home, but consider themselves glorious and victors in looting the chastity of beautiful women, abducting them and looting away valuable objects.

The politics experts in Lhasa suspected that the political future of their country could come into an end. The religious subjects shed tears, resulting from pillage and oppression by a wicked king. The womenfolk considered their youth and beauty a curse for some time. The parents considered their children a chronic ailment. The city of Lhasa was gripped by the fear that it could lose its sovereignty.

In the heaven-like city of Lhasa, the reign of terror spread like never before, robbing people of their peace and sleep. Its denizens outstayed the night, holding their aching hearts and pounded heads. They could not free themselves from the fear of a comet-strike and thunderbolt.

The king's horses and bulls ran their riots in the city. They destroyed all the flowers and gardens in the royal city of Lhasa. Lhasa was stripped of everything. Like the sudden flight of pigeons deterred from the barnyard, the travel team of Timur Khan moved out of Lhasa in a flash and moved toward Beijing, as ordered by the Emperor.

No one could tell what happened in the night and why. Those who were victimized by the pillage kept their woes to themselves and waited impatiently for daybreak timidly. Buddha's name was their only armor hung on every lip.

The roosters crowed. Birds started chirping. The pigeons cooed and the dogs barked. Everyone started singing morning songs to hail the daybreak. The human voice gradually gained clarity from a fuzzy one. The tremble in their hearts slowly subsided. The townsmen, after a spell of terror all night, started feeling alive again. Worship and prayers were resumed in the monastery. The city of Lhasa started feeling that the sound of the band was ushering excitement and peace again. Yet, with the fall of the first rays of the sun, the entire city of Lhasa gathered around the monastery, filling each single inch of free space, to rinse itself of the trepidation and doubt tormenting its mind. It's true that at such an hour, no other place could be a better place for their terror-stricken minds than a religious shrine. Upon reaching the premises of the monastery, everyone felt relived and secure.

The main Lama in the monastery had taken stalk of the pathetic condition of men and women from the time standing in the monastery premises. He was not unaware of the way Timur Khan's traveling troupe and pillaged Lhasa's beauty and its heaven-like peace. He was deeply pained by the plunder and loot the Emperor's men had perpetrated on the settlers of the town.

With a heart filled with utmost compassion, the Lama said, "Emperor Timur, from our friendly neighbor China, himself knows it very well that there was no lacking of any sort in the way Lhasa welcomed and received him and accorded its hospitality. Yet, we were forced to bear his oppression upon the town life. I am of the opinion that he is himself answerable for all this. Our town life is not one of their meadows or gazing areas. I am deeply pained at this consideration."

He stopped for a while and the Lama resumed, "He happened to call off his trip to Nepal and return home from midway. He went back to Beijing. I have an inkling that he returned following information about an earthquake and sudden emergencies at the palace."

He continued, "We don't need to fear anything now. It's all over. I am deeply saddened by the loss and destruction we the dwellers of Lhasa had to bear. I shall make arrangements to compensate the loss physically or financially, whichever is feasible."

He stopped for a while and said, "I also feel that I made a mistake by offering him a stay for one more night as a state guest. If you, my citizens, also feel the same, you must forgive me for my mistake. I beg your pardon."

After hearing the Lama's words, the denizens of Lhasa felt relieved. They started moving toward their own homes, one after another. The sun added polish from its side upon the life of the people beset by sudden calamity and several other questions, and thus made it glorious once again. Before the long human shadows, struck by the slanting rays of the morning sun had stunted, they had reached their respective homes.

***

HARI RAJ BHATTARAI

CHAPTER SIXTEEN

THE PREMISE OF the monastery was desolate. In it, there was only one man standing in the middle. He lumbered in a seemingly tired gait, and threw himself helplessly on the steps of the entrance.

The main entrance to the monastery was on the eastern side. Therefore, the monastery was glittering, having faced the warm rays of the morning sun. The lonely man, who was sitting on the steps, felt the end of his trepidation and started experiencing joy within himself. He considered the refuge of the monastery a divine blessing and took a deep sigh of relief. He also felt a surge of vigor in his body. His countenance reflected the rise of some energy within himself.

A palanquin was brought inside the premises of the monastery. It had the touch of Tibetan art in it.

The four men who were bearing it placed it on the ground and wiped their sweats.

The lonely man sitting on the steps and basking in the sun was observing all the sight.

An old man walked up to him, his hand holding a walking stick. He was in Tibetan dress. He took a sigh of relief. Then he turned to the four palanquin bearers and gestured his thankfulness to them.

The palanquin squirmed. A living thing quivered inside. With help from the four men, that body entered the monastery. As their guardian, the old man was giving instructions here and there.

The man basking in the sun thought, 'It must be a sick person; they must have come here for treatment.' His speculations were plain and simple.

Walking straight up to the main Lama of the monastery, the old man said, "She is extremely sick. She said she couldn't ride and horse, and asked me to drop her here at any cost. I felt her pulse; she seemed critical. I thought she was moving hither for treatment. So I took help of these four men and brought her here."

"Who's she, after all?" the Lama asked.

"No idea. She came up to my village on her own, riding a horse. Seeing that she was sick, I kept her at my own home for two days. But she showed no sign of improvement. So I brought her here, according to her own will."

The old man didn't have any callousness in his speech.

The Lama was in deep thoughts.

"If she recovers, she will take her way," said the old man.

The Lama examined her eyelids, felt her forehead, and checked pluses. After a prolonged thinking, he said to himself, 'It seems her mind is hooked in a young man. She is out to find her man. She will meet him before long. She will recuperate.'

Then he turned to the old man and said, "She will be fine; we don't need to worry. You can rest now."

The old man led the four men out of the monastery and said, "Thank you very much. The daughter will be alright now. I am very happy. I offer you one sheep each; pick the ones you like from my home."

The four men folded the palanquin into a bundle, and left.

The old man thought the Lama was right in predictions. In the meantime, the girl's horse also showed up. She was also meeting her man soon. The old man considered it the blessing of the Lama.

"My daughter! Are you waiting for this young man?" said the old man, pointed at the man who sat like a tramp, basking in the sun on the monastery's footer.

Yangsila moved her head in affirmation.

"I take leave of you now; I have to move toward my village. May all your wishes come true! I have all my best wishes to you," said the old man, showing utmost intimacy.

She looked at the old man with looks of gratitude, knowing that it was the old man who had brought her to the monastery, and had brought her together with Panchashar. The old man, on his part, also showed as much compassion as he could from his eyes, and took his way.

Yangsila walked two steps following the old man and returned, following a brief, secret talk. Signaling Panchashar that she would be back soon, she walked into the monastery.

Panchashar considered this meeting with Yangsila quite unexpected. Yangsila, on her part, had not imagined meeting him here, either.

Yangsila knew well that the primary mission of her tour in this part of the world was to meet the Lama old man and convey to him Melamchi's message. But she wanted to keep this fact within herself at the moment. She knew, to some extent, that she should project Melamchi herself in order to reach up to Panchashar. The Lama old man also believed that it would be best to take Melamchi into confidence in order to reach up to Panchashar, and any other way that bypassed Melamchi would be futile. She contemplated on this issue for a long time, and reached this conclusion.

Panchashar thought, 'Yang must be moving toward Olangchunggola; it's by coincidence we are meeting here."

Yangsila, on the other hand, thought, 'Panchashar was returning to his home country without telling Melamchi. If the old man hadn't brought me to this monastery taking me for a sick woman, I wouldn't have met him.'

Panchashar thought, 'Could Yang be returning to Gola even without taking leave of Melamchi?' He also considered another aspect of the same thing: 'Why would Yang be required to follow Melamchi, who has entered the monastery?'

Yangsila was gripped by a mental conflict. She thought, 'Though Panchashar is my main object of pursuit, how can I close my doors to Melamchi? I know, to some extent, the fact that unless I take Melamchi into confidence, I cannot make my proximity with Panchashar healthy and long lasting.'

She thought even harder: 'This meeting is a coincidence; it's a case of immediacy. It was not a planned meeting. Even if I had made any plan, I would first let Melamchi know, and inform

Panchashar later. So, I think, I must first meet Melamchi and turn to Panchashar later for a fresh meeting. What wrong would it do to me, if I meet her and confess that I came across Panchashar accidentally while I was coming to meet her?'

She tried to land on a solid ground of contemplation: 'I have the Lama old man's message with me and I must convey it to Melamchi. So she is my destination. And this very message is the mantra for me to reach up to Panchashar with Melamchi's help.'

She emboldened herself and thought, 'What's the secret behind the stranger living in the monastery in the guise of an unknown man? Can such a distinguished artist stay here, lost in his own world? Why is he languishing himself in the monastery?'

But the plans Yangsila and the Lama old man had made was for the past. The context had changed altogether now. Panchashar visible to the past eyes was nowhere there now. It was through a strange coincidence that Yangsila had met him. She didn't have the slightest imagination that she would meet Panchashar at such a place. The plan they had made before would come in handy for Melamchi, because they could only tell where Melamchi was. Panchashar was not in any sort of hope to find Melamchi again, because he was aware of the turmoil created in the context here, as a result of the restlessness and anarchy developed inside Timur Khan.

In fact, Panchashar, who had set out for Nepal as a member of Timur Khan's team had found himself at lost, after Timur called off his tour from Lhasa. Finding himself nowhere, he had entered the monastery, forgetting himself altogether. Yet, he didn't engage himself in the search of any thought to bring Melamchi and himself together again. Considering that he had lost the path of his life altogether, he threw himself inside the monastery in Lhasa, having nowhere to go to.

Yangsila was now in deep thoughts. Her thought was never for herself alone. As always, she thought for others; thought for everyone. Whenever she thought only about herself, she felt the guilt of falling quite low and becoming stunted. In life she lived without concealing anything from anyone, she found it painful if she had to keep any secret within herself. At such moments, she grew pathetic with remorse. But at present, something had entered her mind, which she was unable to pick and fling away. Until some time ago, she was a girl of simple and guiltless nature; now she was trying to become a mature person, engaged in serious contemplations.

Yangsila knew it very well that her accidental meeting with Panchashar at the monastery was root to an unpleasant situation. Hadn't she met him there, the conflict inside her mind would not have turned so intense. If someone moving along a simple and effortless path suddenly encounters a crisis, life is gripped by cowardice. In such a case, why should she choose simple and effortless path in the first place? Why should she run away from conflict and struggle?

She analyzed, 'If the stranger is moving toward his home country, I will go with him. For that, I don't have to ask anyone for permission, except himself.'

She further thought, 'If he denies taking me along, I must say, give me company up to Olangchunggola, or find me a companion.' She gathered some guts and said to herself, "No young man can send a young girl with another man along such a long route. From this, one more question will get a natural solution. If the stranger really loves me, he cannot stay away from me at any cost now. I can place before him this very question to know if he really loves me or not.'

Deeper she thought, and landed on yet another question, 'My first task is to convey the Lama old man's message to Melamchi. But that's not the mission of my life. As for my mission, I have spotted it. I am merely a messenger; a post-woman. After I do that, my journey will have no other obligation left in my hand. In reality, my real role will start now. I must myself attain the object of my pursuit. I don't want to receive it as gift from someone else's hand. So I want to see the attainment of my goal as my own success or failure. It's not necessary for others to know about my success or failure. This is an open secret.'

She emboldened her morale further.

With added self-confidence, she analyzed, 'At the moment, the stranger and Melamchi are not making any physical effort to meet each other. Perhaps, they don't consider this time appropriate for that. Melamchi is lost in her own world inside a monastery. The stranger is enjoying his own world in the premises of yet another monastery. They are not impatient to meet each other at the moment. Their minds are not passionate for each other now. They are tormented by problems of different nature right now. Could it be possible that they have pasted each other's images inside their hearts? Should I close my doors toward Melamchi and move toward the stranger?

'It will be best, if I have the stranger as my companion on the way. But if I chose the route along Melamchi's side, I can also reap a negative outcome. But if things do not turn to be as I wish, I will be obliged to choose one from my village, Gola or the monastery. Yet, I should not lose heart. Because in the stranger's eyes, I have seen fifty-one percent of his love in my favor. If that changes into null, it shall still be acceptable to me. But if Melamchi sweeps all cent-percent of it, I won't find it difficult to accept my defeat. So, I must make Melamchi and the stranger meet each other at any cost.'

Changing the stream of her thoughts, she said, 'Where could the stranger be going? How did he reach here? And what is he after? I need to find that as well. Can I bind him to my mission alone?'

Even as these thoughts occurred to her mind, she walked out of the monastery and stood beside Panchashar.

"Yang, it seems you are not quite well. You were lifted to the monastery by others. What's wrong?" said Panchashar, asking with profound sympathy.

"I'm fine at the moment. Now that I have met you, nothing will happen to me. I have been healed."

Panchashar carefully scanned Yangsila's countenance. He thought, a wilting flower was coming back to life.

Yangsila tried to screen Panchashar's direct vision by lowering her eyes. In fact, her soul had been wondering where she might meet Panchashar and when. But she didn't express this yearning. In manifestation, she only said, "I find this sudden meeting quite thrilling; quite pleasant. I have been benumbed by this joy. I have lost control over my own body and mind; I am forgetting myself. I didn't know joy could have such effect. I am experiencing the same for the first time today."

Panchashar gawked, seeming absorbed in Yangsila's words.

"Come; let's move," said Yangsila in clear words.

"Where?" he said, sending her question into quandary.

Panchashar's destination was not clear at the moment. He had gone completely astray. So he had not been able to decide what he would do next. He said to himself, 'It seems, life in a monastery is going to be better than the life of a settler.'

"Let's return to our villages. Let's go to Gola; to Kantipur. These doors will always stay open for us. If nothing works, we can always go to a monastery. However, we should enter one today itself and become dependent. I am not all inclined to that," said Yangsila, quite decisively.

Panchashar said to himself, 'There's no question of returning to the village now. I send my greetings to the old Lama from here. I can no longer return to the palace, for there are signs of revolt in the kingdom of Emperor Timur Khan. So going there is pointless now. Now comes the question of Gola. Is Yang taking me there, or I am giving her my company? If Yangsila is ready, we can't move straightaway to Kantipur right from here? If we choose this option, we can save ourselves from a great crisis. Yes, a great crisis!'

He said the last sentence aloud.

This startled Yangsila.

"A great crisis? What sort of a crisis?" she said, hurling the question on Panchashar.

Panchashar had unknowingly uttered the words 'a great crisis' in the best possible way he could. Yangsila made a question out of them.

"Oh, nothing. I was in my own world. Many thoughts were playing havoc on my mind. It must be a slip," he said with ease.

"Come; let's move away from here. Let's first enter the monastery. Let's bow down, light lamps, and seek blessings."

Yangsila held Panchashar by his arms and pulled him in.

Making the statue of the Buddha a witness, the Lama of the monastery blessed them for love, happy conjugal life, sovereign fame and long lives.

The Lama said in clear terms, "May you have beautiful and glorious children, who can bring laurel to your land and to your community."

The two received the Lama's blessings with lowered heads.

When they raised their heads and faced the Buddha, they felt compassion and peace emanate from his eyes and reach up to them. This made them deeply thrilled, and they got caught into each other's arms, their hearts resonating with profound love.

The community of the Lamas sprinkled water and flower petals on them and concluded their wedding formally. Then they took both of them to the guest room.

"Prince Siddhartha had attained enlightenment by abandoning the bliss of conjugal life and regal splendor. But no Lama is ready to tell this. Why is it so? Have you even given a thought to that, Yang?" Panchashar asked during one of their romantic moments.

"Now is not the time to discuss such a thing, at least on our first night. We will have enough time for that. Let's talk about ourselves now. Let's make our own plans. Shan't we?" said Yangsila, mixing request and plans.

The door to the guest room opened, welcoming the first ray of the morning sun. In the light of the juvenile sun, Yangsila's countenance appeared serene and highly contented. She sunbathed for a while, and naturally, turned her eyes away. She sensed that a dog was waiting for her outside.

A flash of thought occurred to her mind: 'He's not there in the village. But these dogs?'

No sooner had she spelled the word dog than the dog entered the room and started rolling over her bed fondly. It hopped with joy and started sniffing each part of her body. Panchashar considered this sniffing by the dog a compliment to an incident that had occurred in the recent past.

Yangsila's eyes now fell on yet another dog. 'That's a bitch. She must be following her god,' she thought in an obvious way.

Tilké, her horse, was neighing at the stable of the guest house. She was obliged to show her presence in front of it and pour her love. Therefore, Yangsila and Panchashar walked close to the horse in their Tibetan attires. The horse looked, sniffed them and purred, when it was able to recognize them.

Yangsila stroked its ears. She ran her fingers upon its forehead, and showered her love. The horse appeared extremely delighted.

The dogs also teased Tilké. Tilké neighed to the dogs as well. In a while, both the dogs ran away from there. They led Panchashar and Yangsila toward the monastery.

"Pan, did you notice one thing?"

Panchashar, today, loved the informality in Yangsila's address to him.

"What's that?" he asked, curiously.

"This dog had entered the monastery with Melamchi. So it left both its place and its brother. It now moves around with a bitch from the monastery. Didn't you notice that thing too?"

"In that, you saw him move about with the bitch from the monastery. As for me, I see the bitch following him," said Panchashar with utmost modesty.

"That's one and the same thing. Only our views and understanding makes it different. You are trying to cite the male as superior."

"Unless there is a female, the male is devoid of any identity. Isn't it the female that makes a male possible?" said Panchashar by way of flattery.

"By any means, you are trying to put men on the top."

"Not at all. That's what your thoughts infer. But I am obliged to accept if you say so." He added, "I have never imagined that you were so logical and articulate. I am extremely happy."

Yangsila looked elated.

Drawing a conclusion, Panchashar said, "Male and female are equal. There's no hierarchy between the two. The combination of both these counterparts is equally important in personal and social life."

Yangsila appeared equally scrupulous and zealous.

The dogs entered the monastery, only to come out immediately as though they were there to break a piece of information to someone.

After some time, a female figure appeared at the main entrance to the monastery. In an austere face, the figure glittered in the juvenile light of the morning sun and appeared like a fresh embodiment of glory, glittering at the moment like a constituent of the sun itself.

"Look there at the gate! She looks like Sister Melamchi," said Yangsila, drawing Panchashar's attention toward the gate of the monastery.

"Yes, she is Melamchi. She must have become a nun by now," said Panchashar, quite modest in his words.

"Fie, what a thing are you telling? If she hears?" said Yangsila, trying to sound decent.

They walked close to the figure. Panchashar called out at once, "Melamchi!"

"Pan, Yang! You here?"

Melamchi uttered their names in a tone laden with both surprise and excitement. She thought for a while and suspected that something had gone wrong at home and the two had come there looking for her. Then she said, "Is everything fine at home? How did you reach this place?"

"These dogs came to invite us. They led us to this place, and brought us up to you. So the role they have played in making us meet is significant."

Panchashar added with great care, "We have no news from home."

Melamchi led Yangsila and Panchashar into the monastery as though she was its main authority. After they were done with the formalities of worship there, they presented themselves in front of the main Lama. They bowed down to him and sought his blessing.

The Lama looked at them with moist eyes laden with the Buddha's compassion, magnanimity and feeling and said, "I hadn't seen any completeness till yesterday. But I can see interminable completeness today."

Yangsila took in her hand the letter sent by the old Lama man and ran her eyes over it cursorily once. Then she handed it over to Melamchi, signaling her to first read it for herself and then hand over the Lama of the monastery.

After having read it, Melamchi gave the letter to Panchashar. He read it and paid a quick glance on the faces of both. Then he decently handed it over to the Lama. The Lama read the letter:

Melamchi,

I send you warm love from my side as always.

Your grandmother is no longer with us. She passed away. My brother Jetha Lama also left us. It's my turn now. There is no one to look after the household. So I convinced Hwang and brought him down from the animal farm. The house is now under the care of Jimu and Hwang. It would be best if they got settled here permanently. There is no one else I can rely on, once you left me and went away.

At present, I am staying at the home of my elder brother Jetha Lama. I am running quite sick. So I could not come to the monastery to see you. I can no longer force Yangsila to continue staying here. Considering her age, I didn't think it wise to do so. Even if she doesn't meet any one of you, she can take the help of the monastery and reach Gola. I am confident in that.

I have opened up my mind in this letter. Look at Yangsila with love accordingly, and consider her your equal. Yangsila is elder to you by nature and younger by age. To secure your place, you must also learn to give her due. In my view, you will find no other friend and caretaker better than her. This is my message to you.

Convey my blessings to our foreign artist. Before you leave Lhasa, make it a point to seek the blessings of the main Lama at the monastery there. That will make the journey of your life happy.

Your grandfather
Kanchha Lama

The Lama raised his eyes from the letter. They were simmering with love and compassion. He closed them in his bid to hide his tears, and presented himself in silence.

Panchashar continued to stand without any word. Yangsila appeared austere in a placid mood.

Ever since the letter landed on the Lama's hand, Melamchi was engaged in self-musing. She was looking for grounds to suspect if Yangsila had overtaken her. She didn't choose to free herself from the cyclone of speculations and doubt. She thought even harder, 'Is this a dream or reality? Is defeat or deferral the result of my stay in the monastery? If that is the case, won't the faith of devotees in the shrines dwindle? Where's my sole right? Where is it?'

"You do have your right. It's latent inside you," announced the Lama of the monastery, all of a sudden.

Melamchi shuddered and came out of her musing. All three of them were impatient to hear the Lama speak.

"The order in which you are standing here shall not be considered otherwise, anywhere. That shall be considered proper and firm. This is an order you chose or develop yourselves."

The Lama continued, "The seniority granted by time and relation falls on the one standing on the left hand side. Melamchi, as I can see, is standing on the right. Everything on the right falls within the range of your rights. You are the mistress of that part."

It was not easy for them to understand the Lama's cultural and social interpretation. So he made himself simpler and said, "The man standing like Mount Sumeru between the two of you is a great man, an honorable guest of ours."

The Lama threw some light on the personality of Panchashar.

Turning toward Panchashar, the Lama said, "Honorable guest! Yangsila is the resort of your physical personality. For you, no one besides Yangsila better suits for your mental bliss. Her dedication will provide you abundant energy to manage and awaken your need for peaceful rest in order to give continuity to your artistic pursuit and accomplishment. Your harmonious and joyful cohabitation with her shall become for you a resort that shall give you inspiration and success."

Lama wound up his remark on Yangsila's side. All three were equally curious to listen to the Lama's words.

"Guest, it's plain to me that the no other girl can ever have the qualities and power Melamchi possesses. She is a complement to your personality. She has mounted on the site of your wisdom. She is herself contemplation, vision and pursuit in herself. So, she is present in your life as the central force that we imagine beyond a healthy and robust physique."

The Lama was candid in his expressions.

All three of them faced one another and sent forth a peal of satisfaction.

"You shall become renowned all over the world, and in that, Melamchi's company shall be indispensable. As time passes, Melamchi shall become for you a pilgrimage site or a *gurukul*. You shall become each other's complement."

Lama added briefly, "Yangsila shall give you befitting energy and atmosphere. Always place her liberal thoughts and heartfelt dedication on the top of your priorities."

The Lama paused for a while and said, "Your togetherness has attained its completeness today. Let the life voyage of all three of your prove extremely successful. This is my blessing; this is my wish for you."

All three of them bowed down their head and received the Lama's blessings, even as there was an auspicious music in the air.

The life of Panchashar now looked like that of Mount Everest, standing with Kanchenjunga and Annapurna on its left and right hand sides.

Soon the town of Lhasa buzzed with the praise of Panchashar for his skills in architecture and the contribution he made in this field. Many social and cultural events were organized in his honor. In a grand ceremony, the denizens of Lhasa felicitated him.

Panchashar thought from yet another ground, and drew an inference from what the Lama at the monastery had said: It was Melamchi who had brought for him such overwhelming honor from the society there. Else, he would not be so famous here.

After the formalities of the commendation programs were over, the chief of the town placed a proposal, with support from the senior citizens of the town. He said, "Scholarly guest! Can you build an artwork here before you depart for home? That will be a new and historic turn in the identity and friendliness of our two nations."

He said with added modesty and simplicity, "This is not merely a personal wish of mine. It also is the wish of our near ones here, who are great patrons of art."

He ran his eyes on the Lama, who was the patron and the chief of the state of Tibet, and said, "I am myself a monk. By that token, the entire world is my home. I don't need anything exclusively for me. At the moment, the wish of the settlers of Lhasa is my wish too. So I am placing this proposal from their side."

Panchashar stood from his seat and stretched the Tibetan dress he was wearing. He glances at all the people sitting in front of him. He then bowed to the main Lama and other religious leaders, and said in response, "Venerable Lama! With a high degree of honor, I commend your magnanimity and the hearty goodwill you have expressed for your denizens. I can see greatness reflected in each of your words. I also express my honor for your views that befit the present time."

He drew in a long breath and said, "The topographical make and the natural richness in Lhasa are, in themselves, quite artistic and picturesque. It's quite impossible to find a place like this anywhere else in the world. That must be the reason why this entire region is called Trivistapam or Tibet. The city of Lhasa that stands against a backdrop of pristine nature and geographical excellence is in itself a timeless art. Any art that is constructed hereafter can never match its originality and newness. I think I cannot construct any artwork here. If I do, that will be light showing a lamp to the sun. I beg your pardon."

On hearing Panchashar's view, the audience turned listless like a wick lamp that was running out of oil.

Adding further to his speech, Panchashar said, "After six hundred years from now, a great poet will arrive at his place. By describing Lhasa in his words, he shall make the city famous and highly honored all over the world. For doing that, he shall himself be counted among the top-seeded poets of the world. On finding him among you, you the settlers of Lhasa shall find yourselves honored, and shall consider yourselves blessed. I can see this fact coming true from the position I stand at, today."

The listeners were glued to Panchashar's words. They looked contented as though they were realizing the ground reality. Panchashar ran his eyes all over and said, "I am thankful to you for the love and honor you showed to me. I consider myself a member of your own family."

The audience appeared even more curious and impatient. Panchashar added, "I wanted to be monk in the monastery. But I realized much later that I was unfit to become one. You all inspired me to be a householder. That also is acceptable to me."

Panchashar once glanced at Melamchi and Yangsila who sat to his right and left. Then he faced the mass and bowed to it, expressing his honor, and returned to his seat.

The entire ceremony rejoiced in joy. The Lama, the religious head and the state head of Lhasa ran his eyes among all three of them and showered his love.

The program ended in a joyous and hearty manner.

Panchashar's family decided to leave for Kantipur, treasuring in its heart the exhilarating environment of Lhasa, and its memorable meeting with people there. Before they left, they entered the monastery and bowed to the main Lama there, seeking his blessings.

Two pairs of young men and women also decided to move with them as their companions along such a long trail.

The traveling squad appeared divided into several units, probably in consideration of the distance, the environmental condition and the geographical remoteness. A pair of a boy and a girl was in charge of eleven yaks in the caravan, while another pair, again a pair of a boy and a girl, took care of eleven horses. There also was a pair of hunting dogs, and two of their pups moving together with the caravan. Fifty sheep and a pair of shepherds, fifty mountain goats and a pair of shepherds for them, and a dog in each flock kept pace with the moving procession.

This way, the settlers of Lhasa saw off their daughters formally with magnanimous hearts. This way, in the midst of tears and smiles, Panchashar's team left the city of Lhasa in the forenoon.

Panchashar reached Kantipur together with his caravan, having Yangsila and Melamchi on his two sides, the same was as Mount Everest stands, having Kanchenjunga and Annapurna on its two sides.

On the occasion of the Buddha Poornima, the kings of Kantipur, Lalitpur and Bhadgaon organized a grand reception and felicitation of the artisans returning from China, in presence of many other artisans, representatives from the society and government officials, and thus, upheld the glory of the experts of architecture.

Jokhé was missing in this gathering.

***

CHAPTER SEVENTEEN

ON THE NIGHT she reached Kantipur, Yangsila had a dream. In the dream, a goddess came to her, accorded her the honor of a new daughter-in-law in her new family, and ushered her into the house. She blessed her to be brave and glorious, and disappeared from there.

The same goddess returned to her dream another time as well and said, "This is a place where people without noses live. They cannot ensure you honor and security. So you move to a different place. This is both my order and a wish for a happy and healthy life. You have already attained immortality; you shall not lack anything else, either."

Before disappearing, the goddess gave Yangsila a new name: Helambu. She said, "You will be called Helambu henceforth. The new name shall give you safety. The place where you go and live in shall also be known by the same name. I take leave of you. May your journey be a happy one."

When the dream started recurring almost every night, Yangsila moved to a different place in the east, a sunlight garden among the mountains, started living there, together with Panchashar. This place came to be called Helambu later.

In rainy season, Panchashar moved toward Helambu. There he found Yangsila Helambu waiting for him with intense and long-standing thirst. Panchashar stayed there, caught in the love-laden arms of Yangsila. With time, Yangsila gave birth to many beautiful daughters and a brave sons, who grew and spread over the flatlands between mountains. The community of their descendents is famous all over the world today as a community of beautiful daughters and brave mountaineering sons.

They say, Panchashar comes down to Kantipur Valley in winter. There, Melamchi poured her interest and aesthetic touch to the timely refinement and development of architecture, filling it with the glory of concreteness and attraction. This way, Melamchi showed a tireless engagement with Panchashar and their children in creativity and refinement, giving them a reliable guardianship.

The leadership and involvement of the descendents of Panchashar and Melamchi in honing pagoda architecture to the pinnacle of its development, and the development of distinguished architectural patters, especially in Asia, are considered commendable by everyone. For this, Melamchi is believed to have received the honor of Agnigarbha Mata, the mother goddess with inherent luminosity.

The inference was that, for Panchashar, Melamchi was a wife with intellectual merits. It was she who enabled Panchashar to construct buildings in pagoda style.

In order to stay enthusiastic all the time and give the task its continuity, one's body and mind always needed an invigorating retreat. For this, Yangsila Helambu presented herself in person before Panchashar with her romantic offers, giving him a warm and interminable respite. It is said, these resorts and respites are blessings from the Buddhist monastery; they are gifts and blessings for Panchashar.

People sometimes made a mention of a surprising reality: Panchashar didn't look even when his great grandchildren started appearing in his family, nor did Melamchi and Yangsila showed any sign of aging. Had they been blessed with a quality to stay youthful forever? It also is said, the story changed after Panchashar had a strange dream.

But the spark of this story that appeared like a local myth gradually disappeared.

***

Panchashar woke up with a start, when sprays of water fell on his body.

For the past two years, Panchashar had been keeping to himself, deeply lost in his own world. He was in a state of stupefaction, and was pathetic, caught in the memory of Sanjhang and Teejhang. But he thought it unwise to share this fact with anyone else. Instead, he contemplated about it on his own. Finally, he asked himself, 'Why am I pulled so powerfully toward them? Why am I getting restless every moment? What power lies in the land of the Kirats? Why am I drawn so powerfully toward Sanjhang and Teejhang? Or, is it that they are calling me to see if I have forgotten my promise?'

There was a *sadhu*[55] in front of him. He had a *kamandalu*[56] in his hand. Panchashar stood and showed his reverence to the ascetic.

"Panchashar, wake up. The nation is being looted; it's being stripped. The boundary is being encroached. The lopsided treaty, unequal agreements and selfish accords are rendering the state extremely weak and diseased. Centuries passed, but we could never give ourselves a powerful administration. The nation, in the process of becoming a mere memory of the past, has been incessantly slipping toward annexation. This is an outcome of the bad conduct, anti-national thought and behavior of our politicians. The people who give such rights to such wicked people are also equally guilty. Lack of awareness is perhaps a reason. For that reason, you now resume the halted tasks, and give the nation its armor. Wake up!" the ascetic said.

"Revered one! I could not quite get you."

"Remember the words you have given to Siddha Kirat. And act accordingly."

"I could not remember anything. I ask for forgiveness."

"While you were on your way to China, Siddha Kiran had proposed you to construct an administrative building for the kingdom of Kirat. You expressed your inability then. That is a fact. But you had promised him you would do it on your way back. Recall that. Now is the time you should be fulfilling your promise."

'How?' he said to himself.

The sadhu read his mind, for he could easily do that. He said, "The Kirat dynasty is the biggest and the most powerful dynasty

---

[55] an ascetic that moves from door to door, asking for alms
[56] a metal goblet an ascetic carries with him

here. Its three factions—Western Kirat, Central Kirat and Eastern Kirat—should become one. From the unity of the Rais and the Limbus, a powerful, scientific and modern political power should come up. For that, we have our blessings."

Panchashar went on listening to the ascetic, as though in a spell of charm.

The ascetic added, "Foreign powers have started intruding into the nation, with active support from our politicians, and are enslaving us. Those who are inside the country, but are engaged in anti-national and treacherous activities, are traitors. Only the power of the Kirats can vanquish them and make the nation developed and prosperous. This is what we expect from the Kirat people. If they also go astray, fail to recognize their innate power and refused to wake up, we will be obliged to appeal the kings of the Magarat Region for help."

He continued to listen, getting more and more curious.

The sadhu continued, "But we believe that the Kirat Dynasty will perk up; it will surely rise again. No one can decline the appeal of the Kirats. We pray: let the Kirat Dynasty resurrect with all its unity and commitment, and become our protector, jurist and our pathfinder, and save us from perishing. We have full faith in the Kirats."

Panchashar continued in the state he was in.

The sadhu added, "Go and meet Siddha Kirat this moment. He has been waiting for you. He needs your hand in his commitments."

The sadhu stopped for a while and resumed, "Those two Kirat maidens—your friends—also are waiting for you. They are under the patronage of Siddha Kirat, at your request. I hope you haven't forgotten them, have you? You still owe some responsibility toward them.

"I will now bless you with interminable confidence, special vision, matchless strength and successfulness."

Panchashar woke up, when the holy water with special incantations fell from the ascetic's goblet on Panchashar.

'Oh, what a strange thing I happened to dream about?' said Panchashar, as he came back to senses. He resolved, 'I must anyhow go to the village of Siddha Kirat once. I must see him.'

He changed the context and said, 'Sanjhang and Teejhang also must be waiting for me. I had promised them I would go back. On the same occasion, I can also visit Rishi Ashram and Budha Subba Temple, and seek their blessings. That will be matter of great fortune for me.'

***

Panchashar woke up, remembering the images of Siddha Kirat and the two Kirat maidens.

Sanjhang and Teejhang, on their part, were waiting for Panchashar, moving around Gupha-Pokhari, marshes and plains in the mountains, finally making a mountain top their resort. That place carrying the history of their wait later came to be known as Menchhyayem. To welcome their near one, they embellished this place called Milké on the mountain at the top of their village by planting sixty-four different varieties of rhododendron, which bloomed with time, giving the mountain a spectacular hue. The name of Sanjhang and Teejhang is tagged with the rhododendron forest at Milké for all time ever after.

Panchashar, on his part, thought, 'It seems I will be privileged to see Siddha Kirat once again. Else, why would the right side of my body twitch this way?'

Feeling a twitch from the top to the toes on the right side of his body, he started making preparations to move toward the kingdom of Kirat.

Panchashar was about to set out on a journey when Omu showed up. Panchashar knew her as a good friend who always bore positive thoughts about him. Giving their meeting a formal touch, she put a *khada*[57] around Panchashar's neck.

---

[57]   ceremonial shawls made of silk, put around the neck to felicitate or welcome people

She said, "I have come here to give you great news. Listen before you leave."

"Tell. I am impatient. I won't go before I hear."

"Jokhé is still alive. I met him in the village recently."

"The news is so thrilling! It's elixir for me. What can be a better gift for me, Omu? Thank you so much."

Omu said, "The traveling merchants found him on the way and escorted him up to Lhasa. He happened to stay there in a monastery for a few days, until he found some companions and walked home. We are quite happy to find him back."

"In fact, I was in deep pain. You have released me from that."

Panchashar appeared quite emotional.

Omu read the emotions of Panchashar's face and changed the context. She said, "You look the same—still so young. I was shocked to see you after such a long time." She added some mirth to her speech and said, "Youthfulness seems reluctant to leave your body. Melamchi and Yangsila too are still very young."

Panchashar suddenly remembered Siddha Kirat, who had said Sanjhang and Teejhang would always remain young, and anyone getting connected to them would also have the same blessing. She doubted if Melamchi and Yangsila were young on account of being his wives. He started thinking deeply about that.

After thinking deeply for a while, Panchashar asked Omu, "How's Mauni?"

"He's not very fine. He said, he has to talk many things about the Kirat community with you. But he could not come here, though he was willing. I have come here, carrying his message for you. He has sent a paper; in it, he has written some urgent messages for you."

Omu handed over a paper to Panchashar and said, "He said, Panchashar has a lot of trust in the Kirats, and high hopes from them. But I could not add my thoughts in that. Our times were adverse."

Panchashar continued to listen to Omu.

Omu said, "Mauni always says the same thing: in future, this community will squat in others' backyards and fling stones at its own home. So our duty is to give them vision and show them the way as much as we can. The Kirats are the original and the oldest settlers of this place. But they have started risking their own lives by becoming increasingly hostile toward their own soil, life and culture. Theirs is this land, and they are the masters of this region. If we fail to open their eyes when they are blind, they won't hesitate to tender their land to strangers, by keeping the wrong way."

She added something more about Mauni's health: "Since he is speechless, it's his nature to stay contemplating on his own. I think he is sick, thinking about such serious things. He stays quite restless these days. I don't know how I should explain that."

After scanning the grim face of Panchashar, Omu said, "May you have a safe journey! I too will go back now. Mauni must be waiting for me."

After Omu was gone, Panchashar read Mauni's letter. It read:

Brother Panchu,

> *Happy journey!*
> *May you accomplish your mission well! You have my best wishes.*
>
> *Brother, thank you for remembering something you should never have forgotten. You have a lot of trust and honor for the Kirats. I don't want to break that and ask you to reconsider. Yet, I could not infer that this community is strong and wise. You are liberal, and you take others in the same way. That is a salutary thing in you.*
>
> *Was it history that depicted them as great, or their greatness inspired a glorious history? Any of these is possible. We'll discuss about that after you come back.*

If the Kirats want, this country can become dauntless, prosperous, strong and peaceful in future. There is no doubt about that. But as I can foresee now, the Kirats are less likely to continue as they are in the days to come. They shall gradually convert themselves into different people. As a result, it shall fall way down from its royal dignity find itself a miserable, pathetic, foolish, weak and disintegrated community.

For that reason, my brother, if you happen to meet Siddha Kirat, convey him my request: Let not the Kirat community, the crown and canopy of this nation, follow others' dictates and attack its own people with revenge motifs, belittle its own glorious height and blur its own history in front of the world! Let the community receive the blessings of wisdom and intellect from Siddha Kirat so that its high thoughts, liberal views, openness of feelings and helpful culture, concealed by arrogance, jealousy and revenge get revived and manifest once again. That way, let them maintain social harmony again and become able to introduce the true essence of the Kirat community to the modern society once again. But I am shocked:

A cow never becomes a donkey
Nandi was never yoked to a plow
A cat never becomes a tiger
Why is a glorious stock falling low?

After reading Mauni's letter, Panchashar slipped into deep thoughts. He thought, 'Mauni, your thoughts are right in their own place. But I consider the Kirats capable of reclaiming their glory because this community has both strength and human resource. Only that, it must be able to see itself against its own glorious history and cultural background. For that, Mauni, I don't think I hold a conviction contrary to yours. But I can say only this much:

A brave lion can never become a rat
The Tamor cannot shrink to a well or creek
The tall, bright Mountain in fact
Cannot even become stunted at will.

Panchashar set out alone, secretly bowing to Arya Rishi, Buddha Subba and Siddha Kirat. He grew conscious, remembering the words he had given to the animals there. He gave his journey continuity, remembering with reverence Sanjhang and Teejhang, who were waiting for him, letting the entire forest at Milké burst into rhododendron blossoms. This filled him with freshness and enthusiasm.

When he stopped to rest, he took out Mauni's letter and read it again. In his bid to discover the truth, he contemplated quite deep, and got lost in thoughts from time to time. Such was his daily routine on the way.

While he stopped at Mauwa Khola Kharka, Panchashar visited all of its marketplaces, fairs and carnivals, shrines, social and cultural events and festivals. This brought sweet experiences to him.

Sanjhang and Teejhang trained him at every step; directed each of his moves, and made him adaptable to them through their help and dedication. Thus, they kept him extremely pleased. They also taught him new lessons of love and goodwill, and tutored him with sublime lessons of sacrifice and trust.

Everyone appeared quite happy with Panchashar. He received a lot of love from the people's representatives and relatives. He sought the blessings of Siddha Kirat, the ideal personage of that part of the world.

Sanjhang and Teejhang seized a moment and took him to Sabha Pokhari, with an intention to sow the holy seeds. He also projected the pretext of sowing such seeds the following year, and invited them to come to Kantipur for the purpose. They promised they would come.

Sanjhag and Teejhang showed him the rhododendron forest at Milké, walking together with him. They kept him together with them inside their leaf-cottage. He stayed, freeing himself from all worries.

After some days, Panchashar took leave of them and moved toward Kantipur.

When he reached there, he looked even younger. Only Mauni could tell the secret behind his renewed happiness, health and youthfulness. That's because, he was the only witness when Siddha Kirat explained the qualities of Sanjhang and Teejhang and their impact of anyone that befriended them.

So Mauni chose to stay silent though he knew this secret.

People say, even today, the architecture of the Kashtamandap Valley, the beauty of Panchashar and Yangsila, and the rhododendrons at Milké (Sangu) keep remembering Sanjhang and Teejhang. This doesn't mean that Melamchi's position has been backgrounded in this tripartite relation, because the influence of Melamchi's sense of aesthetics on Panchashar's skills can be very well discerned in the images of the buildings he has constructed. The children of Melamchi gave the Kashtamandap Valley altogether new, mature and glorious architectural finery, and this fact established itself as an irrefutable reality. And its influence is seen in all the major countries in Asia.

Other members of the team returning from China ushered a new edition of the human species in Nepal. They ensured the development of a healthy, robust and courageous society in the history of human development. However, this reality remained undocumented in spite of being a reality.

In the tour to China, the team had representatives from people who were forerunners in knowledge, capability, construction and contribution. It also included the senior innovator from our society, our first chancellor, and a very senior professor. But that group could not recognize and uphold its own height and glory.

HARI RAJ BHATTARAI

There was a general complaint: Though they had an opportunity to undertake a tour, study societies, understand cultures, befriend people, enhance friendship, exchange knowledge and uphold a sense of service and harmony, the people in this group did not engage themselves in mental development. Thus, it could never lift itself higher. It always nurtured a feeling of hatred against another class, blinding itself with incurable ailments like pride, avarice, revenge and inferiority complex. So, for want of a healthy development of the mind, this class of experts and academicians make itself a lowly class—Dalit to be precise—and started enjoying the same, embellishing itself with self-acclaimed superiority. Materially, the critical conclusion of the faulty imagination and conduct of these people, who declared themselves superior and prominent and puked poison against others, remained an issue of serious research.

***

Lightning Source UK Ltd.
Milton Keynes UK
UKHW041909300120
357919UK00002B/38/J